To Pluto & Back

BRIDGET L. ROSE

Red Sky Ranch

Silver Creek

Aaron's House

Silver Creek Ranch

Briggs House

The barn

Sunday market

@Snuggleswithtea

Ian's House

Bichell & Flynn's House

Flower fields

Olivia & Hadley's House

orchard hill

Editing: Bridget L. Rose Books Inc.

Cover Design: @ask.the.fairies

Formatting: Bridget L. Rose Books Inc.

Headers, scene break and map: @chapterswithtea

Title Page: @emilyxvrs

Author's Note

Hi my lovely readers,

Thank you so much for being here and taking the time to read my cowboy romance. First and foremost, I want to highlight that epilepsy comes in many different forms. I want to make sure that you know that Tate's experience with epilepsy is not a universal one. Everyone's experience is different. Triggers vary, what medication needs to be taken varies, how a person lives with it and feels with it is different, and so on. A lot of Tatum's fears are rooted in fears I had when my furry son JJ was diagnosed with epilepsy and how I terrifying I think it must have been for him. Plus, while they are entirely different things, a lot of the feelings Tate has are how I feel with my anxiety such as feeling scared to commit to someone and being a burden. I have had sensitivity readers who've told me how seen they feel through Tate's experience, so I hope I have represented epilepsy as best as it could possibly be. I will reiterate that all experiences with epilepsy vary and that readers please keep in mind that I have spoken to people with epilepsy and seizures to represent one version of and one experience with epilepsy in my book.

The same goes for Aaron's experience with panic attacks and PTSD. If you've read certain books of mine, you know that all of the mental health experiences come from my own experience, and I did my best to use what experiences I had with panic attacks and PTSD to create that part of Aaron's story.

The same also applies for Aaron's experience with his grandmother's Alzheimer's. This is my experience and my family's experience with Alzheimer's. My Nonno was diagnosed with it, and recently passed away because of his illnesses.

I wrote this book in part for him and in part for myself. I wrote it because I know this is such a unique grief to every person, and I wanted to assure people they weren't alone in their feelings with it. But it varies from person to person, and it's important to remember that.

Thank you all so much for reading this story.

I hope you enjoy To Pluto & Back.

All my love,

Bridget

Trigger Warnings

The ***trigger warnings list includes***: epilepsy and seizures, PTSD and panic attacks, topics of loss and fear of loss, vulgar language, explicit sexual content, grandparent with Alzheimer's (eventually passes away), and mentions of animal abuse (historical, off-page).

Playlist

Restless Road

Head Over Heels

Growing Old With You

Bar Friends

Tell Me Not To

Go Get Her

I Don't Wanna Be That Guy

You Don't Have To Love Me

Most Nights (feat. Erin Kinsey)

Sundown Somewhere

On My Way

Playlist

you're like - Jamie Fine

Steal The Show - Lauv

Craving You - Thomas Rhett,

Maren Morris

Leave You Alone - Kane Brown

Short Skirt Weather - Kane Brown

Lose It - Kane Brown

Good As You - Kane Brown

Hooked - Dylan Scott

Lover Of Mine - 5 Seconds of Summer

Mind Is A Prison - Alec Benjamin

Falling Like The Stars - James Arthur

Vapor - 5 Seconds Of Summer

Nervous - Shawn Mendes

To my Nonno and to my first furry baby, JJ.

Nonno, I wish you could have read this, but I hope even though you didn't get the chance, wherever you are now, you know how much I love you.

JJ, I wish you could understand that your epilepsy has led me to write a book that I hope will help so many people with the same illness feel seen. I love you more than life.

Prologue

Aaron

PEOPLE DON'T TALK ABOUT the type of grief one experiences when the person you love most isn't dead but gone. When their minds fail them, making it impossible for them to remember who you are. No one talks about the limbo between grieving their loss and not comprehending they're gone because *they're still here*. Their bodies remain while their hearts and souls drift more into the afterlife with each passing day.

This shit isn't talked about enough.

So, when my grandmother was first diagnosed with Alzheimer's, I had no idea how painful it would be. Lorena Blaze raised me, made me the man I am today, and now she hardly ever recognizes me when I visit her at the nursing home. Despite my wishes, it was her demand to be put here before her condition worsened. She didn't want to be a burden while I worked to provide for us. I tried to convince her she wasn't a burden, that I wanted—*want*—to take care of her, but once the woman put her mind to something, there was no stopping her.

It pains me to see her this way. Watching those bright blue eyes of hers shimmer with confusion when she looks at me is like a bullet wound to the chest. It's still remarkable to me how an illness could take away a person's entire existence. Everything that made her the Lorena everyone knew is gone, vanished as if it never meant anything more than a blade of grass getting squashed under a heavy boot.

People still remember her. They remember her kindness, her selflessness. They remember her volunteering from sunrise to sunset at the homeless shelter in town.

1

They remember her saying hello and asking everyone how they were doing without ever expecting to be asked the same questions.

They remember Lorena.

I remember my nanna.

I remember the woman who woke up every Sunday morning at six to drive me three hours to my horse shows. I remember her holding me in the hospital after I busted my knee and couldn't pursue my dream anymore. I remember her cooking for me every single day. No one knew this version of her. No one but me.

"Mr. Blaze? Mrs. Blaze is in the garden. You may see her now," the man at the reception of the home says, and I take off my cowboy hat before nodding my head at him in gratitude.

Every cell in my body fills with dread because I'm fucking scared. Just like I always am.

Will she recognize me today?

Will she look at me and see the boy who's loved her like he's loved no one else?

Will she give me the same confused look I've seen on her face the last three times I was here?

Pain grips my chest. As I said, nothing could have prepared me for losing my nanna this way. All the research I did in preparation didn't tell me about the nausea I'd feel at the sight of her once familiar eyes now turned unfamiliar. She might still be in there, at least that's what the doctors keep telling me, but hope left me long ago. There is no cure for this disease. There is no antidote. There is nothing left to do but swallow down the tears when I see her and...

Confusion crosses her face at the sight of me.

Fuck.

CHAPTER 1
Tatum

WELL, FUCK.

The sign of Silver Creek Ranch blurs past me as I drive my newly purchased, bright-red Chevrolet Silverado down the rocky road toward my father's house. This is the last place I ever thought I'd end up at twenty-seven.

My law degree diploma burns a hole through my backpack, reminding me of what I've given up. It was the right choice, I know it was, but it's still a pain in the ass to think about all the hard work I put into becoming a lawyer being flushed down the drain. All because my stupid chronic illness flares up under stress.

That bitch.

I was diagnosed with epilepsy when I was five years old. The doctors diagnosed me with generalized tonic-clonic seizures. That means, when a seizure occurs, it originates from both sides of my brain.

My life is as normal as anyone else's. Except when there is a burst of electrical activity inside my brain, causing my entire body to seize and shut down. In other words, my brain overloads, signals are sent to the wrong parts of it, and I have to endure thirty seconds of complete loss of motor functions. The postictal period, the time after a seizure, is when I'm usually the most tired. My body aches, red dots appear on my face because of blood vessels that popped, and my head hurts, so, to regenerate, I often have to lie down for a while.

My former boss didn't like that at all.

It's one of the reasons I quit my job. Another was my doctor's warning. Being a lawyer is stressful, so stressful I had two seizures within forty-eight hours. For someone who gets seizures only because of specific triggers, that's a lot. So, I got a warning, telling me if I didn't find a way to reduce my stress, I'd cut my life a lot shorter than others with the same chronic illness.

I have no desire to die. It's always a possibility for people with epilepsy to die prematurely, which is nothing new to me, but if there is a route to spare myself more seizures, I'll change course.

My father almost demanded I move in with him. He said I could work around the ranch, get paid, and take things as slow as I need to. I only accepted because I don't have another option. I love my dad more than anything, but there is a reason I didn't move to Silver Creek Ranch with him when he bought it ten years ago. I stayed in the city with my mom, finishing school, and following in her footsteps.

Staying in Billings also made it easier to see my doctor. Eight years ago, we finally found the right combination of AEDs—anti-epileptic drugs—that helps with my seizures. It allowed me to live a normal life, the only thing causing my seizures being my triggers—whenever I feel claustrophobic, bright lights flashing in my eyes, or any type of alcohol consumption. I guess stress is now part of my list too, but it's something I'll be able to monitor here. In the middle of fucking nowhere. Living with my dad at twenty-seven. Hours from a big city.

Somebody wake me from this nightmare.

Loki, my golden retriever epilepsy service dog, lets out a small yawn in the back seat. I turn to look at him, seeing his dark-brown eyes only half-opened. His gold-colored fur looks shiny as the sun filters in through the backseat window, and I can't help but smile at him. Loki is the best part of my life. Two years ago, my stepdad, multi-billion-dollar company owner Jordan Slate, offered to pay for Loki's training. My puppy's been a great help to me since. Usually, before my tonic-clonic seizures, I will get something called a focal aware seizure. My doctor calls them auras. They're a warning system for people like me, letting me know a much bigger seizure is on the horizon. Loki warns me before my FAS even has a chance to.

However, my FAS are still useful. They're the reason I was allowed to get my driver's license. Since they warn me minutes before my big seizure occurs as my body tenses up and shakes, giving me enough time to pull over, the state of Montana allowed me to get my license. With Loki always by my side, it's even safer.

My dog lets out a low humming sound as if he could look inside my head and agree with my thoughts.

"What the fuck?" I blurt out, my foot hitting the brakes when a herd of cows appears in front of me.

I spot a man on a horse at the back of the herd, his head hung low and his cowboy hat covering his face. His broad chest, on the other hand, is on full display for me. All rugged muscles a person only gets through working with their hands outside every day cover his entire upper body. I can't help the way my mouth waters a little at the sight, at the way his arms look so strong, all coiled with muscles.

I shake my head to regain focus.

"Hey, cowboy, do you mind hurrying this along? I've got places to be," I call out after rolling my window down. His head lifts and... fuck.

His face is even more attractive. The cut of his jawline is sharp, his cheekbones high, and his eyes a bright blue. So fucking blue, I see them from where I'm sitting in my car. His plump lips curl into a devastating smirk as he faces me, one dimple appearing on his right cheek despite the stubble trying to cover it.

"I'm afraid you'll have to wait a little longer, sweetheart. These cows move at their own pace," he calls back, his voice as hoarse and gravelly as I expected it to be. The only thing surprising about it is the strong Australian accent.

"I'm not your sweetheart, cowboy." This gets me a full-faced smile from him. It's breathtaking, almost so gorgeous it hurts.

I only glare at him in response before settling back into my seat and waiting for the herd to move across the road. My eyes keep drifting to the cowboy, no matter how much I scold myself. His body demands attention. Butterflies flutter in my stomach, and I want to strangle them for being MIA for the last five years and showing up for someone as infuriating as the man with the blue eyes.

5

He catches me staring more than once. By the third time, I forcefully drag my gaze away, fumbling with something inside of my bag. It's almost time for me to take my AEDs which means I have to find something to eat soon.

"If you want, I can give you a ride on my horse," a deep voice offers, startling me. I jump in my seat, dropping my medication all over the passenger seat floorboard.

"Great. Thanks very much," I say, not even looking at the breathtaking stranger who has now made his way next to my truck. "Has no one ever told you sneaking up on people is a dick thing to do?" I ask, already leaning over the middle console to retrieve my scattered pills.

Loki growls, clearly unhappy about the cowboy's sudden appearance at my car.

"Has no one ever told *you* a person should buy you dinner before you show them what kind of panties you wear?" the rude man challenges, and I reach backward to feel how high my skirt has risen.

Embarrassment instantly heats my cheeks when I feel my thong-covered ass on display for him. I slowly sink back into my seat, wiping the hair out of my face and taking a deep breath to keep from putting my car into Reverse and escaping this horrible moment.

"That's very old-school thinking, don't you agree?" I ask because it's a lot easier to turn this back on him than linger on the fact that he just saw my pretty-much bare ass. The cowboy lets out a low laugh.

"I guess you're right. I'm Aaron, by the way," he says, extending one of his rough, calloused hands. I stare at it, then at him before cocking an eyebrow.

"And I'm not interested in men who startle me and then ogle my ass." A smirk tugs up the right side of his mouth. It's sexy as hell, something I'm trying desperately to ignore.

"My sincerest apologies for startling you," he replies, retracting his hand. "The ogling I'm not sorry about. You've been doing the same to me since you first saw me," he adds, sending more embarrassment to my cheeks.

"Don't you have cows to herd?" I ask, doing my best not to glance his way again. Instead, I study the forty cows still crossing the road in front of me. I can't help but feel my heart warm at the sight of a mama cow and her calf walking together. It's the reason I'm one of the very few vegetarians in Montana. I love animals too much to be the reason they die.

"Yes, but I'm enjoying our conversation far more." *God, this guy.*

"Not interested. Now, can you hurry this along? My dad's expecting me," I say, finally giving in to the urge to look at him again.

And what a mistake it is because *fuck.*

Aaron is breathtaking. He's a rugged kind of beautiful. The dimple on his right cheek is in full bloom as he grins at me, his perfect set of teeth on display. His plump lips are pulled wide, and his bright blue eyes have specks of silver in them that sparkle in the sun as if the damn star wants me to see them perfectly. He's taken off his cowboy hat, allowing me a clear vision of his raven-black, curly hair. The stubble covering the hard lines of his face only adds to his looks.

"Shit, Old Man Briggs is your dad?" he asks, lifting one of his hands to run it through his sweaty hair.

"Yup, and he hates it when I'm late, screams at me for it," I inform the infuriating man who's currently grinning at me.

"Nah, he's an easy-going bloke. Not even you can convince me otherwise," Aaron says and, damn him, he's right. Nothing bothers him, except when something happens to my sister or me. Frustrated, I roll my eyes and turn to look at Loki in the backseat again.

"Can you leave? I need to pick up what you made me drop and have no desire to flash you my ass again," I explain, looking out my rolled-down window.

"That's too bad. It's a hell of a sight," he replies, the right side of his mouth curling upward once more. Heat immediately rushes to my cheeks.

"Bye, cowboy," I say, willing him away to give my body a chance to untense from the way he looks at me. Like I fascinate him. Like I'm a puzzle.

"See you around, Tatum," he calls out as he trots away on his horse. I'm about to call him back and make him explain how he knows my name when I notice the cows are no longer blocking the road.

Putting the car into Drive, I roll past Aaron on his white horse with brown spots, trying my absolute best not to ogle him or the way his tan, sweaty skin glistens in the setting sun. Or the way the freckles on his back look like a map of stars drawn by a very talented artist. Or... well, the list goes on.

And ends with seven simple words I need to remember:

You can't have him or anyone else.

CHAPTER 2
Aaron

TATUM HAYES IS A devastating kind of beautiful. The type of beautiful painters search lifetimes to capture in their art. The sort of beautiful you stay awake at night dreaming about.

She has pale skin, hazel eyes, brown hair that twirls into curls, and lips I will be thinking about for weeks to come. A gorgeous woman with a curvy body and fiery personality wasn't what I was expecting today. I thought it would be like every other day. Get my work around the ranch done, grab a beer with my mates, and then drop into bed by nine so I can get up at four-thirty to do it all again.

Finally meeting Old Man Briggs' daughter and having the breath knocked out of me was not on my list.

"Hey, Heart-Eyes, we still have to get these cows back in their corral," my best mate, Flynn, calls from where he's sitting on his horse.

"Stop calling me that," I reply, throwing him a dirty look. "I might go have dinner with Briggs instead if you don't."

"Please tell me you're joking. We already made plans with Beckett, Olivia, Hadley, and Ian," Flynn complains, making clicking noises to let Maravilla, his beloved horse, know to move forward and toward me.

"You're the only one who enjoys going to B&B more than having a home-cooked meal."

"Untrue. Beckett loves going out," he replies, running one of his hands over Mara's long, black mane.

"That's because you and Beckett have yet to figure out how to think with your brains instead of your dicks." He smirks at me as soon as the words have left my mouth.

"Why don't you worry less about my dick and more about the fact that the boss's daughter is off-limits. You know how Old Man Briggs feels about his little *honeybee*. None of us are even allowed to think about her or we end up headfirst in the well," Flynn says with a bored shrug and makes his way back over to his side of the herd.

Tatum is off-limits. Briggs has made it abundantly clear after Beckett and Flynn found a picture of her at her university graduation ceremony. I never got to see the photo, but Beckett claims to this day that he's never seen a woman look as beautiful in green as Tatum. Having seen her now, I have no doubt it's true.

"You think one meeting with that woman is enough to throw my world on its head?" I say to Flynn, shaking my head. "Don't be absurd." I have no intention of seeking out Tatum. If I see her again, I see her again. It's not a big deal.

She's just a woman.

"What time are we meeting at Boots & Beers again?" Flynn's mischievous smile spreads across his face until his brown eyes sparkle with something I'm not sure I want to decipher.

"Eight. Don't be late," he warns, bringing Mara to a slow trot. "Last one there pays," Flynn reminds me before calling out to the cows to go faster.

I smile to myself as I follow his lead.

There is hardly a sight more beautiful than the sun setting behind the mountains lining the horizon at Silver Creek Ranch. Every morning, I get to watch the colors explode into existence at sunrise, and every night, I watch them all fade as it sets.

The days I don't get to see both are ones I call "sunny fails." It sounds silly because I invented the term when I was eight years old and Nanna and I still lived on our ranch, Rocking Horse Ranch.

I had to sell it years ago when my grandmother was diagnosed with Alzheimer's to pay for her treatments and now her place at the home. Part of my salary also goes into her rent because these institutions charge a fuck ton of money. It's a good thing she still has me. If she didn't, if she were all alone…

A shiver runs down my spine at the thought.

She has me.

Everything's fine.

I stop by Briggs' before going to the bar because he texted me very cryptically earlier, and when I called him to ask about the fence at the farthest part of the ranch, he didn't answer.

I've been worried about him since then.

"How can I help you?" Briggs asks as soon as he meets me in his living room. He's carrying a bowl of soup with him, placing it on his wooden table before dropping onto one of the chairs.

"I wanted to check in, see how you're doing," I say.

The short man with pale skin, light-brown eyes, and a lean figure furrows his eyes in suspicion. They study me like he can see deep into my soul before he lets out a sigh and slumps back into his seat.

"Ah, hell. You met Tatum," he says with another exaggerated sigh. "I swear to God, boy, if you don't keep your hands off my youngest daughter, I will get a gun after all, just to shoot you," he warns, and I raise my hands in surrender, taking a step back while a nervous laugh bubbles out of me.

All of us at Silver Creek Ranch are strongly against people owning guns. We've seen too many lives lost, too many animals and people hurt.

"Hey, I came here because you didn't answer my call earlier," I explain. The suspicion doesn't leave his gaze, but something else must be bothering him because he switches topics quickly.

"This damn house is fallin' to pieces, Aaron. I was on the phone with a plumber for three hours because I can't get the upstairs toilet to run properly. I tried fixin' it, but the stubborn thing still doesn't flush properly," he explains while playing with a piece of bread. He dunks it in his soup before taking a bite.

"Want me to take a look tomorrow?" Briggs shakes his head before the question has even left my mouth.

"No, I need you to train the new horse tomorrow. She'll arrive early, so don't be out too late," Briggs says and points his spoon my way as a warning.

I grin at him in response.

"Yes, sir." I give him one last nod before heading for the door.

"Oh, and, Aaron?" he asks, stopping me dead in my tracks. "Tatum will be at Boots & Beers with an old friend tonight. I want you as far away from my daughter as the bar allows," he says, and I can't help but chuckle.

"Yes, sir," I repeat and leave before he has the chance to make more demands that I don't know if I'll listen to.

CHAPTER 3
Aaron

Beckett shows up last.

He's in worn blue jeans, his huge thighs straining against the material. Beckett Moore is six foot seven and all muscles. His tattooed, broad chest is covered by a green flannel, and his blonde hair is hidden underneath his usual black cap. He wears it backward because he claims it makes him look even more attractive. It's a pain that he's right, something none of us will ever admit, of course.

Olivia and Hadley showed up together, wearing cowboy boots, shorts that hit just above their mid-thighs, and matching crop tops. Olivia's reads: I'm the criminal. Hadley's reads: I'm the alibi. Which fits them perfectly. Liv always manages to get into trouble somehow, and Hads always pulls her out of it.

I have no idea what I'd do without either of them. The same goes for Beckett, Ian, and Flynn.

My best mate moved to Orchard Hill when he was a year old. His family came from Colombia to Tennessee for a job opportunity. His full name is Rafael Pedro Andrés de Nicolas, but we've been calling him Flynn since we were ten years old. It happened after we all watched Tangled, and he reminded us so much of Flynn Rider, it kind of stuck.

All of us met in fifth grade. Beckett and Ian moved here from out of town the same year Nanna and I immigrated to the US from Australia. Hads, Liv, and Flynn already knew each other since kindergarten, but before the rest of us joined, Flynn never got along with Olivia and Hadley. He didn't have a choice about spending time with them after Beckett, Ian, and I came along though, because we adored those two menaces.

The teachers in school called us the "Delinquent Six." To this day, the thought still makes me chuckle.

God, they all hated us.

My eyes shift toward where Flynn is doing his absolute best to flirt with the bartender, but he seems extremely uninterested in my best friend. So, he turns to the group of people next to him, flashing them his devastatingly handsome smile.

Ian Hamada, who's watching the same scene as me, smacks his forehead with the palm of his hand. He never smiles but the way he presses his lips into a thin line reveals how he truly feels. He finds watching Flynn trying to pick someone up as entertaining as I do.

"Maybe I should show him how it's done," Beckett says as he steps between Ian and me to grab the beer I ordered for him.

"Like you have to do more than stand there, lookin' the way you do," Ian complains with a huff, and I can't help but chuckle when Beckett raises a confused brow at him.

"Are you sayin' my looks are all I have to offer this world?"

"You look like a Greek god, Beckett. Don't play dumb," Ian says, taking a swig of his beer.

Ian is quite tall too, but he's built a lot leaner than Beckett. Then again, so am I. We still have broad backs and strong bodies because it's impossible in our line of work not to, but we don't compare to the giant in front of us. Especially with the way he's been bathed in charm for some reason. I blame his mother.

Momma Moore is the smoothest talker in the entire world.

"I'm flattered you find me this attractive," is Beckett's only reply.

"How's Bailey?" I ask to steer the conversation in a different direction.

"Ah, she's good. Her mom picked her up yesterday and will have her for the next three weeks before fucking off to wherever this woman goes for six months at a time," Beckett says and rolls his eyes, the usual anger he feels toward Charlotte slipping into his eyes.

"I wonder why it didn't work out between the two of you," Ian teases, and I bite down on my bottom lip to keep the grin at bay.

"Because she's a selfish human being? Because our daughter only matters to her when she decides she wants to play mommy?" He takes a sip of his beer as he shakes his head in frustration. "If I had it my way, Bailey would stay with me every single day. I fuckin' hate watching my daughter leave with that woman, that *stranger*. If I could, I'd pull a Rapunzel and lock Bailey in a tower until Charlotte leaves us alone for good."

"That child has you wrapped around her tiny fingers, I hope you know that," Ian says as he stretches his back, cringing at whatever muscle pains him today.

"Yes, she does. She's my little princess, and I'm not afraid to turn into a dragon to fend off any dangers, including her mother," Beckett says, and I can't help but finally smile.

"I mean, you're already as tall as one," I chime in, and Ian snorts.

"Kind of got the face structure, too," he says, and Beck punches him in the shoulder.

"Fuck you," Beckett says with a laugh.

A second later, all of our attention drifts to the door to watch Tatum step through it.

My eyes glue themselves to her full lips, her round face, the way the green dress she's wearing hugs all of her beautiful curves. Tatum Hayes is a thick woman in every way, and fuck, she's beautiful. The way the neon lights of the bar sign turn her hair slightly pink has me a little breathless.

I take a step without thinking.

A broad chest cuts off my view, almost making me groan.

"Absolutely not, my friend. I like you in one piece, not chopped into a dozen," Beck says, using one of his hands to push me backward again.

"Is it because you don't want me in pieces or because you want to talk to her first?" I challenge, crossing my arms in front of my chest.

He's only four inches taller than me, but when Beckett matches my stance and towers over me, I feel tiny.

"It's like you can read my mind," he says and grabs my shoulder, giving it a firm squeeze.

I smile at him as he lifts his beer to his mouth, the immature part of me taking over and tipping his bottle upward until the contents empty all over his shirt.

"Fuck, sorry, mate. You better get cleaned up," I say and slip past him, grinning over my shoulder when I see him scowling at my backside.

Unfortunately, karma has a way of instantly punishing people for their bad actions.

"Do you mind?" her soft voice asks, filling my ears right after I almost mow her down.

My hands barely catch her waist before my heavy body pushes her to the ground. Her hazel eyes meet mine, and while I lighten up at the sight of her, she rolls her eyes at me.

"Of course, it's you, cowboy," she blurts out, taking a step back and severing the contact between us.

"I have a name, you know," I remind her.

Tatum cocks an unimpressed brow at me.

"Congratulations. Now, if you don't mind, my friend and I were trying to have a quiet evening before you ran into me like a—" She cuts off as she looks for a comparison.

"Steel truck? Tree trunk? Something else that's very firm?" I offer, bringing a smirk to my face. I was going for flirty, but Tatum continues to give me the same unimpressed quirk of her brow.

"Sure," she replies and presses her lips into a thin line. "Well, bye."

By the time my mind has caught up, she's rushing toward the bar where her friend is already ordering them drinks.

When I turn back to my friends, Beckett is bent over laughing with Ian shaking his head in disapproval. Olivia and Hadley are both covering their mouths to keep from doing the same as Beckett, and Flynn is holding up his phone, pretending like he was recording my getting rejected.

I glare at each and every one of them, but heat rises up my neck from embarrassment. People tend to like me either because of my accent, my looks, or my personality. Most people also find me nice.

Tatum doesn't seem to share the same inclination to be drawn to me, and I don't know why the fuck I care.

"Don't worry, pretty boy, getting rejected gets easier," Liv says as soon as I rejoin the group.

She moves her dark brown hair over her shoulder and tugs it behind her ears to get it out of her face.

Olivia Williams has sharp features; high cheekbones, a defined jawline, and a pointy nose. Her eyes are as green as freshly cut grass and her skin is light. She's beautiful, and she knows it. Every person here can see it. Just like they see Hadley Clark's stunning dark locks, soft features, brown eyes, and warm brown skin.

"I can't imagine you have a lot of experience in that department," I reply, taking the beer Ian was about to sip and gulping down the entire thing. Hadley flings her arm around Liv's shoulders and lets out a little snort.

"Well, imagine it because while she has great taste in women, Olivia has horrible taste in men. She always chooses the ones that are not interested in more than gettin' their dicks wet," Hads replies, and I flinch at her blatant words, causing me to choke on my drink.

"Man, what's the matter with you?" Beck asks as he slaps my back to get the liquid from the wrong pipe into the right one.

"Nothing. I need another drink," I say, shaking my head.

My eyes shift to Tatum without me meaning for them to, and a bolt of excitement shoots through my chest when I find her watching me already. She looks away, as quickly as someone who was caught staring would, and the grin spreading across my face is entirely out of my control.

It fades as soon as I see Beckett approaching Tatum.

"Is he—" Ian cuts me off before I have the chance to phrase my question.

"Shootin' his shot with Tate? What do you think?" he asks, holding out his hand to bring my attention to the way Beckett's smiling casually, almost lazily, at Tatum.

I hate that fucking smile.

"I vote for kicking him out of our friend group." Hadley lets out a disapproving sound in response.

"No. Way. Beckett is like a big teddy bear. He gives the best hugs and makes the best food. What do you bring to the table, pretty boy?" she asks, and I roll my eyes at the nickname they've all come to call me over the years.

"I'm the one who keeps you idiots alive. If it wasn't for me, you'd all be six feet under because of the dumb shit you always think about doing." Liv opens her mouth to argue, probably remembers the summer I talked her out of going cliff camping, and then shuts it again.

"Fair enough," Ian replies, stretching his arms into the air as he yawns.

"Are we going to stand around all day, or are we finally going to play some darts?" I ask, ignoring the irritation gnawing at me when I think about Beckett hitting on Tate.

CHAPTER 4
Tatum

BECKETT IS GORGEOUS.

He has a southern drawl, pale green eyes, tattoos all over his arms and hands, blonde hair that curls at his nape, and a smile I'm trying my best not to fall in love with. Charm drips off him, but he's not flirting with me. We're having a polite conversation about how long he's been working for my dad at Silver Creek Ranch, and that he'll help me once I start working there, too. My friend, Sage, contributes to the conversation, and I can't help but notice the way Beckett's eyes sparkle with curiosity every time she opens her mouth.

"So, how long have you been livin' in Orchard Hill?" Beckett asks Sage, who gives him one of her flirtatious smiles.

I don't know how she does it, but every single person she meets falls in love with her. And yes, it might be because she's five foot eleven, with toned legs to die for, short blonde hair, and eyes as blue as a clear morning sky. But I'm convinced it's the way she speaks to people. She always chooses her words carefully, catering to people's egos if she wants them to like her, or teasing them if she thinks they'll appreciate it more.

In other words, I might be the lawyer, but she's much better at reading people than I'll ever be.

"I don't live here. I simply came to visit Tatum while she gets settled," Sage replies, taking a sip of her cocktail. Beckett's gaze is glued to her, to the way she licks her bottom lip to get the alcohol she spilled there.

"So, you're not in town for long?" His voice drops an octave as he takes a subtle step closer to Sage. She smiles up at the man she just met, seemingly intoxicated by his presence.

"Yes. Do you have any recommendations on how to make this a memorable trip?" The smirk he gives her in response is downright filthy.

I let out a nervous laugh neither of them hears before excusing myself and slipping away from the bar.

Everything about Boots & Beers screams vintage to me. It's an old Southern-style bar with two dozen people scattered around. There is a pool table in the back and a dance floor in the middle of the place with no people on it. They're all either standing at one of the high tables, sitting on the worn, leather couches that stand off to the sides, or hanging around the bar.

My eyes continue to scan the room until they settle on Aaron at the back of the bar, throwing darts with four other people. They're all laughing and smiling, and, for a moment, I wonder what it's like to have friends like that.

Friends who are family. Who make you laugh and cry in the same breath. Who protect you as best as they can, with everything they've got.

Sage is a wonderful friend, but I hardly ever see her.

At least I have my best friend, Loki.

I grab my phone out of my bag simply to stare at the lock screen, a picture of him at the beach decorating it. Loki loves swimming. I'll have to ask Dad if there's a good place for my baby to enjoy the water.

Leaving Loki at home with my father was very difficult. He's not always working, but tonight is the first time we're this far apart. It's only a ten-minute drive, but I miss him anyway.

"Hey, pretty lady," someone says from beside me, and I turn to see a short woman with deep green eyes and a soft smile. "It's Tatum, right?" she says with a Southern accent, extending her hand.

I return the friendly gesture and shake it.

"Damn. News travels fast in Orchard Hill," I reply, a little freaked out that the whole thing about small towns is true.

"It does, but it's also because I work at Silver Creek Ranch, and your arrival is all your old man has been able to talk about for two days," the mystery woman says, still smiling sweetly.

"Does everyone here work at my dad's ranch because Beckett also said he works there?" I ask not to be rude but because I'm genuinely confused. The woman in front of me lets out an amused snort.

"No, no. Us at Silver Creek Ranch are just extremely nosy," she explains. "I'm Olivia. I mostly work in the stables with the horses and mini cows."

"My dad has mini cows?" I blurt out, for the first time getting truly excited to be here. Since I was a little girl, I've dreamed about having a mini cow.

Olivia beams up at me when she hears the excitement in my voice.

"Yes, I'll take you to see them tomorrow, if you'd like," she says and flings her arm through mine, leading me toward where Aaron and the others are. "Betty is my favorite because she's kind of an asshole at times, like me. Angel is the sweetest animal you'll ever meet. Briggs always jokes they have such differing personalities because I spent most of my time with Betty and Hadley spent most of hers with Angel when they were still babies."

Olivia stops a few feet away from her group of friends, who are still throwing darts at the board. Aaron's eyes have already found their way back to me, opening the cage containing the butterflies inside me. They storm around in my stomach as if I've never felt a man's gaze on me before.

It's ridiculous.

"How good are you at darts?" Olivia asks as she lifts her long, thick hair into a ponytail.

"Not very. Why? Is this a competitive game with you people?" I tease, but she furrows her brows at me in response.

"Didn't you watch me put up my hair?" She points at it, and I almost burst into laughter at her no-bullshit attitude. "That either means I'm about to get into a fight or kick my friends' asses. Depends on the mood I'm in because sometimes those two are the same thing," she says and winks, stepping away before I have the chance to stop my jaw from dropping to the floor.

Okay, it's official.

I like her.

"Okay, Tate, honey, you're going to be on a team with Aaron and Hadley. Ian, Flynn, and I will be on the opposing team," Olivia says, but the other woman lets out an irritated snort.

"That's not fair. I suck at darts, and you said Tatum's not good at it either," she complains.

"Yeah, but Aaron is the best at it," Olivia argues.

They're bickering like siblings. Maybe they are, who knows? It's entertaining either way because it reminds me of the fights I used to have with my older sister.

Remi moved to Singapore when I was sixteen, and I haven't seen her in three years. We speak on the phone every few weeks, but she's very busy running her perfume empire.

"They're always like this, but I've never seen two friends love each other as fiercely as they do," Aaron's heavily accented voice creeps into my ears, and I almost close my eyes at the wonderful sound.

He steps in front of me, an easy smile on his lips. I don't return it. Instead, I merely stare at his full lips and single dimple like they'll tell me everything I need to know about him.

"Ready to play?" he asks, that same easy-going look on his face.

"You'll have to pull more than your weight for our team because saying I suck at darts is putting it nicely," I reply as my feet bring me toward Hadley.

She gives me a welcoming smile before she introduces me to Ian, a tall, lean man with light skin, dark eyes, and even darker hair; Flynn, a man with brown hair, brown eyes, dark golden skin, and a flirtatious smile; and, lastly, herself.

The men are all dressed in jeans, boots, and either a flannel or, in Aaron's case, a polo that brings out his eyes. My favorite are Olivia and Hadley's shirts, though.

I'm about to snort at what's written across them when Aaron hands me a couple of darts. His encouraging smile is as breathtaking as his other ones.

This man is pure sunshine.

I feel like a cloud of rain in comparison. Around people I don't know, I often have a difficult time expressing happy emotions because I've closed myself off for so long, it's become a habit. I probably come across as a total grump.

"Alright, Tatum, do your best. I promise not to hold it against you if the dart bounces off the board instead of sticking to it," Aaron says before carefully grabbing my shoulders to position me in front of the target.

His touch sends volts of electricity through me, making my body hum happily.

"Thank God, disappointing you was my biggest worry here," I say with so much sarcasm, his friends burst into laughter.

"Just take a deep breath and no pressure. You've got this," he says softly, his proximity and words sending wonderful shivers down my spine before he moves away entirely.

Playing darts is as fun as it is embarrassing. I make no shots, not even one by accident. Hadley gives me encouraging words throughout the entire game while Aaron watches me with slight amusement but mostly absolute fascination.

"Well, the outcome is as expected," Olivia starts as she takes a sip of her pint of beer. "We kicked your asses and wiped the floor with you," she adds with a devilish grin. I don't miss the way Flynn snorts in response.

"No thanks to you. You missed most of your shots," he says, rolling his eyes when she places her hands on her hips and turns to him.

"Says the man who can't aim for shit. You know the red spot in the middle is what you were supposed to aim for, right?"

The two of them fall into a session of bickering and throwing jabs at each other.

"They've been like this since the first grade," Hadley explains, grabbing my elbow to hand me my phone. "It's been blowing up for the last five minutes," she adds with a concerned smile, sending a wave of panic through me. My eyes flicker to my screen to see an incoming call from my dad.

I check the bar for Sage only to find Beckett's tongue licking salt off her throat and then downing a shot of tequila. A slice of lemon rests between my friend's teeth, and the tall, broad man captures her mouth with his.

My phone's violent vibrations pull me back to the important things.

"What's wrong?" I ask as soon as the phone is pressed to my ear.

"Loki is growing very restless the longer you stay away. He's barkin' at and scratchin' the front door to get to you, I think," Dad says, getting straight to the point. It's something I absolutely adore about him. He never bullshits. He's always honest, even when the truth sucks.

"I'm coming," I reply and hang up, making my way toward Sage. She picked me up and drove us here, which means without her, I'm without a ride. "Sage, I need to go home," I say, but she barely acknowledges me as she throws me her keys, Beckett's mouth still gliding over hers. "Get my friend home safely, Beckett, or I'll gut you like a fish," I warn, causing him to break the kiss and give me his attention.

"Yes, ma'am," he replies before giving me a lust-hazed smile. He wants to go back to kissing Sage, and I have no intention of making Loki wait any longer.

Sage knows how to take care of herself, and the way she waves her hands to get me to leave is the only reason I manage to do so without a heavy weight on my chest.

By the time I get back, Loki hasn't settled down in the slightest. He throws himself at me, crying a little at how happy he is to see me. I can't lie. I feel the same way about him.

"Next time, take him to the bar," Dad says with a laugh, running a hand along his face.

"I'm sorry he worried you," I reply as I give Loki a kiss on the head and stand up.

Dad's arms wrap around me as soon as I'm upright, and I hesitate for a moment, not entirely sure what brought this on. He cradles the back of my head with his hand, and I finally melt into the embrace. We barely had time to talk today before Sage stormed into the house and demanded I go out with her, so I know he's happy I'm here now.

For the past ten years, we've hardly seen each other. He always came to the city for important holidays, but being so far away from each other for an entire decade isn't easy.

"I'm so happy you're here," Dad says and when he pulls back, I see tears glisten in his eyes. "I've missed you, honeybee," he adds, causing my eyes to tear up, too.

"Dammit, Dad, do you always have to remind me how much you love me?" I ask, and we both let out small laughs before he drags me back against his chest. His warm, familiar scent fills my nose as my arms tighten around him.

"Always. A daughter should never forget how much her father loves her, *ever*." I smile against his chest, feeling like I'm seven years old again. "So, did those troublemakers of mine stay away from you or do I have to start diggin' human-shaped holes in my backyard?" Dad asks, and I burst into laughter.

"They were all really nice to me. So far, I really like Olivia and Hadley. And Aaron—" I cut off, thinking about his gorgeous, single-dimple smile and blue eyes.

"They're all wonderful, honeybee, but do me a favor and stay away from them romantically. They're important to me, but I won't hesitate to fire any of them if they hurt you, you know that," he says, and I smile up at Dad.

"I assure you, I have no interest in complicating anything here." Plus, dating someone, *anyone*, is something I've come to realize is out of the realm of possibilities for me.

"Thank you," he replies, giving the underside of my chin a gentle nudge and stepping away. "Get some rest. Olivia already texted me and said she'll pick you up at five in the morning to introduce you to the mini cows."

A smile stays on my face the entire time I get ready for bed, up until I close my eyes. Maybe moving here won't be as horrible as I've imagined, after all.

Chapter 5
Tatum

"Time to wake up, pretty lady," someone says as they barge into my room, making me shoot up in bed and blink fiercely to get the sleep out of my eyes. Loki jumps up, too, and faces the intruder with his teeth on full display. "Down, boy, I'm not here to hurt Tate. I'm here to kidnap her for the day," Olivia adds with a mischievous grin, and I turn to bury my face in the pillow to groan. "I thought Old Man Briggs told you I'd be here early." She sweeps the blanket off my body in one annoyingly fluid motion.

"He did, but I had no idea how difficult getting up at this hour would be," I admit as I face her.

Olivia is breathtaking. Her long, brown hair is braided into a crown on top of her head, and her green eyes are rimmed with thick black lashes she enhanced with mascara. She's wearing work boots, a pair of gray cargo pants, and a plain black shirt, which exposes a little of her toned stomach. The easy smile on her lips somehow makes her more attractive.

"How do you look this good in the mornings?" I ask, rubbing my face to wake up.

"I think you're going to be my new favorite person," she replies with a wink before leaning down to pick up a pair of black work boots for me. "Get dressed. You have fifteen minutes," Olivia says, still grinning sweetly at me even though her voice means she's not kidding in the slightest.

"Yes, ma'am," I say and slide off my mattress, but Olivia's huff stops me.

"Please don't call me that, it makes me feel old. Only people I take into my bedroom get to call me 'ma'am' and only when they behave," she explains before cocking a brow at me and slipping out of my room again.

For a second, I'm too dumbfounded to move, but after letting out a surprised laugh, I make my way into the bathroom to rush through my routine. Loki watches me with utter fascination, and I stop way too often to pet him or give him a kiss on the head. He wags the entire time, including when we make our way down the stairs exactly fourteen minutes later to find Olivia and Dad in a conversation. Loki isn't working right now, so he runs over to him, nudging my father with his nose to get attention.

"You look tired," Dad says as soon as he looks at me, worry creasing the area between his eyebrows.

"Thanks, Dad," I reply, but he merely frowns at me in response. "I need breakfast, and then I'm good to go," I tell Olivia, but she hands me a lunchbox with a grin.

It has a smiling cow on it that says, 'Good Moooorning.' I pull my lips into a line to keep from laughing.

"I've got you covered."

She leads Loki and me toward a truck, opening the door and stepping back to let my service dog in the backseat. Olivia flashes me one of her devastating smiles as she slips into the car herself, letting the old engine roar to life. The vehicle is rusted and seems to be hanging on by a thread.

Silver Creek Ranch is beautiful this early in the morning. The sun has barely begun to rise. There are horses in a large, gated area not far from the barn, grazing with their tails swishing back and forth. One of them catches all of my attention as it gallops at full speed into view. Its coat is completely brown and the mane and tail are the same kind of raven black as Aaron's hair...

"We're here," Olivia announces. I tear my eyes off the horse to focus on the barn.

The structure, like the rest of my dad's farm, is old. Everything appears to be falling apart one way or another. A row of the wooden panels keeping the barn standing is half broken, and the pink color has faded and is partially chipped in some areas.

Loki bolts for the barn door as soon as Olivia lets him out of the car, sniffing and smelling everything he possibly can. This is all new for him, too. He's never been anywhere near farm animals, but he seems to enjoy the scents because his tail is swinging back and forth. I smile at his happy foot-tapping while biting off a piece of the sandwich Olivia packed me.

"Thank you for breakfast," I say after letting out a satisfied hum. It shouldn't be possible to be so hungry this early in the morning.

"It's my pleasure. Your dad told me you need to eat to take your meds," she says nonchalantly while I stop mid-bite, doing my best to swallow what's in my mouth to speak again.

"Did he tell all of you about my epilepsy?" I ask, scared of the answer.

I hate when people know.

They start treating me differently when there is no reason to. People have a big misconception about what my chronic illness means for the quality of my life. They think I'm a fragile little porcelain doll that breaks at any slight touch. Either that or they have no regard for my illnesses and try to pressure me into drinking alcohol or don't warn me that the video they're about to show me contains flashing lights—it's happened several times in my life and caused a seizure every time.

So, I try to avoid telling people I have to spend a lot of time with. It got difficult to hide when I was working and brought Loki with me every day, which is probably why I didn't have friends either.

It was easier that way.

"Nope. Just me, and I keep my mouth shut about important shit you don't want me to share. Say the word, and I will take it to my grave," she says. Relief floods me almost instantly.

"I'd prefer it if you didn't tell anyone," I admit.

She gives me one of her bright smiles and pushes the rusted barn door open. It creaks and complains, budging only slowly. After swallowing my meds, I ask the one thing that's gnawing at my brain.

"My dad would never tell me this, so I'm going to ask you. Is the farm struggling financially?" I ask, causing Olivia to spin around with surprise on her beautiful face.

"Why would you think that?" Her lips are pressed into a firm line in an attempt to hide her emotions, but her eyes betray her.

"Everything's falling apart. I tried to take a shower yesterday, and the shower head came apart." She sucks in a sharp breath.

"Yeah, the farm is struggling, but I'd try to ask your dad. He explains it better than I do," she says before dismissing this entire conversation by walking away.

My dad is as stubborn as they come. He won't admit he needs help, not even if he were hanging on by a thread. Dad also won't accept help. If the farm is struggling with money, I have savings on the side that could help him. Mom's new husband is so filthy rich that if I were to ask him for a loan to help the farm flourish, he would give it to me in a heartbeat. But my father would lose his mind. Not only does he hate accepting money he didn't work for, but he also absolutely despises Jordan.

"Come along, pretty lady. Angel and Betty are waiting," Olivia calls out, so I chase after her with Loki right beside me.

He's still exploring everything around us like the bales of hay stacked in the corner, the buckets most likely used for food, and the stalls where the horses get fed, cleaned, or whatever else Olivia and her colleagues do. I'm not well-versed in the farm terminology or routines that happen here, but I have a feeling that's going to change sooner rather than later.

The mini cows almost bring tears to my eyes because of how cute they are. If I were the type of person to cry, the image of them stomping their feet happily when they see Olivia would definitely have me bawling my eyes out.

People who've never seen one wouldn't understand just how adorable they are.

"You should take Angel, just to be safe," Olivia says while handing me a lead rope.

Angel is completely white with a thick coat and big brown eyes. Olivia leads me to her to show me how to attach the halter and connect the rope before doing the same to Betty, a mini cow with a deep brown coat, much shorter than Angel's but still quite furry, and eyes so dark, they almost seem black. She shakes her head and moves her jaw as she chews something, and I decide right now to ask my dad if I can be solely on mini-cow duty.

We make our way out of the barn again, passing half a dozen horses on our way, all of them sticking their heads out of their stalls.

"Another mini highland cow is supposed to come soon, and she's going to be yours. Briggs told me this morning," Olivia says, sending a wave of emotion into my chest that I struggle to breathe past. "We rescued her from a family who thought it would be a good idea to keep a mini cow in a one-story home without a barn or proper yard," she adds with a disgusted eye roll.

"All they see is how cute the animal is without thinking about what they will need to be happy," I say and shake my head in disbelief.

"Yep. But it's the least horrible story I could tell you about the animals here. Aaron trains all of our rescue horses, and they've been through hell because of assholes whose privates I'd like to beat up with a baseball bat," she tells me at the same moment Aaron comes into view.

My heart flutters in my chest at the sight of him.

The cowboy is wearing nothing but a tank top and worn jeans with black boots. His muscles are on full display, every hard ridge flexing as he wraps a rope from his thumb to his elbow all the way to his hand again. Over and over. His jeans hang low on his hips and a beige cowboy hat covers his curly black hair. A serious look has his already sharp features looking even more defined, but I can't take my eyes off his full lips or the way his blue eyes seem to sparkle in the morning sunlight.

When he catches me ogling him, he gives me a devilish smirk and a nod of his head before he refocuses on the horse in front of him.

Angel nudges my leg to get attention, dragging it away from Aaron. My hand slides into her fur, ruffling it until she decides she's had enough and drops her head to start grazing.

"The horses are often very distressed and try to hurt Aaron. He's gotten a few bruises and even a broken thumb from this job, so if you get scared easily, I suggest not watching him work," Olivia says as she removes the lead rope from Betty to let her run. I do the same with Angel, and the two of them run away together, getting distracted by the grass a second later.

Olivia makes her way toward Angel and Betty while my feet take me toward where Aaron is climbing over the fence to get to the horse.

I shouldn't watch.

A voice in my head is screaming at me to get as far away from the cowboy with blue eyes as I can, but I can't bring myself to listen.

CHAPTER 6

Aaron

TATUM'S WATCHING ME.

I don't need to turn around to know I'm right when her hazel eyes are lighting my skin on fire.

The mare I'm working with today, Galaxy, stomps her hooves as I take a slow step toward her, warning me not to get closer with a huff and raise of her head. With a step backward, I start moving to the side a little to see if she's comfortable with any direction of movement. Galaxy watches me, her light brown eyes filled with distrust. She's scared of me, I can see it in the shake of her chest as she breathes in, breaking my heart.

Old Man Briggs told me he rescued her from an abusive ranch, where they beat her when she didn't work or do as they wanted. They were going to shoot her when one of the workers at that farm stepped in and said he'd "get rid" of her, which meant going to Briggs and asking if he'd take her in. He's barely keeping his head above water because of how little money and resources he has, but he'd never turn away an animal in need.

"What's its name?" Tatum asks quietly, obviously trying not to startle the scared horse in the pen with me. Her dog is sitting right beside her, not moving an inch.

"Her name is Galaxy," I answer, moving backward to where Tatum is leaning against the wooden fence. "She's been through hell and back. I'm trying to show her she's safe here, but she's not ready yet," I explain, looking through the panels to see her staring up at me.

"So, what are you going to do?"

"I'm a patient man, sweetheart. I'll wait until she's ready," I say with a little smirk that has her cheeks flushing a vibrant red.

She clears her throat before saying, "Sounds good. I hope it all works out."

As Tatum tries to walk away, Galaxy takes a step toward her, curiosity in her big eyes. My hand shoots out to grab my boss's daughter's elbow, bringing her back toward the pen as another piece of information slips into my mind.

Briggs told me Galaxy was only abused by men. I asked Hadley and Olivia if they had time to help me today, but they're both busy. Maybe Tatum's presence will ease the mare's fear.

"What's wrong?" she asks, her eyes moving to where Galaxy is.

"She was abused by men, not women, so I have a theory she'll respond better to a woman," I blurt out my thoughts, watching understanding wash over Tatum.

"Okay. What can I do? Should I get in there with you?" she asks, already putting her foot on one of the panels to climb over. I place my hand over hers to stop her.

"It's too dangerous," I say because there is no way I'm letting her in here with an unpredictable horse.

"You're in there," she argues, and I smile at her again.

"I'm a professional."

Tatum nods several times, keeping her eyes trained on Galaxy as she takes another step toward the woman whose hands I should really stop touching. If it didn't send warmth and sparkling electricity through me, maybe I could.

"Aaron," she whispers. My eyes are stuck on where our fingers are entwined, unable to move.

"Just stay there," I say and step away from her, so confused about what the fuck is happening in my head.

With a deep breath, I shift back around to face the mare. She seems a bit calmer as I step out of the way while she approaches the side where Tatum is standing.

It's unlike anything I've ever seen.

Galaxy uses her big nose to sniff the air with every step until she's right in front of Tatum. The only thing separating them is the wooden fence, which is why I watch the horse even more closely. Her chest rises and expands as she takes a deep breath, bowing her head to look between the panels at Tatum. Galaxy is in desperate need of a bath, her white coat has turned gray from dust and dirt. Her mane needs brushing. Her hooves have to be cleaned, all things I can only do once she trusts me enough to let me get close to her.

Positive association is important, and taking care of her would be a good way for us to bond.

But we have to get there first.

"What do I do?" Tatum asks softly, and I notice she's standing very still behind the fence to let Galaxy study her. Her entire body is tensed up, worry creasing her forehead.

"Don't be scared. I won't let her hurt you." Tatum's eyes flick over to me as the tension visibly leaves her body.

She takes a step toward Galaxy, and the horse cocks her head in suspicion. I see her panic before she has a chance to act on it, so I say, "Back away," to Tatum before jumping over the fence myself.

Galaxy starts running around in the pen a second later, throwing herself against the wood in an attempt to get out, and it makes my heart ache in my chest to see what her trauma does to her.

I'm so focused on Galaxy, I don't even notice Tatum approaching until her hand is on my upper arm. The same concern I feel sparkles in her eyes.

"Is this normal behavior?" she asks, her fingers flexing a little around my bicep. My body almost gives an approving groan.

What *the fuck*?

"Yes, but it doesn't make it easier to watch. It takes a long time to make an abused animal understand they're no longer in danger, to prove to them that you'd never do what their previous owners did." She nods while we stand in silence.

My horse, Firefly, was much more distrusting than Galaxy. He didn't even let me into the pen with him until almost a week had passed and he finally understood I wasn't there to whip him like his previous owners did.

Patience is the key.

"I should go back to Angel, Olivia, and Betty," Tatum finally blurts out, her hand dropping from my arm. "Let me know if there is anything I can do," she adds with a sad look directed in Galaxy's direction.

"Thank you, Tatum."

Her gaze briefly shifts back to me before she turns and walks toward where Olivia is standing, having watched the whole thing.

She wiggles her brows at me suggestively, but I flip her off and spin back around to focus on Galaxy.

There is something very peaceful about stargazing on Silver Creek Ranch. With barely any light pollution all the way out here, the sky is filled with millions of stars. Nature is the only background noise, and I allow my thoughts to wander wherever it pleases them to go.

After a hard work day, this is my equivalent of a hot bath or sitting down with a book to relax, although I don't mind doing the latter either.

Reading is therapeutic for me, even when I want to throw the book across the room in anger.

It's moments like these, when I'm all alone, that my memories plunge to the forefront of my mind. I allow myself to think about Nanna and my parents. My childhood was beautiful, if one doesn't count my parents' passing. All I remember is being happy, surrounded by hundreds of animals.

But the bad memories have a habit of showing up until I'm wallowing in pain, flailing my arms to reach the surface before I drown.

It's right as I'm sinking, my chest constricting as metaphorical water fills my lungs, that I hear her.

"Oh, I'm sorry. I didn't know anyone was out here." She may have only been here for a little over a day, but Tatum Hayes has the kind of voice I could point out in any crowd. It's a unique combination of soft and rough, some words melodic and others filled with a promise of the fire inside of her.

"Don't be sorry. This is your father's ranch. If anything, I'm the one intruding," I reply, turning my head to see her walking toward where I'm standing, her dog by her side again.

A thoughtful expression has taken over her face, and though she tries to hide it, I notice sadness in her eyes, too. I'm too familiar with the feeling not to be able to identify it in other people.

"Are you okay?" I ask once she's beside me.

"Yeah, you?" Her gaze is stuck on the miles and miles of land ahead of us.

"You don't sound convinced. Was your first day not everything you thought it would be?" I ask with a little smile, watching her let out a snort.

"No, it was exactly what I thought it would be," she admits, but I don't think she means it in a positive way. "What about you, cowboy? What are you doing out here so late?" she asks, putting the attention on me. I barely manage to tear my eyes off her to stare at the night sky again.

"Collecting my thoughts. Reminiscing about life. Thinking," I explain, putting my hands in my pockets as a wave of uncertainty fills me.

I'm not entirely sure why I'm sharing this with someone I met yesterday, but the words are out of my mouth before I can think better of it.

"All that at once?" she asks and lets out a whistle. "Careful, Aaron, your brain might explode." I burst into laughter.

"Don't worry, I'm good at multitasking without my head exploding," I assure her, still chuckling. I turn my head to look at Tatum once more, but she doesn't seem amused in the slightest. "What are you doing out here?" I ask as she pets her dog's head.

"Collecting my thoughts. Thinking. Questioning my life choices," she replies and throws me a challenging look that only makes me smile even brighter than before.

"You're something else entirely, aren't you, sweetheart?"

All Tatum does is shrug.

"Nothing special about me, cowboy. I'm just a lawyer turned ranch hand."

I know she's so much more. Everyone is more than their job description, but I don't say it. I don't get the chance to.

"Well, have a good night, Aaron," she says as she wraps her arms around herself, shivering from the evening cold.

Reaching for my jacket and taking it off is instinctual, much like putting it around her without saying a single word.

"Good night, Tatum."

Chapter 7
Aaron

Tired doesn't come close to describing how I feel. After working all week with Galaxy and making little to no progress, I went on to fix the fence enclosure of the ranch in several places and then herded the cattle that got out through the holes I fixed.

Flynn and Beckett decided to show up two hours late for work today because both of them were too hungover to make it earlier. Apparently, Briggs went to the house they share on the ranch—Flynn moved in to help take care of Bailey six years ago—and almost knocked down their door to get their asses out of bed. I wish someone had filmed it.

I'd pay good money to see that footage.

My dog and right-hand man when it comes to farm work, Ash, digs into his food bowl as soon as I place it on the ground. He's been on his feet all day too and deserves to take the rest of it to sleep.

Meanwhile, I promised Briggs I'd go to his house for dinner after he practically demanded I'd show up. Beckett, Flynn, and Olivia said they'd be there too, which is another problem.

However, the biggest one is seeing Tatum after having successfully avoided her for most of the week.

"Ah, Aaron, perfect timing. Do you mind lending me a hand?" Briggs says as soon as he opens the door for me. There are smudges of oil across his right cheek, and he's rubbing his dirty hands on a towel.

"Yes, of course. What do you need help with?" I ask as I remove the cowboy hat from my head and follow him inside.

The door creaks as I attempt to close it, making me cock a brow at my boss. He gives me an easy smile and shrugs.

"This entire damn house is fallin' apart, but I can fix this annoying sound," he explains, handing me the oil. "The rest of the family is going to be here soon, and I need to clean myself up. Do you mind finishin' the front door?" he asks. I force a smile at him because, despite his efforts to sound carefree, the worry is evident in his features.

"No problem, Briggs. Go freshen up," I reply, grabbing his shoulder to give it a reassuring squeeze.

"Thanks, son."

Briggs runs a hand through his thick, gray hair as he struts away, leaving me to fix the creaking.

Right as I press the oil to the hinges, Beckett pushes the door open, almost slamming it into my face.

I jump out of the way in time to see him cringe at the sight of me.

"Fuck, sorry, Aaron. Didn't mean to slam the door into that pretty face of yours," he says before bursting into laughter and giving my back a firm slap.

"Do you ever knock?" I ask, my heart still beating a bit out of rhythm. Beck merely furrows his brows.

"When people invited me to their home? Absolutely not. You tell me to come, and I barge into your home. That's the Beckett way," he explains before leaving me to scout out the food situation.

"Hey, Beckett." My head shoots up at the sound of her voice, distracting me from everything else.

"Hey, Tate. Do you know what's for dinner?"

Tatum appears at the bottom of the staircase wearing nothing but a dress showing off all of her curves. The fabric hits just above the middle of those thick thighs of hers. It flutters against her skin when a gust of wind comes through the opened door, and I choose that moment to look away again, focusing on oiling the hinges.

"I'm gonna throw you into a steamin' pile of horse shit the next chance I get, Rafael," Olivia's voice fills my ears. She's the only one who calls Flynn by his real name, and, for some reason, it pisses him off even more.

"Do it. It'll be far more pleasant than spendin' another second in your company, *pesadilla*," my best mate replies.

I roll my eyes at their ridiculous bantering.

"You'd smell better afterward, too," she adds, forcing a snort out of me.

"Whose fuckin' side are you on, *cabrón*?" Flynn asks with a glare directed my way. Alright, switching into Spanish to call me an asshole is not a good sign.

"No one's because you're both acting like children," I reply while continuing to fix the door. Neither of them speaks to me again, they both just flip me off over their shoulders.

"Must you walk so close to me?" Flynn asks as they make their way to the dining room.

"You're the one on my heel like a damn dog."

Drowning out the rest of my friends' argument, I kneel down to fix the bottom hinge. My stomach growls because it's been empty since breakfast this morning, but once I start a task, I can't leave it half-completed.

I have to finish it.

"Why don't the two of them fuck and get it out of their system?" Tatum says as if she was asking me what the weather will be tomorrow.

A chuckle slips past my lips, but I don't look at her. She's blindingly beautiful, and if I want to keep my shit together, I can't look at her.

Then again, I don't seem to listen to myself when it comes to Tatum.

"Probably because they hate each other," I manage to reply.

"Hate and desire go hand in hand. Just like forbidding and desiring," she says as she takes me in, those eyes of hers traveling over my face, then to my hands.

Instinct takes over as I stand up, barely leaving an inch between our chests. My head tilts down a little and Tatum moves hers to meet my gaze, her chest rising and falling quickly. If she was anyone else, if she wasn't my boss' daughter, I wouldn't be fighting this hard to ignore how gorgeous I think she is. I wouldn't fight feeling attracted to her.

But she isn't anyone else. She's Tatum Hayes, Briggs Hayes' daughter, and she's off-limits.

"Is that so?" I ask with my best flirty smirk.

Well, I'm almost proud of myself. I made it one week without flirting with her. I avoided her well, but I knew dinner with her would complicate things.

"Yup. It's why you can't take your eyes off me when you think I'm not looking. My dad probably told you to stay away from me, and now you want to do the complete opposite," she says.

"That's where you're wrong, sweetheart. I already couldn't take my eyes off you before I even knew who you were," I reply shamelessly, watching her eyes sparkle at my admission.

"You don't even know me," she argues.

"What if I'd like to?" A little smile finally slips onto her face, but she shuts it down and steps back before I can truly enjoy it.

"You shouldn't want that, Aaron."

Something changes in the air between us. It shifts from crackling to uncomfortable.

"Why—" She cuts me off by shaking her head and taking another step back.

"Dinner's ready. My dad made his famous pasta salad," she says and walks away while I try to process what the fuck just happened.

"Hittin' on Tate is a dumb idea if you want to keep your balls attached to your body, man. How many times must I tell you the same thing in one week?" Beckett asks as he approaches with two beers, holding one out for me to take.

"I wasn't hitting on her," I defend and take a sip of my drink. Beckett flings his arm around my shoulders and smiles.

41

"Whatever you say, pretty boy." He shoots me an amused look. "I am *hungry as fuck*. Do you think you could manage not to hit on Tatum again until after we've eaten?" I slam my elbow into his ribs hard enough to make him wheeze a little.

CHAPTER 8
Tatum

DINNER WAS FUCKING AWKWARD, and that's putting it nicely. Aaron hardly spoke, confusion painted across his face the entire time. Flynn and Olivia shot daggers at each other, and at one point, I even confiscated her knife because she looked ready to stab the man across from her. Beckett was too busy enjoying the food to speak to anyone, and I felt too shy to pick up a conversation with any of the mostly new people to say a word either.

Which left my dad, who couldn't stop talking about everything that had to be done on the ranch.

It's now been eight days since then, and we've had three more dinners, which were equally as strange.

I've also become a pro at taking care of Betty and Angel. Dad told me to stay away from the cows, llamas, and horses for now to make sure I don't get overwhelmed and stressed out learning too many new things at once. It's sweet to see how much he cares, but I'm still trying to make him understand that it stresses me more when people cover me in bubble wrap.

Learning new things is something I need to stay happy. It stimulates my brain, especially on a farm in the middle of fucking nowhere.

Dad putting me solely in charge of Betty and Angel has left me with a lot of time to observe every little thing going wrong with the ranch. The fence surrounding the farm is rusted to the point where it keeps breaking in different spots. Some of the animals keep getting out, making more work for Aaron, Hadley, Olivia, Flynn, Beckett, and Ian.

All of them had to abandon their other duties yesterday to hunt down some of the horses that got out and fix the fence on the far east side.

Obviously, Dad is struggling to keep this ranch alive and thriving, and with all of the free time my brain has to overthink—pointedly not my interaction with Aaron before our first dinner—I've come up with a solution he might be on board with.

So, I made a PowerPoint presentation, researched distributors, and created a plan for the ranch, which, if executed well, could make Dad a lot of money. In turn, he could finally fix up everything that's falling apart, including the house he lives in. I may have a law degree, but I majored in business, too.

"Dad, can we talk?" I ask after we've both settled down at the table for dinner. It's just the two of us tonight, giving me the perfect opportunity to pull up my presentation. He watches me lift my tablet with furrowed brows and half a smile.

"Should I be scared?" he teases, but I give him an unimpressed look. Dad chuckles before shoving a forkful of meat into his mouth. "Talk to me, honeybee."

"Promise to keep an open mind?" Dad holds up his pinky, wiggling it at me until I laugh and hook mine around his. "I would like to make you a business proposal."

Surprise widens his eyes and forces his eyebrows to shoot up. Creases appear all over his forehead as I slide my tablet across the table toward him.

"You are supposed to be relaxin' out here, Tatum. What are you doin' making business proposals?" he says, a little frustration slipping into his voice. "This is not keepin' things stress-free." I fight back my own irritation before responding.

"Dad, you're going to lose this ranch if we don't do something about it."

My father leans back in his chair, touching his thumb and index finger to his temples and massaging the areas. He's worried. About me. About his home. About everything he's built here. But that's where I come in, me and my idea.

"It's not somethin' I want you worryin' about, honeybee," he replies, but I slide my hand on top of his with a comforting smile.

"Well, too late. I want to help, and as much as I love spending time with Angel and Betty and soon the new mini cow, I'm more useful with things like this," I say and point at the PowerPoint.

"Fine. Lemme hear it," he blurts out after a moment of complete silence.

"Turn Silver Creek Ranch into a visitable farm with events like flower picking, strawberry picking, all the picking you want," I say, causing Dad to chuckle. "Let's grow things we can sell, have events where people can attend by paying a small entrance fee. Pumpkin patches, Christmas markets, Halloween haunted mazes, whatever your heart desires. These types of farms are becoming more and more popular, and I'm sure Orchard Hill would love to have one as close to home as Silver Creek Ranch is."

I pause to give him a chance to process my words, and when he doesn't immediately object but seems to think about the proposal, I go on.

"There is a lot of potential here, Dad. I already found cheap seed distributors. It'll take a while until we can start the picking aspect, but we can still host the events. Maybe every Sunday, we can do a market where other farmers sell their products and pay a small fee to have a booth."

I take a deep breath, Dad watching me so closely, I wish I could look into his head and hear what he's thinking.

"Like I said, Silver Creek Ranch has potential, and I don't want you to lose everything you've built here," I go on, holding my breath as I wait for him to say anything.

Dad leans forward to slide through the statistics and charts I made. He's silent for so long, sweat starts collecting at the back of my head.

"Where is the money comin' from for the initial purchase of these seeds and other goods?" he asks, and I roll my lips, thinking about avoiding the question when he shifts that detective gaze on me.

"I have some savings," I explain, but Dad immediately shakes his head.

"Not happenin'." He goes to stand up, but I place my hand on his again to stop him.

"Don't be stubborn, Dad. You'll lose this farm if you don't accept my help."

"I know, Tatum! The fuckin' bank's after me because I can't pay the mortgage anymore. I've been warned that if I don't prove I'm capable of turning things around, they'll take everythin' away. This was my dream, and I could lose it all in six months if I don't figure a way out. All because some damn teenagers thought it'd be funny to set some of my crops on fire last year during a fuckin' drought. Burned everything we had and damaged the land so badly, we couldn't grow 'em this year either. I've been using my savings, Tate, but they've long run out, and I'm not taking what you've worked for your whole life in an attempt to save somethin' we might not be able to save," he rants, slumping back in his seat.

My heart shatters into a million pieces.

"I'm so sorry, Dad. I didn't know about the crops," I reply as I get up and squat down next to him. His hand moves to the top of my head before dropping to my shoulder.

"I didn't want to worry you." Of course, he didn't.

"I'm twenty-seven years old, not seven, Dad, not anymore. You don't have to protect me when I can help you. Let me help you," I say while he massages my shoulder absentmindedly.

"This will be too stressful for you, Tate. I'm tryin' to get you away from stress so you don't have more of those goddamn seizures," he whispers the last part, and I frown up at him.

"Worry less about my epilepsy and more about the fact that I came here to live with you for good. That can only happen if you let me use my savings to pay off a little of your mortgage and get us the supplies to turn this ranch into a visitable farm. Will you let me do that? Will you let me invest in our future?" I ask and wrap my fingers around his wrist next to my head.

"Damn your brain. It always comes up with exactly the right thing to say." I can't help but beam up at him.

He's letting me help.

"Six months is all we've got," he adds after a moment of silence passes between us.

"Six months is all I need. We've got this, old man," I tease with a smile so big, it hurts my face. Dad places his hand on my cheek with a thoughtful expression.

"If it gets too stressful, if you have a seizure because of this, you're off the project immediately. Deal?"

"Deal," I promise.

"And I'm puttin' Aaron on this with you. From now on, you'll be working with him. He has the most experience with plantin' seeds and growin' 'em. I'm also pretty sure he and his grandma used to have similar events like the ones you were describin' on their farm years ago. You should speak to him," Dad says, letting out a heavy breath and turning to his food again.

I stand up and move back over to my chair, ignoring my fluttering heart.

We finish dinner in silence while I panic about the fact that Aaron and I will be working together for the next six months. Just him and me. All of my efforts to not see him these past two weeks will have been for nothing.

Not that I was successful anyway.

Every morning, Olivia, Angel, Betty, and I walked by him training Galaxy. She's still not letting him go near her, but he's been making progress. Every day, he takes one step closer without her getting scared. Every day, she feels a bit safer with him.

"Is there a place I can take Loki swimming around here?" I ask to distract myself.

"Yeah, it's about eight minutes north walking distance from the house, close to Aaron's place." Of course it is. "It's called Silver Creek, the river the ranch was named after," Dad explains with a wink as he takes our plates and carries them to the kitchen.

"Thanks," I say and make my way outside with Loki for our daily evening walk.

My dog storms off into the distance to do his business when another furball makes its way toward me, running with its tongue flopping in the wind. The animal with the gray, black, and brown coat stops right in front of me, plopping its butt down to wag aggressively.

"Why, hello, sweets," I say, bending over at the waist to let the dog sniff my hand.

"Ash, heel," Aaron's voice fills the night, making my heart skip several beats. "Goddammit, Ash, where did you go?" I can't see him, but he's definitely walking toward me.

Meanwhile, Ash has come closer and decided sitting on my feet is the best idea.

"Over here, cowboy," I call out, ruffling the fur between Ash's ears.

"Tate?" he asks.

"Yup," I say, watching him stroll up the hill of the house with a bouquet of flowers in his hands. He's dressed in a pair of jeans and a copper flannel that brings out his eyes. The smirk on his lips sends a wave of shivers down my spine.

"Sorry about that, Tatum. Ash has always had a weakness for gorgeous women," he says, causing my cheeks to fill with heat.

"That smooth-talking mouth of yours should be illegal," I blurt out before my brain has a chance to process the words. He cocks an intrigued brow but doesn't say what we're both thinking.

Aaron stops a few feet away from me, the bouquet still clasped tightly in his hand.

"So, who are the flowers for?" I ask to change the subject.

"It's Beckett's mom's birthday. She's having a little celebration and I'm already late, but Ash decided I needed to be even more so," he says with a small laugh and looks at the flowers in his hands before picking out a red one. He spins it as he closes the distance between us to hold it out for me. "Would you like to come with me? I'm sure they won't mind," he offers, but I merely take the flower from him while shaking my head.

"Maybe next time. I have some work to do, which, by the way, we need to discuss tomorrow." Aaron gives me a confused smile but doesn't question me.

"Over dinner? Sounds wonderful," he replies and pats his leg to get Ash to heel.

"I never said anything about dinner," I call out once I regain my ability to speak.

"I'll cook," he shouts back, and I take several steps in his direction because he's already too far gone for me to have a proper conversation with him.

"I didn't say yes!" I argue.

"See you at seven," he says before walking down the hill with Ash trotting by his side.

CHAPTER 9
Aaron

IT'S EASY TO SUPPRESS the grief and denial in my chest when I'm working. My head is too busy focusing on the tasks in front of me to think about anything else, and, by the time night rolls around, I'm too tired to do anything but fall asleep.

Day in, day out, it's the same routine to keep me from being stuck in this bloody limbo.

Should I grieve her and accept that my nanna is gone when I can still see her whenever I want?

Should I cling to hope she'll remember me when she sees me, even though she hasn't recognized me for the past month?

What is the right choice, the one that'll protect me from the most pain?

The last question repeats itself a lot in my head before I visit Nanna. Once a week. It's all I allow myself, no matter how desperately I want to see her. It hurts too much to reintroduce myself every time like I'm a stranger and not the grandchild she's loved for over three decades.

Like I'm no one to her.

"Mr. Blaze? Mrs. Blaze is ready to see you. She's in the garden," one of the nurses, Freddy, says as he approaches me, and I nod appreciatively at him. The same sad and comforting smile he always wears rests on his face as my feet bring me past him and toward the big glass doors.

My attention drifts to where Lorena Blaze sits at a small table, a cup of tea in her hand and looking more at peace than I've seen in a while. I remove my cowboy hat as I walk up to her.

49

When her gaze shifts to me and recognition turns her eyes soft, I almost take a knee to let out a breath of relief so strong, it would shake my whole body. She might not recognize me tomorrow or the day after, but if I'm allowed one more day with her when she remembers who I am, I'm grateful.

"There you are, Aaron. I've been waiting for you," she says, and I glance down at the watch around my wrist to see it's ten past three in the afternoon. When I first helped her move in here, we agreed to see each other every Friday at three. She remembers. For today, she remembers, and I barely keep from tearing up in response.

"I'm sorry I'm late," I say as I place my hat on the opposite chair so I can pull her into a fierce hug, one I've needed for the past month.

When I'm a stranger to her, all I get from the person I love the most is a casual conversation she forgets as soon as I leave.

"That's alright, my angel boy. You're here now," she replies with a small laugh. Tears sting my eyes, but I blink them away, leaning back and pressing a kiss to the top of her head.

"I've missed you," I mumble, unable to stop myself.

"I've missed you, too. Now sit and tell me how work has been going," she demands with her bossy tone, the one I'd grown to love and hate all the same when I was a child.

"Busy days and exhausting evenings with Beckett, Flynn, and Olivia getting themselves into trouble every week," I tease, watching my grandmother's eyes sparkle with amusement.

"Well, nothing new there," she replies after taking a sip of her tea.

"Yeah," I say with a watery chuckle. "I also recently met a woman I can't seem to stop thinking about," I admit because after meeting Tate, my first thought was how desperately I wanted to tell Nanna how beautiful she was.

"What's her name?" she asks with a suggestive wiggle of her brows. My cheeks heat under her gaze and at the thought of the woman I'd very much like to get to know better.

"Tatum. She's Briggs' daughter," I explain, causing her to suck in a sharp breath.

"Jesus, Aaron, of all the dumb things you could do, finding your overprotective boss's daughter attractive is one of the dumbest," she says, but not in an upset way. This amuses her.

"Don't worry. She's not interested in getting to know each other anyway," I say and grab the cup of tea in front of me, taking a sip to give my hands something to do before they start fidgeting nervously.

"Did she say that?"

"Not in so many words, but—" Nanna cuts me off.

"That's too bad," she says, and I nod in agreement.

"Yeah." I take another sip while Nanna shakes her head.

"No, I mean it's too bad I raised an idiot," she says, slowly standing up to walk over to the flower garden. I watch her with utter fascination before joining her near the wildflowers. "You are a good-looking, kind, charming man, Aaron, and far from stupid. You know what you've got to offer, and if you want to get to know her, then do something about it," she adds, that bossy edge back in her voice.

"Well, I did invite her to dinner tonight because she wanted to discuss something work-related," I defend, and Nanna looks over her shoulder to grin at me.

"You cookin'?" I smile at the way her Australian accent fades to give way to the Southern one I often struggle to prevent from taking over as well.

"Of course," I say, relishing the fact that it's so easy to slip back into the role of her child despite not having been able to be him in a month.

"Good. Make her the Lorena specialty. No one can resist the person who prepares a meal that good. Just ask your grandfather," she says with a wink, but her words break my heart into a trillion pieces.

Fuck.

"Will do," I say and swallow hard to get rid of the lump in my throat. My arm snakes across her shoulders before pulling her against my side and kissing the crown of her head.

"Do you know when he'll come home? I've been waiting for him all day," she adds, making the stinging in my chest even worse.

"I'm sure he'll be back soon," I lie because there is no point telling her Granddad died when I was little.

There is no point in reminding her of the heartbreak of losing her husband to a heart attack when she won't remember it tomorrow or in an hour. If anything, it would probably cause her to break down, for an episode of paranoia to overtake her. She's been struggling with those since her Alzheimer's started, and I don't want to be the reason she has another.

Today is supposed to be a good day.

"I love you," I say after we've been standing in silence for a moment.

"To Pluto and back," she replies because the moon was never far enough for her.

"To Pluto and back," I echo, kissing the top of her head again and letting a single tear escape my left eye.

It's three minutes past seven. I'm stirring the sauce I made before moving over to the pasta pot. I didn't demand Tatum show up for dinner, I'd never fucking do that, but part of me is very tempted to go up to the main house, throw her over my shoulder, and carry her here.

Ash barks up at me, and I give him a small smile. Right as I give him a bone to make him happy, there is a knock on the front door.

My heart somersaults in my chest at the sound.

I wipe my hands on the cloth draped across my shoulder while rushing toward the door.

Disappointment washes through me at the sight of my best mate on my porch with a six-pack in his hands.

"Damn, don't look too excited to see me. It might just kill me," he teases with an easy grin, but I'm in no mood to joke around.

"I'm expecting someone for dinner," is all I reply before moving back over to my stove because I forgot to turn down the heat and something smells like it's burning. "Fuck. Shit," I blurt out as I lift the sauce off the burner.

"Tatum? Yeah, I saw her walkin' over here with Loki by her side and somethin' that looked suspiciously like a bowl of salad," Flynn says, making my heart flutter again.

"Get out. You already made me burn the sauce. I won't let you ruin my evening with all your—" I gesture at all of him, hoping it's explanation enough.

Flynn places an offended hand on his chest.

"Pardon me? I'm a fuckin' delight. I'm sure Tate won't mind my bein' here. I did bring beer, after all," he says, but I merely shake my head at him.

"First of all, no, you're not. Secondly, ever notice she doesn't drink alcohol? We've had dinner with Briggs and her four times since she moved here, and she didn't touch a single drop of alcohol." I've also noticed she doesn't eat meat, so I did my best to prepare a full vegetarian meal.

"Shit, man, you've put a lot of thought into tonight," he says with an amused smirk I'd like to knock off his face.

"Well done, Nancy Drew. You figured out I want things to go well, now fuck off. I need to go change," I say after spotting a drop of sauce on my polo.

Should have known my best friend never does what I tell him to, though.

"Hey, Tate. You look phenomenal." Flynn's voice comes from my front door. Panic grips my chest as I storm out of my bedroom.

"Aaron should be right out. He's just changing his shirt," he goes on right as I walk up to them.

For a moment, breathing becomes impossible. Seeing Tatum in jean shorts that barely hit a third of her thighs and the simple green shirt she's wearing makes me weak in the knees. Her dark hair is loose, those beautiful curls more defined today than I've ever seen them before. Her hazel eyes sparkle with something I can only identify as desire as they land on me.

Flynn's attention drifts to me before he presses his lips into a line.

"Or leaving a shirt off entirely." I furrow my brows at him and stare down my body, realizing he's right. I'm half-fucking-naked in front of the woman I wanted to impress tonight.

Fuck.

"Get. Out." I enunciate every word carefully, directing my irritation at him.

"Sure thing. I have shit to do anyway. This story isn't going to spread through town by itself," he replies before giving Tate's shoulder a quick squeeze while my cheeks heat from embarrassment.

Fantastic.

"If I'd known this was a nude dinner, I wouldn't have worn this many clothes," Tate jokes, and while I'm convinced it's a way to make me feel better, I can't help the visual of us having dinner completely naked storming into my mind. "You should probably put on a shirt. We have business to discuss, and I won't be able to focus with your eight-pack on display," she says and places the bowl into my hands, her eyes traveling over my body appreciatively.

"Or we could make it fair, and I could take off your shirt, too," I suggest, but she's already on her way to the kitchen.

Loki gives my leg a nudge before following Tate.

"Not gonna happen, cowboy."

CHAPTER 10
Tatum

AARON'S LITTLE HOUSE IS beautiful.

His kitchen has the newest appliances, but the dark wooden cabinets give it a rustic sort of look. He has a kitchen island with a stove built into it where two pots are currently on simmering heat. A delicious scent mingles with the scent of food burning, but it doesn't look like it's in any danger at the moment.

His kitchen leads to a living room with a small leather couch, a fireplace with a television hanging above it, and a coffee table. It's cozy and homey, the perfect place to make you feel like you belong somewhere. I've never felt this way in any of the places I lived, but I can imagine being the type of person to own a small house like this and be perfectly content.

The veranda and view don't hurt either, of course. There is a single rocking chair on it which overlooks the mountains. The backyard is nothing but greenery, and I'm pretty sure the creek Dad told me about isn't too far from here, too.

A dog nudges my legs as I admire the view, and I squat down to greet Ash, Aaron's Australian Shepherd. His tail swings back and forth from excitement as I massage his ears and then pet his sides. He craves attention, and I'm more than happy to give this dog whatever he wants, especially to distract myself from what happened a few minutes ago.

I don't know what came over me, flirting with Aaron like that.

Having a chronic illness like mine where a simple trigger can shut down my entire body for thirty seconds makes committing to someone extremely difficult. I don't want to burden them with the fear of losing me at any moment. I don't want to frighten them by making them watch me seize. I don't want to fall in love with someone without being able to give them a future.

Flirting with Aaron was a mistake, but it doesn't feel like that when he stands in front of me, all sculpted muscles and devilish smirks.

"What would you like to drink, Tate?" Aaron asks, and I lift my head to see him leaning against the veranda door with his arms crossed in front of his chest and an easy smile on his lips. His black hair is ruffled and a little all over the place, but it somehow makes him look sexier.

"Some water would be great, thank you," I reply, and he gives me a swift nod before disappearing inside again. Ash follows his daddy while Loki makes his way over to me.

He sniffs the air around me, causing panic to grip my system. It's never a good sign when Loki's nose starts wiggling as he takes in my scent. It's usually the first sign that I'm about to have a seizure, but he doesn't nudge me or alert me of one. I let out a relieved sigh as he sits down in front of me, wagging his tail and smiling a perfect dog's smile.

"Good boy," I praise.

Loki and I join Aaron in the kitchen where he's grabbing two plates. The glass of water he filled for me is already on the table in the dining room.

"I wouldn't forgive myself if I didn't say this, Tate, so bear with me," he starts before turning his head to face me. "You look breathtaking." He takes a step toward me, and I find myself holding my breath and inching closer, too.

"So do you, even with the shirt on."

Get a grip, Tatum.

Stop flirting with the damn cowboy.

Aaron chuckles softly, his electrifying gaze traveling over my face. He turns back to the food without another word, letting me breathe again.

"How come I didn't see you on the ranch today?" I ask, hoping it's a casual enough question. Aaron's features fall a little as he walks into the dining room with the pot of pasta in his hands.

"I was visiting my Nanna. She's been living in the nursing home twenty minutes outside of Orchard Hill ever since she was diagnosed with Alzheimer's," he says while wiping his hands on the towel that's resting over his shoulder.

"Shit, I'm so sorry. I know how difficult watching a grandparent you love forget you, it's—" I cut off, looking for the right word when Aaron appears in front of me with a sad smile.

"Torture," he finishes my thought, and I feel like wrapping my arms around him to comfort him. "Nanna or granddad?"

"My grandfather. He passed away five years ago when the final stage of Alzheimer's set in," I reply, feeling a familiar same stinging sensation in my chest.

"Fucking Alzheimer's," Aaron whispers, his gaze fixated on mine.

"Fucking Alzheimer's," I echo.

The left corner of his mouth twitches a little, as if he would smile if the topic of our conversation wasn't so damn depressing.

"You wanted to discuss business, let's discuss business," he says after we've been staring at each other for several long moments, neither one of us breathing or breaking eye contact.

Aaron disappears into the kitchen again before bringing the sauce into the dining room, too. Loki and Ash join him there, so I do the same, trying to keep my heart from racing. He's right, we should be discussing business, but I find myself wondering about things like where he was born, and if or when he moved here. Why he's working at my dad's ranch, and anything else you'd ask on a first date. But this isn't a date, so I have no right to voice any of my curiosities.

"You're thinking awfully hard over there, sweetheart. Anything you'd like me to take care of for you?" he asks, sending heat straight back into my cheeks.

"I was thinking about the food you made and that I forgot to tell you I'm a vegetarian," I lie.

"Don't worry, I already knew that." My brows furrow at his smug smile, so he decides to elaborate. "I'm a very observant man."

"Is that so?" I ask while he pulls out a chair for me and then pushes it back in once I'm seated.

"Yup. It's why I know you also don't drink alcohol," he replies, stepping away and taking his body heat with him. My lips are parted in surprise as he sits down, moving toward the table. "May I make a plate for you?" he asks, ever the gentleman. I hand him my plate with a "thank you" and watch the muscles in his forearms flex as he moves.

He smirks when he catches me.

"I spoke to my dad about the ranch not doing well financially," I say after a few minutes of us eating in a weirdly comfortable silence. Aaron reaches forward to top off my glass of water.

"This is where the business part comes in, I'm assuming?" he says, bringing a smile to my lips. His eyes attach themselves to my mouth instantly, awe crossing his features.

"What?" I ask. Aaron clears his throat with a grin so bright, it makes his eyes twinkle.

"This is the first time you've smiled around me," he points out, clearing his throat. "And, well, you have the most beautiful smile I've ever seen in my entire life."

A blush paints his cheeks pink, and I feel heat rushing into mine, too.

"Oh," is all I manage to reply because what do I say to that?

So do you, Aaron. And I adore that you give it away so freely because it somehow manages to brighten up a person's day"?

"Back to what you were saying before your smile distracted me. The ranch is struggling and you have a plan. Where do I come into that?" he asks.

"Yeah, so, um—" I stutter because he's thrown me so off balance, I'm not even sure if I'm still sitting or floating somewhere.

"Did my compliment make you stutter like that?" His brows are drawn together in confusion, but the hint of a smirk remains on his lips.

"Absolutely not." We both know it's bullshit. Aaron's blue eyes narrow a little.

"I guess I gotta make a habit out of complimenting you then. Help you get used to it," he clarifies, and I let out a nervous laugh before slapping a hand over my mouth to keep it in. I hate that nervous laughter is my go-to bodily reaction when I don't know what the fuck to say.

"Maybe you shouldn't compliment me at all," I fire back instead of acknowledging my outburst of laughter.

"Maybe, but I want to," he says, and I can't help the smile spreading across my face.

"You're impossible. Can we get back to this?" I ask and hold up my tablet to point at the chart I made.

"Of course. Anything you want, Tate." Aaron takes the device from me, his attention on the screen.

He lets me explain my plan for Silver Creek Ranch, listening closely and scrolling through the presentation I created. It takes a lot longer to describe my vision to Aaron because he keeps asking more questions, trying to get the full picture. I'm so passionate about this entire project, I find myself talking and talking and talking until I have to take a sip of my water because my voice is cracking.

"What's the timeline?" Aaron asks as he hands me back the tablet, his face serious.

"It will take the flowers a few months to grow, so we should get on that as soon as possible. Halloween is over five months away, and I'm anticipating we need approximately four months to make the decorations ourselves to keep the costs low. Then, I thought for the other holidays before and after we could set up a market where people could have stands of food, games, drinks, or little self-made trinkets. Whatever people in Orchard Hill come up with. Entry can be free, but we could charge vendors a percentage of their profits, a small one."

Aaron thinks about my words for a moment, his eyes shifting from my right one to my lips and then back up to my left. Half his bottom lip is tucked between his teeth as he processes everything.

"What if we have riding lessons for kids at these events, too? Maybe a supervised petting zoo with the mini cows and horses to make sure everyone is safe but also to make more money?" he asks, and I write down all of his suggestions.

"Yes, that's good. Maybe then I can get a riding lesson, too," I say with a small laugh, but he tilts his head in a contemplative manner.

"I'll teach you whenever you'd like me to."

Another tense moment of eye contact passes between us because I don't know what to say to that and Aaron doesn't seem to mind simply looking at me.

"We also have to plan in that I'm still training Galaxy. I'm making so little progress with her, I can't risk losing it all," he says, starting to clear away the plates.

"Of course. I also have my responsibilities with Betty, Angel, and the new mini cow we're getting tomorrow," I reply as I follow him into the kitchen with one of the pots.

"So, should we meet after lunch then?" he asks before turning to take the pot from me. "Unless you'd like us to have lunch together," he adds.

"After lunch is fine. I don't want to get sick of you when we're going to have to spend the next six months working together," I tease, making him grab his chest as if I'd deeply offended him.

"I'm wounded, Tatum, and I even made dessert. Guess I'll have to eat the strawberry shortcake all by myself," he replies, and I barely manage to catch my jaw before it drops.

"Strawberry shortcake is my favorite. How the hell did you know?"

"Old Man Briggs never stops talking about you. I brought him some once, and all he could talk about for the rest of the night was how much you adored it." My heart warms at the thought of how much my dad loves me before Aaron steals all my attention by tugging a runaway stray of hair behind my ear. "He also said you're a remarkable woman with a brain like no one else's, and he was spot on about that, too, so I decided he's a reliable enough source."

"You should really stop flirting with me, cowboy. We're going to be working together from now on, and I don't fuck people I have to see every day. It complicates things." It's complicated enough that my heart keeps stuttering around him.

"Fair enough. I guess I'll wait six months to ask you out then," he says and turns back around to the sink to do the dishes.

After taking a deep breath, I join him and start drying what he hands me.

We work in silence until he breaks it, but I welcome his voice.

"How was law school?" he asks, handing me a plate.

"I think it took several years off my lifespan," I tease, watching a brilliant smile take over his face.

"That bad, huh?" he asks, handing me a glass to dry this time.

"It was exhausting. The amount of work I had kept me awake most nights, and even after I graduated and became a junior associate, it never stopped." Aaron nods thoughtfully at my words.

"I watched Suits. I've seen the workload they put on the junior associates," he comments, and I shake my head, biting my tongue to keep from laughing.

"Who was your favorite character?" Aaron stops washing his plate to think.

"Harvey, without a doubt, but I did like Jessica, too. I have a thing for powerful women," he explains, throwing me a sheepish grin.

"I don't blame you. I was in love with her right until she left the show," I reply, enjoying this entire interaction. I can't remember the last time I had a friendly conversation about something as simple as a show I loved. "But Harvey was my favorite, too," I reply, drying the plate he hands me.

Aaron keeps asking me more questions like what my favorite music genre is, and what my mother does nowadays. In turn, I ask him how long he's known Beckett, Flynn, Hads, Olivia, and Ian, and he shares some of his childhood stories with me.

It's easy and comfortable, two things I've never felt with anyone.

Halfway through dessert, which we eat on his veranda, him on the chair he took outside and me on the rocking chair, I realize we're going to be spending *a lot* of time together. I knew that, of course I did, but truly understanding what it means only hits me when he talks about having to take it a little easier because he has mobility troubles in his left knee.

I don't usually tell people about my epilepsy, but Aaron should know in case I have a seizure while we're together. Not knowing about my chronic illness would make him handle the situation a lot more poorly than if I told him. Even if I don't want to. Even if I know it'll change the way he sees me now. Even if I'd rather no one knew so they didn't treat me like I'm incapable of being a member of society in the same way a person without a chronic illness is.

"How long have you had Loki?" Aaron asks, giving me the perfect opening.

"Two years. My stepdad got him for me and paid for his service dog training," I explain while Aaron takes a bite of his shortcake, which is absolutely phenomenal, just like dinner was. It shouldn't be allowed for a man that handsome to be a good cook, too.

"That explains why he hasn't left your side all night," the cowboy replies right as Loki places his big head on top of my feet. I smile down at my best friend.

"Yeah. I have epilepsy, so he warns me before I have a seizure and he's been incredibly helpful ever since I got him," I go on, and Aaron smiles at my dog.

"Are you the best boy?" he asks, so Loki starts wagging his tail. He loves attention, but so does Ash, and he's not happy about his daddy giving my dog any of it. The Australian Shepherd jumps to his feet to start licking Aaron's face. "Yes, you are, too," he says with a chuckle and kisses the top of Ash's head.

"Loki knows exactly what to do when I have a seizure, so, should it happen while we're working together, which it won't as long as I don't feel claustrophobic, stressed, have any alcohol, or see flashing lights, don't worry. He helps me through it," I rant because saying the words fast makes it easier.

Aaron nods along to them, still petting Ash.

"Is there anything I can do to help when it happens?" he asks, and I almost hug him for asking a helpful question instead of the useless, pitiful comments I get when people find out.

Oh no, you poor thing. That must be horrible. Yes, having a seizure isn't fun.

Can't you just take something to prevent it from happening? No, that's not how it works. There is medication to help control the seizures, but if triggered, they still happen.

Why don't you just avoid your triggers so it doesn't happen? Because I can't always control my environment, and, for fuck's sake, I can't control my stress levels every single minute of my life.

"No. I've been living with it for twenty-two years, I know how to handle my seizures," I reply, my hand reaching out to scratch Loki between the ears.

"Okay. Thank you for trusting me with this," Aaron adds with a hint of a smile. "I'm assuming you don't like people knowing, considering no one at Silver Creek Ranch has mentioned it, so I promise to keep this to myself," he says, sending my heart into a frenzy.

"I'd appreciate that."

"You got it, sweetheart." He winks at me before finishing his dessert and putting his plate aside.

His eyes drift to the starry night sky, but I can't help watching him instead of the beautiful picture nature creates. The cut of his jaw, the column of his throat, the line of his cheekbones, the stubble on his face, and the way his broad chest strains against his shirt are things I'm tracing over and over with my gaze. Almost like I'm trying to memorize every ridge and muscle and freckle I can spot.

His attention shifts back to me, fire sparkling in his eyes as he finds me ogling him. Aaron leans forward, elbows resting on his knees and his hands clasped together as he studies my lips. His gaze sends desire rolling down my spine until my heart is beating so rapidly, I'm convinced he can hear it, too.

"I should get home," I blurt out.

"I'll walk you."

Despite my telling him not to worry, that Loki and I will get back to the main house fine by ourselves, Aaron brings me all the way to the front steps. My dog bolts through the door as soon as I open it while I'm stuck on the porch, trying to find the right words to stay.

"Thank you for dinner. It was... nice," I manage to say, and Aaron gives me half a smirk before stepping closer and pressing a kiss to my left cheek.

"Good night, Tate."

He walks away without another word, leaving the skin on my cheek tingling.

CHAPTER 11
Aaron

TATUM HAS ONLY BEEN at Silver Creek Ranch for about three weeks, but there is no denying how much happier she seems every day. Her mood improves even more after we work on our projects. Like yesterday when we were sending out emails to all of the ranch owners close by as well as the community chain of Orchard Hill. Zelda Remin emailed back straight away, demanding to know all of the information so she could tell everyone at the library today.

Olivia and Hadley agreed to help us prepare our projects, telling us they will drag Ian's, Beckett's, and Flynn's asses into this project as well. I almost burst into a fit of laughter imagining Beckett doing the delicate work of sewing materials together with those big hands of his or Flynn and Olivia sitting long enough to create something without starting a physical fight. But, my family promised, and I'm so grateful to them.

This plan of Tatum's will work.

I know it will.

Right now, Tatum and I make our way to where Firefly is. My horse of five years with his white fur covered in brown spots nods his head in excitement as we approach him. He's always excited to see Ash and me, and I can't wait to introduce him to Tate. My animals mean the world to me, and I want to show her how sweet and incredible they are.

There are several animals on the ranch I have a close connection with who are mine even if Briggs brought them here. Firefly, Ash, a llama called Flames that I rescued from being euthanized for biting the owner—who deserved to have his entire head bitten off for abusing Flames—and, slowly but surely, Galaxy. That mare is fighting her way into my heart with every interaction between us, even if she's not sure of me yet. It's okay.

What I told Tatum was true. I'm a patient man. I'll wait until she's ready for me.

"What are we doing here?" Tatum asks as she studies my horse with a soft look in her eyes.

"I wanted to finally teach you how to ride a horse. You've been here for weeks. It's unacceptable that no one has taught you yet," I say, hearing a snort from behind us. I turn just enough to see Beck with a shovel in his hand, about to muck out the stables. "What's funny?" I ask. Beckett smiles like he knows something I don't.

"Hard to teach her when you keep the woman so busy doing God-knows-what," he says with an insinuating chuckle, and Tate throws an unimpressed look over her shoulder.

"As a matter of fact, Beckett, *I'm* the one in charge, the one keeping *him* busy." Damn right she is. "I'd be more than happy putting you to work, too. How would you feel about mowing the grass area in front of the main house? We're planning to have the Sunday market there starting this week, and it's a mess. There are weeds, and they are angry."

Beckett halts his movements, his eyes going wide at the horror of what she's asking him to do. Out of all the chores in the world, mowing grass is by far his biggest nightmare.

"Didn't think so," Tate adds with a smile, and I'm so close to bursting into laughter, I have to suck in a sharp breath to keep it at bay. I'm used to this bossy side of Tate by now. We've spent a week working together, and she hasn't held back her commands or softened her instructions. When she needs something done, she'll tell you as dryly as possible.

"Well played, Tate," Beck finally replies, taking off his baseball cap, the one he always wears backward, and bending slightly as he holds it out. "I respect the feistiness. My daughter is like you in that way," he says with a grin before walking away and leaving Tate's mouth to drop. She smacks my shoulder in disbelief before grabbing my arm.

"Beckett has a daughter?" She's whisper-screaming as if it's a secret no one but us knows.

"Yeah, her name is Bailey. She's six and the sweetest little kid, which is surprising considering she's part Beckett and part evil," I say, but Tate merely gives me an unimpressed look. Her hand is still on my arm, touching me absentmindedly.

When she realizes she's still squeezing my bicep, she shifts her attention to inspecting it more closely before shaking her head and removing her hand. I don't comment on it, but it's a close thing.

"So, what horse am I riding?" she asks, and I step behind her to grab her shoulders and spin her to face Firefly completely.

"Only horse I trust with you," I say. "Mine."

Tatum looks over her shoulder at me, surprise all over those soft features of hers. I could get lost in those hazel eyes and the way one is lighter than the other. The way her lips are so round and full, kissing her must feel like heaven on Earth. The way her chest is rising and falling more quickly when she realizes I'm staring at her mouth.

"Firefly has a good nature and is very patient. He didn't use to be, but now, I trust him with my life, just like he trusts me with his," I explain as I place my hand on Firefly's long nose. He nudges my hand and lets out a content huff.

"He's magnificent," she says, staring at where I'm scratching my horse's forehead now. "Are you sure you want me near him?"

Gently, I grab her wrists between my fingers and lift them to where Firefly is. I guide the backs of her hands to his nose, and he sniffs them immediately, booping them once.

"This is called a horseman's handshake," I explain. "When the horse touches the hand you offer them, it shows they're comfortable with you." Tatum is smiling brightly as she moves closer to Firefly, still holding out the backs of her hands to make sure he's okay with her.

I, on the other hand, can't take my eyes off her face. Her smile is the type of breathtaking that actually steals your breath, seizes it in your chest because you're not allowed to do anything apart from study it, memorize it.

Eventually, I tear my gaze away before moving over to where the saddle is.

"First lesson. Learn how to carry this," I say and point at the black leather saddle.

The only color on it is the blue thread used to stitch it together. Olivia got it for me when I first started working here because it reminded her of my eyes and hair color. The horse stitched into each flap is also made of blue thread.

"Is this yours?" she asks, and I give her a firm nod before placing it into her arms. She almost drops it as she lets out a small grunt, clearly surprised by how heavy it is. "You could have warned me. Fuck," she says as she holds it up higher again.

"I have to keep you on your toes," I reply and reach out to brush a curl out of her eyes. She blows air upward and removes it before I have a chance, finally forcing a laugh out of me.

"You're an ass," she says, and I shrug.

"It's a good thing you're an ass woman then, considering I've caught you staring at mine on several occasions," I reply, winking at her and leaving her so I can open the door to Firefly's stable.

I feel the daggers she's shooting into my backside with her eyes, and I'm having a hard time reining in my smile.

"Tate, you need to be careful. Steam's coming out of your ears," Beckett teases as he makes his way back over to the entrance of the barn where all of our saddles are. He lifts his, a light brown one with dark highlights on the flaps and pummel, from where it usually hangs on the rack mounted to the wall.

"It's Aaron's fault," she replies, but Beckett merely booms out a laugh.

"It usually is. He's a special breed of annoying, that one," he says as if I'm not even in the bloody room. Tate flashes me a wicked smile before she answers.

"Infuriatingly so." Beckett snorts but doesn't say another word as he makes his way over to Pegasus, his horse.

The animal is sixteen hands—about six foot three—and completely brown with a longer coat around his legs and hooves. It's short everywhere else, except for his magnificent mane and long tail. I'm a firm believer in the saying that owners and their animals resemble each other because the way Pegasus and Beckett make sense is almost ridiculous.

Tate joins me at the door leading to Firefly. She walks inside first, and I instruct her to place the saddle over the wooden panel as I grab everything we'll need to prepare Firefly.

"First, we have to brush his coat and clean the dirt out of his hooves," I explain as I hold out the curry comb.

"Will you show me how?" she asks, and I smile at her uncertain expression.

"Of course, Tate. You don't have to do anything by yourself unless you feel ready," I promise, and she nods, letting the reassurance remove the tension in her shoulders. "Start at his shoulder and move it toward his flank in circular movements," I instruct, taking her hand to show her exactly what I mean.

She repeats it by herself, smiling at the horse when he tilts his head to look at her. Firefly is used to my confident and sure strokes, not the extra soft ones Tate is using, and he looks a bit confused.

"I like this," she says as I point to his neck and then tell her to keep moving the brush in circular motions.

"Brushing Firefly?" I ask as I step back to let her do her thing, crossing my arms in front of my chest. God, it's so fucking impossible not to smile at the image in front of me, at the way Firefly places his head on the crown of Tatum's while she brushes his neck, just like he always does with me.

"Taking care of him. He seems to like it, too, don't you think?" she asks right as Firefly places his nose in Tate's curls and sniffs.

"He likes you," I blurt out as she giggles, the sound filling my veins with liquid joy.

Tate brushes his stomach next before I guide her gently toward Firefly's hindquarters. She brushes his left leg first, careful and thorough the entire time. Tate doesn't half-ass things, and I can't help but adore the care she uses on my baby.

"Okay, important rule: when you walk behind your horse, keep a hand on his croup to make sure he knows where you are. Accidents happen if you don't," I warn, and Tate looks at me, her eyes studying my face as she processes the words.

"Otherwise, he could kick me, right? I've heard about that," she says and places her hand where I show her before walking behind Firefly to get to his other leg.

"Exactly." *Smart woman.* "Next, we use the dandy brush," I say and hand it to her.

We go through that process and then through the body brush's process to make sure Firefly's coat is all nice and shiny. Then, I show her how to use the face brush and lastly, the finishing brush.

Tate is watching me carefully as I lift one of Firefly's hooves and use the hoof pick to get rid of the big pieces of dirt and then the brush to remove the rest. She's a bit more uncertain about this step, so I show her again with another hoof and supervise closely as she tries one by herself.

"Almost. Wait, let me show you," I say and step behind her. "May I?" I ask.

She gives me a little, breathless "yeah" before I close the distance between us entirely. My body comes to life with her pressed against me, but I do my best to focus on the task at hand to keep from revealing how much I enjoy the way her soft body feels against mine. My hands fly on top of hers, wrapping around them completely to show the downward strokes I use to clean hooves.

"Just like that," I say, my voice barely more than a whisper.

Her floral scent fills my nose, and I step away to let her finish it on her own, my entire body overheating.

All this time I'm spending with her is really fucking with my head. I wanted to stay away from her, not press my body against hers to show her how to clean hooves. Not spend every available second I have working with her on the project she came up with.

"First, we place the pad down," I say and hand her the soft, black cotton material. "Then, we place the saddle on top," I go on, and she does as I instruct her. "Lastly, we attach the cinch. It loops in here"—I lift the flap on the right side and point at the hooks—"and stretches across his stomach to the other side where there are more."

"Okay, what now?" she asks once she has fastened it, clearly content with her work.

"Now, I teach you how to ride," I say and step toward Firefly's head, doing my best not to notice Tatum's blush because of my words.

Loki makes his way into the stable, wagging when he spots Tate.

"Hey, Loks! What are you doing here? I left you with Dad so you could get some rest," Tatum says, bending down to greet him.

Firefly watches the interaction with interest. He loves dogs. He's best friends with Ash, but my dog wanted to go herd the cows with Flynn this morning and refused to come with me.

"He doesn't always work?" I ask, a little unsure what a service dog's work schedule looks like.

"No, not always. As a matter of fact, when I'm not driving and don't run the risk of encountering one of my triggers, I do my best to give Loki as much free time as I can," she explains, running her hands through his golden fur.

"Loki! I'm too old for this shit. My hip's gonna need replacing after I'm done runnin' after you," Old Man Briggs calls out through the barn, and I can't help but smile at the fondness I hear in his voice.

That man has a soft spot for animals. There isn't a single creature he'd turn his back on if they needed help.

I'm like him in that way.

"Oh, there you are," Briggs says as he steps into Firefly's stable, looking all shades of out of breath. "This dog of yours, honeybee, has serious separation anxiety from you," he adds while Tatum kisses Loki's head.

"It's okay. I have it with him, too," she replies, most of her attention still on Loki.

"What have y'all been up to?" he asks me with a small smile, clearly regaining the ability to breathe evenly as he finally stands.

"I'm teaching Tate how to prepare and ride a horse," I reply, gliding my hand down from Firefly's shoulder to the middle of his leg. He stomps it once before stepping against me, nudging me. I smile at him in return.

"Thanks, son, I appreciate you showin' my daughter how to do that." I give him a small nod before my gaze shifts down to Tate, but he doesn't like that at all. "Honeybee, you tell me if Aaron can't keep his hands off you," Briggs says, throwing me a warning glare.

"All touching I do is with permission given," I assure him, but he narrows his eyes at me.

"Dad, please stop it. I'm not a child," Tatum says as she stands upright, glaring at him.

"A little reminder never hurt anybody," he says, calling Loki to his side so he can put a leash on him. "Let's go, little man. Tate will spend her whole evening with you," Briggs promises the dog, disappearing out of the barn.

I turn to Tate, but she's not looking at me. She's staring at the toe of her shoe as it digs into the dirty ground.

"Shall we?" I ask, gesturing toward the door.

"Sure," she replies, shaking her head a little to get rid of whatever dark thought was pulling down her mood.

After I hand her the lead rope, Tate starts guiding Firefly out of the stable and toward the fenced area outside where I usually train the horses, but she stops halfway, looking up at me with uncertainty written across her features.

"Usually, he doesn't give a shit about who I choose to spend my time with as long as I'm happy, but it's different with you, Aaron," she starts, her eyes drifting to my chest before she lifts them to mine again. "He loves you, and he doesn't want anything to ruin that because I'm always going to be his priority. That's why he's like that, so protective. It's not because I'm his daughter and he wants to prevent me from dating. It's because he loves us both and is scared of things changing for

72

the worse," she explains and tugs a strand of her hair behind her ear. I watch the motion with utter fascination.

"Sweetheart, I'd treat you better than anyone else has ever treated you. Briggs shouldn't be scared," I say, but a sad smile tugs at the corners of her mouth as she steps away from me.

"You're not the problem, Aaron," she replies as she turns to Firefly and runs a hand along his mane. "Alright, are we going to stand around all day or are you going to teach me?" she asks, placing her fists on her wide hips and cocking a brow.

"Almost ready," I say before strolling over to where Olivia placed the helmet I asked her for an hour ago. It's atop a ball of hay, and I retrieve it before placing it on Tate's head.

"Must I wear this?" she asks with a frown. I place my index finger under her chin to tilt her head up. It takes me a moment to fasten the clasp, part of me too distracted by the way this woman is watching me, looking up at me through those thick lashes of hers.

"Safety first, Tate."

Chapter 12
Tatum

My ass cheeks hurt.

I've been cursing Aaron out all day in my head for making me ride for an hour yesterday until I got it right and felt more comfortable on Firefly. He called me a natural, but he said it with a slight chuckle and amusement sparkling in his eyes. It was his failed attempt at making me feel better, but I really wanted to kick him in the shin.

I'm walking on wobbly and aching legs today, thinking about different ways to strangle the cowboy.

"What are you thinking about?" he eventually asks, his usual smile placed firmly on his lips.

"My legs and ass are fucking sore, and it's your fault," I explain, but Aaron only flashes me a sinfully filthy smirk.

"Not the first time I've been told that." My cheeks heat immediately.

Ulma chooses that moment to approach us with our food, clearly having heard us.

"You kids have to be careful. I tore my ACL trying out a new sex position," she says and shudders at the memory. Aaron chuckles at her words, but I'm too dumbfounded to do anything but let my mouth form an O-shape.

"Don't worry, Ulm, nobody would even be able to dream up the shit you try out," Aaron replies with a grateful smile as he hands her the cash for our lunch.

"Only because none of you read the book I wrote last year," she complains before her eyes drift to me. She bursts into laughter at the shocked expression covering my face. "I didn't formally introduce myself, did I?" she asks me, and I shake my head.

She hadn't even spoken more than three words with me before disappearing into the kitchen with our order.

"Hi, I'm Ulma. I own this diner, but I used to be a sex therapist when I lived in California. I'm happily married, twenty years now to my beautiful wife, and I'm very sex-positive," she says as she sticks her hand out for me. I shake it with a smile slowly spreading across my face.

"It's a pleasure to meet you, Ulma. I'm Tatum."

The curvy woman places her hands on her hips, her soft features pulling into utter contentment as her brown eyes stare directly into mine. The buzzcut she's sporting shows off her thick eyebrows, high cheekbones, and full lips. Ulma is in her mid-forties with light-brown skin and laughing wrinkles around her eyes and mouth.

She's beautiful.

"I know who you are, angel, you are the talk of the town and have been for the past few weeks," she replies with a wink before handing Aaron his change and throwing us both a grin as she heads back into the kitchen.

"She's right about that one, hun," a woman says from beside us, and I turn my head to get a glimpse of the person demanding my attention. I'm met with a welcoming smile I've seen earlier when we passed by the library.

"Zelda, I assume," I say, causing her to lighten up even more.

There is so much life here in the people, in the town, in the way they know each other better than I know my family at this point. Orchard Hill may be small, but I don't feel as confined here as I thought I would. So far, it feels like I've finally found a place to call home. A place where I can thrive and be truly at peace.

My days don't feel wasted because I'm always doing something I adore. Yesterday, after my riding session with Aaron, I went with Olivia and Hadley to check on the calves of the herd on the east side of the ranch. Then, Aaron and I cleaned up the yard area in front of the main house for the market we're hosting on Sunday.

At the end of each day, I feel accomplished in a way that filing and completing stacks of paperwork never made me feel.

It shouldn't be possible to fall in love with a place in three weeks, especially since I had no faith I'd even like living here.

I couldn't have been more wrong.

"Listen, kids, there are a bunch of people who want to have a booth for the market on Sunday. Do you want me to email you the list of names and their contact information?" Zelda asks, and Aaron looks at me to see if I'd like to respond or if he should. I give him a small smile.

"That would be great, Zelda, thank you," he says with his usual charming smile entirely directed at her. The woman's pale cheeks blush under his attention, and I roll my eyes at the cowboy. He knows exactly what he's doing. "Will we see you at the market on Sunday?" Aaron asks after he enters my email into Zelda's phone so she can forward me the list.

"Of course. I'll bring my granddaughter, too. She always enjoys seeing you," Zelda adds before refocusing on her food and lifting a spoonful of soup to her mouth.

I give Aaron a look, but he merely drapes his arms across my shoulders as if it's the most natural thing to do before leading me out of the diner, throwing a "See you then, Zelda!" over his shoulder.

His casual affection disappears as soon as we're out of sight, and now I have two things I need to ask him about.

We walk toward my new truck, where Loki's nose is poking through the cracked window, and Aaron hops into the passenger seat with the food still in his lap. I jump in as well, turning to him as soon as I'm seated. He's already waiting with a fry extended, another between his lips. I narrow my eyes at him but take it and plop it into my mouth. The salty taste immediately sets my taste buds on fire, making my stomach growl. I think about snagging the bag out of Aaron's grasp and digging into the food, but we promised Beckett and Hads we'd have lunch with them.

"Sorry about that whole arm thing. Alice, Zelda's granddaughter, has had a crush on me since high school, and Zelda desperately wants us to give it a go," Aaron explains without me having to voice the question. I appreciate that I don't have to ask, that I don't have to worry about jealousy creeping into my tone and him hearing it.

"So why haven't you?" I manage to reply as I pull out of the parking lot of the diner. My eyes briefly note that there's a bowling alley with a big apple carved into a bowling pin. The words *Orchard Bowling* are written directly next to it in white and green letters.

"I'm not attracted to her," he replies, and, damn him, my curiosity has me speaking before my mind can step in and seal my lips shut.

"What kind of person *are* you attracted to?" I ask, my eyes skipping to him as he cocks an eyebrow.

"I have a thing for curvy women who want me but pretend they don't," he says, and I roll my eyes at him for the second time today.

"Good thing I'm safe then," I reply, and he snorts like he knows I'm full of shit.

"What about you?" he asks, causing my heart to flutter.

"I'm pansexual, which means I'm attracted to people no matter what gender they identify as, especially if they come with a good heart and great personality," I explain, trying to ignore the way Aaron is watching me as closely as I'm watching the street in front of me.

"So, are you attracted to me?" His question has me shifting in my seat. We're slowly making our way down the gravelly path leading to the main house where Beckett and Hads are waiting for us.

"Are *you* attracted to *me*?" I say instead of answering.

It's a lot easier to divert the attention from me than it is to admit that I've been physically attracted to him from the second I laid eyes on him. Let's not even talk about the emotional attraction I've felt since we've had dinner.

"Very much, sweetheart." Well, fuck. That answer doesn't help me in the slightest.

"Is that why you put your arm around me for everyone at the diner to see?"

"Maybe," he says and grins, ever the sunshine man. I let out a dry laugh.

"FOOD'S HERE!" Beckett yells as soon as he sees us drive up to the main house. My windows are down, but I'm convinced I would have heard him either way. The whole of Orchard Hill probably heard him.

"Jesus, Beck, they're right there. I can see them," Hadley replies. I can't help but grin at both of them.

"I'm hungry, and they took forever. Normal people would understand my excitement," he says with his drawl as I jump out of the truck, welcoming the distraction.

"Define normal," Hads challenges, and Beckett smiles in response. He crosses his tattooed arms over his chest.

"People that need food to survive."

"I don't need food to survive?" she asks, crossing her trained arms over her chest to mock him. She's amused by this conversation, I can see it in the way her eyes sparkle with defiance and entertainment. Beckett is hungry, and she's trying to get under his skin.

"Hads, I say this with as much love as I could possibly muster: you're a pain in my ass." She blows him a kiss as Aaron and I join them at the small table Dad keeps on his porch.

Lunch passes quickly, Beckett leaving first to get back to whatever it is he does on the ranch. I have yet to ask him the details, but every time I remember to voice the question, he's already leaving. Hadley follows soon after she devoured her burger, telling me she's going to join Olivia in adding fencing to give Galaxy more space until she's comfortable enough with Aaron for him to exercise her.

I'm still working on my fries when an email lights up my screen, catching my attention. Aaron follows my line of sight before his gaze skips back to my face, a question lingering in his eyes.

"Zelda sent the list of people," I explain, opening the email to read him the information. "A lot of the farmers from the surrounding ranches want a booth to sell their produce. Linda Reed wants a booth to sell her self-made jewelry, Carol Fall wants one for her artwork, and Jamie Garcia wants to sell his baked goods," I say, a smile creeping onto my face at the amount of people who are interested in our makeshift market.

"Fucking hell, Tate, you did it. You set the first part of this plan into motion. Successfully. This is happening," Aaron says as he places a hand on my shoulder and squeezes it proudly. Tears almost jump into my eyes at his words because he's right.

We did it.

"It was a group effort," I remind him with a grin.

"No, sweetheart, this was all you. You and that big, beautiful brain of yours," he says and places his index finger on my temple, tapping it once. I finally shift my attention to him, watching his gaze attach to my eyes. "I should head back to Galaxy. I haven't trained with her today," he says and steps away, popping one more fry into his mouth before cleaning his mess and asking if I'd like him to take my garbage too.

His thoughtfulness still catches me off guard. It's small things like holding the door open and letting me go first every single time. It's ordering my food first and his last. It's not arguing with me when we're discussing projects but simply giving me his input without pressuring me to do as he says. It's always greeting Loki when he sees him because he knows how much he means to me.

"Thank you," I say as he takes my burger wrapper. He winks at me one last time before walking inside.

Dad strolls out of the house a second later, dirt all over his hands and clothes. Sweat drips down his temples, and he wipes it away before he beams at me.

"Hey, honeybee. I didn't know you were having lunch here today. Olivia finally let you out of her sight?" he asks, and I can't help the little chuckle escaping me.

"Yeah, after she made me clean out every single one of the stables and only because Aaron and I had some business to get to," I say as he sinks down on the chair opposite me with a small grunt. "Actually, I'm glad you're here. I have some very good news," I say as I hold his gaze. His light brown eyes sparkle with interest.

Aaron comes out of the house with empty hands, his phone clutched to his ear. He's frowning at whatever the person on the other end of the line is saying, rolling up his sleeves as he walks past me, giving my shoulder one more quick squeeze as a way of saying goodbye without using words.

Dad tracks the movement with narrowed eyes, but I don't give him a chance before diving into the story of meeting Zelda today, and letting him know there will be a market here on Sunday with lots of vendors and hopefully attendees as well.

I place my chin on my intertwined fingers and wait for him to process all of this new information. My father leans back in his seat, crossing his arms in front of his chest before running a dirty hand over his face. Three lines of dirt are painted across his forehead and cheeks now. I grin at him, making him realize what he did.

"Ah, hell, it's all over me now, isn't it?" he asks, and I nod with a laugh before grabbing a napkin and making my way over to him.

"Let me help you," I say, still grinning. Using the napkin, I start following the lines of dirt to remove them. "So, what do you think? Are you happy?" I ask, but my father's hand wraps around my wrist to stop my movements.

"Are you?" I drop into the seat next to his.

"More than I've ever been," I admit. Dad seems to consider my response, tracing my features with his eyes in search of deceit.

"You don't think I ruined your life by convincing you to move here?" My eyebrows shoot up in surprise.

"What? No, Dad, not at all. I feel good here. My body feels good, less tired and stressed. I'm enjoying the ranch work, even the jobs where I have to shovel shit, and this project, Dad, is exactly what I needed to keep my brain happy. So, no. You didn't ruin my life. In all honesty, I think this decision saved it." Tears fill his eyes before they drop down his cheeks and he wraps me up in a bear hug.

"I love you so much. You know that, right?" I nuzzle my face into the crook of his neck as if I could hide from his affection because I'm so unused to any type of it, I still don't know what to do with it.

"I love you, too, Dad."

Dad and I used to be very close when I was young. He took me everywhere with him, taught me how to paint my nails and change the oil on my car so I never needed to depend on anyone to do it for me. He learned how to braid hair and then showed me. He took me to my first Formula One race where I was glued to the fence, watching the cars race by. He tried to do the same things with Remi, but she was always with Mom, learning everything she could about the business world.

"Alright, come with me. I want to introduce you to my horse," he says, and I jump out of my chair with excitement.

"Shit, really?" Dad merely grins at me before waving his hand in the direction of his ATV.

Loki is right beside me, bouncing on his feet.

Dad and I have both been so busy, he hasn't had time to show me Silver Creek Ranch from his perspective.

"I should warn you. Rusty is moody as hell," Dad says as he takes a seat on his green ATV, holding out a hand for me to help me get on. I take it before slipping into the space behind him and holding onto the seat handles beside me.

"Will he bite me?" I ask, but Dad merely chuckles as he lets the engine roar to life.

Loki is next to the vehicle, wagging and ready to run beside us. When we were still living in the city, we went on almost daily runs for both of our exercise routines, but here? Here he really gets the exercise he needs. He gets to run until he's sick of it.

"Nah, he won't bite, honeybee, but he will head-butt you if he doesn't get his way," he says, releasing the clutch so the ATV starts moving.

There is nothing but land in front of us, some horses in the fenced area to our left and soon, Silver Creek appears on our right. I focus on the glorious sight that is Loki running at full speed beside us. He's magnificent. The way his fur flies with every step he takes, all of his paws floating off the ground is so mesmerizing, I take out my phone to record him.

"Good boy," I say as soon as we arrive at the barn and Loki comes to a stop next to us, breathing hard but smiling a perfect dog's smile. I bend down to pet his head, scratching behind his ear.

"Let's go, Tatum. I've got other things I still have to take care of before falling into bed and sleepin' for a week," he jokes, but I can tell he desperately needs it.

He needs at least a few days off where he doesn't have to worry about anything but recovering and letting his body recharge. He's so worried about my epilepsy and me, but I'm worried about him, about his health. Dad tends to forget that stress isn't just dangerous for people with a chronic illness like me, but that it can cause health issues for everyone.

When the worry about the ranch is finally gone, when we've made enough money to sustain ourselves, I'll buy him a ticket to somewhere humid and with a beach. Maybe I'll buy him a ticket to go see Remi. Hell, I'd get myself one too.

I miss my sister.

"Ah, there he is," Dad says, holding out his hand for Rusty. The horse wastes no time to get to Dad, nudging his hand with his head for attention. It's the same one I saw the first morning Olivia took me to meet the mini cows.

"He's magnificent," I mumble, waiting behind the fence because I don't want to approach Rusty the wrong way.

"Don't let his looks fool you. He's stubborn as hell," Dad says, holding out his hand for me in a gesture that says he'd like me to come closer.

I do as he instructs, then remember what Aaron showed me and hold out my hand, waiting for Rusty to boop it with his nose. Dad gives me a proud look before watching his horse complete the horseman's handshake. I slide my hand over his nose and forehead, my chest warming at the way he accepted me already.

"I want one," I admit, more to myself than Dad, but he hears me anyway.

"Soon, honeybee, I promise. For now, you're going to have your hands full with the new mini cow and the market on Sunday," he reminds me, and that thought alone brings me nothing but true joy.

CHAPTER 13

Aaron

"SWEETHEART, YOU HAVE TO—" I cut off, placing my hand over my mouth to keep from laughing. Not at her, never at her, but at the mess she's made in front of her.

"I know what I'm doing," she scolds and swats my hand away when I offer it to her.

"Tate, please, give me the rake. I'll show you again. We're trying to prepare the earth, not butcher it," I say, and she leans back with her mouth falling open in offense.

"I'm doing it the way you showed me to," she insists and then waves the rake around. I can't help but smile at her grumpy scowl.

"I know you are. Obviously, I'm a horrible teacher." She studies me, searching my face for a second before bursting into laughter and covering her face with her arms.

"No, I'm a horrible student. I'm sorry, Aaron. Fuck, I don't know what I'm doing," she says and hands me the rake.

Tate walks over toward my truck, grabbing her water bottle and taking a long sip, watching me approach as she swallows.

"It's okay not to be great at everything right away," I say, but she hands me my water, frowning like I've personally offended her.

"In our case, it's not okay, because we want to start planting the seeds, and we need to make sure we've properly prepared the ground," she argues, wiping the dirt off her hands. "I'm sorry I can't get this right. I know we're on a tight schedule."

84

"Do you know how I'm so good at this?" I ask, and her eyes lift to my face as she gives me her attention. "Years and years ago, when my Nanna and I had our own ranch, she grew flowers there, too. Not for people to visit the farm, but for herself. She taught me how to do this, and it took a year until I finally knew how to do it properly. It definitely took more than a single day, Tate. Have some patience with yourself, would you?"

A small smile finally stretches her lips.

"What kind of flowers did she grow?" My chest tightens a little at her question, but I push past it as I step in front of where she's sitting on the truck's tailgate.

"Wildflowers. They were her favorite," I say and push a strand of Tate's hair behind her ear without thinking. Her breathing stops entirely as I do it, so I drop my hand again, shaking my head to ignore what the fuck I just did.

"Did you always want to work on a ranch?" Tate asks, clearly trying to bring us back to a safer topic.

"No, but it was the only option I had after—"

I cut off, but she doesn't push me to talk about what happened either. She merely watches me with big, curious eyes. Those hazel eyes I get lost in every single time I look at her. My attention shifts to my knee, a phantom pain shooting through it as I remember what happened all those years ago.

"What about you? Was ranch hand your second choice after being a lawyer?" Tate snorts at my question, bringing the grin back to my lips.

"Absolutely not, but I must say, I enjoy it far more than I thought I would," she replies, and I slide onto the tailgate next to her, turning my body so we're looking at each other.

"Why did you become a lawyer?" Her attention shifts to where Loki is sleeping in the trunk bed under an umbrella I opened so he'd have shade.

"Because I wanted my mom to be proud of me. I wanted to find something that would make her want a better relationship with me, but after I declared I'd study to become a lawyer, I hardly saw her. She got busier, spoke to me less, and when she did, it was only to ask how my studying was going and then lecture me." The sadness in her voice is like a sharp knife slicing across my chest.

"Your mother sounds like she never wanted to be a mother in the first place," I blurt out before catching myself and regretting the words immediately. I don't want to upset Tate, but she merely shrugs, soothing my worries.

"She didn't want to be a mother, but my dad wanted to be a father. So, they adopted Remi, and I was a little bit of an accident." She cringes at the thought, but I lean back against the side of the trunk bed, watching her with a grin.

"I'm going to need to thank Briggs for forgetting a condom, otherwise I wouldn't have a stubborn as hell project partner right now."

"Eww, Aaron! I don't want that visual in my—" She cuts off, and I throw my head back in laughter.

Her phone ringing tears us out of our conversation, and Tate looks down before groaning and placing her phone against her ear.

"Hello?" she says, listening to the person on the other end of the line. "No, that's not going to work. We need our whole order, not half." She listens, then adds, "Fine, but if the other half isn't here within the next week, I want a discount on future purchases because I was promised fast delivery of my *whole* order."

I'll never, ever get tired of watching the fire inside of Tate come to the surface and spill over until I feel the heat of her against my skin.

"You want me to pay for delivery twice?" she blurts out, surprise evident in her voice. "We are not paying for it twice because you don't have our entire order ready." She hangs up without giving the person another chance to speak, groaning. I simply sit next to her, dumbfounded and amazed. "What?" she asks with a shy smile.

"You are remarkable." Tate nudges me in the side before shaking her head. A blush creeps onto her cheeks.

"No, I'm sick of people trying to keep this ranch from flourishing."

Her fingers disappear in her backpack before she takes out her tablet and starts hitting her screen, adjusting her entire plan. I watch her fix the timetable, shifting the dates and tasks we have to complete before she turns her tablet off again. It's still fascinating to me how quickly her brain works, how she solves problems as soon as they arise so swiftly, like finding out her dad's ranch is in trouble and creating a whole business plan to fix it.

"Alright, I'm ready to try again. Show me one more time," she says and jumps off the tailgate, grabbing the rake and making her way back over to the soil we were working on. "But you're not allowed to laugh anymore, okay? If you laugh, I'll hit you with the handle of the rake," she warns, bringing a smirk to my lips.

"I won't laugh if you promise me not to hack at the ground like you're trying to kill it." She glares at me, grabbing the handle of the rake lower so she can use the top half to whack it my way. She's too far away, which means she's merely warning me.

"I don't see the difference between what I did and what you showed me," she says, placing one of her fists on her hip and staring me down. I hold out my hand and wait for her to place the rake in it before showing her a gentler way of preparing the earth.

"Don't pretend the ground is Flynn. Pretend it's Hads or Olivia," I say and carefully rake through the dirt, noticing a warm smile slip onto her face as she studies me.

"Your grandmother would be very proud of your technique," she says, and I find myself grinning at her words instead of feeling the usual sadness.

"Thank you. She'd probably never let you go near her flower patches if she saw yours." Tate and I scowl at each other for a brief moment, her genuinely and me teasingly, until we both burst into laughter.

"Fine, I think I got it now," she says, and fuck me, she really does a good job afterward.

We continue in silence for a while until I decide to share more childhood stories with her about the Delinquent Six.

Her laughter fills my ears, so free and happy, I can't help but sink into it, letting it consume me until all I hear is that melodic sound.

CHAPTER 14
Aaron

TODAY IS THE FIRST Sunday Market Silver Creek Ranch has ever hosted. Tate and I worked tirelessly yesterday to make the booths—a few tables we borrowed from the library and makeshift canopies we built out of bamboo sticks and old linen Briggs had in his closet.

I made a poster to hang below the Silver Creek Ranch sign at the entrance of the ranch. Tate doesn't know about it because it isn't the prettiest thing I've ever created. The purpose of it is merely to make sure everyone knows where they're going.

"Yikes. You let a second grader make this?" Beckett asks as he and Flynn approach me. They were out checking the fences for damage this morning.

"No, I made it," I reply through gritted teeth, and both let out a laugh.

"Cute. Did you use your feet or why does it look like that?" my best mate chimes in, and I flip him off over my shoulder as I get back to attaching it under the sign.

They're right about it being ugly, but they don't have to point it out. I'm well aware this looks like I told Firefly to do it and he understood me enough to stomp his hooves all over the green poster.

"I think he's tryin' to impress Tate with it," Beckett says to Flynn as if I'm not even here.

"Yeah, no shit, but that's not the way to do it, unless he wants her to pity his artistic skills," Flynn replies, and I roll my eyes at both of them.

"No, it's thoughtful. Our pretty boy has a massive crush on the boss's daughter," the father of the cutest kid says, and I wonder yet again how Bailey turned out so well when her father is such a dick.

"Nah, I think he's way beyond crushing on her at this point. What's it been, four weeks? Aaron is definitely in his 'like' stage already."

There is no point in denying the truth. I like Tatum. I like her a lot. Not just in the romantic way either. I like her as a friend. I like her as a person. I like *her*, period. It's impossible not to after three weeks of spending almost every day together when Tatum is by far the coolest, funniest, sweetest, most badass woman I've ever met.

She made a man cry yesterday after he cut off another woman in the line at Jamie's café and then had the audacity to insult her, too. Tatum and I watched it happen, and right as I was about to knock the man on his face for his disrespect, she placed a hand on my chest to hold me back. I stayed back and watched her go all lawyer on his ass. He started yelling at her, but she merely stood there with her arms crossed in front of her chest. Unimpressed. Unfazed. And unimaginably hot.

"Are you two dipshits finished making fun of me or do you need another few minutes before I ask you for a favor?" I say once I'm sure the poster won't fall.

Beckett and Flynn are both on their horses, looking down at me.

"We can take a break for now, but we're never gonna stop," Beckett says right as Ian approaches in his truck, rolling down his window with a scowl on his lips. His dark eyes are covered by a pair of black sunglasses and his black hair is hidden beneath a cowboy hat.

"Howdy, fellas," he says before tilting his head to look at something over my shoulder. "Did you ask Bailey to make that? I thought she was still with her mom," Ian adds, and Beckett bursts into laughter.

"She is. Aaron made that for Tatum," Flynn explains, Beck still laughing half-slumped over Pegasus.

"How sweet. Better not show her that. All it's gonna get you is a pity fuck at best." Ian's rare hint of a smirk is evil, but Beckett is wiping away tears of laughter because of how thoroughly he's enjoying this.

"More than he's gettin' now though," Flynn adds with a shrug.

"Is there a reason you're all at an all-time-high dickhead level, or am I just not used to you three anymore?" I ask after walking over to remove the poster again because they made me feel like shit about it.

"Come on, don't do that. Leave it there. Tate will like it. We're just acting like this because we miss you, man. You've abandoned us for the new project these last few weeks," Ian says. I turn back around to see Beckett's laughter stopping immediately and Flynn straightening out his back, his attention clearly captured.

"Why would you tell him *that*?" he asks and Beckett gives the man in the truck a disgusted look.

"Yeah, now he's gonna think we care about him and shit."

"When you first got Bailey, who was the person you called?" I challenge with a hint of a smile tugging at the right corner of my mouth.

Beckett grits his teeth.

"You."

"Exactly," I reply and walk back over to Firefly where I bound his lead rope to the Silver Creek Ranch sign. I mount him before signaling him to move into a trot. Ian drives off while Beckett and Flynn appear on either side of me. "I'm sorry I've hardly seen you. I know you depend on me for your happiness," I tease, and Flynn flashes me a smile while Beckett rolls his eyes.

"Nah, we depend on you for entertainment. Makin' fun of you is by far one of our favorite ways to spend our time," Beckett says and guides Pegasus into a canter.

He's gone within a minute.

"Wanna grab a beer tonight?" Flynn asks, placing one of his hands on Mara's head and running it down her mane.

"Yeah, I'd like that."

The main house comes into view after a few moments of silence pass between us. Tatum's curvy figure appears in my field of vision, making my heart stutter.

"I think your art skills are going to be a major deal breaker for her." He presses his lips shut to keep his laughter inside, but as soon as I narrow my eyes at him, it bursts free anyway.

"You know what? Let's find out," I say and guide Firefly into a gallop.

Tate's gaze shifts to us as soon as we're close enough for her to hear, a small smile stretching those full lips of hers. Uncertainty and confusion mingle with amusement as I race toward her, only stopping once Firefly and I are right beside her. She places her fists on her hips and looks up at me, half her bottom lip tucked between her teeth. She's so fucking beautiful, I don't think I'll ever tire of looking at her.

"Can I help you?" she asks, Olivia and Hadley appearing behind her.

"As a matter of fact, yes. I need to show you something," I say and extend my arm to help her onto Firefly. She gives me an unsure look, so I wiggle my fingers at her. I slip my foot out of the stirrup so she can put hers in there.

"People are about to arrive. Is this going to take long?" she asks, but she's already slipping her hand into mine and placing her foot in the stirrup, letting me pull her onto my horse.

"Not long, I promise." I guide Firefly into a turn, waiting for her arms to move around me, but they never do. "Hold on tight, sweetheart," I say, but she merely snorts.

"I think I can stay up here without help, thank you," she replies.

A smirk spreads across my face.

"Alright, if you say so."

I click my tongue once for Firefly, urging him into a trot. Tate's hands are still firmly placed on her legs, right until Firefly starts cantering at full speed and she grabs onto my hips before wrapping her arms around my torso and sliding her hands onto my stomach. Her fingers dig into the fabric, holding on tight. I chuckle, but she pinches my stomach.

"Shut up," she says loud enough for me to hear.

Then, all of my amusement disappears as I feel the side of her face press against my back. She absentmindedly strokes her thumb along my stomach, apparently completely unaware of how close her hands are resting to the waistband of my pants, how good her touch feels. Her pinky finger glides back and forth, as if she's trying to memorize the feel of my abdomen to the best of her ability with the clothes in the way.

I take a deep breath, hoping it will help.

It doesn't.

I'm convinced only submerging myself in an ice bath would calm my body at this point.

We slow down to a trot again, my breathing embarrassingly ragged.

"Aaron, are you okay? You've gone really stiff." That's certainly one way of putting it.

"I wanted to show you what I made," I say, avoiding her question because I don't want to lie to her nor do I want to tell her how fucking turned on I am.

"What did you make, cowboy?" she asks and looks past me. When her eyes catch the sign, she covers her mouth with her hand. "You did this?"

"Yeah. Beckett, Ian, and Flynn hated it, but I thought you might like it." Well, not thought, but I hoped.

"They're assholes. This is adorable. I love it," she says and squeezes my bicep once. "Thank you for making it," she adds before leaning forward just enough to press her soft lips against my cheek.

The whole way back to the booths, I wear a smug look, feeling like a smug man. Flynn catches my expression and shakes his head with a smile, clearly realizing what must have happened. I can't lie. I'm surprised she liked it, but I shouldn't have doubted her either.

Tate enjoys thoughtful gestures.

The market is a booming success. Almost everyone in Orchard Hill is here, ready to spend some money. Tate and I agreed that we'd ask for a small percentage of the profit the vendors make, so the booth is free and how much we get is based entirely on how much the people make. Everyone signed an agreement, and the entire town showed up for us and our project. They seem to be having a great time, too, chatting and laughing with each other.

Jamie is selling his coffee and baked goods, just like he would at his café, and I'm so grateful to him for closing his shop to do this today.

Ulma and her wife, Helen, are here with their daughter, who is selling her crochet animal figurines. Gina is only fifteen, but the kid is incredibly talented with those crochet hooks.

Bernard and his wife from the ranch next to Silver Creek Ranch, Red Sky Ranch, are selling their produce. Tomatoes, corn, cucumbers, salad, and apples catch my attention.

Carol Fall has her artwork displayed and her partner, River, is doing their best to get people interested by talking to them as they pass by the artist's booth.

Linda Reed is selling her jewelry, and I walk past to see the different kinds of flower necklaces she has. They're mostly all types of wildflowers, some of my Nanna's favorites too, but there is one that catches my attention. It's a crystal the color of Tatum's eyes, carved into the shape of a horse. I run my fingers over it before smiling at Linda.

"How much?" She tilts her head before studying her box full of cash.

"Take it. It's my honor for the host of this event to take something from my stand," she says, her gravelly voice a side effect of the decades she's been smoking.

Considering she's only Olivia's aunt, it's ridiculous how much they look alike. Linda has the same green eyes, the same brown hair, and is just as short.

"I couldn't possibly," I reply, letting go of the necklace.

"Then I probably shouldn't tell you that Tatum saw it earlier and wanted to buy it but couldn't because she didn't have any cash on her. When I told her to take it, she refused, too," Linda replies. She gestures to the piece of jewelry, almost lazily. "It would be a waste for her not to get something she desires because you're both stubborn."

The way she chooses her words so carefully to make a person feel like an idiot without having to say the words is a skill I've only ever seen one other person have. Her niece.

"I'll take it," I blurt out, and she flashes me a smile. As soon as I heard Tate wanted it, this became a no-brainer. I'd have paid for it, but if Linda insists, I won't insult her by forcing my money on her.

"Wonderful. Glad you came to your senses," she says, making me chuckle. I watch her drop the necklace into a pink, see-through satin bag.

"Thank you," I say as she hands me the necklace.

"I've made more money today than I have in the last six months combined. Thank *you* for this opportunity, Aaron. I know it's probably for Silver Creek Ranch, but for many of us here, this is a great way to get our products out there." Her response warms my heart because I hadn't even considered how beneficial this market would be for small artists.

"It's our pleasure." I give her one last smile before walking away again.

There are a few other farmers from further away who are selling their produce and products. I know it's good for them too, but it's mostly to help Silver Creek Ranch. No one knows the specifics about the farm's struggle, but people talk. Briggs' bank advisor is Lucinda, Jamie's wife. She's not supposed to share information, but something must have slipped at some point and rumors started circulating. Not to mention, everyone knows about the fire that burned the ranch's crops.

"Aaron!" I must have heard this voice over a hundred times since I started working at Silver Creek Ranch.

"Bernard, how are you?" I ask politely, extending my hand. The tall, lean man shakes it a moment later, smiling brightly.

"Yeah, alright, son. I love what you've done here. It's a great idea," he praises, clapping me on the shoulder once before pointing at his booth. "Sofia loves being able to sell what she embroiders," Bernard adds, grinning at his wife who is currently deep in conversation with Tate. My project partner even smiles at Sofia, but I can tell it's forced. She's not used to the friendliness of the people in Orchard Hill.

"Thank you. I appreciate the support," I say, dragging my attention from Tatum to look at Bernard again.

"Course. We can't wait to visit the flower field too, once it's ready," he adds, squeezing my shoulder once before leaving me to wonder who the fuck told him about that project. Nothing stays secret in this little town.

"Hey, Aaron? Could you get another table? This one here has a wobbly leg," Olivia says and I give her a brief nod before walking around the house where Tate parked her truck.

There are two more tables there, both still folded for easier transportation, and I slide one off the bed before lifting it into the air. I twist to start walking again when my knee resists the movement, causing lightning bolts of pain to burn up and down my leg. I drop the table and press my lips together to keep the curse words and pain-filled sounds inside.

I collapse against the side of the house, sliding down and waiting for the wave of agony to subside.

"Fuck, again?" I hear someone ask, but my brain can't focus enough to make out who it is.

All I can do is take deep breaths through gritted teeth, press my eyes shut as if I could hide from what is happening, and wait for this sensation to disappear.

"Stay right there, I'll get your brace," the person says and disappears again.

Panic invades my chest, constricting my breathing. Memories of the day I lost my dream fill my head until I'm drowning in darkness. Getting thrown off my horse. Landing on my knee. Hearing the crack and feeling the tear. All of it bombards my brain until my senses don't know what's real and what's a flashback. I can hear people yelling, cheering that dissolves into panic as I hit the ground. Paramedics rushing toward me. My leg bent at a horrifying angle.

Shivers rake across my arms and back until I'm shaking. I'm not entirely sure if I'm still in pain or if it's all part of the memory replaying in my head. It doesn't matter. The panic attack is much worse than the physical pain would be. *That* I can understand. It's a thing I can touch, a place I can find on my body where it originates from. The panic attack on the other hand? It's a formless thing, not able to be grasped or pinpointed. It's simply everywhere, consuming me.

I don't want to go through the surgery again.

I don't want the endless months of recovery.

I don't—

"Instead of just wearin' the damn thing like the doctor keeps tellin' you to," someone mumbles, their voice so close, I realize they're right in front of me now. "Come on, son, it'll be okay." *Briggs.* "Take a deep breath. You're okay. You're not back there, you're here, at Silver Creek Ranch," he says, trying to help, but I'm too far into the attack to listen.

"Can't. Focus."

"Is that Tatum walking around the corner?" Briggs says, and my eyes shoot open from fear.

She can't see me like this.

But Tatum is nowhere to be found. Meanwhile, her father is currently staring at me with a scowl. "My daughter, Blaze? Really? That stops you from spiraling?"

I manage to slow my breathing, to let go of the panic. Briggs said her name to see if it'd get me out of my head, and it worked. I hate that it did as much as I want to hug her right now.

"Wear the brace, son. It might not be comfortable, but it's there for support. And it'll help prevent those goddamn attacks before they even happen," he says and grabs my knee, attaching the brace to it with care.

"I can't stop thinking about your daughter," I say, and he stops mid-movement. "I've tried, but it's impossible, and not because I'm always around her. She's just in my head, all the damn time." I'm not sure why I'm telling him this, I haven't even admitted this to any of my friends.

"Is this your way of saying you're quittin'?" he asks, a hint of a smile on his lips despite what I told him. I know he's trying to lighten this moment, but part of me is scared he'd really draw an ultimatum. This job or Tatum. Currently, that's a no-brainer. Even if I like her, I wouldn't give up this job for her.

"No. This project means the world to Tate, and I'm not letting her do this by herself. And I love all my animals here and I'd never leave them."

"Good," is his only reply before he finishes attaching the brace and then stands up. "I'll grab the table. Take your time," he says and stalks over to it, lifting it and walking back toward the entrance to rejoin the market.

It takes me another few minutes to fully regain the feeling in my legs and arms. No one at the market is any wiser about my knee problems or my panic attacks, and I can go straight back to pretending I'm invincible. I know I shouldn't hide either of these things, but it's easier than admitting I need help sometimes.

"Aaron?" Her voice is like warm honey filling my veins in the most pleasant way. She appears in front of me with a bright smile.

"Yeah, sweetheart?"

Her head turns in the direction of the market where Jamie's wife, Lucinda, is now plugging speakers into an extension cord. Music blasts through them a second later, and everyone starts cheering at her choice of song.

"They're having a great time, don't you think?" she asks, and I can't help but smile at her excitement.

"They are," I assure her. Tate's eyes find me before dropping to my knee brace.

"Are you in pain?" I'm about to respond when she takes my hand. "You should sit down, Aaron."

She tries pulling me in the direction of one of the chairs, but I plant my feet firmly into the ground, causing her to fly back against my chest. I let out a laugh as her shoulder presses into my torso, but the amusement is knocked out of me at the sight of her looking up at me through those thick lashes of hers. Her eyes are full of concern, and the desire to place my mouth on hers to take it away almost threatens to make me act without thinking.

"I'm fine, I promise," I tell her.

"Hmmm, I can see that," she says, not believing my bullshit.

My hand slips into my pocket to grab the necklace I got her. She watches my every move with utter fascination. Even as I turn her back to me, she throws me a curious look over her shoulder.

"What are you doing?" she asks as I fumble with the clasp.

"This belongs around your neck, Tate," I explain as I lift her hair, placing it over her shoulder.

The charm falls against her sternum as I fasten the clasp and then step in front of her again. The hazel color of the crystal is complemented by her pale skin tone, but I only get a second to admire it before she lifts her hand to wrap her fingers around the charm.

"Why?" Her eyes reveal a combination of softness and uncertainty.

"Why, what?"

"Why do these sweet gestures if you're not going to get anything out of it?" she asks, her question taking me completely aback.

"I don't do these things expecting something in return, Tate. Is that how people have been treating you in the past?" Her eyes drift from my face, so I move closer to her again.

"Well, yeah. Isn't that normal? People always have an ulterior motive. They do something nice, and you think nothing of it, and then *bam*, they ask you to help their niece write a paper for her class on family law." My eyebrows shoot up at the very specific example.

"Well, that's not how we operate here. We don't do things expecting something back. We may ask for help every now and then, but we don't expect it as a way of repaying."

"That's going to take some getting used to," she admits with a nervous laugh. I touch the underside of her chin with my index finger, nudging it once to get her attention. Her gaze drifts back to me.

"I think you're doing a great job adjusting already." Tatum had her entire life turned upside down, yet has adapted without a single complaint.

"Flattery, Mr. Blaze, will not make me like you more," she says and crosses her arms in front of her chest.

"That's too bad because I quite like complimenting you."

She rolls her eyes as she walks away, leaving me to stare after her.

CHAPTER 15
Tatum

OUR HALLOWEEN DECORATIONS ARE coming along slowly, mostly because Beckett is helping out too, and it takes him half an hour to shove the thread through the eye of the needle. Not that I can blame him. It takes me half that time to do the same. Aaron, on the other hand, is a natural at sewing.

"How are you so good at that?" I ask, pointing at where he's sewing two pieces of fabric together.

"A master sewer never reveals their secret," he says with a grin, but Flynn gives him an unimpressed look.

"You're not a fuckin' magician, Aaron," he replies, and I bite down on my bottom lip to keep from laughing.

"Count yourself lucky. If I were, I'd make you disappear," Aaron says and I finally burst out laughing. The cowboy watches me with utter self-satisfaction for getting that response out of me.

"How the fuck do I do this?" Beckett asks, tearing our attention away from a frowning Flynn.

"Let Aaron do it," I suggest and Beckett hands him the thread and needle.

I watch Aaron push the needle through the tiny hole in one try, tying a knot so the thread doesn't accidentally slip out again. Beckett gives him an appreciative smile before going back to fighting with the fabric in front of him. I let it happen for another few minutes before telling him to move to the painting station with Hads and Liv instead.

"Thank God," is all he says before throwing the needle on the table.

Liv has a smudge of paint on her cheek, which Beckett laughs at before wiping it off for her. Flynn's entire body tenses visibly as his friend touches his *archnemesis* or whatever they call each other. He glares at Beckett, but when he catches me smiling at him, he bites down on his bottom lip and turns away, storming out of Aaron's little house without another word.

"What's his problem?" Ian asks, scowling as always.

"Don't know," I mutter, grinning to myself.

Aaron throws me a questioning look but I merely shrug and go back to fastening the white fabric around the styrofoam head. I'm attempting to make a ghost, but, as of right now, it looks more like a used tissue than anything else.

Another hour or so passes before Beckett, Olivia, Hads, and Ian all decide they're done for the night. Aaron grabs the things in my hands too, putting them down and telling me to go sit outside while he whips up something for us to eat.

I drop into the chair on his back porch, watching the last remaining rays of sun before it disappears completely. My mind wanders to the numbers and the amount of money we've made at our first Sunday market, trying to determine what we can do with it to expand our market or invest it into one of the other events.

"What are you thinking about?" Aaron asks as he hands me a plate with a sandwich, some veggies, and cream cheese to dip them in. I look at this simple, five-minute meal he threw together, feeling emotional because no one's ever really taken care of me like this before.

"The project," I reply when I remember he asked me a question.

"Your brain never stops, does it?" he asks with a sweet smile, sitting down on the chair he brought outside. He's next to me, his dimple on full display.

"No, it's one of my many great qualities," I say with a smirk, and he gives me a small nod.

"Great, yes, but you should also find a way to shut it off every now and then," he reminds me, making it my turn to nod.

"Yeah, I guess." I stare down at the sandwich, smiling when I think about the one thing that used to let me shut off my thoughts, that consumed me.

Pleasure is a very good distraction.

"Alright, eat. Then, I want to try something that might help," he says, and I do as I'm told for once in my life.

Once we're both done, he takes my plate to bring it inside. He returns a moment later with two cushions, placing them on the ground before us. Aaron gestures for me to sit on one of them, so I do. Then, he merely sits there with me, doing nothing but studying every inch of my face. My thoughts run wild, my heart races, but I take several deep breaths to control my breathing.

"What are we doing?" I whisper, and Aaron grins at me before taking my hands in his. I don't pull away, even though I should.

"Nanna used to do this with me when I got overwhelmed. She used to sit me down and wait for me to be ready to talk. Once I was, she'd ask me a million questions to take my mind off what was stressing me out," he explains, rubbing his thumbs over the back of my hands until a shiver runs down my spine.

"I doubt that'll work," I reply, but Aaron shrugs.

"No harm in trying, right?"

"I guess not." He leans back with a satisfied look, then stares at the night sky, thinking about something.

"Alright, these will be quick fire, so you have to answer fast. Ready?" I nod once, giving him the go-ahead. "First question. What's your favorite animal?"

"Mini cows."

"Favorite color?"

"Green."

"Figures," he says and chuckles. "Favorite food?"

"Lasagna."

"Favorite artist?"

"*From Angels to Devils*."

"Favorite place on the ranch?"

"The creek."

"Favorite person you've met at the ranch?"

"You." As soon as the word is out, I realize the mistake I've made. "Fuck, I didn't mean that," I blurt out quickly, but Aaron isn't even paying attention to me anymore.

"It feels like I just won the lottery," he says, so I grab my pillow and smack his arm with it. Aaron chuckles as he takes it from me and hugs it to his chest. "Best thing I've ever heard," he adds, and I roll my eyes.

"Your turn," I announce, readjusting the pillow under my ass again. "Favorite animal?"

"Horses."

"Favorite color?"

"It's become green." My heart stutters a little at his response. His grip on my hands tightens, and I feel like retracting them to keep my feelings at bay.

"Favorite food?" I ask, trying not to think about his previous response.

"Mac and cheese."

"Favorite artist?"

"Kane Brown."

"Favorite place on the ranch?"

"Also the creek." I stop there, but Aaron won't have any of it. "Ask me the last question." I bite down on my bottom lip but don't voice the question. "You are, Tate. You're my favorite too."

"That's only because you didn't meet the rest of The Delinquent Six on the ranch," I argue. He opens his mouth to respond to that statement, but I'm scared of what he'll say, so I change the subject. "What's your biggest fear?" I ask, trying to keep the questions going.

"Losing my memories like my Nanna one day," he admits, looking at something past me. "What about you? What's your biggest fear?" he asks, not allowing either one of us to linger too long on that terrifying thought.

"Falling in love," I admit before I can manage to keep my mouth shut.

Aaron's eyes soften as he studies my face. It's not in a condescending way either, as if he was questioning how someone could possibly be afraid of that. No, he looks at me with complete and utter understanding.

"It's called falling for a reason. You're supposed to be scared while it happens, so I get it."

"Really?"

"Yeah, but I also think that the right person will catch you mid-fall and open the parachute for both of you so that the fall doesn't kill you," he says, which makes an uncomfortable feeling spread through my chest.

Not because of what he said. It originates from the fact that... I might want exactly what he's describing.

"So, did your brain shut off the work part of it or do we have to try again?"

A smile breaks out across my face.

"It worked, but I'd like to keep talking."

CHAPTER 16
Tatum

GETTING UP AT FOUR in the morning should be illegal. If I didn't want to take Loki swimming before work, I wouldn't force myself out of bed either, but he deserves this. He deserves me getting up at the ass crack of dawn to take him somewhere he can do what he loves most.

Chase after his toys in the water.

Loki's head lifts from where it was resting on my feet as soon as I sit up. He gives me a sniff before going back to sleep. I chuckle before ruffling his fur and stepping into the bathroom to get ready.

"Come, baby," I command after putting on a bikini and a light, summer dress, grabbing two towels, one for him and one for me. Loki trots beside me, yawning as I pack some food so I can take my medicine soon.

We walk toward the creek with nothing but the chirping of birds and crunching of my shoes against the ground to break the silence.

It's been almost an entire week since the Sunday market. We made a small sum, but it was a lot more than I expected, so Aaron and I were both quite happy. A lot more people signed up to have tables for tomorrow, even emailing to say they'll bring their own to take some of the workload off Aaron and me.

While I've been here for over a month, it'll probably take another twelve until I'm finally used to the way people treat each other in Orchard Hill.

Aaron and I have also started planting the flower and strawberry seeds yesterday, but they've only delivered half of them so far.

My phone rings in my pocket at the five-minute mark of my walk, my sister's name flashing on my screen. A smile slips onto my face as I slide upward on the screen to answer her call.

"Hey, troublemaker," I say, and Remi snorts into the phone.

"When the fuck were you going to tell me you moved to the ranch to live with dad?"

Well, shit.

"Does right now count?" I ask, but my sister's exasperated sigh tells me it doesn't.

"My job was causing me stress. Stress became a trigger for my seizures. I had two of them in forty-eight hours and was advised to cut down on my stress immediately. Now I'm here, trying to do my best to relax and take things easy," I explain, getting straight to the point because I know she appreciates efficiency above every other quality.

"Fuck. You make it impossible to stay mad at you for keeping me out of the loop, do you know that?" she asks, and I can't help the way a sad smile tugs at the corner of my mouth.

"I didn't mean to keep you out of the loop. You're busy running your perfume empire, and I don't want to worry you when I've got everything under control," I say, and Remi lets out an annoyed laugh.

"You're the younger sister. *I* am supposed to be the one who doesn't worry *you*, and *you* should be dumping all your problems on *me*," she replies. I stop dead in my tracks for a moment, taking a breath for courage.

"Okay, here is a problem. Dad is about to lose the ranch if I can't pull off the master plan I've come up with," I say before going a bit into detail about what is happening here.

"I can send money. You know I've got it. How much does Dad need?" she asks, a rustling sound coming through the line.

"He's not going to let you give him money. He reluctantly accepted mine, and only because I reminded him this is my home, too. So, now, Aaron and I are working to turn this farm into a visitable one," I explain, the way I linger on his name and how I say it with so much fondness catching her attention.

"Who's Aaron?" she asks.

"No one," I lie, desperately trying to ignore how quickly my heart is beating.

"Yeah, right, just like Talia was no one in law school. Next thing I know, Mom told me she caught her sneaking out of your dorm room," Remi says, sending me back to four years ago. Talia and I had a lot of fun.

"He's one of Dad's workers, so no one like *that*," I say, hating the way the words still taste wrong on my tongue.

Loki tears me out of my conversation with a quiet whining noise, his nose moving as he sniffs the air and probably takes in the scent of the creek. It must be close. We take a few more steps with Remi telling me how much she doesn't believe me when, suddenly, I see him.

Aaron Blaze is standing at the creek with his back facing me, wearing... nothing. He's standing there buck ass naked, emphasis on ass because *holy damn*.

I've never seen a more magnificent ass in my entire life.

My body gives an enthusiastic hum as I study this man's glorious one, unable to look away even though I really should. Even though if he turns around and catches me, it'll make working together a hell of a lot more complicated than it is at the moment.

But I can't get my eyes to move away from Aaron.

"Remi, I'm going to have to call you back," I manage to whisper into the phone, swallowing hard when Aaron stretches his arms into the air, causing all of his muscles to flex.

"Why?" my sister demands to know, but my brain is so cloudy from the view in front of me, forming sentences becomes impossible.

"Muscles, so many muscles," is the last thing I mumble before letting my arm drop to the side of my body.

Desire licks its way up my spine in the form of flames. Need fills me until the most inappropriate images fill my head, but I can't stop the intrusive thoughts. I'm just glad he isn't turning around because I don't think I'd be able to handle looking at his front right now. At least not without throwing all of my morals and rules out of the fucking window.

Loki bolts toward the creek where Aaron and Ash are standing, dragging me out of my desire-filled trance. Panic grips me by the chest as I take a step in my dog's direction and call him back. Since his training is great, he stops halfway, making his way back to me. Unfortunately, Aaron has clearly heard the whole thing and turns his upper body a little to look over his shoulder at me.

"Tatum?" he calls out, and I immediately turn around before he can accidentally flash me his naked front.

"Yeah?" I yell back, my head dropping backward as my eyes flutter shut. Fuck. Shit. Fuck.

I hear movement behind me until footsteps seem to get closer and closer.

"I'm so sorry, no one's ever out here this early," he explains, but it doesn't help the heat in my cheeks or the one that's settled all over my body.

"I was ogling your naked ass, and you're apologizing?" I blurt out, almost slapping a hand over my mouth.

I didn't have to tell him that, did I?

He's in front of me wearing nothing but a pair of black boxers a second later. My eyes drop to his very impressive bulge for the briefest moment until his chest captures all of my attention. The hard ridges of his stomach making up his eight-pack should be illegal.

"Fair's fair," Aaron says, dragging my attention to his lips.

The smirk on his face makes me a little breathless as I remember the first day we met, the way I accidentally flashed him my thong-covered ass.

"I'm sorry," is all I manage to say, my cheeks so hot from embarrassment, it feels like I'm going to burst into flames any second now. My head drops again while I try to hide it, but Aaron slides his index finger under my chin, lifting it until I'm looking into his eyes. There is no amusement left.

"Don't be. It's a fucking turn on to know you couldn't keep your eyes off me, Tatum," he replies, the corner of his mouth curling into another smirk.

"I turn you on?" *Stupid, stupid question.* Aaron's finger trails along my jaw until I'm barely holding myself back from shivering.

"All the damn time, sweetheart."

"Oh," I blurt out while his thumb slips onto my chin and pulls down ever so slightly, just enough to keep my lips parted.

"Is this okay?" he asks, his mouth somehow coming closer and yet the distance is still too much.

"Yes," I say, my voice barely a whisper. Aaron's blue eyes are wonderfully complemented by his black hair.

"That's both good and bad for me," he blurts out with a soft chuckle, taking a step closer until our upper bodies are barely an inch apart.

"Why?"

"Because I want to touch you, but I really shouldn't," he explains, his attention zeroing in on my lips. "I want a taste, Tate, and I'm not allowed one," he admits, and my body inches even closer to him until we're pressed against one another.

He's hard and hot, and no part of me is equipped to fight this magnetic attraction between us. His arousal presses into my stomach, and I have to fight back a whimper at the need swelling inside of me.

"See, I told you. Desire and forbidding go hand in hand," I say, and he smiles down at me, closing the distance between our faces until I'm swallowing hard. My hands lift to his hard chest, his skin hot and tight underneath my fingertips.

"This is a bad idea," Aaron says, but my eyes are already fluttering shut at his proximity. I barely manage to open them again to see his eyes studying the way his thumb traces my lips. It's like he's hypnotized by me. "The things I want to do with this mouth of yours, Tate," he says, biting down on his bottom lip.

"What things?" I ask, my heart thundering in my chest. I want him to tell me, describe every filthy thing he's picturing.

"Things we're not ready for," he replies but brings his mouth closer.

My phone vibrates a second later, tearing us out of the moment. I jump back while Aaron reluctantly lets go of my chin. Both of our gazes drop to my screen where my alarm is blaring, reminding me to take my medicine.

"I should go," I say and grab the strap of my bag tightly in my hand.

My eyes drift to where Loki is still patiently waiting to go swimming next to me. Ash has decided to lie down with my dog, pawing at him for attention. Loki merely lets out an annoyed growl but doesn't move away.

"I'll see you at lunch when we get back to work."

"See you," I mumble, watching him walk off with my eyes stuck to his round ass. I hate that it looks phenomenal with and without anything covering it. "Let's go, Loks," I say once Aaron is out of my line of vision.

Loki immediately bolts toward the water when I throw the toy in there for him, trying not to think about Aaron naked.

I fail miserably.

CHAPTER 17
Tatum

ON MONDAY, LUNA, OUR new mini cow, joined the family at the ranch, and I've been spending all of my spare time with her, trying to make her feel comfortable and loved here. Loki seems to adore her, too. He tried playing with her yesterday, but she merely looked at him like he was annoying before continuing her grazing.

"Hey, pretty lady," Hadley says as she walks into the barn where I'm sitting on the ground with Luna's head on my lap. I use the opportunity to brush her face and down her shoulder and back.

"Hey, Hads," I reply, looking up at her to see the gorgeous woman dressed in a short jean skirt, a red bralette with a lacy pattern that barely covers anything, matching red cowboy boots on her feet and a cowboy hat in the same shade. "You look incredible," I blurt out as soon as words make their way back into my brain.

"Thank you," she replies with a smile, hovering over me with an unsure expression on her face. "Why are you still covered in dirt?" she asks.

"What do you mean? Why wouldn't I be?"

"Tonight is the annual Boots & Beers fundraiser. They collect money and then the town votes on what to invest it in next year. Usually, they give it to the schools or the library to further the educational system," she explains, holding out a hand for me to take.

"So, people just give money or is there an auction or gambling?" I ask as she pulls me off the ground.

"Five contestants are asked to chop as much wood as they possibly can within a minute. The winner is the one who chopped the most." I dust off my dirty hands

111

on my equally filthy pants while Hads pushes me toward the entrance of the barn. "It's great. Not only because we get to see all of those hot as hell people putting their muscles on display, but they're also chopping the wood the older folk in Orchard Hill will use in the winter."

Hadley and I make our way outside in time to see the sun setting behind the acres and acres of land stretching in front of us. An explosion of color paints the sky. Hads touches my elbow to signal we have to get a move on.

"So, who's competing this year?" I ask, ignoring the way my heart is racing at the thought of Aaron wearing nothing to cover his chest, sweat glistening on his skin, and his muscles moving as he swings an ax into blocks of wood.

"Yup, you guessed it. Aaron is last year's reigning champion and will be competing this year, too," she says as if she read my thoughts.

"How the fuck did you know I was thinking about him?" I cross my arms in front of my chest and stop walking, but it only takes her three steps to notice my absence.

"Please, Tate, your body tells me everythin'. Every time you think of Aaron, there's this combination of softness and indescribable desire pooling in your eyes." Heat fills my cheeks, but she simply chuckles as she keeps walking toward her truck to take me back to the main house.

"That's because he's hot and I haven't had sex in a while," I defend, but Hads gives me an unimpressed look, clearly not believing my ill-attempted lie.

"If that was all it was, you would have chosen to focus on Flynn or Beckett, or even Olivia. They're all drop dead-gorgeous and not into relationships. They would have given you a meaningless fuck and moved on, but you don't want them. You want Aaron," she says, and, damn her, there is no arguing when she lays it all out like this.

"Must you be such a know-it-all?"

"It's one of my best qualities," she replies with a huff, letting the engine roar to life before racing back toward the main house. "Olivia, Beckett, and Ian are also competing, as well as Landon Cole from Red Sky Ranch. Liv won the competition two years ago, and Beckett won it the year before her."

"And then people bet on who they think will win?" Hads gives me a few nods. "So, who are you betting on?"

"I'm supporting Olivia all the way, even if I'm not sure she has a chance against Aaron. The way that man moves is—" She cuts off, looking for the right words. "Almost otherworldly. He's fast and precise, not easily distracted," she replies.

My heart is still thumping unevenly inside of my chest as Hads speeds over the pathway to the house. I do my best to force my thoughts toward what the hell I'm going to wear tonight, but there is no stopping my body from giving a needy throb as soon as I think about Aaron.

"Olivia is already at your place, ready to spend the next half hour turning you from swamp princess into the goddess you usually are," Hads teases, gesturing at my current state.

"Hey, this is not my fault. Flynn made me fall into the hay I was distributing to the horses," I reply, but Hads is already chuckling before I'm even finished with my story.

"I know, he told us. He felt so bad he got you a pair of brand new cowboy boots for tonight." My jaw almost falls to the ground.

"He didn't," I say, making her tilt her head my way.

"He did, and they're gorgeous."

The boots dangle from Olivia's fingers as we drive up to the main house, and I can't quite keep from gasping. They're a combination of black and green with flowers in a deeper shade of green painted across the leather material. They'll reach a few inches higher than my ankles and will go perfectly with the tight, green dress I own.

My mother once told me a dress like that isn't meant to be worn by thick women like me, but I don't want to let her ruin it for me anymore. Especially not one that will fit perfectly with those cowboy boots and hopefully have Aaron's eyes glued to my body all night.

"Good God, I think we're going to need more than half an hour," Olivia says as soon as I approach her. She's wearing long cargo pants and a simple black shirt that is cut off at the belly button.

A smile curls the corners of her mouth, but I just snatch the boots from her grasp and make my way up the front porch.

"We most certainly will if you're going to stand there all evening," I fire back over my shoulder.

Olivia and Hadley both chuckle before following me into my room. Loki is right by my side, too, but I leave him outside while I shower and get rid of the dirt that was giving the two women outside of my room gray hairs.

The next half hour is spent pampering me from top to bottom, adding makeup to bring out my eyes and highlight my lips and cheekbones. Olivia and Hadley both agree the dress I picked is a knock-out, so I put it on, along with the boots Flynn bought before standing in front of my mirror and admiring the way I look.

"Holy shit, Tate, you look sexy as hell," Olivia says, and Hads gives an agreeing nod.

"You look like the embodiment of why I'm bisexual," Hadley chimes in, and I grin at both of them.

"Thank you," I reply and take a deep breath for confidence. "And thank you for your help," I add and brush my hands down the sides of my dress, over my wide hips, and down my big thighs.

"Any time, pretty lady." Olivia stands up from my bed and claps her hands together. "Let's go."

I give Loki a kiss on the top of his head before leaving him at home with Dad, who is already fast asleep on the couch. I don't wake him, but leave a note so he knows where I've gone and that Loki is with him.

Then, Olivia, Hadley, and I make our way to Boots & Beers.

CHAPTER 18
Tatum

BOOTS & BEERS IS the place to go on Saturday, but I wasn't expecting this many people to show up for the fundraiser. Five giant logs of wood, the bases for the competitors I assume, are planted in a row with piles of wooden blocks behind them.

Beckett, Ian, and Aaron are already standing at their designated places, wearing nothing more than muscle shirts and plain jeans. It's almost like all three of them coordinated their outfits.

"Lord have mercy," someone says from beside me, and I turn to see Flynn studying me with his mouth hanging open. "Tatum, I didn't think I'd ever ask anyone this, but would you do me the honor of marryin' me?" he asks, and I burst into a fit of laughter at his ridiculous question.

"No, I'm good. I'm never getting married, even if you're pretty. But thank you very much for the boots. I love them," I say, and Flynn flashes me a flirtatious grin.

"You're welcome. And that's too bad. Havin' a wife as hot as you would be nice," he replies as he throws his arm over my shoulder.

"Take a hint, Rafael. You're not her type. She's got better taste in men," Olivia chimes in, bumping her shoulder against Flynn's. A challenge sparkles in his eyes as he tilts his head toward her.

"Says the woman who keeps fuckin' piece of shit dudes who leave you hangin' after one night." I smack his stomach at the flash of hurt in Olivia's eyes before she shuts it down. Flynn is unfazed by my warning, his attention firmly set on the woman he claims he despises.

115

"When you watch me win this competition today, just know I'm imaginin' your face on every single piece of wood," she says as she walks over to where Beckett, Ian, and Aaron are.

"You know, you can be a dick to her all you want, but you're not fooling anyone," I tell him after watching him stare after her. I slide out from under his arm as he narrows his eyes.

"I have no idea what you're talkin' about," he replies with a shrug before stepping toward the double doors leading inside of the bar.

"Don't bother. He's in denial," Hads says as she approaches me, holding out a bottle of water.

"Well, some people are scared of their feelings," I say, feeling a bit defensive now.

"Yeah, but fear is precisely what keeps you from livin' more often than not. You can be afraid, but you gotta do what scares you," she says, taking a swig of her beer.

"It's not always that easy."

"No, it isn't. Good things aren't easy. They take work and commitment, but they're also worth the effort."

Her words hit me straight in the gut, whirling around there until I'm nauseous. Part of me is screaming she's right, but that fear she was talking about, the type I need to overcome, it's stronger than all rational thought. Aaron represents all of my fears at the moment. Aaron and that smile of his. Aaron and that thoughtfulness, affectionate touching, and body sculpted to perfection. It's almost sad how badly I want to walk over to him and bury my face in his chest to get a whiff of his woody and fresh scent. How desperately I want to tell him that I'm terrified of spending my days with him because the more time we spend together, the less I want to keep pushing him away.

Having epilepsy has taken away too much from me throughout my life. I can't ever get drunk. I can't be in elevators because if they break down and I get stuck, my claustrophobia will set in and make me seize. I can't go to concerts or other events without running into the risk of flashing lights triggering my epilepsy. I've adjusted what I eat, given up my job to reduce stress, and more. I've terrified my family more times than not.

I don't want it to take more from me. I don't want it to keep me from living. I don't want it to be the reason I'm not in a relationship. It should be my decision based on what I desire, not what I think is for the best.

But it takes a lot to change a mindset I've had my entire life.

Aaron throws his head back in laughter at something Beckett says to him, and I study the column of his throat, the way his Adam's apple bops. I study the shape of his lips, the dimple in his cheek, the stubble covering the lower half of his face, the swoop of his lashes, and the veins in his neck.

His eyes catch mine as he continues laughing, almost as if he's trying to share his amusement with me from afar. My heart flutters at his joy, and I smile in response. I adore the way his attention always drops to my mouth when I smile, grin, smirk, or simply just because he wants to study my lips. I've never had a person look at me the way he does, and, damn him, the feelings it evokes inside of me are addictive.

"You must be Tatum, Briggs' daughter." A tall, muscular man steps in front of me, stopping me from getting my fill of Aaron.

Not the best way to introduce himself to me.

"Yup, that's me. Who are you?" I ask, and the tattooed man extends one of his hands in greeting.

"Landon Cole. I work at Red Sky Ranch," he replies, finally piquing my interest.

I shake his hand, watching his eyes scan my features. Landon flips a lighter between his fingers, the symbol of a hawk painted across it. He pulls out a cigarette and lights it before shoving the pack and lighter back into his pocket.

"I heard you are one of the five competitors tonight. I'd wish you good luck, but I'm rooting for Olivia," I say, and he gives me an understanding nod, the easy look on his features never wavering.

"In all honesty, I bet on her too," he replies before giving me one last polite smile and then joining my friends.

As soon as Landon is out of the way, I catch Aaron's irritated glare, which he's directing entirely at the cowboy from the other ranch. He looks jealous and a little possessive, but when he turns his attention back on me, he forces a smile to pretend Landon speaking to me didn't bother him.

I wrap my hand around the charm of the necklace he gave me and twist it from side to side, causing his gaze to drop before he rakes it down my body and then back up again.

Heat replaces any sign of jealousy.

Beckett claps him on the shoulder, and Aaron turns his head slowly, keeping his eyes on me until the very last second before looking at the person demanding his focus.

"Good evenin', people of Orchard Hill!" Mayor Lucas Xavier says as he stands in front of the five contestants.

Flynn appears next to me again, placing his arm back around my shoulders and whispering in my ear to look at Aaron. As soon as the Australian's eyes settle on us, the same possessiveness reappears, and I feel my heart giving a happy thump at how much he wants me.

"I saw the look he gave Landon and couldn't resist. He can't stand seeing anyone close to you," Flynn says and squeezes my side while I do my best not to grin a little.

I like seeing Aaron this way, as if he'd love nothing more than to storm over here, throw me over his shoulder, and carry me someplace quiet.

"You should probably let go of me so he can focus on the competition," I tell Flynn, but he gives me a one-shoulder shrug. The way he's touching me is so casual, almost lazy, and I don't mind it one bit. It's the kind of easy affection friends show each other, and, while I'm not used to it, I can't lie... it feels pretty amazing.

"Nah, it'll help him win," Flynn says before looking down at me and furrowing his brows. "Unless you want me to. I'm very touchy with my friends so you gotta tell me if you don't like that," he adds, but I merely nuzzle myself against his side and place my head on his shoulder.

"I don't mind."

Aaron's hard gaze turns soft at something he sees in my face, and I'm almost convinced he notices how much I needed this from someone, anyone, even from the last person at Silver Creek Ranch I would have expected this embrace.

"You know, Olivia and Aaron are both picturing your face on the wood now. You might as well have participated yourself considering how big of a part you're playing in this competition," I tease, and Flynn blurts out a laugh next to me.

The mayor, who was in the middle of his speech announcing all of the competitors, throws the cowboy beside me a dirty look. Flynn raises his hand to pretend he's zipping his lips shut and locking them before taking my hand and placing the imaginary key in it. My lips hurt from how hard I'm pressing them shut to keep from causing a scene myself.

"One minute on the clock," Mayor Xavier says, and I watch Aaron, Beckett, Olivia, Ian, and Landon pick up their axes and prepare to start.

The determined gleam in Aaron's eyes tells me no one else has a chance tonight. When he flashes me a smirk right before the start, my breathing stutters.

"GO!" the mayor calls out, and I watch in utter fascination as all five of them move in perfect synchronization for the first ten seconds. Then, chaos erupts.

Beckett swings for a piece of his wood, but instead of breaking apart, the piece flies off the block base it was standing on. He watches after it for a millisecond before taking another piece and hitting it with so much precision, it doesn't take more than one swing to half it.

Olivia is strong. Precise. Deadly. As she swings her own ax, the muscles in her arms flex in a way that I've never seen before. It's glorious.

Ian and Landon are clearly only doing this for the fun of it because neither of them is quick enough to keep up with the other three. While they split open one piece, the others have gone through five.

Aaron is magnificent. He's fast, precise, and his movements are smooth and calculated. My mouth waters at the way his muscles flex. My body aches at the way soft grunts escape his lips because of how much force he's using. My knees go weak at the way his black hair clings to his now sweaty forehead, his skin glistening. The tight muscles coiling his body shift in a way I didn't even think was possible. I could happily watch him forever, but a minute isn't very long.

Before I know it, it's over. I didn't even pay attention to how close the race was. Beckett and Olivia's piles look identical. Aaron's isn't far off either, and from this perspective, I can't tell who won.

"Aaron won," Flynn says as if he could read my thoughts.

"How do you know?" I ask as he releases my shoulders to stretch out his back.

"I was watching 'em all," he replies and nudges my shoulder with his. "Weren't you?" He cocks a suggestive brow, and I shove him right back.

"The winner is Aaron Blaze!" Mayor Lucas confirms minutes later.

Aaron is already grinning at me when I turn to look at his reaction at hearing he won. My cheeks heat under his attention, and I realize everyone must know that he can't take his eyes off me at this point. I mean, he isn't even trying to hide it. His gaze jumps to the mayor as he hands him a small trophy, but as soon as he's released, he makes his way to where Flynn, Hads, and I are standing.

"I won," he announces as if I wasn't watching him intently the entire time.

"I saw," I reply as I stare into his beautiful blue eyes.

"For you," he adds, using his index finger to wrap it around the horse charm around my neck. He tugs on it until I take a step toward him.

"For me?" I ask with a smile, feeling myself inching closer even when he's not tugging anymore.

"Yup. Was trying to impress you," he admits, lowering his head just enough so we're at eye-level. "Did it work?" Aaron's smile makes me forget about the world around us.

"No," I say, jutting out my chin and inevitably bringing our mouths closer together. He doesn't lean back, doesn't shy away. Instead, he licks his lips as his eyes fall shut halfway and he focuses entirely on my mouth.

"Oh yeah? Then why are you thinking about kissing me right now?" he asks after I take another step closer.

"Because you have pretty lips, cowboy." His hand slips onto my throat, a gentle touch but demanding either way. He attempts to bring me closer, to diminish the distance between us entirely, but Beckett, Ian, and Flynn drag him backward before he has a chance to.

I watch them lift him onto their shoulders, celebrating his win with loud cheers.

Liv glares at Aaron like he attacked her entire family, so I throw an arm around her shoulder like Flynn did to me earlier, offering her comfort with a small squeeze.

"You'll get him next year," I assure her.

"Yeah, right. That'll only happen if you manage to distract Aaron to the point where he doesn't care about participatin' anymore." She pouts right up until Hadley appears in front of her with two shot glasses.

"You're not going to spend the rest of the night being bitter. You lost. Suck it up. Go find a good fuck to distract yourself," she says as she hands the first glass to Liv, who downs it without a second of hesitation.

"You're right. What's the impression you got from this Landon guy?" the brunette asks before her green eyes find my face.

"He was nice," I offer, but she scrunches her nose at that. "What's wrong with nice?"

"Nothing is wrong with nice. Nice is the ideal, but my downstairs only seems to be attracted to the not so nice people," she explains before taking the second shot from Hads and placing the glass against her lips. "Fuck it. I'll give it a try. Maybe he's good with his mouth," Olivia adds and throws the glass at Hads, who catches it easily, clearly used to this.

"That woman needs someone to treat her right," I say, taking a swig of my water.

"She definitely does, but she has to be ready to let them in, and she isn't. Not yet. Not after what she went through with her first ex," Hads replies, crossing her arms in front of her chest and looking after her best friend with concern in her eyes.

"What happened?"

"That ain't my story to share, especially when Liv hasn't even told anyone but me. Otherwise, Beckett, Aaron, Ian, and Flynn would have ensured her ex was six feet under already," she replies. "Not everyone can be lucky enough to catch the eye of someone as amazing as Aaron Blaze. That man would move heaven and Earth for the people he cares about and, lucky for you, that includes you now, too."

"I'm not sure I deserve it," I admit, staring down at the tips of my shoes.

The green flowers shine in the neon lights of the Boots & Beers sign and rope lights that Hank, the owner of the dive, arranged so we could see the competition play out even in the darkness of the night.

"You do, Tate." Hads steps into my view, pointing at Aaron and tilting her head as a compassionate smile spreads across her face. "Can I give you a piece of advice?"

"Sure," I reply.

"Don't fuck this up, whatever it is you have with him. This man looks at you like you're the very reason the sun shines every single day, and I sure as hell know that if anyone ever looked at me that way, I'd hang on tight, even if the ride might get messy," she says, placing her fingers on the horse charm hanging from my neck.

"I've never been in a relationship," I say with a shrug.

"And I promised myself I'd never follow in my dad's footsteps and work on a ranch. Now, here I am. Sometimes, the choices we make don't align with the ones we've made in the past, but that doesn't mean they're the wrong ones." She inhales deeply, then lets out the breath in the form of a sigh. "They might just be the best ones you could ever make."

With that, she leaves me standing by myself and walks toward Beckett, Ian, Flynn, and Aaron.

My eyes latch onto the man I haven't stopped thinking about, noticing he's put on his cowboy hat. He looks like a fantasy I never allowed myself to have, and when he notices Hadley approaching without me, he searches the crowd until he finds me standing by myself. He extends his hand in invitation.

But I can't control my fear. I can't control the way sadness creeps in because I'm supposed to be alone. I'm not supposed to drag someone down into the worrying that comes with my epilepsy. I'm not supposed to let someone care for me and depend on me in a way a partner would. It's not fair toward Aaron to keep playing into this attraction between us, these feelings, when I'm too terrified to ever act on them.

I don't join them. I don't let myself immerse myself in the joy of these celebrations. I don't do anything I want to do, but, instead, I give in to what I think I'm supposed to do and distance myself until I'm sprinting toward my car.

"Tate!" His voice makes me stop dead in my tracks. "Please, sweetheart, stop running. You don't have to do that here," he says, his tone pleading and soft.

"I have to, Aaron, it's all I know how to do. I run and don't stop until I've chased everyone away. Fucking ironic, isn't it?" I ask, spinning around to show him the tears streaming down my cheeks.

I haven't cried in so long, I was almost convinced I wasn't capable of doing it anymore.

"You're not going to chase me away, Tate. I told you I'm a patient man, and I meant it. You don't have to be ready right now, but I know you want to explore whatever is between us as badly as I do. And that's scary, fuck, sweetheart, I know it is. I feel the same, but running won't make this go away." He gestures from him to me with his index finger, and I feel my heart lurching uncomfortably in response. "Exploring it is the only way we'll find out if it's all simply some built-up sexual tension or if it could be more."

"How long are you gonna be patient for, cowboy?" I challenge, placing my hands on my hips and trying my best to ignore the way the tears are still dripping down my cheeks.

He walks toward me until he can take my face in his hands, tilting it up until I have no choice but to meet his blue eyes.

"Until you're ready, Tatum."

A sob claws its way out of my mouth as he presses a kiss to my forehead, a gesture so sweet and gentle, everything inside of me melts into a puddle. I fling my arms around him before I can stop myself, but he hugs me back as fiercely.

"Until you're ready," he repeats in a whisper, too much raw emotion coming through in his voice for me to handle.

I push away from him and jump into my car, hating myself as I watch his figure getting smaller and smaller in my rearview mirror.

Once I'm completely out of sight, I pull the car to the side and start bawling my eyes out.

This has never been a problem. I never wanted someone so desperately, it made me question whether or not I should go against everything I've told myself I should be doing. When the doctors identified my triggers, I accepted that my life would have limits. It was worth it if it stopped the seizures from happening. But Aaron isn't a trigger. He isn't something I need to deny myself, only something I *should*.

The feeling of loneliness I've grown so accustomed to over my life starts to creep in, and I find myself sobbing even harder, crying until I lose my voice and the ability to feel my face. Everything goes numb until I sit in my car, staring at the dark road ahead of me and wondering for the hundredth time in my life what I've done to deserve any of this.

Most people get to make decisions about whether or not they want to be with someone dependent on how they feel. If they like someone and they like them back, that's it. They start dating, get married, start a family, or whatever it is their hearts desire. I don't get to make these decisions so light-heartedly.

Some choices about my future were taken away long before I was even allowed to make them. Choices everyone should be allowed to make. Choices about whether or not they want to carry a child, grow it inside of them. Women and people with uteruses are supposed to be allowed to make these decisions, not have them made for them by nature. Choices like allowing someone to be let in, to let them take your heart and either care for it or destroy it.

But, like I said, some choices were already made for me, never mine to make.

CHAPTER 19
Aaron

GALAXY ISN'T GROANING AT me today. I take a step toward the horse, and she's finally ready for me to approach her, so she stays where she is, watching me closely. My heart is hammering, hope blossoming in my chest as her head moves forward a little while she sniffs me. Whatever it is, my scent becoming familiar to her or her realizing I would never hurt her because I've given her time and space to be comfortable, allows me to bring my hand to her nose with a sigh of relief.

Progress.

We're making progress.

My mind is still stuck on this little step when her voice, a voice so smooth and sweet like honey, fills my ears as the mare and I step into the barn.

"Hey, cowboy. How's Galaxy doing?"

Tatum appears in front of us, looking devastatingly beautiful in a simple black shirt and green cargo pants. Her curls are tied back into a messy bun, making my fingers twitch with the desire to pull it out and run them through her hair. Her full lips have a glossy shine to them today, and it takes everything in me to fight against my body's wish to taste her lip gloss or lip balm or whatever the fuck has her mouth looking so damn kissable.

It's been almost a week since the woodchopping competition where I saw her cry for the first time. We've met every day since to water the seeds we planted, walk the length of where we will plant the rest that are coming today, and find more cheap materials we're going to use to make the Halloween decorations.

125

We haven't spoken about what happened again, but I promised her I'd wait, and I always keep my promises. There is no rush. I'm not pressuring her to find out what she wants. If she needs us to pretend nothing happened for now, then we'll do that.

"Good, we're making progress. She let me touch her today," I say, proving my point as I place my hand on the side of the horse's face.

"Aaron! That's amazing," Tate says as Galaxy shifts her focus to where she's keeping her distance to not spook the horse.

"How's Luna?" I ask when I notice she's holding a bucket of water with Loki standing beside her. I smile at him, making him start wagging his tail. I can tell he's working right now, so I'd never walk up to him, call his name, or pet him.

"She loves Betty and Angel," Tate replies with a small smile. We both turn to look at where the mini cows are walking around in their stable, and I spot Luna, our newest addition, chewing on some fresh pasture.

"And you. I saw her flopping her head down on top of your lap yesterday," I say, bringing a grin to Tatum's face.

"Yeah, I guess so." Tate's eyes meet mine, and we hold a look for several moments too long before she stares down at Loki again. "I'd better get back to her. I'll see you later," she adds before leaving Galaxy and me.

I shouldn't watch after her as she walks away, but I haven't been able to take my eyes off her when she's near. It's getting even harder with every day we spend together.

"Mine is definitely bigger than yours," Beckett says as he and Flynn walk through the barn doors with saddles in their arms.

"How old are the two of you?" I ask, catching their attention. "Comparing dick sizes like you're still in high school." Flynn bursts into laughter while a wicked smile crosses Beckett's face. I'm well aware they were probably discussing their saddles, but I can't help messing with them.

"No one would start that comparison with me. Have you seen me?" Beckett says and points to all six foot seven of him.

"Height don't mean you've got a big co—" Flynn cuts off when Briggs steps into the barn, his eyes going wide at our boss's unimpressed expression.

"Really, Flynn?" Briggs asks, and I almost start howling with laughter as my best mate starts pointing at me.

"He started the dick talk, not me," he defends, but I merely shake my head.

"I did no such thing. Those two were already discussing who has the bigger one when they walked in here," I reply, and Beckett bursts into laughter.

"Just use a damn ruler and measure so you can get the fuck back to work," Briggs says before stepping toward where Tatum and Olivia are tending to the mini cows.

"You're such an asshole," Flynn tells me, but Beckett still hasn't figured out a way to stop laughing.

"Briggs walking in was bad timing," I admit, but I don't apologize for throwing him under the bus.

"You think?" Flynn hisses, his face now bright red from embarrassment. I press my lips into a thin line to keep from smiling, but it only works for a split second.

"Want me to get the ruler for you?" I tease, and Beckett plants his ass on the ground as he starts laughing even harder.

Flynn is still glaring at me when I guide Galaxy back to her stables.

Once I'm done brushing Galaxy, I make my way outside, wiping sweat from my forehead with the back of my hand. It's incredibly hot out today.

"This is only half of what we're missing from our order," is the first thing I hear when I meet Tatum and the supplier at the main house. She looks calm but pissed off as the man throws bags of seeds from his truck.

One of them almost hits Tatum, and all I see is red.

"This is the rest. Not my fault you're stupid and didn't check how much you were orderin'," the man says, and I watch Tate take a step forward after dodging another bag of seeds he's throwing down.

"In total, I ordered thirty bags of various seeds. Fifteen were delivered, all of which were sunflowers and strawberry seeds. I'm missing fifteen where about half is lavender and half is wildflowers. You are telling me you are here to deliver only seven bags. Let me do the math for you. Fifteen minus seven equals you owing me eight fucking bags, sir," she says so calmly, no one would ever suspect she'd just insulted him and his intelligence more efficiently than I've ever seen anyone do.

Then, the man throws another bag, this one brushing against Tate's hand, making her lift it to her chest with a curse.

"You little—" I step up to the truck and get in the man's face before he has the chance to finish his insult.

"I suggest you don't finish that sentence and apologize for hitting her with one of these bags," I say, poison laced in my voice. His eyes narrow at me, but I don't back down. The protective part inside of me wants to knock out a few of his teeth for the way he spoke to Tate, for hitting her with a sack of seeds.

"Maybe you should back away before I hit you instead," the delivery man says, and I nod along to his words before stepping away and picking up the bags, throwing them right back into his truck. "What the fuck are you doing?" the man barks, but I don't answer at first, not until every single sack is back inside of his vehicle.

"We will be taking our business elsewhere. Be sure to let your boss know we're expecting a full refund and written apology unless he wants my buddy, chief of police Owen Grim, to knock on his door," I say, stepping in front of Tatum to be a protective wall. Her hand reaches out to touch my back in comfort, causing a bit of tension to leave my shoulders.

"Fuck you," the delivery man says before slamming the back of his truck shut and storming toward the driver's side.

He races off without another word, so I finally spin around and take her hand in mine to check how badly she's hurt. There is only a faint red mark, but it makes me angry nonetheless.

"Don't worry, it doesn't hurt. It just startled me a little," she promises, rubbing her index and middle fingers over her temples.

"I'm sorry if I overstepped," I quickly say, hoping she isn't upset with me.

"You didn't. It just sucks because that was the cheapest supplier in the area and we couldn't afford the other one," she explains and walks toward the front porch to sit down on the stairs and drop her face in her hands. "Sunflowers won't be enough to get people to visit more than once." She blows out a breath and shakes her head. "I don't want my dad to lose this farm, Aaron."

"He's not going to, I promise. There was another supplier with cheap prices. I'll drive there and pick up the bags myself," I say, making her head shoot up in surprise.

"That supplier was a thirteen-hour drive from here," she reminds me, but I merely shrug.

"It's fine. I like road trips."

Maybe not by myself, but it'll give me time to think and clear my head about this whole wanting Tatum situation.

"You're not going by yourself. This is my project, so I'm going with you," she announces as she pulls out her phone, and all my plans dissipate into thin air.

"What are you doing?" I ask as she starts hitting the screen of her phone with determination.

"Getting us motel rooms so we can split the trip into four days," she says, always the planner.

Her bottom lip slips between her teeth as she works, and I barely manage to keep my thumb from lifting to her mouth and pulling it free so I can bite on it instead.

"You don't have to book a motel room, sweetheart, we can just stop when we feel like it." One of her eyebrows raises so high, it almost touches her hairline.

"Would you like to spend a night in a place infested with bed bugs?" I shudder visibly at her question. "Exactly, so let me do my research."

Her brows furrow as she skims through reviews, doing her best to filter places with bad ratings so we don't end up somewhere cockroaches live.

By the time she's done, we found three motels to stay at and made a plan that'll have us on the road for four days.

Just Tate and me.

All alone.

Confined in one car with lots of time to connect.

If this isn't going to be the sweetest torture anyone has ever experienced, I don't know what is.

CHAPTER 20
Tatum

"So, you two are going on a road trip for four days?" Dad asks Aaron and me during dinner. The cowboy gives him a tight nod.

"Yes, sir. We're driving to Oklahoma to pick up some cheaper seeds," he explains while Flynn leans forward on the table with his chin placed on his intertwined hands.

"And you both have to go?" I know him well enough to know his intentions by now. Almost two months of regular dinners with Flynn, working with him, and spending evenings at Boots & Beers have taught me to always expect the worst.

"Yes, because this is our project," I tell Flynn with a firm tone, warning him not to turn this into something it isn't.

Something I haven't been able to stop thinking about since Aaron and I made our road trip plan.

Something I'm still not ready for, especially not after what happened at the bar.

"Interestin'," Flynn mumbles before taking a swig of beer and smiling at Aaron.

"They're gonna fuck," Olivia whispers to Hadley next to me.

"No, we're not," I say quietly enough to prevent Dad and everyone else from hearing me.

"You so are. You look at him like you've never seen a hotter man, and he looks at you like he wants to ruin you for every other person," Hadley says before lifting her hands as if to weigh both statements. "Take a and b and you get Aaron and you doing the dirty in his pickup truck on your way to Oklahoma."

Beckett catches her last sentence and chokes on his food a little, coughing while picking up his beer. I shoot him a glare, but he returns it with a wink.

"You have to keep us updated, Tate. Please. Nothin' interesting ever happens here," Olivia says, still whispering so Dad, Aaron, Ian, and Flynn can't hear. Not that they're paying attention. They've fallen into their own conversation.

"Maybe we should make a group chat," Beckett suggests, leaning forward on the table.

"Oh yes! That would be a lot more efficient," Hads replies as she pulls out her phone.

"Do I get a say in this?" I ask, but all three of them shake their head. "Fine, but don't get your hopes up about me texting that group chat because, no matter what happens, I'm not informing the three of you," I add before taking a sip of my iced tea.

"Booo," Olivia blurts out, grabbing everyone's attention at the table. She freezes in response, playing it off with an easy laugh. "Tate said she's not going to bring back any souvenirs," she lies to cover up, and I fight back a smile.

"I'll bring you a beer opener, Liv," Aaron promises his friend.

"And that's why you're my favorite," she says before digging into her food with a happy wiggle of her shoulders.

Aaron's eyes find mine across the table, something unspoken in those blue depths. I break eye contact first, unwilling to let him get under my skin with a single look, *again*. Spending time with him doesn't make it easier to keep an emotional distance. Two months is all it's taken for my stupid heart to flutter and warm every single time I think about him.

I... *like* him.

I haven't liked anyone in years, but I like the off-limits cowboy.

"Tate, mind passin' the beans?" Dad asks, his brows furrowed in suspicion at my red cheeks.

"Sure," I hand them over to Aaron because he's closest to my dad, trying to ignore the way a swift touch of our fingers has goosebumps cascading down my spine and arms.

"By the way, it's a good thing you found that ruler and got all your work done today, Flynn. I was a bit concerned I'd have to rip you a new one," Dad says after a few moments of silence.

A grin stretches his thin lips wide while I watch the way Flynn's face heats from embarrassment. Beckett has a hand clamped over his mouth, and Aaron is chuckling beside his best friend.

"Ruler?" Hadley asks, and Dad looks over to Flynn with a mean smile.

"Yeah, you see, Flynn here—" He cuts him off before my father can finish his explanation.

"Aaron went skinny dippin', and Tatum saw!" My eyes go wide in an instant.

"Flynn," Aaron hisses before smacking his arm.

"Sorry, man, I'm not goin' through earlier's embarrassin' moment again," he says, but Beckett slams a hand on the table, catching all of our attention.

A bright smile covers his face as he almost screams, "What?" He leans back in his chair, his eyes drifting between Aaron and me. "Goddamn, this is the best thing I've heard all week," he mutters to himself while Olivia and Hadley's heads both cock to the side as they wait for an answer.

"I don't think this is appropriate dinner coversa—" Olivia cuts Aaron off before he can finish that sentence.

"Tell me, is his ass as phenomenal as it looks in those jeans he wears?" she asks, and Beckett leans a little forward, clearly interested in the answer to that as well.

I open my mouth to respond, not with the truth—there is no way I'll tell them I've never seen a more muscled, round, glorious ass in my life—but to say anything to get these nosy people to change the topic.

Dad speaks a moment before me.

"You showed my daughter your naked ass?" he barks at Aaron, who turns a bright red. Flynn and Beckett have burst into laughter, Beckett leaning forward, his forehead pressed to where his arm is resting on the table, preventing anyone from seeing his face. Flynn's head is thrown back and Ian is shaking his head in disapproval.

"No. Well, kind of, but not on purpose," Aaron defends, and I wish I'd find my voice again. But I'm trying to hold back my own nervous laughter.

"Kind of? You told me you were buck fuckin' naked," Flynn says, digging a deeper hole for Aaron. I'm about to get a shovel and carve out a space beside him for myself. Or maybe I'd shove Flynn into the hole. Who knows?

"Would you shut the fuck up?" Aaron hisses while my father rubs his temples, clearly trying to get rid of the visual of a naked Aaron or the headache we're causing him.

"How the hell have you kept this from us for so long?" Liv demands, and I shoot her a warning look she completely ignores.

"It was none of your business," I fire back, but she merely dismisses my comment with a wave of her hand.

Olivia, Hadley, Beckett, and Ian start discussing all the possibilities of what happened or what could have happened while Flynn smiles at Aaron, who's glaring at his best friend.

"Lord, give me strength not to kill this boy," Dad whispers under his breath, but Aaron and I both hear, causing the cowboy's eyes to go wide.

"Briggs, I promise, I'd never voluntarily show your daughter any part of me she didn't ask to see," he points out, his eyes shifting to where I am, pleading with me to say something.

"I think you're overreacting, Dad. So I saw Aaron's ass, and what? I'd already forgotten until Mr. Let-Me-Change-Topics-To-Avoid-Having-Mea-sured-My-Dick-With-A-Ruler-Talk brought it up," I say, leaning back in my chair and flicking an imaginary fluff off my arm to seem unbothered.

I'm lying through my teeth. I've dreamt about Aaron's naked body on multiple occasions since I've seen it. It's not something *anyone* could ever delete from their brain.

"You measured your dick? How old are you?" Olivia asks Flynn, who immediately starts scowling at her.

"You're one to talk. I caught you laughing at a guy who walked into a pole because he was staring down at his phone," Flynn replies, and Olivia gives an unamused snort.

"That was fuckin' hilarious," she points out and lifts her index finger to shove it in his face. He smacks it away with an eye roll.

"And order's restored," I say to Aaron with a small, victorious smile as Olivia and Flynn lay into each other again.

He grins at me in response, and I internally scold my chest for warming at the sight of his happy expression.

It's early. Way too fucking early. The only reason I'm out of bed at three-thirty is because I wanted to make sure Luna was taken care of before Aaron and I left for Oklahoma today. The mini cow with a light brown, furry coat and white spots looks at me like I hung the moon for her.

She's calm and cuddly and does this little jumping thing where she kicks her hind legs into the air as soon as she touches the grass outside. Luna gets excited about any type of affection and attention and food. She taps her feet every single time I place the food in her stables. Angel and Betty also seem to adore the new addition to their little family, and Luna never leaves their side anymore.

"Would you stop fussin'? I'm gonna take care of your little princess," Olivia says, and I startle a little at the sound of her voice.

"What the hell are you doing up this early?" I ask, clutching a hand to my chest as if it could calm my racing heart.

"I often come here when everything's still quiet. Gives me a moment to breathe," she explains before walking over to Betty and ruffling the fur between her ears. "And shouldn't you be packin'? Aaron said you were leaving at six," she points out while Loki struts over to her. Liv's attention shifts to my dog before a bright smile covers her face.

"I already packed yesterday," I reply as I brush over Luna's coat.

"I'm sorry about dinner yesterday. I know you know this, but we're a very chaotic bunch who have yet to figure out how to keep our mouths shut with each other. Don't get me wrong. It hardly ever leaves the group, but all of us will eventually know every little detail about each other's lives," she explains with a little shrug. "We're family. It's what we do," Olivia adds with a sad smile while I make my way over to her, settling on the ground beside her.

"I adore it," I start, and she lifts her gaze so our eyes can meet. She doesn't believe I'm being sincere, so I decide to elaborate. "My mom and her new husband are so busy with work, I've become invisible to them over the years, apart from a few holiday dinners. My sister lives too far away for us to be closer than the occasional phone call, and I'm just now reconnecting with my dad. I've never had the kind of family you have with Aaron, Hadley, Ian, Beckett, and Flynn. So, yeah, it's nice."

Loki, sensing how emotional I've gotten, trots toward me.

"I know what you mean. My parents shipped me off to my aunt and uncle when I was still a baby. They wanted to travel the world for work, not raise an accidental child. My aunt and uncle did their best, but they didn't know what to do with me for most of my teenage years. I was a horrible child, always sneakin' out and breakin' the rules. Once, I stole my uncle's truck and tried to run away, but all it did was give me a juvenile record and a month of being grounded," she says, eyes wide and lips pulled into a thin line.

"You being a troublemaker as a kid makes so much sense to me," I reply, and she bursts into laughter, blinking away the tears that have collected in her eyes.

"Yeah, I guess I haven't changed as much as I wish I had. Just changed my habits from stealing cars to fucking emotionally unavailable people," she says and shudders a little.

"Sounds like a downgrade." My response earns me another burst of laughter from her. Her green eyes sparkle with gratitude as she faces me again.

"I'm really glad you moved here, pretty lady. It feels like you've completed our group." Fuck. Now tears are shooting into my eyes, and I promised myself after crying until no tears were left a week ago that I wasn't going to do so anymore.

"Dammit, Liv," I say and stare up at the ceiling, willing the tears to stay inside.

"Sorry," she replies with a snicker.

"Y'all having a party without me?" Hadley's voice fills my ears, causing my head to shoot in the direction of the barn doors. She walks in wearing a pair of shorts and a crop top. It doesn't look like she slept, but, somehow, she's full of energy and seems ready to start her day.

"More like an emotion-fest," I say, and Olivia buries her face in Betty's side to hide her chuckle.

"Sounds perfect. I could use a good cry," Hads adds as she plops onto the floor next to Olivia and me.

"Sorry, can't. You have the best parents and we were bonding over feeling like we never belonged in our families," Olivia explains, causing Hadley to push her bottom lip forward in a pout.

"My brother used to make fun of me when I was a kid. Does that count?" Hads asks, but Olivia shakes her head with a grin.

"Nope, because he also made fun of me." I'm smiling so hard, my cheeks are beginning to burn. "Plus, your brother is a sweetheart nowadays. Remember when he brought all of us dinner after our fifteen-hour day?" Olivia asks, and Hadley rolls her eyes before pointing at her friend.

"Yeah, he's great now that he reached thirty-three and decided maturity was the right path."

"Not to mention, he is *gorgeous*," Olivia adds with a dreamy look filling her eyes.

"And gay, thank God, otherwise you'd have made our interactions with him a hell of a lot more awkward already."

I could listen to them all day, lose myself in the way they love each other so much and know each other so well. I want something like they have. A best friend you can go to whenever something's wrong. A best friend who makes you feel better about a shitty situation. A best friend who could tell me what the fuck I'm supposed to do about Aaron. My head and heart are in agreement, somewhat, but my body? My body is telling me to ignore everything and give in to what it craves. One night. It's all it'd take for us to get it out of our systems, to go through it instead of running away, like he said, but I'm not stupid enough to believe I wouldn't become addicted to Aaron.

Not when I already adore the way I feel around him. Safe. Comfortable. Alive. Heated with desire so intense, I've never felt anything like it in my life.

"She's thinkin' about Aaron," I hear Olivia whisper.

"Oh, definitely. Look at how red her cheeks are," Hads chimes in.

"And how fast she's breathin'."

"And the way her bottom lip is tucked between her teeth."

I pick up some hay from beside me and throw it at both of them. They start laughing because they know they have me.

And I can't help but enjoy how they saw right through me.

CHAPTER 21
Aaron

FIREFLY NUDGES MY ARM with his nose. I brush over the coat on his neck and mane, trying to ignore the stabbing guilt for leaving him. Flynn promised me he'd take care of him while I'm not here for the next four days, but it's not the same. I kiss his forehead once before repeating the same process of brushing with Galaxy. I feel even guiltier leaving her with Hads and Olivia, even though I made sure yesterday she was alright with both of them.

At least that's what I keep telling myself.

Once I've finished, I make my way back to my house, grabbing my keys and bags before hauling the latter into the backseat of my truck. I've packed snacks, water, pillows, and a blanket, in case Tate would like to sleep in the passenger seat during any point of this drive. I've even made a playlist for us on my phone, but I'm not sure what music she'll want to listen to, so I'll leave it up to her whether to play it or not.

Ash gives me a sad whine, making more guilt shoot through me. He's staying with Briggs because I didn't want him to distract Loki while he's working the next few days.

"I'm sorry, buddy," I say right as I knock on the main house's door. Briggs opens it a second later, looking grumpy and sleep-deprived. "You doing alright?" I ask with a laugh, and Briggs lets out an annoyed groan.

"It's six in the morning, and I didn't sleep well, worryin' about you and my daughter going away together for a few days."

His words have two effects.

One, more guilt shoots through me than I was already struggling with.

Two, annoyance joins the feeling.

"With all due respect, Briggs, I understand Tatum is your youngest daughter, but what we do is none of your business. Nothing's happened yet, but I told you I can't stop thinking about her, and I wasn't lying. She's the most incredible woman I've ever met, and if she says she wants me, too, then that's our decision to make," I blurt out because I'm getting a bit tired of him trying to keep Tate and me from exploring whatever's between us.

"I meant worry in the sense of the long journey," Briggs says as he straightens out his shoulders. Fuck me. "However, I hear what you're sayin', and I'm gonna have to give you an ultimatum here, son. It's either datin' Tatum or workin' on the ranch. You can't have both," he says, sending a stinging pain through me.

"That's cruel." I need this job to pay for Nanna's medicine, her room at the home, and her medical bills. Insurance covers some of it, but not nearly enough for me to be jobless. And all of my animals are here.

"It's me protecting my daughter's heart, Aaron. Yours, too." Briggs gives me a sad smile, and it almost makes me believe he isn't doing this to be mean and meddling. Almost.

"You don't trust her to make these decisions for herself and handle the consequences. That's what it is," I reply and move backward a little, trying to get away from the man I used to admire.

The only parental figure I have left.

Tatum appears in the door with a bag slung over her shoulder and Loki beside her.

"What's going on?" she asks when she picks up on the negative vibe between Briggs and me. I take the bag off her shoulder, never breaking eye contact with her father.

"Nothin' you need to worry about," Briggs says, but that also doesn't feel right, him keeping this shit from her.

"Oh, so you didn't tell Aaron to stay away from me or you'd fire him," she blurts out, and my eyebrows rise in response. "Dad, I already promised nothing will happen between Aaron and me. Let it go," she adds, causing every muscle in my body to tense.

"Honeybee, I—" Tate cuts him off before he has a chance to come up with excuses.

"I'll see you in a few days, Dad. Try not to fire anyone else for even having breathed my way," she says and, despite being upset with him, kisses his cheek. "Let's go, cowboy. I need breakfast," she says and brushes her hand against my arm to get me moving.

"Please take care of Ash," is the last thing I say to Briggs before following Tate and Loki to my truck.

The first hour of our drive passes in silence. I picked up some drinks for us at Jamie's café, who threw in breakfast on the house. Tate eats it quietly before taking her medication and then staring at the playlist I made. She hits shuffle, sending a country melody through my truck before Kane Brown's voice follows. I catch the faint smile on her lips as the song plays, tapping her feet to the rhythm.

We don't talk at first, and I do my best not to stare at her at every red light we stop at.

"I promised him I'd never let things go further than friendship between you and me because I don't want to cause my dad more of a headache than I already have in my life," Tate says once we hit the one-hour mark of our twelve-hour drive. She tilts her head my way, so I take my eyes off the road for a brief moment to meet her sad gaze. "He's always been so worried about me, I don't want him to have to worry about you and me," she explains, causing my grip on the steering wheel to tighten at her words.

"Why would he even be worried if all you had in the past is casual relationships?" I point out. Tatum looks out of her window for a beat before staring down at her hands.

"I don't know. It's all I can give someone. It's why I've been running from what's between us, too," she mumbles before taking a deep breath. "I can't imagine dating someone with epilepsy to be ideal. You're constantly worried your partner will have a seizure, the one seizure that might end their life prematurely. They're called SUDEP, you know. Sudden unexpected death that happens to someone with my chronic illness," she goes on while my chest tightens. "There are so many restrictions to what I can do. For example, my favorite band *From Angels to Devils* is coming to Tennessee in three months, and I can't see them because it's too risky they'll have flashing lights at their concert. I always have to check which movies I can watch, which meals I can eat, plan around taking my pills, and, and, and."

I'm convinced I stopped breathing, but she doesn't seem to notice.

"It's a burden. I *feel* like a burden, even when I know I'm not. My chronic illness doesn't take away from who I am as a person, but it's easy to acknowledge that and harder to internalize it, especially when society tells you the opposite."

Silence fills the car again as I try to process her words, her pain.

"That's why you were crying. You think you'd be putting me through hell if we were dating," I point out, trying to piece everything together.

Tatum gives me a sad nod.

"Yeah, pretty much," she says and blows out a breath. "So, there you go, cowboy. Don't wait for me to figure my shit out. Stay away from me," she says with a nervous laugh, obviously getting uncomfortable with this situation.

"To be completely honest with you, sweetheart, I'm long past the point of being able to stay away from you, and you have yet to give me a good reason why I should," I reply, stopping at another red light. I turn my head her way, but she has her brows furrowed in confusion.

"I just did," she argues, but I shake my head.

"No, you haven't. You've told me how you feel, but you don't get to decide what I want, only I do, and your epilepsy doesn't change how I feel." Tears fill her eyes, but she rapidly blinks them away.

"You don't mean that. You can't," she says, her voice firm.

"Only way to find out is to try."

"Aaron—" Her voice breaks off at the same moment someone honks behind us, telling me the light is green.

I step on the gas as I say, "Do me a favor, Tate, and don't live your whole life in a cloud of what-ifs when I'm right here, willing to prove you wrong," I say before flashing her a smile she doesn't know what to do with. Her eyes narrow, so I smile more brightly. A sigh slips past her lips a second later.

"What am I going to do with you?" she says and drops her face into her hands.

"Whatever you want," I reply with a chuckle, making her throw a napkin at me with a laugh.

"God, you're impossible."

"Can't argue with that," I reply and pick up my coffee to take a sip.

"Well, it doesn't change that my dad would fire you if we even went on a date," she points out.

"So, we go on a date and tell nobody. Tate, you want me, and you don't have to fight it."

"Aren't you full of yourself?"

"No, but you could be full of me." Her face turns bright red but a smile fights its way onto her face anyway.

"Aaron, stop talking," she says with a breathless laugh.

"Why? Am I convincing you to go out with me?" I ask, and she sighs again.

"Yes." *Fuck. Yes.* "But it's not happening. God! We're project partners, and that's it."

"For now," I reply, too happy with this development to mind the uncertainty still lingering between us. "Have you thought about what you'd like to do tonight? I heard there is this fun honky tonk next to our motel. We could go there, do some line dancing," I offer.

"You dance? What about your knee?" she asks, and I make a *pfft* sound.

"My knee will be fine," I assure her, although it's mostly a reassurance for myself. I've been wearing my brace, which is helping more than I'll ever admit to Briggs.

"If you don't mind my asking, how did it happen?"

We finally hit the highway, which means now it's just going to be us and the open road for the next few hours.

There is no question about whether or not I want to open up to Tate about my injury. She's been so open and honest with me, I want to give her the same in return. But I'm not nearly as strong as she is. Every time I think about what happened, I want to crawl out of my skin to get away from my mind, away from the knee that failed me moments before I made it big. I want to tell her, but I can't manage to form the words.

The usual panic threatens to take over me, to shut down my entire system.

I take a deep breath instead, finding courage somewhere deep inside of me. Courage that's long overdue because that heartbreak, the one of losing everything I worked for my entire life up until I was twenty-four, is long in the past.

"I used to be a show jumper, and I was damn good at it," I start, turning on the cruise control and shifting my foot to hover over the brake pedal.

"It was the day of the championship finale in the country. I was number two. Winning would have made me number one. I was so close, all it took was one perfect run," I say. "My horse at the time, Phoenix, got startled mid-jump by a member of the audience using flash while taking photos. He bucked and threw me off his back, and I landed right on my knee. The entire bone shattered, tendons snapped. They reconstructed my knee and left it looking like a wolf had torn into it," I try to joke, but it falls flat.

Tate covers her lips with one of her hands.

"I'm so sorry, Aaron," she says, but I shrug off her comment because if I acknowledge it, I might actually shed a tear.

"Don't be. It was a long time ago. I only get the occasional cramps that take me out for a few minutes," I explain, ignoring the stabbing sensation in my chest.

"Maybe it's better if we don't dance," she says, but I snort in response.

"At least if it starts cramping, you'll have an excuse to comfort me," I reply as I switch lanes and slow down to take a sharp corner. "Maybe I'll even pretend to faint so you'll give me CPR," I add.

"Is that really how you'd like our first kiss to go? While you're pretending to be unconscious?"

"No. I'd like our first kiss to be when neither of us is able to fight this attraction anymore." I don't know what compels me to say it, but it's too late to take it back.

"We're entering dangerous territory again, Aaron. I think we should play a car game instead," she suggests, and I give an agreeing nod.

"Open the glove compartment. I put some trivia games in there," I say, and she does as she's told, her curls bouncing beautifully with the movement.

"I'm going to destroy you in these, I hope you know that," she says with a smile directed my way, and I cock an amused eyebrow at her.

Her fingers struggle with the plastic around the metal box that holds the cards, but she slaps my hand away when I offer her help.

Ever the independent woman.

She's used to doing things by herself, and it'll take time for her to see she can rely on me.

"Got it," she mumbles with a victorious, quiet, "Aha!"

"Alright, let's see who can get the most answers. Winner gets to choose the other person's outfit for tonight," I offer before extending my hand in a deal-making manner.

"Oh, you're on," she says before clasping my hand and shaking it.

Easiest game I've ever won.

CHAPTER 22
Tatum

"WHAT DO YOU MEAN there's only one room?" Aaron asks while my entire body freezes. "At least tell me there are two beds," he says to the man at the reception, but he only gives the cowboy a bored shrug.

Loki huffs out a breath, catching the receptionist's attention. He scrunches his nose at the sight of my dog until I point at his service dog harness to keep him from commenting. The same uncomfortable look I've been flashed my entire life covers his face.

"Nope. Should have booked in advance. We're in our busy season, everybody knows that," he replies with an eye roll.

I'm about to punch him in the face when Aaron places his arm around me from the front, pulling me behind him. The ray of sunshine I've gotten to know disappears as he leans forward on the wooden desk to ensure the receptionist pays close attention to his next words.

"I need another bed. Arrange it. I'm not going to ask again," Aaron demands, his voice rough and low, sending a wave of shivers down my spine.

"Fine," the receptionist says and shoves two room keys Aaron's way. He swipes the cards off the desk and takes my hand before storming toward where our room is.

"What a dick," I blurt out once we're inside, shaking my head in disappointment. "The eye roll? I almost fucking decked the guy," I say. Aaron lets out a laugh before flopping onto the bed.

"Me, too." I can't help but snicker at his exasperated sigh. "I get it's not the best job, but fuck, would it kill him to not be a jerk?"

"Probably. Did you see his face? He's probably never said a nice thing to anyone," I reply, crossing my arms and moving to stand in front of him. He spreads his legs, an invitation for me to step between them, and it takes everything inside of me not to give in.

"Yeah, I saw that, too," Aaron says with a chuckle, his hands slipping onto his knees as if he's looking for a way not to touch me too. His eyes trail over my hips, confirming my suspicion when his fingers dig into his legs. "I don't think I could survive sharing a bed with you when I'm not allowed to touch you." His admission sends a thrill through me.

"We'd probably accidentally touch each other throughout the night, Aaron. I wouldn't be against that." Or any other touching he'd like to do.

"That's not what I meant," he says, heat turning his gaze molten with desire.

My heart pounds as he finally gives in and brings his hand to my left hip, tugging until I'm between his legs. My fingers fly onto his neck for stability, and he grins at the way I curl them around the hair at his nape.

"What did you mean?"

"You know what I meant, sweetheart. Don't make me describe all the things I want to do to you if you're not ready for me to actually do them," he says with an easy smile.

"You must know that after one night, one time of us getting it out of our system, we wouldn't be this attracted to each other. It's only because we're not supposed to," I remind him, and he drops backward onto the bed.

"Speak for yourself, Tate." I let out a chuckle and nudge his good knee with my hand.

"I'm going to go get ready," I say before stepping into the bathroom and taking a deep breath.

After showering and putting on the outfit he insisted on buying me on our way here—camouflage green cowboy boots, jeans that hug all of my curves too well, and a flannel shirt—I step out of the bathroom to find Aaron completely dressed, too. And I curse him internally because fuck, he looks like a wet dream in his jeans that hug his ass in a sinful way. His feet are shoved into black boots, and he's wearing a white dress shirt he barely buttoned to show off his tanned chest. A matching black cowboy hat to his shoes rests on his head. I'm convinced I'm drooling like a dog with a piece of meat in front of it.

His blue eyes find mine, a dangerous smirk lifting the right side of his mouth. Maybe I'd be able to resist this man more easily if we didn't spend six hours in the car together, laughing at the questions on the cards. Maybe I could keep my heart from getting involved if we didn't spend all our time together. Maybe I could prevent myself from liking him if he wasn't thoughtful, kind, honest, and good with animals. Maybe I wouldn't want him if his mouth wasn't as dangerous, sexy, and seductive as it is.

"You look like all of my fantasies combined into one person," he says, and my breathing hitches.

"And you look like you should model for Calvin Klein," I say. "Cowboy Edition," I add with a little smile. Aaron's face lights up with a grin so bright, it almost knocks me on my ass.

"Is that your way of saying I should undress so you can take photos of me?" he asks and I grab his arm to lead him out the door.

"Not today, Aaron." He throws a smirk over his shoulder.

"Tomorrow work better for you?" I fight back a grin.

"Shut up, cowboy."

"As you wish, sweetheart."

CHAPTER 23
Aaron

THE HONKY TONK IS full of life. The dance floor is covered in attendees line dancing, the bar is occupied with people on every stool, tables are buzzing with conversation and laughter, and the music playing is upbeat. The scent of fried food and alcohol fills my nose, and I notice Tate ever so slightly swaying her hips to the music. My fingers twitch with the need to touch her, grab her hips and pull her to me to grind our bodies together to the rhythm of the music, but I suppress the urge.

"Can I get you a water or iced tea?" I ask after placing my hand on her arm and leaning down enough to hover my lips over her ear.

"Water. I'm going to need to hydrate if you make me line dance," she says with a small smile, and I grin.

"On it." I make my way through the crowd to get us our drinks.

By the time I've secured my beer and Tate's water, she's found a standing table and is chatting with someone. He's short and lean, and his smirk is a little too flirty for my liking. Tate, being who she is, gives the man an unimpressed look with one of her brows cocked and the corners of her mouth a little downturned. She shakes her head at something he says, and when he takes a step toward her, I barely hold myself back from crushing the can of beer in my hand. I don't know how dense this man is, but anyone who looked at Tate could see she is not comfortable with the conversation he's trying to have with her.

"Oh, come on, baby. One dance. I promise to be good to you," the man says as he leans toward Tate.

"I already said no. Are you not competent enough to understand that word?" she asks with a scowl, and, if I weren't pissed at this man's behavior, I'd laugh.

"Come on. I only bite when I'm asked to." He flashes her another smile, but Tate gives him a disgusted look.

"Do you also go away when asked to?"

As soon as her eyes find me, relief spreads across her face and tension seems to slip out of her shoulders. The reaction is so sweet, it makes my insides twist and turn in the best way. She trusts me. She feels safe with me.

I place myself right behind the disgusting man.

It's not that I think Tate isn't an independent and strong woman that can deal with this guy, but when men are pigs and refuse to hear a woman say "no," they're only going to get the fuck away if another dude shows up. I'm often taller and more muscular than them, so one look at me is enough to scare them away, especially when I place that frightening Blaze scowl on my face.

My grandmother used it so much when I was a kid, I never misbehaved around her.

"She asked you to leave, and I suggest you do so before I lose my temper," I suggest, even if I'm not the biggest fan of violence. Flynn and Beckett are the fighters, not me, but I'd gladly change that to get this disgusting man away from Tate.

The man in the polo shirt with the expensive watch and gelled-back hair straightens out his back to reveal he's about a foot shorter than me. He stares at my wide chest for a moment before his eyes trail up and he has to lean his head back to look into my eyes.

"Shit, sorry. Didn't know she was your girl, bro." He slaps a hand on my shoulder in a casual sort of way, but when I narrow my eyes at him, he removes it.

"Yeah, she is, so you better leave, *bro*, because I don't fuck around when it comes to *my girl*." She isn't mine, but damn, it feels good to say.

"Chill out. I'm leaving," the stranger says without another glance in Tatum's direction.

I watch him walk away to make sure he's truly gone before spinning back around to catch Tatum staring at me with the biggest grin on her face. It's the most amused look she's ever given me, and I take a second to appreciate the way she offers me these expressions now. She opens up to me like a wildflower when the sun shines brightly on it. It's mesmerizing and breathtaking in a way I've never experienced before, especially because to the rest of the world, she's an adorable grump. It's only when she cares about you that she lets you see there is a whole lot of sunshine inside of her.

"Thank you, I appreciate you doing that," she says and takes the bottle of water I hand her. "Even if you called me *your girl*," Tate adds with a snort. I step toward her, only stopping once our chests almost touch.

"You don't wanna be my girl, sweetheart?" I ask and take a sip of my beer, watching her closely as she thinks about what to answer.

Tate places a hand on my left pec, her nails digging in ever so slightly. She drags her hand down, down, down, until her fingers slip into my belt loop. My entire body lights on fire as every drop of blood rushes to my cock, demanding her hand go even lower.

"No, but if you play your cards right, I could be your good girl later," she teases and shifts her weight onto her tiptoes, bringing her lips close to mine. She's playing with me, but I'm more than happy to participate in this game.

"Oh yeah?" I ask with a smirk, moving lower until our mouths almost brush. She sucks in a sharp breath and leans away, my body moving with her without meaning to.

"Too bad you have alcohol on your lips. Otherwise, I'd kiss you, and show you I'm being serious," she says before shrugging. Fuck. I didn't even think about that. "Let's go, cowboy. I was promised you'd be dancing, too," she says and grabs my hand to lead me to the dance floor.

I'm not sure how much time passes, but I've never felt so carefree, or laughed so much, in my entire life.

At first, I tried to teach her the simple moves at the sidelines. She seemed to be picking them up easily enough before we went on the dance floor to join the three dozen other people that were line dancing.

Then, everything went to shit in the funniest way possible.

Tate is awful at line dancing, and whenever she missteps, she bursts into laughter and pulls me right out of the step sequence with her. It happens so often, at one point, I'm bent over at the waist laughing with her because she stepped on my foot and I had to catch her.

She's so busy trying to catch her breath, she doesn't even notice when I drag her away from the dance floor so the people around us stop giving us funny looks. I lead us far enough away that the music becomes a dull background noise. It allows me to hear Tate's laughter, unfiltered and raw, a beautiful sound I do my best to memorize. The softness and melodic tone of it, the way her eyes sparkle, and the shape of her lips.

She's so fucking beautiful.

"I'm so sorry," Tate says once she's caught her breath, but she's still laughing. "God, that went so much worse than I thought it would."

"I thought you did great." She wipes under her eyes to get rid of the tears of laughter, smudging a bit of her mascara on her cheek.

"Liar," she says, but I'm moving forward now, my finger darting toward her to wipe away the mascara. Her breathing hitches, but her smile never fades. "Are my mascara and eyeliner a mess?" she asks, still grinning up at me.

"Not yet," I reply, imagining all the ways I could ruin her makeup while she takes my cock, fingers, or mouth.

"Is that a promise?" she asks, grabbing me by my belt loops again.

"If that's what you want."

Tate looks up at me, her right hand reaching out to grab my cowboy hat and slipping it onto her head instead. Everything inside of me catches fire from desire. I'm not entirely sure if she knows what she just did, but I merely hold my breath as she adjusts it and then wets her lips. My cock gives a needy throb, unbearably hard because of the way Tate is looking at me.

It's intoxicating.

"You know, I've heard about the cowboy hat rule. Wear the hat, ride the cowboy, right?" she says with a smirk.

"You don't want me," I remind her. Tate slips her hands onto my stomach and clutches at the fabric there.

"I do want you. I keep trying to convince myself I don't, but it's useless." My heart races so wildly, it's close to jumping out of my chest. "I want one night. One night of us giving in to whatever is between us, and then we can finally move on."

"What if you're right and it goes so horribly, we won't be able to look at each other anymore?" I argue because I want her, but I want more than one night. Hiding that is pointless.

"I want you. God, Aaron, I don't think I've ever craved another person the way I crave you." If it weren't for my fear of still having alcohol on my lips or in my mouth, I'd kiss her right now.

"Sweetheart, I can't give you what you want. One night won't be enough for me. One taste won't be enough. Tate, you're the kind of woman a man like me doesn't get over. Don't ask me for one night when I can't promise it wouldn't change everything between us." Honesty. I know it'll kill the mood, but it's the best route.

My grandmother used to say, "Lying will only get you so far because if your lies are uncovered, everything you built on them starts to crumble."

"I'm so scared," she admits, not letting go of me. Her smile has faded, fear and need in her eyes. I want to take away what scares her. I want to reassure her. And I want to give her everything she needs.

"Of what, sweetheart?" Tears jump into her eyes, so I cup her face, preventing her from hiding from me.

"Of wanting something I've never allowed myself to have. Aaron, this isn't me trying to be cruel. I want more than one night too, but I can't give you a relationship.

I can't give you the promise of years. I can't even give you the reassurance that my next seizure won't result in irreparable damage. Security. That's what I cannot give you, and no one should have to live like that. You wouldn't be able to be happy, not fully," she says and takes a step back, taking her heat with her. It leaves me cold.

"Tate, you can't know that unless you let someone in. I know it's scary, but—" She cuts me off.

"I can't have babies, Aaron! Okay? I can't give you marriage, babies, all that stuff people want. I can't. My doctor told me that for me personally, being pregnant could trigger more seizures, so I made the choice to be sterilized to prevent the risk of accidental pregnancy when I was twenty years old. To spare myself more seizures that could potentially risk my life. Nothing would be ordinary with me, and that? Giving up what you've probably wanted since you were old enough to understand the concept of having your own family? That's not something you get over because you like me, Aaron."

She storms away from me when nothing but silence lingers between us. I don't mean to be at a loss for words. I mean to tell her something, *anything*, but I'm so overwhelmed by her display of vulnerability, I feel like sinking to the ground and hugging my knees to my chest.

By the time I manage to regain the ability to walk and talk, Tate is making her way through the front doors of the honky tonk. I run after her, pushing through people without so much as an apology because I can't leave our conversation like that.

I don't want her to ever feel unwanted because of her epilepsy.

"Tate!" I call after her, but she doesn't so much as turn around. "Fuck," I mutter, picking up my pace. "Tatum, wait a damn second, please!" Why the hell is she so fast?

"I've said everything I needed to say, Aaron," she calls back over her shoulder. I finally manage to catch up to her, placing myself in front of her to stop her from walking.

"Good, then you can listen," I say, hating the way a tear is falling down her face. I wipe it away, but another one rolls down her other cheek. "One day at a time."

She furrows her brows at me in confusion.

"We'll go slow, take it one day at a time without thinking about marriage and babies and every other stupid fucking societal expectation people have on relationships. I'm in no rush to start a family, nor do I even know if that's what I want. What I do know for certain is that I'd really like to take you on a proper date."

Her gaze shifts from my eyes to my lips and then back up. Tate is considering what I'm saying, probably thinking about a way to push me away again, but I'm here to stay.

Her epilepsy isn't an obstacle we need to overcome.

It's part of her, and I want all parts.

"Okay," she whispers, and I barely hold back my sigh of relief.

"Okay?" I repeat.

"Yeah," she says and wraps her arms around herself. "But we won't be able to tell anyone if we go on a date because I don't want to be the reason my dad fires you," Tate adds, but I'm so happy, I can't stop smiling.

"It'll stay between us when it does. Until we're ready," I promise. "But, like I said, we can go as slow as you want."

"We're about to share a bed. I think that'll make taking things slow a bit more complicated." Her hazel eyes turn softer, letting me in again.

"They'll have arranged for another bed."

"We're capable of sharing a bed without fucking, aren't we?" I love the way a little, naughty smile creeps onto her lips.

"I am. Are you?" Tate merely shrugs.

"I guess we'll find out."

CHAPTER 24

Aaron

AFTER A SHOWER, BRUSHING my teeth, and slipping into my pajama pants, I slide under the covers to listen to the sound of Tate singing in the shower. It's not loud, barely more than a whisper, but I close my eyes to enjoy the softness of her voice. I didn't know she could sing.

Another little piece of Tatum to add to my list of reasons why I like her.

As expected, the receptionist didn't get us another bed and the woman working there tonight said she could have something arranged by tomorrow, which obviously doesn't work. I offered to sleep on the ground, but Tatum was very firm about neither of us doing that.

We'll be sleeping in one bed.

Fuck me.

"Loki, come," she says, and I realize I didn't hear the shower turning off. I was so lost in my own thoughts, I didn't notice she was about to join me in the bed.

My heart stops beating at the sight in front of me. Tatum walks over to her suitcase in silky pajamas with a polka-dot pattern painted across the fabric. Her shorts are *short*, hugging her ass and thick thighs in a way that should be unlawful. Her tank top reveals a little bit of her stomach and barely contains her breasts, sending a wave of arousal straight to my dick.

I roll onto my side and groan into my pillow.

"What?" Tate asks, all feigned innocence and danger.

Alarm bells start going off in my head, telling me to get out of the damn bed before I pull her on top of me and kiss her senseless.

Slow.

We're going slow.

"Those pajamas, Tate, they're a gorgeous, little tease, baby. I'm going to need you to stay as far away from me in bed as possible," I say after rotating my head enough to make sure my voice comes out clear. She chuckles at my dramatic words.

"Relax, Aaron. Haven't you ever platonically shared a bed with a woman?" she asks, crossing her arms under her tits, pushing them up until they're almost spilling out at the top of her shirt.

"Nope. Unlike what you may believe, I haven't been in a serious relationship before either. I'm just not as opposed to them as you are," I say with a smile, and she shoots daggers with her eyes in response. "All I'm saying is I haven't taken a woman into my bed if she didn't scream my name in ecstasy at least once before we went to sleep," I explain, and, if I didn't know better, I'd say there is a bit of jealousy in her gaze.

"Only once?" She clicks her tongue in boredom. "Part of me expected more from you," she teases, her easy flirting attitude back. I welcome it.

"I said at least. It all depends on the person and how much time I've got," I reply and watch her roll her eyes at me. It's not the first time she's done it, and I'm sure it won't be the last.

"Cocky cowboy," she mumbles as she slides under the covers, finally giving me a chance to breathe. "Far enough?" she asks as she arranges herself at the very edge of the bed.

Panic settles in my chest at the thought of her rolling and accidentally falling off the bed. I throw every single worry out of the window and pull her back flush against my front, keeping my hips far away to prevent her from feeling my cock against her ass. No matter how desperately I'd like to do the opposite.

"You don't know what the hell you want, do you?" she asks but nuzzles herself into me anyway.

"Not exactly, to be honest. You've turned my world so upside down, I don't even know left from right anymore."

"Don't blame me for that," she mumbles. I trace circles on her soft stomach, enjoying her warmth while inhaling her sweet scent.

"But it is your fault."

She nudges her elbow backward, but I catch it and guide her arm forward again until my fingers slip between hers, our arms pressed right below her breasts. Dangerous. So fucking dangerous.

But I don't care.

"Aaron?" God, the way this woman says my name.

"Yes, sweetheart?"

"Is it easy for you to talk about your grandmother?" she asks, trailing her nails over my arm until goosebumps spread across my skin.

"Not always, but it feels easy with you," I admit, and she turns around in my arms to bring her gaze to mine.

"Will you tell me about her?" Her eyes search my face, seeing if her question makes me angry or uncomfortable. It makes me neither. I want to share stories about her, share how incredible she was.

"When I was five years old, both of my parents died in an accident," I explain, feeling the usual bit of sadness. I don't remember my parents well, and, still, I miss them. "My grandmother took me in and we spent another year in Australia before we packed up our house and moved to Orchard Hill. She bought the ranch next to your dad's ranch."

Tatum's full attention is on me, watching me carefully as she slips one of her hands on top of where one of mine lies on the pillow.

"Red Sky Ranch?" I give her a nod, grabbing her fingers and guiding them to my lips so I can press a kiss to the back of them.

"It was called Rocking Horse Ranch when we owned it, but we sold it when she got diagnosed, and I used that money for her medical bills, housing, and general living costs."

Tate nods along to my words, not interrupting me once because she's too invested in the story.

"She was everything to me. She was my rock for most of my life. It didn't take me long to realize I wasn't the only recipient of her kindness and love. Everyone in the community adored her, even your dad. They used to have coffee every Sunday morning to discuss distributors, what had been happening in the world, or anything else that came to mind," I go on, enjoying that I get to speak about my grandmother like this.

"She sounds like a wonderful person," Tate says after I've been quiet for a few moments.

"She is," I reply with a sad smile.

Tate's finger slips across my jaw, tracing it until she reaches my neck. Her thumb runs down the length of it until my eyes flutter shut. I barely manage to open them halfway. I've never been this vulnerable with anyone before.

"Do you visit her often?" she asks after shoving her hands under her head and resting it on top of them.

"Every Friday at three," I say. Tatum thinks about that for a moment, chewing on her bottom lip as she does.

"Does she recognize you?"

"Sometimes. Less and less as time goes on," I reply and roll onto my back.

"It was the same with my grandfather, only I wasn't as close with him. We didn't share as many memories together, so I think that's why he forgot me first," she explains, and I turn my head just enough to watch sadness cross her features. "I'm sorry she's forgetting you," she mumbles, pain in her tone. I nudge the underside of her chin with my fingers, lifting her head until she's looking at me.

"Life happens however it decides to. Nothing we can do to change it. All we can do is find the pleasures in life that make it worth living. I can't change my nanna's illness, so I do my best to cherish whatever time I have left with her, even if she doesn't recognize me. You can't change your epilepsy, but you're a warrior, taking on life in a way that mesmerizes me every single time I look at you." She rolls her lips as tears fill her eyes again, but she blinks them away quickly.

"I'm not as strong as I pretend to be," she whispers.

"You're right. You're even stronger."

"I get scared a lot," she admits, and I roll back onto my side to be closer to her again.

"That doesn't make you weak. It makes you human, sweetheart." She studies me, her eyes drifting all over my face in search of deception, but there is none to find. "I get scared a lot, too. Every single time I step in a room with Olivia and Flynn, I'm scared they'll set it on fire," I joke to lighten the mood, and Tate gives me a beautiful smile.

"Understandable," she says.

We fall into a comfortable silence, still facing each other, when Tate's eyes start fluttering shut every few seconds until she's fast asleep. Loki scooches closer, only stopping until he's right between us, serving as the pillow wall I wanted to build earlier. I pat his head and he falls onto his side, nuzzling into me and placing his paw on Tatum's hand.

My eyes trail over her face for a while longer, memorizing every single freckle, birthmark, lash, and wrinkle I can find until I fall asleep, my dreams filled with Tatum's laughter.

CHAPTER 25
Tatum

MY LEG AND HALF my body are draped across Aaron's chest while one of his arms is wrapped around my back, his fingers slightly digging into my hip. He's leaning a bit toward me, meaning his crotch is perfectly lined up with mine, and my nipples are rubbing against his chest.

I should have known we'd end up this way. It's impossible not to when Aaron is a cuddler and I can't help wiggling closer to him any chance I get.

We said we'd go slow, which means, no matter how good his morning wood feels pressed against my needy pussy, I will not wake him and beg him to rub it against me until the uncomfortable ache between my legs is eased.

Aaron shifts in his sleep, thrusting his morning wood against my clit so hard, I have to bite down on my bottom lip to keep from moaning. He, on the other hand, isn't awake enough to bite back his pleasure and groans softly, his fingers grabbing my hip more tightly. I try to move away, to prevent it from happening again, but my head is spinning from pleasure.

"Tate?" Aaron asks, sending my heart into a frenzy.

He's awake. I could tell him not to stop, to keep going until we're both a panting mess, but that would go against the plan we made. I can't bring myself to care as he shifts a little again. My nails dig into his torso as I gasp in pleasure.

"Tate, we should stop this."

"Aaron, please."

Please what, Tatum? This is dangerous territory, and I should stop this right now. *Should, should, should.*

"You're so hot and soft against me, baby, if you beg again, I don't think I can stop until I've made you come," he says, his voice husky and sleepy.

"You feel so good," I mumble against his chest, trying to hide my face as heat fills my cheeks. I roll my hips against his dick again, seeking the friction I need. "I want you to touch me." Fuck. Well, there's no turning back now, not that I want to.

"Give me your mouth first, then I'll use mine to make you come," he says, and I tilt my head to do exactly that. His hand slips around my throat, applying just the slightest bit of pressure as he guides my mouth to his.

Aaron wastes no time claiming my lips with his in a hungry kiss. It isn't anything like I thought kissing him would be. It isn't soft and comforting. It's demanding, possessive almost, as if he's trying to imprint himself on my mouth until my lips will never want another person's but his.

Aaron tastes like the kind of drug the most strong-willed people in the world would become addicted to. The kind I will become addicted to if I let this kiss go on, but I can't stop. I can't push him away when I don't want this moment to end.

His thumb slides across the line of my jaw before settling on my chin, tugging it down to part my lips. My body comes alive as his tongue slips inside my mouth, massaging it with his. Every cell inside of me explodes in euphoria like tiny fireworks until he puts them back together with a gentle stroke of his index finger over my neck. Shivers trail down my spine, need coiling into a knot in my stomach.

All because of one damn kiss.

I roll my hips to get back the friction my clit is aching for, but Aaron grabs them to stop me as he groans into my mouth.

"Fuck, Tate. You're gonna make me come before I've had a chance to taste your pretty pussy," he says, kissing along the length of my jaw before tilting it so he can work his way down my neck.

"So?" I manage to blurt out, but the sound turns into a moan as he licks along the length of my neck before sucking on a soft spot I didn't even know existed.

"You're not allowed to, not until I've had my face buried between your legs," he replies as he guides me onto my back and pins me down with his heavy, muscular body.

He kisses my lips again while I bury my hands in his raven-black hair, tugging on the strands every time his exploration of my mouth sends a bolt of electricity through me.

"Tate, I need your shirt and bottoms off," he says, but it's not a demand. It's a statement. He needs them gone as much as I need his pajama pants and boxers to be on the floor.

"Take them off," I say with a little smile. Aaron rewards my words with a kiss to one of my covered nipples, nipping at it until my back arches from pleasure. His mouth is so hot, I feel its heat through the fabric.

"And then, can I taste you? I've wanted to for weeks now, baby. It's been driving me wild," he says, working his way down my body until his face hovers over where he wants to be most, where *I* crave him to be.

"Yes, please. I got tested before I moved to the ranch. I'm all clear, so yes, please do," I beg, and the smirk he flashes me in response is so filthy, my heart rate skyrockets.

"Me too, baby, and I can't wait to slip my cock into your pretty mouth later."

He slides up my body again to wrap his lips around mine, and I welcome back the full weight of his body. My knees move to his hips, squeezing to keep him in place. His hard cock rocks against me in the most delicious way until I'm trembling under him, whimpering his name.

His right hand slips under my shirt, his fingers splayed across my left rib cage as his tongue licks my lips before pushing into my mouth again. Aaron rolls his hips, rubbing against me as his hand shifts higher and higher. My fingers slip into his hair, wrapping around his thick, black curls. I tug, trying to get him closer, trying to tell him to move his touch to my breast, but he's quite content taking his time exploring every single inch of me at his own pace.

"Aaron."

His name leaves my lips in a plea and demand. His mouth moves to my jaw and then my neck right as his big hand cups my breasts and squeezes, forcing a low moan from my lips.

"Don't rush me, Tate." His words are followed by another roll of his hips, grinding his cock against me. "This little tease of a pajama had me hard since you put it on," he says, biting down on the lacy part of the top and dragging it down until my right breast bounces free.

A groan vibrates off his chest and through me as he lowers his head to my pebbled nipple. He blows a single breath on it, watching the skin tighten even more before he sucks the nipple into his mouth and pulls.

"Oh my God," I moan, my back arching and shoving my tit further into his face. He gives an agreeing hum as his other hand frees my left breast, his fingers pinching the nipple as he continues sucking on the other one.

"You fit so well in my hands, Tatum, like I was made to explore your body," he says, trailing kisses along my cleavage to wrap his mouth around my other nipple

"Aaron, either you make me come, or I'll do it myself," I blurt out, too desperate for my release to give a fuck about him wanting to take his time.

He pushes himself to hover over me, a smile on his lips as he studies my determined features. No part of him is touching me anymore, so I slide my hand down my body, attempting to slip it into my panties to relieve the tension, but Aaron's fingers wrap around my wrist to stop me. He lifts my hand, pressing a soft kiss to my pulse point, then trails kisses down my upper body.

"Remove your shirt, Tate," he instructs right as he pulls my shorts down, leaving me only in my thong. His blue eyes zero in on my pussy as he licks his lips. "God, you're so fucking wet, sweetheart, you've drenched your panties," he says, placing his thumb on the wet spot before circling right above where my clit is.

"Fuuuuck." The moan slips free before I know what has hit me.

"Your shirt, Tatum. Take it off," he reminds me, and I practically rip it off. "Is my good girl as desperate for my mouth as I am to taste her pretty pussy?" His question sends another wave of arousal straight between my legs. I attempt to push my legs together, but his big, muscular body is in the way.

"Yes," I say through gritted teeth, staring down at him to see his attention has shifted to my panties again.

"Knowing you wear these little things has been keeping me up at night," he says as he runs his thumb over the fabric again.

"Did you fuck your hand to the thought of me in them?" I manage to ask, my curiosity stronger than the spell of pleasure he's put me under.

"Fuck yes, Tatum. Does that turn you on?" I nod with a smile before he circles my clit and a moan crawls out of my throat and past my lips. "Good girl," he mumbles before pushing my thong to the side. "Fuck, sweetheart."

His mouth moves to the inside of my thigh, nipping at the sensitive skin there. One of his arms wraps around my right thigh before the other does the same to my left one and the next thing I know, he's on his knees in front of the bed and I'm on the edge, perfectly in position for him to eat me out.

"Holy shit," I say as his mouth leaves wet kisses along the inside of my thigh, closer and closer to where I need him most. My entire body trembles with anticipation, pure desire coursing through my veins until it lights everything inside of me on fire. "Aaron," I complain, and then, *finally*, he presses his lips to my clit.

A combination of a sigh and moan leaves me as he drags his tongue along my pussy, stopping at my clit to use the tip of it to circle the swollen area. My fingers dig into the sheets as he repeats the same motion over and over until my back arches off the bed again, my hips rolling and grinding my pussy against his mouth to get more relief.

"You taste like my new favorite habit," he says, dragging his tongue lazily up my pussy.

"More, Aaron," I demand, and, a second later, he pushes a blunt finger inside of me, testing how tight I am. It's been a while since I've been with anyone, and I don't do more than clitoral stimulation to get myself off. So, I suck in a sharp breath at the sensation.

"God, you're so fucking tight," he says as he sucks my clit into his mouth. I feel myself relaxing from the pleasure. "There you go. You're doing so well, baby. You think you can take another finger?" I nod eagerly, my eyes glued to the view of him playing with my clit and shoving two fingers inside of me.

"Fuck," I moan, my hands slipping into his hair to guide his head to my clit.

The tip of his tongue flicks over it again and again, faster each time. His fingers match his switch in pace until I'm shaking. My orgasm tightens everything inside of me, ready to take over every nerve ending.

"So pretty and wet and swollen," he says, licking my clit again and thrusting his fingers inside just to curl them at the perfect spot again. "Just"—*lick*—"for"—*thrust*—"me."

My orgasm slams into me. An explosion of stars appears behind my eyelids like little fireworks going off inside my brain, carrying me so high, I wonder if I'll ever come down again. Aaron doesn't stop eating me out either, he keeps going, sending wave after wave of pleasure through me and dragging out my orgasm until I'm screaming so loud, I clasp a hand over my mouth to stop myself from waking every other guest here.

"Nuh uh, sweetheart, hand off that pretty mouth I wanna fuck later. I want to hear your screams," he says as he slows his movements.

Aaron presses soft kisses on the inside of my thigh as he waits for me to recover, but then his mouth is right back on my clit, his tongue fucking me straight into another orgasm I didn't think I could have this quickly after my first.

"Aaron. God. No more, cowboy," I manage to blurt out between deep breaths.

"What if I told you I've been fucking my hand this entire time while eating you out, Tate? What if I told you I've never tasted a pussy and wanted to spend the rest of my life licking it? What if I told you I can't wait to bury myself in your tight, little cunt, to feel your walls hug my cock? Will you give me another orgasm?" My sore clit gives another needy throb from his words, the ones he chose carefully, knowing exactly it would spike my desire again.

"I was right," I say, running my fingers through his soft hair again.

"About what, sweetheart?" he asks while placing more kisses on my inner thigh.

"Your mouth should be illegal," I say, shivering when he kisses my clit.

"Never claimed you were wrong," he replies and makes his way up my stomach, leaving a trail of nibbles, licks, and kisses on all of my sensitive areas.

"Cocky," I mumble, forcing a snort out of him.

"What am I going to do with you, Tate?" he asks, placing his hands on each side of my head and hovering over me, looking a hundred different types of sexy.

"Whatever you want, cowboy, as long as you finally take those pants and boxers off." His mouth drops to mine as soon as the words have left me, something territorial and possessive cursing through me as I taste myself on his lips.

"What do *you* want, Tate? Tell me, and I'll give it to you. I'll give you everything you ask for," he says between kisses, his heavy body slowly sinking on top of mine again.

"I want to—" I cut off, a moan replacing any words when his hand grabs my tit again, his index finger and thumb pinching my nipple just shy of painfully.

Fuck, that feels good.

"Use your words."

"Suck your cock," I finish my sentence through gritted teeth. He releases my nipple, bringing his gaze to mine. "I want to suck your cock."

"You're going to be the death of me."

A smile covers his entire face, and as much as I'd like to focus on that, I can't help but admire the thick outline of his cock in his pants.

I reach for it at the same time as my alarm goes off, telling me to get the fuck out of bed, grab some food, and take my damn pills. I think about silencing it, ignoring the reminder and doing exactly what I told Aaron I wanted to do, but his attention drifts to my phone, reading the name of the alarm before I can turn it off.

"Alright, sweetheart, up you go. We gotta get some food in you so you can take your meds," he says without a moment's hesitation, completely ignoring the way his hard cock is still straining against his bottoms.

"You're not mad?" I ask after my stupid alarm completely ruined the mood. Aaron looks at me with shock on his handsome face.

"Why would I be mad? This is important, Tate, and whatever we were going to do isn't going anywhere." I narrow my eyes in disbelief, but he merely presses a soft kiss to my lips. "I promise, I'm not upset. You come first for me, and if we get interrupted by something as important as you taking your meds, then so what?" he says as he cups my cheeks and tilts my head up to look at him. "I'm planning to spend the foreseeable future exploring you, fucking you, worshipping you, Tatum. I want to find every single way your body falls apart and claim them all for myself, but I'm not in a rush," Aaron adds with a smile. The one I'm beginning to distinguish from the other ones he offers people. The one where his entire face lights up with joy as if I make him truly, wholeheartedly happy. It's my one-dimpled smile, I've decided. Only mine.

"Dammit, cowboy. Why do you have to make me like you even more?" I ask because it complicates the situation far more if I start developing stronger feelings for him.

Unfortunately, I came to the conclusion yesterday that I don't want to run anymore. I don't want to close myself off and prevent myself from living. I don't want to be alone. I want to give this sunshine of a man the chance to steal my heart and keep it because I know, deep down, that's exactly what's going to happen if we go down this road.

"I want to treat you right, in the way no one ever has before. If that makes you like me more, it's an added bonus," he says with a mischievous grin before placing a kiss on my forehead and going back to packing his things.

"Loki, come here," I say.

As soon as I throw my legs over the edge of the bed, he comes running to greet me. He plants his head on my right thigh and starts wagging.

"I have to ask. Why 'Loki'?" Aaron says before squatting down. My dog runs to him in a heartbeat, whining happily as he throws himself at the cowboy's chest.

"He's my favorite anti-villain. Plus, I used to have a huge crush on him when Tom Hiddleston played him," I explain and Aaron cocks a curious brow at me.

"You mean you had a crush on the tall, black-haired, light-eyed character with an English accent?"

I open my mouth to respond, but all that comes out is a nervous laugh. They look nothing alike, even if they have similar features. Aaron is a lot more muscular, has fuller lips, and his hair is shorter. They're incomparable, but I do see his point.

"Well, I like the name. You should get another and name him Heimdall," he says as he scratches Loki's belly.

"I thought you were going to say Thor," I reply with a laugh.

"Nah, I like Heimdall more." Aaron's grin warms places inside of me I didn't even know could be unfrozen at this point in my life.

"My dad says I'm gonna get my own horse soon. Maybe I'll name it Heimdall," I say, my voice barely more than a whisper.

"Actually, I have a horse in mind for you." The way his eyes sparkle with a familiar fondness tells me exactly who he's referring to.

"Galaxy," I blurt out.

"Yes, I've been training her, but I've realized that I've been training her *for you*. I wanted to discuss it as soon as we got back."

"I thought she was going to be yours," I say and hold my breath, feeling more emotional than before.

"So did I, but I know you'll take good care of her, and she can be good for you." He stands up and makes his way over to me, running his thumb over my bottom lip once.

"Thank you," I croak out, fighting back the emotions threatening to overwhelm me. He's still tracing my mouth, studying it like he's never seen a prettier sight.

"Pack so we can get some food and continue what we've started," is the last thing he says before disappearing into the bathroom and leaving me to fall backward on the bed with a giggle.

He said I'd be the death of him, but he might just be the one to finally make me feel alive.

CHAPTER 26
Aaron

WE'RE AN HOUR INTO our six-hour drive of the day. Tate has eaten and taken her meds, and is sitting next to me, happily singing along to the new album Restless Road, her favorite country band, released. Her voice is so beautiful, I find myself resisting the urge to close my eyes to take away one of my senses to heighten the other.

To only listen to her.

The taste of her lingers in my memory, too. My dick is unbearably hard at the sound of her moans replaying in my head and the visuals that come with them. The way she arched her back and ground her beautiful pussy against my mouth. The way her breasts shifted with every move, her nipples wonderfully hard. The way she fell apart, so free and wild and fucking loud, I have to readjust in my seat to find a position that gives my cock more room in my pants.

Fields over fields of greenery pass by us and little to no cars are on the road. It's too early in the morning, and I can't imagine many people taking this road on a daily basis. Nothing to take my mind off how badly I want to kiss the woman beside me again, memorize the way she fits against me.

"I was thinking we could plant the wildflowers in front of the sunflower patch. Then, the lavender seeds can go to the left so we can make a path between them," Tate says as soon as the song she was singing comes to an end.

Work talk is good. Work talk is safe. Work talk might be what my body needs to calm the fuck down.

"That sounds great. We have to spread them out though, make sure the roots have enough space to grow. I think we might have placed the sunflowers too close together," I say, and she nods along to my words, reaching forward to adjust the temperature.

"Yeah, that's what I thought when you planted them, but I didn't want to say anything," she replies, her tone light and teasing. I tilt my head her way, watching a challenge glimmer in her eyes.

"Is that right?" I ask right before cursing when the lights start flashing at the train crossing we're approaching and the barriers drop.

Great, this could take a while.

"Hmmm, looks like we're stuck. In the middle of nowhere. Not a single car in sight. What to do, what to do," she says as she unbuckles her seatbelt and crawls halfway over the middle console.

Surprise has my heart skipping a beat as her lips attach to my neck, her teeth nipping at my sensitive skin.

"Sweetheart, what are you doing?" I ask with a smile. Tate leans back enough to trail her hand down my chest before hovering it over my hard bulge.

"You've been hard since this morning, cowboy, and I'd very much like to take care of that for you," she says, so I grab her hand and shove it firmly against my groin, giving her the permission she was waiting for.

"Right here? Where people could see you suck my cock?" I ask, and she smiles as she palms me through my pants. Pleasure shoots through me until I grit my teeth and hiss out a curse.

"Yes, right here," she says, her hand lifting to my belt buckle, working on it until it's out of the way. She slides my zipper down, and I almost sigh in relief when it no longer presses against my erection.

"Then suck me off, sweetheart. If you do a good job, I'll slip my fingers back inside your tight pussy and make you come, too," I say, hearing her let out a small whimper. Her bottom lip slips between her teeth as she works on getting my cock out of my boxers.

Tatum loves dirty talk. The filthier the words, the harder she trembles for me. I noticed it this morning, just like how hard she came for me when I took control. When I praised her. When she was mine to fuck however I wanted. I love the way she trusts me to make her feel good.

"If you don't touch me, Aaron, I'll touch myself because I love giving head." Fuck. Me. I grab her chin between my fingers and kiss her lips before lifting my hips to shove my pants down enough.

"I'll touch you until you're screaming around my cock and coming right alongside me," I promise, and she flashes me one last smile before her head drops a little as she slips my underwear down and my dick jumps free.

"Fucking hell," she mumbles as she stares at the size of it. Her head lifts once, revealing the way her throat works as she swallows nervously. "You're a lot bigger than what I'm used to. I don't think I can take you all the way," she admits, absentmindedly stroking her index finger along my length. It's a soft touch, barely there, but it has me shifting in my seat because it's Tate touching me. The woman I want more than I've ever wanted anyone else.

"You'll get used to me, sweetheart," I assure her, trailing a thumb across her jawline. She shivers visibly, her eyes closing. "Until then, take me as deep as you can." Tatum's hazel eyes reopen as she gives me an eager nod and drops her head once more.

Despite her worry that I won't fit all the way into her mouth, Tate wastes no time taking me as far down her throat as possible before her gag reflex sets in. The wetness and warmth of her mouth as it wraps around me has me groaning so loudly, she chuckles with the head of my cock still in her mouth, the sound vibrating through me and tightening my balls even more.

"Goddamn, Tate," I curse under my breath, wrapping her curly hair around my fist and tugging gently to get her off my cock for a moment. I need my orgasm to back the fuck off because she got me way too close with a single suck. "Take it slow, baby, or I'm going to come down your throat before I've even had a chance to fuck you with my fingers," I admit.

Her tongue darts out and licks my tip even though I'm holding her back a little. A shiver trembles through me.

"I don't care," she says, so I release my grip on her enough for her to swallow me down again.

My head falls against the headrest behind me as I do my best not to thrust up and deeper into her mouth. She feels too fucking good, and I want more, *need* more of her.

"You make me weak, Tate," I say before moaning as she lifts her head to swirl her tongue around the head of my cock.

"Can you take me a bit deeper, sweetheart? Just a little," I say, stroking my free hand along her jaw and then her lips where they rest around my cock. She releases me to respond, but I can't help placing a kiss on her mouth to taste myself there. Something possessive stirs in my chest, but I welcome it, welcome the warmth spreading through me at the thought of her tasting like *me* and no one else.

"Thrust up into my mouth, Aaron. Let me give you everything you need," she says before pressing another swift kiss to my lips and then lowering her head once more.

I do exactly as she wants. As constrained as it is to thrust upward in my seat, I manage it well enough. My hips roll upward, shoving my cock deeper into her mouth until her gag reflex sets in again and I lower myself. Tate's left hand is firmly pressed against my stomach now, holding herself up to give me space to thrust into her mouth.

It's heaven.

Her right hand drops down to my balls, cupping them and sending a wave of pleasure through me so strong, my muscles turn to putty for a second.

"Hand off my balls, Tate, please. I can't handle you touching them right now," I say, and she chuckles around me before giving them one last gentle squeeze and wrapping that same hand around the base of my cock.

My vision blurs as I continue thrusting into her, chasing my orgasm as it builds deep inside of me.

"Touch me," she says before pushing my hips down, clearly more confident taking me deeper by herself.

She licks from the base of my cock all the way to the top and circles the tip. Her hands glide along the part of my cock that doesn't fit inside of her mouth, jerking me off as she bops her head up and down. My muscles tighten, making me reach for the steering wheel so I have something to hold on to.

"Fuck, Tate, you're doing so well for me," I say as I use my hand closest to her and slide it over her beautiful, round ass. "Where do you want me to finish?" It's almost embarrassing how rough my voice is from pleasure, but I don't care.

It has never felt this good.

"In my mouth. Let me swallow you down," Tate replies, unraveling me entirely.

I grab onto her thong and wrap my fingers around it, pulling on the fabric so it rubs over her clit and makes her moan with my cock still deep inside her mouth. My fingers lower until I find her soaking wet entrance, groaning at how turned on she is from sucking me off.

Tate switches between licking and sucking while I work my finger inside of her tight pussy, loving the way her walls hug my fingers. It's impossible not to imagine her doing the same to my cock as I sink inside of her, into the warmth of her. While she's on top of me or under me or in front of me. Anywhere is fine as long as it's Tatum I get to lose myself in. As long as it's Tatum's pussy stretching to fit me.

My orgasm blindsides me, the fantasy I was playing out combined with her expert way of sucking my dick sending me straight over the edge. My fingers thrust inside of her frantically, stroking along the spot that makes her scream around my cock. She drinks me down while trembling through her orgasm, her nails digging into my stomach until I'm sure marks will appear. I flick my fingers inside of her, playing with her G-spot until she's sucking me harder again, causing a strange sensation of more pleasure and a little bit of pain to shoot through my system. It's a heady feeling, and I want to stop her as much as I want her to keep going.

"Oh God," she blurts out as she releases my cock.

My eyes briefly shift to where the train is passing, noticing that it's almost completely past us now. I attempt to catch my breath while she lifts her head to show me her pink, swollen lips and the smirk resting there. A cocky smirk she earned because that was the best fucking blow job I've ever gotten.

I guide my hand out of her pussy and place her thong back where it belongs before rubbing my hand over her beautiful ass. I might be obsessed with it, but not quite as obsessed as I am with the woman it belongs to.

Her eyes sparkle with happiness and satisfaction as she looks at me like I've made her happier than she's ever been. She looks at me like I built the world for her and crowned her queen, which she should be. Tatum should rule the world, and I'd worship her on my knees.

"You're so devastatingly beautiful," I say as I cup her jaw and bring my mouth to hers.

I want to plant her in my lap, cuddle her to my chest and kiss her for a bit longer, but the only aftercare I can give her for now, for the next thirty seconds before I'll have to keep driving, is through my words and this kiss.

"You really enjoyed that, didn't you?" I ask after she leans back to smile at me and trace her finger over the single dimple in my cheek. Then, she drops her hands back to my pants and pulls my boxers back into place, reaching for my zipper again.

"I told you I do, and I enjoyed the challenge you presented even more," she replies with a naughty grin. She buckles my belt before kissing my cheek. Tate shifts back into her seat, smoothing out the fabric of her summer dress. It's green, shows off her curves, and has me licking my lips while more highly inappropriate thoughts swirl around in my head.

"You really will be the death of me," I say, shifting the car into Drive before placing my hand on Tate's thigh and squeezing it. Her fingers immediately cover mine as she presses her legs together.

Tate puts on some music as she smiles from ear to ear, the blush of her post-orgasm still lingering on her cheeks and cleavage.

I'm surprised to find her watching me.

"What?" I ask as I drive over the railway tracks.

There are still no cars in front or behind us, which is a relief because the possessive part inside of me wants no one else to see Tate come, especially not while she sucks my cock. That's for me, no one else.

"Are you going to be my secret boyfriend now?" she says with a small chuckle.

"Sweetheart, I'll be whatever you tell me to be," I reply, squeezing her thigh once and making her press her legs together again.

"My dirty, little secret," Tate adds, and I burst into laughter.

"I think I prefer 'boyfriend.'" She considers that for a moment, rolling her neck and then scrunching her nose a little.

"I've never had a boyfriend, girlfriend, or significant other, so I'm going to have to get used to that term," she admits with a shrug.

"If you don't like it, you don't have to use it," I assure her with a laugh. I think it's cute how unsure she is about something I've never considered a big deal. Now, "boyfriend" seems like a stepping stone to something a lot bigger.

Something a lot better.

"I want to." Tate thinks for a second, then adds, "I want you."

"I want you, too," I reply without hesitation. "In whatever way I can have you."

CHAPTER 27
Tatum

SOMEHOW, AARON AND I make it all the way to our destination without getting distracted again. .

Beckett, Olivia, and Hads stayed true to their promise of making a group chat and have been texting me all morning, asking for updates.

Olivia: Have you seen him naked yet?

Hads: Apart from the time at the creek of course ;)

Olivia: Obviously. Still can't believe you kept that from us for a month!

Beckett: They've hooked up by now

Hads: How do you know?

Beckett: Aaron has definitely made a move

Olivia: For sure, I mean, he's been making some at home for weeks now

Hads: Yes OMG did you see the two of them after the wood chopping contest? Aaron was so gonna kiss her

Beckett: I'm gonna text Aaron to see if he'll gimme an update

Me: Leave Aaron alone, he's driving

Hads: So you are getting these messages!

Me: I regret giving you all my number

Olivia: Don't be like that, pretty lady. We just want to know if his dick is as big as we think it is

Me: Oh my God. I'm blocking you all

Beckett: It's definitely big.

The sacks of seeds are so heavy, Aaron lets me carry one before he asks me to wait in the car so I don't hurt myself. I give him an unimpressed look and pick up a second one. Aaron practically runs the bags to the car to make sure I don't carry too many, causing a laugh to bubble out of me as I watch him.

"You're so protective," I say right after we place the last two sacks in the trunk bed.

He pulls me against his chest and covers my mouth with his. The way he can't help but touch me, wanting us as close as possible, is intoxicating. I'm as drawn to him as he is to me, welcoming the way his mouth glides over mine in a frenzy to taste me, to memorize me.

"And you're stubborn. Are we going to keep listing things we like about each other or get to the hotel so I can finally remove this dress and replace it with my hands?"

He nibbles on my earlobe, then trails kisses down my neck before nuzzling his face in the crook of it. He's so tall, he has to bend his knees a little to wrap his arms under mine. I lift my hands to his nape, sliding them into his hair to twist my fingers around his curls.

"You're going to have to find a way to stop touching me, cowboy. As soon as we get back, we can't be like this," I say, guiding his head closer anyway.

"The only way you'll get me to stop is by telling me you don't want me to touch you."

"I don't want you to touch me," I say to test it, and when he attempts to pull away, I drag him straight back against me. "I *need* you to touch me," I add, and he lowers his hands to my thighs.

He lifts me into the air briefly to place me on the tailgate, moving between my legs before placing his hand on my throat and pulling me close to kiss me.

"We should get to the hotel before you do whatever it is you want to do right now," I remind him.

"No need, I'll do it right here," he says before covering me with his big body, pushing me backward into the bags of seeds.

Laughter bubbles out of me. He joins in until we're both breathless. Aaron pushes himself up and grabs my hand to tug me with him, the ringing of his phone the only thing stopping him from saying whatever it is that made his lips part.

He stares down at the caller ID before panic fills his eyes.

"Give me one sec," he says before pressing a kiss to my temple and hitting Answer, taking a few steps away from me to get privacy. "Fuck," Aaron curses a moment later, his hand flying to his hair where he grabs a handful and tugs. "When did this happen?" he asks, and I notice his hand trembling now as he covers his mouth.

I jump off the tailgate and make my way over to him, placing a comforting hand on his arm and squeezing gently. He grabs hold of my fingers, his gaze far away as he listens to whatever the person on the other end of the line is telling him. The muscles in his jaw flex as he fights back the wave of emotion I see flashing through his eyes. Concern creeps into my chest until I'm holding my breath.

"I'll be there as soon as I can," is the last thing he says before he hangs up and shoves his phone into his pocket. He squats down, his face dropping into his hands as I lower myself to be on the same level as him.

"Aaron?" I ask, wrapping my fingers around his wrists. "I'm here. For whatever you need."

My sunshine man lifts his hands off his face to show me the tears in his eyes. He blinks until he's got them under control as he studies me.

"My nanna had an accident. She fell and hit her head so hard, she has a concussion. They're checking her for internal bleeding now," he explains, causing my heart to sink to the bottom of my stomach.

"Okay," I reply, thinking about what to do. "I'll take the first half of the drive, you'll take the second. Try to rest so that we can switch in about six hours," I say, standing up to walk back over to his truck. I lift the tailgate, closing it and making sure the bags of seeds are secured before arms wrap around me from behind.

"I'm scared, Tate," he admits, his forehead falling against my shoulder.

"I know." I still remember the way it felt to hear about my grandpa falling and hurting himself. I remember the way my heart stopped beating for a breath whenever my grandma called us. "I've got you, okay? We're going to get there as soon as we can, even if it means driving all night, I don't care. You'll be there for your grandma when she wakes up," I promise, spinning around in his arms to show him my serious look.

"Okay," he says. "Thank you."

I place a brief kiss on his lips before making my way over to the driver's side and jumping in. Loki gives me an unsure look. I scratch behind his ears once before turning the key in the ignition and letting the engine roar to life. Aaron buckles his seatbelt before pressing on his screen with one hand, probably texting Flynn or Hads to send them to the hospital.

I focus on the road, desperate to get us back home and Aaron to his grandma.

Aaron has been sleeping for the past three hours after spending the first five bouncing his leg up and down from worry. He stared out the window until he fell asleep on his hand, looking as vulnerable as he probably feels with the lingering pain in his chest. The same pain I always worried my family felt whenever I had to go to the hospital.

Part of me is screaming to get away from him, spare him more worry and heartbreak. It's what I did with everyone else in life until I was so alone, I lost all sense of what having friends and family felt like.

Until I moved to Silver Creek Ranch and everyone showed me how much I was missing.

However, the part of me I got so used to, the one drenched in loneliness, that's the one telling me to distance myself. It's the part of me saying Aaron deserves better than a girlfriend he'll always have to worry about on top of everything else that's going on with his grandma and the ranch.

I swallow the lump of emotion in my throat to keep from crying.

"Tate?" His voice fills my ears, all sleepy and hoarse. His head is already turned my way, and I realize he must have been looking at me for a while. "I need to tell you something," he says while I swallow again, hoping it'll get rid of my tears.

"Tell me," I manage to say, my voice sounding strange.

"I have to pee," he replies, catching me so off-guard, I burst out laughing.

"There's a gas station in two miles," I promise him, and he nods, a hint of a smile resting on his lips.

"There's something else I need to tell you," he says after a few more moments of silence where he simply studies my face.

"If you gotta do anything other than peeing, you don't have to tell me," I warn, making it his turn to laugh.

"No, nothing of the sort." He reaches out to pull my hair out of my face and tug it behind my ear. "I wasn't ready to go back. I don't want to have to pretend you're not mine and I'm not yours. I want the rest of the world to know." He caresses my cheek as he says the most beautiful words anyone's ever said to me. Possessive, yes, but also beautiful.

"We haven't even been on a date," I remind him, and he trails his thumb across my jawline.

"We have been. The first week you were at Silver Creek Ranch, we had dinner. The second week, I showed you how to ride a horse. We've been having lunch together almost every day. Yesterday, we went line dancing. I would argue that at least one of those instances qualifies as a date," he says, but I cock an eyebrow and tilt my head just enough to show him my expression.

"Yesterday, you said to me, 'I'd really like to take you on a proper date,'" I remind him, and he nods in agreement.

"Exactly. A proper date. That means we've had others," he says, making me shake my head with a smile.

"You're sneaky, cowboy, I'll give you that," I say and shift into the right lane to take the next exit.

Aaron's hand drops to my neck where he runs his index finger down the length of it, waiting for me to park at the gas station pump to fill his tank and for him to use the washroom.

"You know what you are?" he asks, his fingers holding my chin to keep my face turned toward his.

"What am I?" I ask, his blue eyes a darker shade in the dim lighting of the gas station. He rolls his lips for a moment, which brings out his dimple.

"You are a dream." His voice drops an octave as he adds, "My dream."

"Nightmares are dreams, too," I say, but the tears that drop down my cheeks reveal how his words make me feel. Aaron tugs on my chin before slowly moving my head from side to side.

"You know that's not what I meant," he says, releasing me and opening his car door.

He's halfway out of the truck before he turns back to me with a thoughtful look on his face.

"Don't run again, okay? I saw what you were thinking, but you're wrong. You convince yourself caring for you wouldn't be worth it, but you're worth every single feeling you evoke in me." My heart flutters at his words, at the emotion in his voice. Aaron pats his door once before adding, "Plus, worrying is what I do. I'm always concerned Beckett and Flynn will fuck around and get themselves either killed or murdered."

A laugh bubbles out of me while I do my best not to sob. Aaron smiles as he shuts his door and makes his way toward the bathroom. I watch him walk away, stare at his glorious ass move in those jeans I love, and wonder how the hell he saw right through me. Then, I feel like crying all over again because I don't *want* to run away. Quite the opposite. I want him to hold me, hug me, kiss me, and touch me until we're both sick of it. I want to belong to him and him to belong to me.

Most of all, I want to allow myself to fall in love with him, and I want to let him fall in love with me.

CHAPTER 28
Aaron

THERE IS A DESPERATION inside of me to take Tatum's hand, to reach for it and lace my fingers through hers to get the warmth and comfort only she can provide for me right now. Not knowing if Nanna is going to be okay has my heart hammering in my chest from fear so raw and powerful, it has taken over my entire body.

She has to be alright.

Tate and I storm through the sliding doors of the hospital, rushing toward where Flynn is sitting. His head is on his hand as he dozes in one of the uncomfortable chairs here. I've been to this hospital often enough since Nanna was diagnosed to be familiar with the backache-inducing seats.

Guilt shoots through me at the thought of Flynn having spent the entire day here, waiting just like I always did, like I will do until I no longer get to. Until what I fear most comes true and I leave this limbo. The limbo where I'm grieving my grandmother but at the same time can't comprehend she's gone because she's still here. The limbo where I can tell myself she'll still recognize me the next time I visit her. The limbo where I've built a house, and I'd rather stay there instead of losing her forever.

"How is she? " I ask as I shake my best mate awake, making him shoot up and out of the seat. He's disorientated for a moment, then his face relaxes from fear to relief.

"Nah, they didn't tell me anythin'. I've been waiting for about three hours, but they wouldn't let me know what's happenin'. I think it's because I'm not her biological relative or some shit like that," Flynn says, rubbing his eyes to get rid of the sleep in them. I place a hand on his shoulder and squeeze gently.

"Thank you for trying and being here. You can go home now, if you'd like," I say, but he straightens out his back and frowns at me.

"Are you jokin', Aaron? I ain't leaving until they tell me if *abuela* Lorena is alright."

Because she's like a grandmother to him, too. Because Nanna picked him up from school and took him to our house so we could hang out every time his parents were busy with work. Because he still visits her at the nursing home every week even though she doesn't know who he is anymore.

Because he loves her.

"Okay, let me go check in with the nurses and see if they have an update," I say, watching Flynn turn to Tate before pulling her against his chest and placing his cheek on the crown of her head.

She wastes no time wrapping her arms around his torso. Her eyes are on mine as my best friend relishes in the comfort she provides. She mouths "I've got him" to let me know Flynn is going to be fine with her. I want that comfort, too. I want to kiss her and hug her because I'm terrified out of my mind. But I can't. Not right now.

Later, when we're all alone, I'll take whatever she gives me.

My feet bring me to where a nurse is sitting behind a desk, scrolling through information on her laptop.

"Hi, my name is Aaron Blaze. My grandmother, Lorena Blaze, was admitted to this hospital after sustaining a head injury. Is there an update you can give me on her current state?" I ask, my voice quivering from emotions.

I would love to be strong and steady right now, but I can't bring myself to be the Aaron everyone has started depending on. The Aaron that always had everything together. The Aaron who fixes messes instead of becoming one.

At this moment, I'd give anything to be able to be him. Maybe then I could stop from feeling the same creeping sensation of a panic attack I always experience when my knee acts up, but it's there, lingering in my chest. It's threatening to take over and force me to crumble into a ball in the corner of this hospital waiting room.

Suddenly, the lights are too bright, voices are too loud. My head is pounding, screaming in protest. Everything inside of me is shutting down until I'm breathing so hard, the nurse in front of me cocks a concerned brow. My vision blurs and I take a step back, trying to find the strength to fight off the attack.

That's when I feel it.

A hand slipping over my back, soothing the building tension there. I melt into her touch, taking a deep breath and letting it out through gritted teeth. My body shudders, but Tate's hand runs up and down my spine, reassuring me and comforting me with the motion.

"You're alright, Aaron. Feel the ground under your soles. Focus on the breath in your lungs. Acknowledge that I'm here, my hand pressing against your back. Come back into the moment," she coos, and I find myself obeying, doing what she tells me to do.

I take another deep breath until everything inside of me settles. A strange type of calm swoops through me while I place my hand on Tate's neck, giving her a thankful smile.

"Mr. Blaze? Your grandmother is going to be alright. She got a few stitches on her forehead and a concussion, but there is no other injury in her report." A breath of relief *whooshes* out of me.

"Can we go see her?" I ask, and the nurse lets us know her room number before we turn to walk back to where Flynn is standing.

"Aaron, I should go home. This is family business, and I'm not the biggest fan of making Loki wait in the car for longer than he already has been," she says and steps in front of me to prevent me from walking.

Her hazel eyes lift to my face, making every part inside of me yearn to touch her. I want to beg her to stay, but she's right. Loki shouldn't be waiting in the car, and I don't want to overwhelm Nanna with another stranger.

"Take my truck. I'll catch a ride with Flynn later," I say and place my keys in her hand, lingering there for longer than necessary. My gaze meets hers, drowning out everyone else here.

"You can't look at me like that in public," she mumbles before putting distance between us. "I'll leave your truck at your house, but you'll have to come get the keys from me later." Something like longing plays in her eyes, drawing me in.

"Go get some rest and then meet me at the creek at five in the morning," I say, and she gives me a small nod before turning on her heel and giving Flynn a pat on his chest. He smiles down at her then turns the amused expression on me.

I attempt to walk away before he can get to me, but he clasps a hand around my bicep to stop me.

"You've looked at her like she's the most beautiful woman in the world since you first laid eyes on her, but something's changed. There is more intimacy, like you've been allowed to explore her in a way not many people have," he points out, and I feel like punching him in the arm to get away from this conversation.

"I have no idea what you're talking about. I like her. It's not a secret." Certainly not one I've been trying very hard to keep.

"I know you do, but somethin' happened between the two of you on that trip. If you're not tellin' anyone, you got to shut down your expressions around her better. If you don't, everyone at Silver Creek Ranch will know you had your mouth on her within an hour." This time, I slap the back of his head, earning an elbow to the ribs. "I'm tryin' to keep Briggs from murdering you, *cabrón*," he says, then starts cursing in Spanish.

"No one can know," I say in a low voice, and Flynn slings an arm around my shoulders with a laugh.

"I've kept worse secrets than you datin' the boss' daughter, man. Remember the time you stole Owen's dad's truck and crashed it into the creek?" he asks, making me flinch at the reminder.

Owen's dad was the Chief of Police of Orchard Hill for the better part of fifty years before he retired five years ago. Owen got promoted to chief the same year.

"To this day, no one knows it was you," Flynn reminds me.

"Fair enough." I wasn't worried he'd tell anyone. I trust him with my life, and this secret isn't an exception.

"I can't believe Tate really decided to give you a shot," Flynn teases as we make our way to Nanna's room.

"I hate you."

"Yeah, I know. Hate is often born out of jealousy," he says with a wiggle of his brows.

"And what do I have to be jealous of? I have fewer wrinkles than you and the most gorgeous girlfriend," I say, and he lets out a hurt gasp.

"How dare you throw my age and singleness into my face? Those are my two biggest insecurities," he says as he places a hand to his chest to imitate being hurt.

"I thought your personality was one," I tease and he shoves me forward, ripping a laugh out of me.

The sound dissipates as soon as my eyes land on my grandmother.

There are stitches on her forehead. Blue, red, and purple surrounds the swollen wound, and I feel like my heart drops out of my body at the sight of her.

"I should have been here," I say, guilt piercing through me until my knees threaten to give out.

"And what difference would it have made?" Flynn asks, standing in front of me and placing his hands on his hips. Not seeing Nanna hooked to machines and an IV temporarily allows me to breathe.

"I would have been there for her," I argue, making Flynn's eyes turn sympathetic. He slides a hand onto my shoulder and squeezes.

"She probably wouldn't have recognized you, man. Don't feel guilty. You're here now, which might be better considering you won't scare her more than she must have been with a head wound like that."

I appreciate my best friend's words, but the stabbing sensation in my chest doesn't subside, if anything, it only gets stronger when I step around Flynn again to stride over to the chair next to Nanna's bed.

"She shouldn't have been alone, Rafael," I say, and Flynn raises both his eyebrows at my use of his real name instead of the nickname everyone, even his own mother, has adopted.

"She wasn't alone. I was here, and they didn't even let me see her," he reminds me, and I nod along to his words, dropping into the chair beside the bed.

I want to reach out to touch her hand, wrap my fingers around it, but if she wakes and doesn't recognize me, she'd only be scared a stranger is touching her. It's a horrible feeling, as if the person I loved most my whole life suddenly became a stranger that never knew me in the first place. But my memories aren't dissipating into nothingness. There is no black hole where they're all getting pulled into, not how there is for her.

"How am I meant to move out of this grief when she's still here? How am I meant to go from denial to acceptance? How can I accept what's going to happen sooner than any of us thought it would?" I ask my best friend as he steps closer to Nanna, standing on the opposite side of where I'm sitting. Tears linger in his eyes as he takes in her appearance.

"I don't know," he admits.

Neither one of us has an answer because this is bigger than us. This is about finding a way to accept your grief as a permanent part of yourself instead of something to overcome.

It hurts. Fuck, it hurts worse than anything else I've ever experienced, but that's what I need to come to terms with. The stages of grief aren't as straight-forward as people claim. Especially not when it comes to the family members of people who suffer from Alzheimer's. It's a cycle of stages that repeats itself over and over.

"But you don't have to bear the burden of your grief alone. I'm always here when you need someone to lean on," Flynn promises, and I manage to force a small smile.

"I appreciate that." Tatum's face reappears in my head, and a realer smile slips onto my lips.

"Thinkin' about Tate?" Flynn asks, and I shoot him a mischievous look I didn't even know I was capable of while my chest felt this constricted.

The thought of her lets me breathe easier.

"Yeah, I'm always thinking about her now. She's like an addiction to sugar. I'm always wondering when I'll get my next rush," I admit, the corner of my mouth tugging upward into a small smirk.

"You're so wrapped around her finger, man, it's disgusting," Flynn teases, and I flip him off at the same time my grandmother's eyes flutter open.

She looks disorientated, blinking rapidly to focus her vision. Her gaze shifts to Flynn first, confusion turning her lips downward as she regards him. Panic floods through me at the thought that she might not recognize me either.

"Who are you?" she asks, her voice gravelly and husky. Flynn puts on his best smile, pretending like it doesn't bother him that she doesn't remember him.

"I'm here for entertainment," he says, making her blink rapidly as she tries to process that information.

Then, she turns her attention to me, and I feel like sobbing like a baby when she furrows her brows at me and winces because of her wound.

I want to reach out and touch her, comfort her because that's always how I expressed my feelings, but her next words stop me.

"And who are you?"

CHAPTER 29
Tatum

DAD HAS BEEN SILENT all through dinner. Something is weighing heavy on his mind, but I know better than to start a conversation about his feelings before he's ready to share them. He'll simply pretend he's alright, that nothing's bothering him. Unfortunately for him, I know him better than that.

The creases in his forehead speak louder than any words ever could.

He was excited to see me when I first got home, hugged me until I couldn't breathe anymore. It surprised me a little considering our last conversation, but he didn't seem to even remember it. I'm not exactly happy with the ultimatum he gave Aaron, but until my cowboy and I have figured out if we work together for longer than one steamy road trip, I won't bring it up. If we make it all the way to Halloween in a few months, I'll broach the topic with Dad, hoping he'll ignore that I broke my promise and focus on my feelings. Because, as scared as I am, I've never felt so alive in my entire life. Aaron with his thoughtfulness and filthy—yet incredibly skilled—mouth makes me happy.

Shaking my head to refocus on the present, I turn to Dad with a small smile.

"How was your day?" I ask after placing my spoon back inside the bowl.

"Fine. Luna is doin' well, by the way. She's eatin' and runnin' with Betty and Angel. She seems very happy," Dad says, and I nod along to his words, grinning because I can't wait to see my baby tomorrow. Maybe I'll even go check on her after dinner.

"How about Galaxy?" I ask. Dad's features reveal surprise at my question.

"She's doin' alright, why?" I shrug, picking up my spoon again to give myself something to do with my fingers.

"Aaron has been working with her for a long time, so I wanted to make sure she didn't lose her progress because he wasn't here." I don't tell him that Aaron mentioned she'll be my horse soon.

"Yeah, she's fine, but I think she'll be very happy once Aaron is back with her tomorrow," he explains, and I try my best not to let heat rush into my cheeks.

"Anything else happen today?" He takes our bowls before disappearing into the kitchen, returning a moment later with dessert.

"The bank called today," he says right after placing the pudding he made on the table. Understanding washes through me.

"They don't want to give us more time to come up with the money?" I ask, my hands starting to shake from fear.

"Quite the opposite. They loved the business plan you came up with and were more than happy to give us more time to pay the mortgage," he replies, confusing me.

"So, what's with the foul mood, old man?" I tease, and Dad takes back the plate of dessert he just gave me.

"No dessert for daughters who call me old." He shoves a spoonful of the pudding he plated for me into his mouth, and I let out an annoyed gasp.

"Hey, that's not fair. Everyone around here calls you *Old Man Briggs*. Why am I the exception?" I ask, making him chuckle as he slides his full plate toward me. He grins around a mouthful of pudding, and I welcome back his playfulness. It leaves a moment later as he prepares to tell me what's truly weighing heavy on him.

"Remi and your mother are coming to visit to check on you." My spoon drops into my plate.

"To *check* on me?" I blurt out. "Tell them they can stay wherever they are" —I mean my mother, not my sister—"and leave me alone. I'm happy. I don't need them"—Mom—"fucking with what I'm building here."

"Honeybee, they're coming whether we like it or not. Remi is always welcome, and if the spawn of Satan has time off from torturing innocent souls, then let her come, too. I'd never close my home to my family," Dad says, and I can't help but burst into laughter at the comparison he made to Mom.

"Fuck. When?" I ask after pulling myself together.

"They don't know yet, but they said soon."

Kill me now.

Loki jumps excitedly beside me as we make our way toward the creek. The summer weather has the temperature pleasantly warm even this early in the morning, and I inhale deeply to let the scent of freshly mowed grass fill my nose.

My heart is racing at the thought of finally seeing Aaron again.

The keys of his truck are in my hands. I ate something and took my meds before leaving the house to ensure we won't be interrupted again. Especially considering he wanted to meet at the creek and I have a feeling it wasn't so we'd be having a conversation with our clothes on. As a matter of fact, I didn't even wear anything underneath my shorts and t-shirt.

My dog runs toward the water as soon as I give him the go-ahead, and, a second later, my eyes catch Aaron's beautiful face and muscular shoulders as he floats in the water, throwing a toy for Ash. I can tell by his smile how happy he is to be at home with his son again. Then, he turns that bright, sunshine look on me, and I feel like everything in my life, every dark corner, gets lit up.

"Hey, cowboy," I say as I remove my shoes.

"Hey, sweetheart," he replies, moving closer until half of his body is out of the water.

The V-line created from either side of his hips dips low until it disappears in the water, but enough of him is outside of it to tell me he's naked again. Just like he was the first time I caught him here. My mouth waters at the glorious sight of his chest and abs, my fingers itching to run down his torso.

"Clothes off, Tate. Make this fair," he says, and I realize he wants to ogle me the same way I'm ogling him.

My fingers wrap around the fabric of my t-shirt before I lift it over my head and discard it. Aaron's eyes flare with lust and desire as I shove my shorts down, leaving me completely naked.

"No bikini?" he challenges with a smile, and I grin as I gather every little bit of confidence and stroll over to where he is in the water.

It's a little chilly, but it does nothing to cool my skin from the heat of his gaze. I want him, I *burn* for him, for the first time in my life understanding what it means to burn for someone. Like every inch of your body is consumed by liquid desire that curls around your limbs and insides until you feel like you're on fire. The flames aren't meant to hurt but heat you until you feel nothing but them.

"It would have just gotten in the way," I reply, watching his breathing speed up. His eyes never leave me, not even once as I stalk toward him, closing the distance with each second that ticks by.

"In the way of what?" he asks, placing his hands on my hips as soon as I'm close enough. He pulls me against his chest, his hard body rubbing against me as he drops his mouth to mine, hovering above it to give me a chance to answer.

"Of feeling your skin against mine everywhere," I reply before wrapping my arms around his neck and kissing him.

We stay in the water for a while, nothing but the sound of birds chirping and the wind howling filling the silence. I enjoy the way he holds me, the way our naked skin is pressed together, more than I should.

"How's your grandmother?" I ask, pressing my nose to his when sadness flits through his eyes.

"She's going to be alright. It'll take some time, but she'll heal," he assures me, his left hand running up and down my spine in lazy, soothing strokes. "She didn't remember me. She was in pain and confused, and I couldn't comfort her because she had no idea who I was." His words send a stinging sensation through my chest.

"Do you think she needed the comfort or you did?" Aaron tilts his head back so his gaze can meet mine. He looks thoughtful as he considers my words, his eyes dropping to my lips before he brings them back up to my eyes.

"I guess I did, at least a lot more than she did," he replies, so I cup his cheeks and plant my lips on his.

"I know it's not the same, but you can always get comfort from me," I say, and he gives me one of his pure sunshine smiles.

"You like me," he points out, and I roll my eyes.

"You already knew that," I reply while he plants his mouth on the corner of mine and kisses a line toward my jaw.

"You haven't told me yet." He nips at the sensitive skin on my neck.

"I like you, cowboy." The words are past my lips before I have a chance to stop them.

"I like you, sweetheart, with every fiber of my being."

His mouth moves over mine as he kisses me, letting me taste his feelings. And they taste amazing. They taste like I finally belong to a person who will treat me right, who will be there for me even though I tried to run away because of how scared I am.

"Will you tell me a happy memory you have with your grandmother?" I ask, hoping to replace some of his sadness with a good memory, something he can cling to.

Aaron considers my question for a minute as we float in the water.

"We went to a planetarium when I was seven. We looked through a telescope and were told about all of the planets. At the time, Pluto was still considered a planet, instead of a dwarf planet like nowadays. I was fascinated by it, couldn't stop talking about it, so my nanna eventually started saying, 'I love you to Pluto and back' and it stuck. We still say it to this day, at least when she remembers me," he explains, and I lose myself in the memory he shared, smiling as I imagine his grandmother and how much she loved him.

"Can I meet her?" I know I overstepped, I must have. This is a sensitive and delicate situation, and I shouldn't be blurting out a question like this as if it's so simple.

"I'd love that. She might not remember me when we go, but she's still the same Lorena she's always been, just without her memories," he explains, rubbing his nose over mine.

"Then I can't wait to meet her."

Aaron kisses me once more before diving into the water, releasing me for the first time since he dragged us into a deeper part of the creek. I move my arms to stay afloat, waiting for him to resurface. When he does, he's right behind me, wrapping his arms around my torso to lift me a little out of the water. I spin around in his arms as soon as he puts me down, loving the way he doesn't release me either.

"There is something we should talk about that's going to complicate our whole sneaking around thing," I find myself saying after another moment of silence passes between us.

"Going to complicate? Tate, I hate to break it to you, but it's already complicated," he teases, and I squeeze his torso between my legs in response.

He chuckles but lifts me out of the water enough to place his mouth on the top of my left breast, trailing kisses up the length of it until he reaches my neck. His warmth contrasts the breeze, sending goosebumps across my skin.

Well, it's either the breeze or the sexy as hell cowboy holding me against him.

"Aaron, please, we need to focus," I say.

"You can talk, baby. I'm the one with my lips on this beautiful neck of yours," he says as he moves over to the other side and gently bites down on my soft spot.

"Aaron," I warn.

"I'm obsessed with your body, Tate. It's a dream," he says and cups my ass to guide me further against his chest. The compliment only has my legs clenching against him harder.

"Aaron, I can't concentrate like this," I admit, a small laugh escaping me.

"I don't know when I'm going to be able to touch you again. I want to use every second we have right now to the fullest," he says.

"But I need to tell you something, and I don't want to talk about them while you're kissing me," I reply. He stops abruptly, cupping my jaw to force my gaze to him.

"Tell me," he says, sensing how serious my tone has gotten.

"My sister and mother are coming to visit. They don't know when, but it could be soon." Aaron furrows his brow, clearly not seeing the problem. "We won't be able to be alone until they're gone again. My sister loves spending every spare second with me when we're together, and my mother, while impassive when I'm not around, is incredibly nosy as soon as I'm near her."

Aaron considers my words for a moment as the fingers on my face stroke the skin there absentmindedly.

"Maybe by then we'll be ready to tell everyone about us," he says with a grin.

"Or we'll be tired of each other," I reply with a laugh that has him frowning at me.

"I don't see how I'd ever tire of you." He kisses my lips so gently, I melt against him.

Chapter 30

Aaron

Beckett slaps my arm and lets out a surprised laugh.

"I can't believe you did it!" he says, and I punch him in the shoulder. He lets out a grunt before raising his hand to the spot I hurt and frowning at me. "Remember who you're punching, little boy. I've got height and muscle weight on you," Beckett says, proving his point by taking a step toward me and tilting his head down.

"I'm more agile," I reply with a cocky smirk, but he merely shoves my shoulder, making me stumble. "Careful!" I bark, barely keeping from stomping on what has me so excited.

A little sprout from a sunflower shot out of the ground, pointing at the sky. It's green for now, but I'm so excited to see the first hints of Tate's vision coming true.

"Tate will want to see this," I say, glancing over my shoulder to see Beckett narrowing his eyes with amusement playing on his face.

Tate and I have been doing our best to keep our relationship quiet since we got back, which has been surprisingly easy considering Old Man Briggs has been keeping her so busy, she's too exhausted by the time night comes around to meet me. It's as understandable as it is frustrating. I want to ask Briggs to give her a day off because as much as I enjoy our stolen kisses when we're alone, I miss her body wrapped around mine. I miss the laugh she shares only with me. I miss the way her eyes sparkle with adoration at the sight of me. She is much better at locking down her feelings than I am. It's a good thing that I've always looked at her like she hung the moon, the stars, the goddamn sun, otherwise, people would be even more suspicious than they already are.

"You keep saying nothin' happened, but you must have at least kissed her," Beckett says, crossing his massive arms in front of his massive chest, and I roll my eyes.

"Don't you think I'd be telling the whole world if Tatum and I were dating? Don't you think I'd want to tell every other person to back the fuck off because she's *mine*?" God, I fucking want to.

Beckett still doesn't look convinced, but he doesn't push it either.

"Bailey wants to go horse ridin', but Briggs asked me to drive to Red Sky Ranch to check on our half of the shipment of supplies," he starts, shifting his weight from one foot to the other. "You mind takin' her later when she gets back from her friend's house?"

"Not at all. Unlike you, your daughter is actually nice to be around," I tease, and he flips me off, thanking me in the same breath.

Our conversation is interrupted by Owen Grim's Dodge pulling into the main house's driveway. He flashes his lights briefly to get our attention, and I notice him waving me over as soon as he's out of the car. I walk toward Firefly, placing my foot in the stirrup and swinging my other leg across his back. I adjust in the saddle and then guide him into a canter, rushing toward the chief of police.

My old friend's brown hair is all over the place, his brown eyes sparkling with concern and pity. He's dressed in his uniform bottoms and a white dress shirt, his gun strapped in the leather holster he wears around his back. He looks like he's ready to fight crime every single time I see him. The guy is about an inch shorter than me, but he's got muscles from going to the gym almost every single day. His facial hair is questionable, but I've never been the biggest fan of mustaches.

"Hey, chief. Still sporting that God-awful mustache I see," I say, trying to keep my tone light. Owen scowls as soon as the words have left me, but I'm grinning at him.

"It ain't that bad, asshole," he insists.

"Yeah, it is. Looks like you've glued my Pop's nose hair on your upper lip," Beckett chimes in with a laugh, and I can't help but join him as Owen scrunches his nose in disgust.

"You're revoltin', Beck," Owen says, then shakes his head. "Fuck it, I'm shavin' it." He runs two fingers over his mustache thoughtfully.

"How can we help you, chief, apart from helping you make better life decisions?" I ask with a teasing smile, and he straightens out his back, remembering that he came here to discuss something.

"The department's closin' the investigation. They said we can't waste any more resources to try and figure out who started the fire that burned y'all's crops," he says, causing my shoulders to sag in disappointment.

"But we don't know who did it yet. How can we keep them from attacking the ranch again if no one's trying to find them? Plus, what about compensation for everything Briggs lost?" I ask, waving my hands around at the farm.

After the crops were burned down, Owen promised us he'd find who did it and make them pay. If it were teens like Briggs thinks, their parents should pay for the damage. Hell, Briggs is drowning in bills and his home is slowly falling apart. He doesn't have money to fix any of the things going wrong in his house because he invests it all in trying to make sure the fences are secure and the animals are fed and taken care of. Animals that he rescues and takes care of. If there is one person in Orchard Hill who least deserves all of this pain and stress and worry, it's Briggs. Him and that big heart of his.

We may not have spoken since he gave me his ultimatum, but I care a shit ton about that stubborn man.

"I'm sorry. I tried to put my foot down, but the people above me, the ones fundin' my department, they're not gonna give us more money to 'waste' on this investigation. Their words, not mine," he says, crossing his arms and leaning against his Dodge with a frown. "Off the record, I'm not gonna stop lookin' yet. I'll use my spare time, and I'll find out who did it. That's my job and I ain't done with it until the people responsible are held accountable," he goes on and Beckett claps me on the shoulder, making me realize he dismounted Pegasus to stand with us.

"We appreciate it, man." Beck nods at Owen, who gives him a bored shrug.

"Yeah, y'all can appreciate me with a couple of beers and a night out at Boots & Beers," he says and pushes off his car to open his door.

"How does Monday work?" Beckett asks and I roll my eyes at him.

"Perfect. I'll have some more updates for you by then," he adds before letting his car roar to life and driving off again.

"Should we tell Briggs?" I ask, but Beckett shakes his head.

"Nah, he didn't even know the investigation was still happenin'. I didn't want to give him hope in case somethin' like this happened," Beckett says, and I nod along to his words. "Anyway, Landon is expecting me. I better hurry before he goes about his day and I'll have to track him down." He claps me on the shoulder once more before getting back on Pegasus and riding toward the barn.

"Hi, pumpkin," I say as soon as Bailey gets lifted out of the car by Jessica's mother.

When she sees me, her dark green eyes light up and she starts running my way, screaming, "Uncle Aaron!"

My heart warms at the sight of the little goofball smiling so brightly at me. I crouch down so she can run into my arms. I haven't had the chance to see her since her mom dropped her off again a few weeks ago.

As soon as she's in my arms, I lift her off the ground and place her on my left hip. She wraps her small arms around my neck while I flash her friend's mom a thankful smile and then turn toward Firefly and Cookie, her pony.

"Your dad told me you wanted to go horse riding," I say as I place her on the ground in front of Cookie. She approaches the small horse with a giggle.

"Yeah, but Daddy said not today," she replies, taking Cookie's nose between her hands and laughing more when he blows out his breath and her hair goes flying everywhere.

"Only because he didn't know if I had time to take you today," I say as I pick up the helmet I brought her and the riding boots Beckett bought her two months ago. I attach the helmet first, then help her into the shoes. "Ready?" I ask once I've double-checked her helmet is on properly.

"Ready," she replies. She stomps her feet before raising her arms to signal she wants me to lift her onto Cookie.

I place her on the saddle at the same moment I notice Tatum, Olivia, and Hadley transferring the llamas from one pen to another. It's almost like my gaze on her calls her attention, and I love the way she brings her eyes to me before a bright smile takes over. She gives me the cutest, little wave I've ever seen before focusing on my llama, Flames, again. I introduced her to Flames two days ago after we planted the rest of the seeds. Tatum, being who she is, fell in love with the animal as soon as she saw her.

"Uncle Aaron?" Bailey asks, poking my stomach to drag me back into the moment and away from where Tate is petting Flames.

"Yes, pumpkin?" I ask, for a split second remembering the day when she was only three and stuck her head into the pumpkin Beckett was about to carve. She pulled her head out to reveal seeds stuck in her hair, but she was laughing like she'd never done anything more entertaining.

"I'm a little hungry," Bailey says, and I give her helmet a wiggle before making my way to Firefly and grabbing his lead rope and then Cookie's.

"I'm sure Briggs has some snacks," I assure her before starting to make my way toward the main house.

I feel Tate's gaze burning my skin as we walk, but I do my best to focus on Bailey as she tells me about her day at Jessica's house and how much fun she had feeding the bunnies they have.

When I really can't help myself anymore, I let my eyes drift back to Tatum. She catches me staring, longing in her eyes.

"Aaron, can you stop starin' at Tatum's ass and help me for a sec?" Ian calls from the porch of the main house, his head down as he fixes the top stair. He must have not seen Bailey because the little girl looks at me confused.

"What's ass?" she asks, and my eyes widen.

Beckett's going to kill me, then Ian, bring me back to life, and kill me again.

"Hey, Ian. Bailey is asking what that word you used means," I say when Bails and I are in front of the porch.

Strands of his black hair fall over his eyes, but I can still see his brown pools filling with regret as he realizes Bailey heard him.

"Well, Bailey, that word has actually been outlawed by me and may only be used by me. If you say it, the tickle police will come and tickle you for five minutes," he says, making Bailey giggle and bounce a little in her saddle.

"But I already said it and didn't get tickled," she says, so Ian pins me with a look, and I burst into laughter as I lift Bailey off the pony and hold her out for him. He rushes over and tickles her until she's squealing and laughing.

"Are you ever going to say that word again?" Ian asks with his index fingers pointed high, warning her that if she says yes, he will tickle her again.

"No," Bailey replies with another giggle, so I pull her against my chest and away from Ian. He lets out a string of curse words in Japanese, I'm guessing out of relief, and I smile at him as he goes back to fixing the step.

"Come. I need your arms to lift up the stone while I add the cement underneath," he says, so I lift Bailey up the porch to avoid having her use the stairs and encourage her to go inside and ask Briggs for a snack. She practically runs inside while I move over to Ian and lift the stone step.

"Where's Flynn?" I ask, turning my body ever so slightly to check on Tate, Liv, and Hads.

Considering I've had this knee problem for years, one would assume I'd remember to wear my brace or keep from twisting my knee awkwardly until pain latches onto me and panic fills my chest.

Unfortunately, I'm an idiot.

"Move your hands!" I scream at Ian, who doesn't waste a second to do as I've asked.

I drop the stone and stumble backward as my knee cramps up and forces me to the ground. I try to get my breathing under control, but panic latches onto me until my vision blurs and then turns black.

"Aaron? What the hell's happenin'?" Ian asks and jumps down the porch to get to me.

"Nothin'," I lie, but we both know it's not true.

"Aaron?" Her voice is full of panic while I hear footsteps sprinting my way.

There is nothing I want more than to get up, to pretend I'm fine because I want to be strong for her. I don't want her to see my control slipping through my fingers because my knee is acting up, but I can't. I can't do anything but wait for the sensation to pass or for my panic attack to drag me into the darkness.

Chapter 31
Tatum

ALL I HEARD WAS something dropping, making a loud, almost bone-shattering sound. Then, I saw him wobble on one leg and drop to the floor.

It's his knee, I know it is, and I'm running as fast as I can to get to him.

My breathing is uneven and shallow as I drop down in front of Aaron, watching his chest rise and fall too quickly. His hands are shaking so violently, I wrap them in mine as I take in the way his breaths are also coming in shallow.

He's having a panic attack.

When he opens his eyes, they have a faraway look in them, as if he isn't in the present anymore but somewhere deep inside of his memories, reliving something.

Reliving his injury...

The thought has me grabbing his hands tighter and inching closer to him.

"Hey, cowboy, I'm gonna need you to breathe okay? Breathe," I say firmly, but he's still not with me.

He's fighting to get to me, I can see it in the way his entire body shakes, but the memory of the day he lost his dream has him wrapped tightly in pain and fear. My eyes attach to the sight of his knee, which isn't in a brace, so I look over my shoulder where Hadley, Olivia, and Ian are standing. They're scared too, but I'm used to a body shutting down. I know how to handle this, which means giving them something to do so they don't feel as helpless watching Aaron fight through his panic attack.

"Ian, get me his brace. Liv, go get some water. Hads, get me a wet towel." They all nod at me before sprinting inside. I turn back to Aaron, his hands still pressed between mine. "Alright, listen to me, Aaron. You're okay. You are not back there. You are here with me. Okay?"

"I can't—" He breaks off before he can tell me what he can't do, but that's alright. I know he can't breathe. I know he can't focus. I know he can't push out of the memory.

"Yeah, you can. You can breathe because I need you to, okay? I need you to breathe for me, baby," I say, and his eyes shoot open at the pet name, filling with something other than panic. They soften until his shaking subsides a little too.

"I'd do anything for you, sweetheart," he says a moment later, taking a deep breath and blowing it back out through gritted teeth. I smile as his hand lifts and rests on my neck, his thumb tracing my pulse point. "Your heart's racing," he points out, and I let out a small laugh. "My heart is also racing. Maybe that means we're connected now," he says with a soft smile, ever the sunshine man, even when he's in pain.

"Or maybe you're—" He cuts me off by pressing the thumb that was rubbing over my neck to my lips.

"Don't ruin it," he whispers, bringing a grin to my lips. His eyes are only half opened because the panic attack has clearly made him tired.

"I wasn't going to ruin it," I reply, but we both know it's a lie.

"You called me 'baby' for the first time, so, honestly, I don't really care about anything else right now," he says as he removes his hand and rests his head against the porch, his eyes remaining on my lips. "Say it again."

"Say what again, baby?" The left side of his mouth curls upward in a perfect smirk.

"I like that a lot," he admits and closes his eyes, taking several deep breaths. I slide my hands over his thighs in a soothing motion, anchoring him and myself at the same time.

"How often do your panic attacks happen?" I ask, and he opens his eyes to show me the uncertainty in them.

He doesn't want to tell me. He doesn't want to destroy the image of the independent, indestructible cowboy he presents to the world, but he's also Aaron. He's the guy that loves to talk about his feelings and be open.

It's one of the many things I like about him.

"Usually only when my knee acts up, but I also almost had one at the hospital, so I don't know anymore," he admits and places his hands over mine.

Footsteps from inside the house make me retract mine from his thighs. He drops his head backward again, closing his eyes as his fingers twitch a little, almost like he's holding himself back from reaching for me again.

"Goddammit, boy, how many times before you learn?" I hear my father ask as he storms out of the house, anger veiling over his concern. "Honeybee, Imma need you to move, please."

Then he's at Aaron's knee, securing the brace around it without saying a single word. All he does is scowl at my cowboy.

"This is the last time. Wear your damn brace, Aaron. I know it restricts your movements and makes you appear weaker on the outside, but it helps you. It prevents the pain." Dad's voice is a lot softer now, and I place my hand on his shoulder to assure him everything will be alright.

"Yeah, I'm aware," Aaron says through gritted teeth as Dad adjusts the strap of the brace a little harder than necessary.

"Are ya?" Dad asks and stands up, looking down at Aaron and shaking his head.

"If you don't mind, Briggs, I've just had a panic attack and experienced a hurricane of pain. I can't handle your disappointment right now," Aaron admits, placing his hand over his eyes and rubbing his temple to probably get rid of the headache that comes with having a panic attack.

"I'm not disappointed, Aaron, I'm wondering what the hell I'm gonna do with you."

"Nothing. I'm not your problem. You've made it abundantly clear my position at this farm is dependent on your rules and that you'd have no problem taking away my livelihood if I were to break them. Before today, you hadn't even spoken to me since

Tate and I got back. Therefore, your answer is nothing. I'm a disposable worker at your ranch, nothing more, and that makes my problems mine, not yours."

A surprised gasp threatens to spill past my lips, but I manage to swallow it down. Dad's back tenses, and so does mine. In a way, I'm so proud of Aaron for sharing his feelings with the stubborn man who raised me, but, on the other hand, I frown a little because Dad loves Aaron. My cowboy is hurt, I know he is, but he's accusing my father of something that isn't true.

Or is it?

"That ain't fair, son, and you know it." Aaron merely shrugs. "I'm tryna protect both of you from makin' a horrible mistake because you, my boy, want a spouse to devote yourself to. You want to make them your life and grow old with them. That ain't Tate. She's a runner."

I don't know if he forgot I'm standing behind him, but his words shatter my heart into a million pieces. He's not wrong. I've run from love my entire life because I was too scared of it to ever let it consume me, but that doesn't mean I'm incapable of falling in love. It doesn't mean I wouldn't be able to devote myself to someone.

At least that's what I keep repeating in my head until his words stop suffocating my heart with their death grip. Dad isn't cruel on purpose. He doesn't make plans to hurt people or say things to deliberately bring them pain. He didn't ask me to stay away from Aaron because he thought it would hurt. He did it to protect us, at least in his head.

"Fuck," I hear Aaron mutter. My gaze drifts to him to see his eyes on me as he gets up from the ground, but I lift my hands to stop him.

"I'm fine," I croak out right as a tear slips down my cheek.

I run from them to protect my heart from further damage, becoming exactly who my father accused me of being.

Luna's head is resting on my legs as I run a brush her coat. Her eyes are closed as she enjoys the groom, and I do my best to stop sobbing. Loki is right beside me, too, his eyes on me as he feels my sadness. Dad has been giving me space since he said what he said, but Aaron has been sitting in front of me with Betty beside him in silence ever since he found me in the barn. He hasn't said a word, merely started brushing Betty. He smiles at me every time he catches me looking at him, which only makes me cry harder and him frown.

I hate crying.

"What he said hurt my feelings," I manage to admit after silence stretched between us for several more minutes. Aaron's full attention immediately shifts to me as he starts nodding.

"I know, sweetheart." He stands up only to gently place Betty's sleepy head on the ground and settle down in front of me. His knee almost brushes mine, and I welcome his proximity.

"He wasn't wrong when he called me a runner, and I hate that he wasn't. I hate it even more that I ran from you so often, you're probably worried I'm going to do it again. Hell, even I'm worried I will," I admit, allowing myself to express all of my concerns for once instead of keeping them inside.

Aaron's blue eyes are fixated on me as he listens closely, processes my words, and then responds.

"I'll simply chase after you, Tate. I don't mind. As long as you want me, I'm not letting you go," he says, and it feels like a weight lifts off my shoulders.

"But you want a wife, Aaron. You want to grow old with someone. I don't know if I can give you that." He thinks for a moment, and I adore the way he doesn't dismiss my words with meaningless promises.

"That's okay, Tatum, because I want you *more*."

The way he pronounces the last word is so full of emotion, raw and real, it brings more tears to my eyes.

"One day at a time, sweetheart. Don't let your dad pressure you into thinking that has changed. I'm not in a rush. I don't want anything more than to spend every single available second with you." He twirls one of my curls around his fingers before tucking it behind my ear.

"What he said doesn't bother you?" I ask while he cups my cheek in his hand.

"No, it doesn't, at least not in the way you think. It bothers me because he upset you," he replies, his hand dropping to the side of my neck. His thumb rubs along my pulse point softly.

"I really want you to kiss me right now," I whisper, but as soon as he smiles and leans forward, the creaking of the barn doors opening causes him to jump back.

"What if they're bangin' in one of the empty stables?" Flynn asks, and I hear Beckett snort.

"Nah, Aaron isn't that kinky. He's not into public sex," he replies, and I watch Aaron cock a brow while a sinful smirk tugs up the right corner of his mouth. He winks at me before standing up and stepping out of Luna, Betty, and Angel's stable.

"Do the two of you ever get tired of being so goddamn annoying?" Aaron asks, and I can't help but finally smile for the first time in hours.

CHAPTER 32
Aaron

SLOWLY BUT SURELY, THE first sunflowers Tate and I planted are starting to come to the surface. The last two Sunday markets we hosted were an absolute success, with more and more people from the town and neighboring ranches coming to sell their goods. We're making enough money that we invested some of it into buying pumpkins to have a pumpkin patch from September to October, but not enough to get the bank off Briggs' back, at least not yet.

We've received donations for our Halloween decorations, but tonight, all seven of us at Silver Creek Ranch are planning to make more.

For now, I'm trying to find Tate so we can finally start the process of allowing her and Galaxy to familiarize themselves with one another. I find her carrying a bucket of water right beside the hose outside of the barn. It dangles between her legs, clearly incredibly heavy. I rush to her side to help.

"Give it to me," I say, placing my hand over hers, but her happy smile at seeing me soon fades into irritation.

"I can do it," she protests as I try to pull it away, the water swishing back and forth in response.

An evil idea slips into my mind, but who can blame me? It's been two weeks since we were at the creek and I had Tate's naked body pressed against mine, and ever since then, all we had time for were a few kisses here and there. So, I grab the bucket and pour the water all over her and me, soaking our clothes—okay, mostly her clothes because by the time I tilt the bucket my way, it's practically empty. Tate lets out a gasp as the cold water covers her, and I try my best not to burst into laughter.

"Oh no, now we have to go change our clothes," I say to try and make her understand why I did that. Understanding washes over her as she looks at me but slowly backs away.

"Well, I certainly do, but you don't. At least not yet," she says, pointing at the single circle of water turning the left side of my jeans a darker shade of blue. I furrow my brows at her, studying the way she continues to back away until she's right back at the hose.

"Don't you dare," I warn, but she picks up the green pipe while her hand fumbles with the valve, twisting until the water is on. "Tate, I'm warning you. You spray me with the hose and I'll take you across my knee and spank you until you can't take it anymore," I warn.

I should have known that would only encourage her more.

"Ooops," she sings right before directing the spray of water my way.

It soaks my shirt within seconds, so I walk over to her slowly, almost like a predator, and she giggles at the top of her lungs as she watches me.

"Guess now you have to change, too," she says right as I stop in front of her, lowering the pipe so the water only hits my legs.

Tate lets me take the hose, her chest rising and falling because she feels the anticipation as strongly as I do. I turn off the water before leaning down, inhaling her sweet scent for a brief second before backing away again.

"You have thirty seconds to decide between getting your ass into my truck so we can drive to my place or running there." It's only about a two-minute run from the barn. "I'll give you a headstart if you choose to run, but I'll take you right then and there in the open if you don't make it to the house before me, not giving a single fuck who will see us," I say, her smile the only response I get before she starts running toward my little cottage.

Good lord, this woman.

Loki chases after her, and I give her thirty seconds—and myself because my cock is growing so hard at the thought of finally sinking deep inside of her, it's making even standing painful. Then, I chase after her, looking around to see if any of my friends are watching what's happening, but Beckett is at Red Sky Ranch today, Olivia and Hads are out fixing the fence on the far west side, and Flynn and Ian are herding the cows from one place to another so that Briggs can fertilize the area.

There is no one near the barn except for us, and that only encourages me to run faster.

I catch her right before she makes it up the stairs to my porch, wrapping my arms around her from behind and pulling her into the air. She lets out a laugh combined with a squeal, filling my veins with her joy and bringing a grin to my face. The sound quickly turns into a moan when I set her back on her feet and step into her, pressing my hard cock against her big and beautiful ass. God, I love her ass. I love everything about her body.

"Almost, sweetheart, you almost made it inside," I say as I brush a strand of hair off her forehead, gliding the tips of my fingers down her cheek and to her neck. She lifts her head to give me better access, so I wrap my hand around her throat, not pushing down but merely feeling how quickly her heart is racing.

"I love it when you hold me like this," she admits as she brings her hand up to wrap her fingers around the wrist that's near her throat.

"I know," I reply, leaning down to nip at her earlobe. "Get inside. As much as I would love to fuck you on my front porch, nothing's going to interrupt us while I sink my cock deep inside your tight, perfect pussy for the first time," I whisper into her ear, feeling her shiver from pleasure.

Tate rushes up the stairs, using the key I told her hides under my flower pot to unlock the front door. As soon as she and Loki are inside, getting greeted by Ash who is still mad at me for not taking him to work after he sprained his paw yesterday, I close the door behind us, locking it to make sure no uninvited guest decides to walk in—yes, I mean Flynn.

She spins around and places her mouth on mine before I have a chance to think about whether I want to rip her clothes off or ask her to strip for me. One of her hands slips into my hair as her other one reaches for my groin.

"I want to touch your cock," she admits, and I smile as I kiss her lips again.

"Touch me however much you want, Tate. I'm yours to play with." She returns my smile as she palms me, moaning at the hardness of my cock.

Her hand wraps around my bulge, and my hips thrust forward without me meaning to.

"Fuuuuck," I grunt, pleasure clouding my brain as she rubs me until I see stars. "I need your clothes off," I say while she continues to palm me through my jeans.

"Take them off. Take whatever you want. I'll tell you 'stop' when I don't want something and you do the same," she says, and I nod once before planting my mouth back on hers, pushing my tongue inside of her to taste her.

My hands reach for her soaked shirt, pulling it over her head before bringing my lips back down to hers.

Kissing should be the thing taking away your ability to breathe, but it feels like the opposite whenever I kiss Tatum. It feels like, for the first time in my life, I'm finally able to take a deep breath and give my body the very thing it needs to survive.

Tate gives my cock a rough rub, forcing pleasure through me until my hand snakes back around her throat. I force her head up so her swollen lips are easily accessible. It's also to get her attention away from touching my cock because with a few more rough strokes, I'll come in my pants without her even properly touching me, and that's not happening.

"Strip out of the rest of the clothes, then wait for me on the bed," I say.

The shy smile playing on her lips is the only response I get before she rushes into my bedroom and leaves me standing in the middle of my entrance with a hard cock and my restraint so far gone, I tilt my head back and close my eyes to try and reign it back in.

My fingers fumble with the buttons of my wet flannel as I make my way into the bedroom to see Tate completely naked on my bed, grinning at me. She's keeping her legs pressed together, but that won't do.

"Touch yourself while I watch. I want to see how you fuck yourself," I say, moving toward the edge of my bed where her feet are. "But don't make yourself come."

She gives me a naughty smile before letting her thighs fall apart and exposing herself to me. My cock gives a needy throb in my pants, but I ignore it as I continue to undo the buttons of my shirt.

Her hand drops to her pussy where she runs a single finger along the length of it, only letting it dip inside of her enough to coat it with her arousal. Tate brings it back up to her swollen clit, rubbing tight circles that have her head falling backward. She moans so loudly, I can't help but smile.

I let my shirt drop to the floor as I say, "You like being watched, don't you? You like me standing here, getting even harder at the sight of you playing with your pretty, little cunt, don't you?" My words force another moan out of her, answering my question without her having to say anything.

"Only when you're watching, baby," she pants, and I smirk as I unbutton my pants and pull them down, right along with my boxers.

"Damn straight, sweetheart."

Her back arches, another moan filling the room. The way her legs tremble a little and her hand starts moving more frantically lets me know she's close. I sink to my knees in front of her, gently grabbing her wrist to stop her from falling over the edge. She whimpers in complaint, but I trap her hand in mine, preventing her from reaching for her clit again.

"I want you to play with your tits, Tate. Make yourself feel good while I eat you out," I instruct, placing each of my hands on her thighs to spread her wider for me.

My eyes trail over every inch of her, watching as she lifts her hand to touch her beautiful breasts, rolling her nipples between her fingers. Finally, I reach her face, noting the way half her bottom lip slips between her teeth as she stares down at me with desire glazing over her eyes.

"You're so beautiful," I say, watching a shy smile cross her features and a blush settle over her cheeks.

"Aaron—" She cuts off as I lick along the length of her pussy once, using the tip of my tongue to flick over her clit.

"You are breathtaking," I go on, bringing my mouth to the inside of her thigh and trailing open-mouthed kisses toward her pussy, wrapping my lips around her clit and sucking hard a moment later. She cries out, almost screaming my name as I work her clit.

"You are absolutely devastating," I say. "Tell me you know that, and I'll make you come."

"I know," she moans.

"Such a good girl for me, Tate."

Then, I shut up and play with her clit until her back arches and she's begging me to slip my fingers inside of her. I obey, curling them at the perfect spot and making her clench around me. My other hand reaches down to wrap around my cock. I thrust forward with each time I slip my fingers inside of her, imagining how it will feel to replace my fingers with my dick. The fantasy almost has me coming in my hand. I let go of my cock when my balls pull even tighter, groaning against her clit so hard, she comes right as I suck on it.

Her walls clench around my fingers again as she trembles through her orgasm. Tatum's back arches off the bed as she grinds her hips and rolls her pussy against my mouth, riding out her orgasm. I pin her down, my tongue moving more frantically over her clit until her hands reach for my hair, tugging on it until I remove my mouth and bring it to hers instead. She moans as soon as she tastes herself on my lips.

"I need you inside of me," she says, reaching around me. Her fingers dig into my ass cheeks, pulling me down and bringing my cock to her entrance. "I've thought about whether or not I want to use a condom," she says, bringing back the memory of me asking her a few weeks ago what she preferred. I've never had unprotected sex in my entire life, but I want to with Tate. I want nothing between us as I claim her for myself and she claims me in the same way. But I told her to think about it. To take her time and decide.

"What do you want, baby?" I ask, trailing kisses from her mouth down her neck and licking over her soft after sucking on it.

"I don't want to use one. You're negative and so am I, so I don't want anything between us either." Her hand wraps around my cock at the same time as she says the second half of her last sentence, and my hips thrust forward without me meaning to.

"Fuck, Tate," I curse as the head of my cock pushes inside of her. She clamps down on me, and I suck in a sharp breath. I manage to slide a few more inches inside of her, but she squeezes me so hard, I have to stop halfway.

"God, you're so big," she moans, tugging on my neck to bring my lips back down to hers.

"Tate, I need you to relax a little, sweetheart. I'm not fully inside yet," I say, trailing kisses down her neck to her breasts.

"You're not?" she pants, and I shake my head.

"Not yet." I slide out of her and bring half my hard length back inside, feeling her loosening up with each stroke.

"Fucking hell," she curses right as I wrap my mouth around her pebbled nipple and tug.

"You're so wet for me, Tate, so ready to take my cock all the way. Don't you want it buried deep inside of you? Don't you want to squeeze my entire cock with your beautiful cunt?"

My words combined with a soft lick over her nipple have her loosening up until I can thrust deep inside of her. Her pussy hugs me entirely now, both of us moaning at the way we fit together. It feels like sliding into paradise. It feels like sunshine and rainbows and everything good in the world. I've never fucked a woman without a condom, never wanted to, but this? This is so much better than I could have ever imagined. Feeling her warmth, feeling every little inch of her around me, it's addictive.

It feels like coming home.

"You're doing so fucking good, sweetheart, taking all of me," I praise, lowering myself enough so our chests press together. I haven't found the ability to move yet, trying to give both of us time to adjust to the sensation.

"Aaron, please move. I need you to move and make me come again," she begs, but it sounds like a demand all the same, and when Tatum wants something, there is nothing in this cursed world that could stop me from giving it to her.

"So fucking greedy," I mumble as I pull out of her again only to thrust into her, harder than before. Tate screams my name, but I kiss her hard, not wanting anyone to walk by and hear how good I make her feel.

"Oh my God. Oh my God," Tate repeats over and over with every single thrust while I worship her breasts, using my mouth to play with her nipples. "It's too much," she says, and I lift my head to look into her eyes.

"Do you want me to stop?" I ask.

"No," she replies so quickly, I can't help but smirk.

"Then you can take it, sweetheart," I say, dropping my mouth back to her nipple and bringing my right hand to her clit.

I start rubbing in tight circles, combining it with my rough and deep strokes. My balls draw tighter and tighter, pleasure consuming me as I get closer to my orgasm. It feels too good to try and fight it off, and when her walls squeeze me again, I fucking lose it.

My thrusts become frantic as my orgasm builds in my cock before taking over my entire body. Tate clamps a hand over her mouth to scream into it as another orgasm shudders through her, too, following me straight over the edge.

My arms are shaking, sweat rolling down my spine. It takes several deep breaths until I find my way back into my body.

I look down at the mess we made, the smirk still firmly set on my face. My strokes slow to give her time to catch her breath and tremble through the aftershocks of her orgasm. A low, satisfied hum leaves her as I sit back, pulling out of her to run my fingers over her pussy.

"You're perfect, sweetheart. Absolutely perfect." I press a kiss to the inside of her left thigh, rubbing my hands over her calves. She gives me a lazy smile as she props herself up on her elbows.

"Aaron?" I bring my gaze up to hers, noting the emotional rollercoaster going through her reflecting in her eyes. "Kiss me."

"With pleasure."

I bring my mouth to hers, kissing her until she breaks it and buries her face in the crook of my neck.

We stay in each other's arms for a while. I let go of her reluctantly to grab a wet towel and clean us up before bringing her naked body straight back against mine. She shivers a little, so I wrap my throw blanket around us, dragging her even closer. My hands run all over her while I enjoy this moment of peace between us. I whisper how perfect and beautiful she is in every variation of the English language, and she smiles from ear to ear, looking more content with each second.

Our relationship being a secret is difficult. I won't pretend it's ideal, but I will take whatever I can get with Tate. If it weren't for Briggs' ultimatum, I don't think she'd want to keep it secret at this point either, but she's doing it for me. To protect my job. To protect my income that I use to pay for Nanna's care at the nursing home.

"We should probably leave soon," Tate eventually says, and I look down, rubbing my nose over hers as I do.

"Why?" I want to stay in bed with her. No other responsibilities in the world. It could be her and me, in this moment, forever, and I'd be happy.

"Because we have to make sure no one finds out that we're both gone and start asking questions. We can't risk anyone else finding out," she reminds me right as someone clears their throat from the doorframe of my room.

"Might be a lil late for that, honeybee."

CHAPTER 33
Tatum

MY HEART STOPS BEATING. Panic fills me from head to toe, causing me to jerk my head in the direction of the very familiar voice.

"Briggs is gonna kill you. Then, he'll lock Tate up to prevent anyone else at the ranch from going near her." A bit of relief floods through me. "I mean, I had a feeling you two were fuckin', but seeing it is truly somethin' else," Olivia says, and I think about throwing one of the pillows I'm lying on at her head.

"What the fuck are you doing in my house?" Aaron barks, shifting his body in front of mine even though his blanket covers me entirely.

"I needed to pee and your house was the closest. I didn't think anyone was home," she defends, crossing her trained arms over her chest. It seems to piss Aaron off even more.

"That's not what your key is for, Liv. It's for emergencies."

"It was an emergency! I almost peed my pants and it was either you or hiding behind a bush. I didn't feel like getting a tick on my ass cheek today, so I came here." A laugh bubbles out of me before I can stop it, and Aaron shoots me a confused look in response.

"I'm sorry, but I'm so glad it's Liv and not Beckett because that man cannot keep his mouth shut. Olivia, on the other hand, can keep shit to herself," I explain, running a soothing hand over Aaron's arm. He relaxes a little under my touch, but he's still mad.

"Give me your key," he says to Liv, who rolls her eyes as she digs her hand into her pocket.

"I'm just glad I got here after y'all were done fuckin'," she says, and I smack my forehead with the palm of my hand. The jangling of keys is the only sound I hear before Aaron's body moves, probably catching it mid-air. I lift my head again to see his features pulled into a scowl. "So, are you datin' or just fuckin'?" she asks, sending a wave of heat straight to my cheeks.

"Get out," Aaron demands right as I throw a pillow at my friend.

"Fine, God. If y'all wanna go back to your coital shenanigans, you could have said so," she says with a wicked grin.

"Coital shenanigans? Really?" Aaron asks, but I merely throw another pillow Liv's way. She laughs the entire time before we hear the soft *click* of the front door closing. "Shit," Aaron curses, but I'm giggling so hard, tears are coming out of my eyes. "What's so funny?" he asks, finally bringing a smile to his lips. God, I love his smile, love the way the dimple imprints itself into his cheek.

"Well, like I said, I'm not worried she'll tell anyone, so all I can focus on is the fact that we got caught. I feel like a teenager who snuck out of their house after curfew," I say, still laughing.

This is so stupid. My father is treating us like we *are* teenagers who have no idea what we're doing.

Aaron gives me another confused smile.

"I know it's been *a lot* longer for you since you were a teenager, but—"

He cuts me off by tickling my side until we end up with him on top of me, pinning my hands to the bed. He's smirking down at my chest, rising and falling abruptly from anticipation. I was trying to tease him, especially because there are only four years between us, but now I'm the one getting teased as his hard cock presses against my clit.

"Careful," is all he says before spinning me around so that I'm on my stomach. "Naughty women get spanked."

I'm not entirely sure how almost the entire town of Orchard Hill has made their way to the library to help us with our Halloween decorations tonight. No one seems to mind that Halloween is still months away. They're all here to help us make Aaron's and my vision come to life.

Carol, the woman who sells her art at our Sunday market every weekend, is putting her skills to use as she paints a face onto the human-looking-figure that Flynn made out of hay and old clothes, tied together by some rope.

Ulma and her wife are busy untangling lights that were given to us by Bernard and Sofia, the owners of Red Sky Ranch. Landon is by their side, helping them. He flashes me a smile when I look over, and I give him a small nod.

Jamie is busy bringing everybody coffee and commenting on our work, cheering us on by telling us how amazing we are. Linda, the woman who sells her jewelry at the market, helps him distribute the caffeine.

Zelda and Alice are stitching fabric together to make ghosts. I don't miss the way Alice keeps looking over her shoulder at Aaron. He doesn't pay any attention to her, but it bothers me nonetheless. It shouldn't because we aren't even dating officially. She's allowed to look at him like she wants him. It's fine. Totally fine. Doesn't irritate me at all. Nope.

"You doin' alright?" Owen, the chief of police of Orchard Hill, asks, and I turn my head his way.

"Just peachy," I reply through gritted teeth, fighting back the disgusting feeling of... jealousy?

"I'm a cop, darlin'. It's my job to know when people are lyin'," Owen reminds me, flashing me an easy smile that I'm sure has made people fall headfirst for this man.

"Well, chief, you mind not doing the detective thing with me because I'm not in the mood to get arrested for kicking a cop's ass."

It's bad enough that Olivia and Flynn—yeah, Aaron told me his best friend found out—know about us dating. I don't need the chief of police to have his nose in my business.

"You know, even threatening a cop could get you in handcuffs," he warns, but there is something downright sinful about the smirk that follows when he realizes what he said.

My cheeks heat and a nervous laugh bubbles out of me. It catches my cowboy's attention right away, but I force my gaze from him and back to Owen.

"Sorry. It wasn't what I meant when I said it, but the second I heard it, I knew it was too late to take it back." His eyes sparkle with a combination of mischief and embarrassment.

"That's alright, officer," I assure him.

Owen studies my face for a moment as he leans back and puts down the hot glue gun he was using to attach cut-out drawings of pumpkins to a piece of wood. We're planning on making it the welcome sign to hang at the entrance of the ranch.

"I think it's remarkable what you're doin'," he says and gestures to everyone at the library.

"Thank you, but I don't think it's anything to call remarkable. This is me trying to save my dad's ranch, save the life I've grown to love here. It's actually quite selfish," I reply as I move my weight from one foot to the other, wishing there were more chairs so we could be sitting down.

"If you say so," he replies with a shrug, clearly not agreeing with me. "My momma used to say that if your intentions are good and the end result benefits more than yourself, you're still doin' the right thing. It's okay to be selfish sometimes, Tatum, necessary even. You gotta do what makes you happy first, then you can focus on everyone else," he says, and I stare down at the pumpkin I was about to color in.

"I think you're the only person I've ever met who thinks that way," I point out, making Owen chuckle, a deep and rough sound that has Carol on the opposite side of the table blushing.

Owen and I continue our conversation, my attention drifting to Aaron a few moments later.

It doesn't go past me that everyone else here is drinking, but he's been sipping on water all night long.

He looks irritated and angry as he regards the cop beside me, and I furrow my brows at him. I don't have a chance to find a way to ask Aaron what's wrong when a finger appears on my cheek. I jerk my eyes back to Owen, who is leaning forward and touching me softly, tenderly.

"Sorry, you had a bit of glitter there," he says, immediately pulling his hand away.

"Oh, thanks," I manage to croak out, feeling a warm, hard chest pressing against my back a second later.

Well, fuck.

"Hey, Aaron," Owen says, a little unsure and a lot amused. I'm about to remind Aaron that we're not alone, that my dad is sitting at a table beside the one we're standing at with most of the town here, but I can't bring myself to say the words.

"Chief," Aaron grinds out. I feel the anger in the way his chest vibrates against my back. I take a small step forward to break the connection between our bodies.

"I didn't know y'all are datin'," Owen says, clearly picking up on Aaron's emotions.

"We're not," I blurt out quickly, but Aaron merely steps toward me again until his chest is firmly pressed against my back. I can't lie, I thoroughly enjoy the way this tells Alice and every other person who might be interested in Aaron that he isn't looking at anyone but me. No matter how dangerous this territory is.

"Might wanna tell your human shadow," Owen replies with the same easy smile he's been carrying since I first met him tonight.

"Might wanna back the hell off, chief, because I'm pretty sure Tate didn't ask you to touch her," Aaron says.

"Alright, gentlemen, I need to finish this before Olivia bites my head off for being the slowest," I joke to take away some of the tension.

Owen is still smiling at Aaron while my cowboy is probably scowling at the cop. I remember Aaron mentioning he was friends with Owen a while back, but I'm not so sure he will be if this situation doesn't get defused soon.

"Aaron, do we have any more paint in your truck?" I ask as I turn around.

His blue eyes drop down to my face, softening as he takes in the smile I only ever give him. His black curls are all over the place in a perfectly sexy mess on top of his head, and his stubble has me remembering that I still have some slight beard burns between my legs he's responsible for.

"Yeah, I think so," he replies, watching my lips and eyes with utter fascination.

"Want to help me carry them up here?" I ask, already making my way toward the exit of the library.

No one seems to have noticed the exchange between Aaron and Owen. They're all too busy focusing on their projects to pay us any attention. Olivia may have something to do with my father not having noticed anything, too, because she's hovering over him and laughing like he's the funniest man in the world. I flash her an appreciative smile, and she winks at me.

Aaron follows me out the door but pulls me down the corridor and into another room instead. I can't help but gasp as he shuts the door and stalks toward me, backing me against the wall. My heart is racing in the way it always does when Aaron is about to kiss me, pure excitement and anticipation coursing through my veins. His arms lift to each side of my head, the muscles in them flexing as he tries to restrain himself from whatever he wants to do to me right now. I wish he wouldn't. I wish he'd take everything he wanted because no matter how many times he touches me, it's never enough.

He lets out a string of curses as I place one of his hands around my throat. He applies exactly the amount of pressure I love before finally kissing me, his lips demanding and firm as they press against mine. He groans into my mouth as he cups my face and my hands slide under his shirt. I run my nails down his abs while his tongue demands entry.

"You're mine," he says after pulling back, completely breathless. "Mine to kiss, mine to touch, mine to worship. Unless you decide it to be otherwise, that is how it is, sweetheart," he says, softly kissing along my cheek to get back to my mouth.

"I'm yours," I reply against his lips. "And you're mine." He pulls me close and kisses me until nothing but him remains.

"I've been yours since you stepped foot on Silver Creek Ranch, Tate. I only want you, no one else." He seals his words with another hard kiss that has me melting against him. "I don't know why I feel this way, so... so possessive of you." His admission makes me smile.

"It's okay, I feel the same way about you. Whenever Alice looks at you, I want to march right over, sit down on your lap, and kiss you until she gets the hint," I say, and he smiles at me like he's never heard better words.

He rests his forehead against mine, the heat of the moment subsiding a little. I slide my hands into his thick, soft hair, enjoying the way his scent fills my nose. I love the way he smells. All woody and fresh and delicious.

"I think it'd be easier for us if everyone knew," I mumble, and he gives an agreeing nod.

"Yeah, because if everyone knew, Owen fucking Grim would keep his hands off you," he replies, letting out an annoyed huff that I find more adorable than anything else.

"I don't want Owen Grim," I say. Aaron runs a hand down my left cheek, then my side until he rests it on my hip.

"You want me." It's a statement, a damn cocky one, too, but he's right. I want him and only him.

"We're being reckless," I remind him, but he merely smirks and shrugs.

"Don't care. Need another moment," he says and grabs my chin between his fingers.

"For what?" I ask as he lowers his mouth back to mine.

"To make sure you taste nothing but me for the rest of the night."

Once I'm back at my station—where someone has finally put a chair for me—I feel a pull on my sleeve. I look down at my side to find a little human staring up at me with beautiful dark green eyes, black curls, and a shy smile.

I've only met her once at dinner a few days ago, and she was so tired from spending the day helping Dad brush all of the horses, she could barely keep her eyes open.

"Hey, Bailey. How can I help you?" I ask and she raises her hands in the air to get me to lift her onto my lap. I do as she wants, placing her mostly on my right thigh.

"Can I sit with you?" she says, pressing her little, short fingers against my cheeks and studying my face so intensely with her big eyes, it feels like she can see a lot more than I'd ever expect.

"Of course," I reply.

She helps me color in the pumpkin I didn't get to finish earlier, laughing and sharing stories from her friend with me. I listen attentively, but she stops a story halfway when she spots her daddy again. She runs toward Beckett as he strolls into the room all casually and looking like he should be the runner-up for *People Magazine*'s Sexiest Man alive, second to Aaron, of course.

"Hey, sugar. See anythin' you like?" he asks me with a suggestive quirk of his brow after Bailey runs to my dad to show him the drawing of the pumpkin I gave her.

"Yes, but it ain't you, *sugar*." He places a hand over his chest in mock hurt before winking at me and continuing to make his way to where Aaron is sitting.

My cowboy pretends not to notice his friend's approach, but once Beckett is close enough, Aaron *accidentally* shoves an elbow into his ribs as he pulls tight on the rope he is using. Beckett lets out a choked breath and bends over as he touches his hand to his side while Aaron looks at me and smirks.

CHAPTER 34
Aaron

THE BRACE AROUND MY knee makes it harder to move around, to try and fling my leg over my saddle on Firefly's back or squat down when I have to fix something. I know it's best I wear it, to prevent my knee from shooting an electric bolt of pain through my body, but it irritates me. It irritates me how hard simple tasks become because of this thing keeping my knee in place.

I call Ash to my side and make my way through the barn and toward Galaxy's stable. She's a lot more comfortable with her surroundings and me, so much so that she actually comes to see me as I approach. I grab her lead rope, her bridle, reins, and bit before grabbing the saddle I had custom-made for Tatum. It's black with green highlights woven into it the same way the blue color is integrated into mine, through the threads that hold the piece together. It matches my saddle, including the horse stitched into the side of the saddle.

It was my plan to wait another few days to show her, wait until a moment presented itself when it's just the two of us and I could make it romantic, but I need to see her right now. This longing to constantly be near is almost driving me to do something reckless.

I love my life here. No part of me wants to give any of it up, but with every second I spend in Tate's presence, with each kiss and piece of her she shares with me, it becomes more difficult not to find a new job.

I want to go to the creek, dip my head underwater, and scream, like a real adult with frustration bubbling inside of them that they don't know what to do with.

After shaking my head several times, I rub my hand over Galaxy's nose and forehead before making my way out of the barn and toward the pen I trained her in. Tatum is carrying a bale of hay while Beckett walks beside her, laughing his carefree laugh and bringing the fresh pasture with him. She catches me staring at her as soon as she walks outside, furrowing her brows at my expression. I gesture toward Galaxy, and Tatum practically drops the hay to run to me, Loki following closely behind her.

Everyone but Olivia and me still assumes Loki and Tate are simply inseparable because they spend so much time together, not because he's also her service dog that alerts her before her seizures. Tate told me she prefers it that way, but I can tell she's getting more and more comfortable with everyone at Silver Creek Ranch. I have a feeling she'll soon tell the rest of them about her epilepsy, and I will be there to support her.

"Sorry, Beckett, but the day has finally come!" she calls over her shoulder while I chuckle at the confused expression taking over his face.

He mouths "what the fuck?" so I nod my head toward Galaxy. Understanding washes over him before he smiles, picking up what Tate dropped. Then, I finally bring my eyes to my woman, watching her ponytail swish back and forth as she sprints toward me. It shouldn't be possible for someone to be as stunning as Tate, especially while running. But there she is, alive and glowing, and here I am, wondering when watching the sunrise and sunset became secondary in my priority list of things I need to see to have a good day.

"Hey," she says as soon as she stops in front of me.

Tate wipes the sweat off her forehead before placing her hands on her hips and taking a deep breath.

"I'm ready. In a few minutes," she adds with a joking smile.

The urge to kiss it, taste it on my lips, is overwhelming, but I manage to hold myself back because Beckett is still nearby, and Olivia and Hadley are currently feeding the llamas to the left of us. So, I can't touch her. I can't kiss her, can't sweep her into my arms and whisper all the dirty things I want to do to her before reminding her how much I adore her.

"You ready?" I tease with a grin after she takes another deep breath to even out her breathing, and probably slow her racing heart. Loki sprints over to where Ash is slowly making his way toward Beck. Noticing his friend approaching, my son spins around and meets Loki halfway.

"Ready," Tate assures me, poking my side when I give her an unsure expression.

I burst into laughter as we both turn to look at Galaxy. She's walking around in the pen, but not as fidgety as she was when she first came in months ago. The mare takes a step toward us as we move inside the pen to be with her. Tatum stays behind me, clearly waiting for instructions, showing me she respects my work as a horse trainer and trusts me to guide her and Galaxy through this.

"Okay, you can do the handshake. Like I taught you," I tell Tate, moving to the side to give her a chance to lift her hand to Galaxy.

My woman does exactly as I told her to approach a horse, waiting until the mare presses her nose against Tate's hand. She does so almost immediately.

There is something about Tatum that Galaxy is drawn to, something that makes her feel more comfortable than she does with most people.

"I think she'll be okay to let you ride her," I assure Tate after a few moments of her merely petting Galaxy and allowing the mare to familiarize herself with my girlfriend.

"Are you sure?" she asks before Galaxy nudges Tate to get more attention.

"Yes, I'm sure." If I weren't, Tate wouldn't be anywhere near Galaxy. I'd never risk her life or well-being.

Tate walks around to Galaxy's side and is about to place her foot in the stirrup when the saddle catches her attention. She runs her fingertips along the length of the horse embroidered on the side before following the green line of thread across the saddle. Her hazel eyes rest on the fabric for so long, my heart palpitates out of fear she hates it.

"Aaron," she whispers, her voice barely audible. Raw emotion filters into it, but I have no idea if it's in a good way or a "you fucked up, Aaron" way.

"You don't like it?" I ask, shoving my hands into my pockets to resist the pull she has on me.

"Aaron," she repeats, sucking in a sharp breath and blinking rapidly. "This is the most thoughtful gesture anyone has ever done for me," Tate says, still running her fingers over the green color of the horse.

It's at this moment that I decide this is one of many gestures I will do for her. If she is as unused to them as she is to my compliments, then it is about fucking time somebody allows her to get used to these concepts. Gift-giving and words of affirmation. Physical touch, quality time, acts of service, I will give this woman every form of love language she never got but has always deserved.

"I love it so much," she adds, pulling me back into the moment.

"I'm glad," I say and force a smile, itching to touch her.

Why is this so fucking hard?

"You really want to kiss me right now, don't you?" she asks with a sweet grin that turns her cheeks a wonderful shade of pink.

"More than anything." Her eyes fall to the ground as she continues to grin to herself.

"How about a hug?" She brings those hazel eyes back to me, and I watch the sun bring out the different colors in them. Brown, green, and yellow all fight for dominance in the sunlight.

"If you hug me, Tate, I can't promise you won't end up pinned against one of those wooden panels with rope tying your hands over your head and my mouth between your thick thighs."

"A hug is all it takes?" she asks, the blush remaining on her cheeks.

"When you look at me like you are at the moment, yes," I reply with a shrug while she laughs and shakes her head.

"You're impossible, cowboy."

"Get on the horse, sweetheart, before I throw you over my shoulder, to hell with anyone who sees," I warn, and she doesn't waste a second to place her hands back on Galaxy, making sure the horse knows she's about to have a human on the saddle on top of her.

Tate places her foot in the stirrup, going slowly so that Galaxy doesn't get spooked. I admire her patience, watching the mare closely as I hover my hands behind my sweetheart in case she needs help, which, of course, she doesn't. Even if she did, she's still too stubborn to ask for it.

"Is Galaxy okay?" Tate asks as soon as she has adjusted herself and feels comfortable in the saddle. My hand moves in front of the mare, a few treats waiting there for her, and she vacuums them up immediately, bobbing her head up and down as she chews.

"Yes. How are you doing? How's the saddle?" I ask, causing her to drop her face into her hands and let out a barely audible, excited squeal.

"Yeah, good."

She rolls her lips into a thin line, but I can tell how much she's loving every second of this. Tate's been waiting for her own horse since she got to Silver Creek Ranch. A few months ago, while we were working on the project for the ranch, she shared with me that she's always wanted a mini cow. And a horse. The horse comment was a bit of an afterthought, but it made her face light up in a way I wasn't entirely used to by then.

This is a big moment for her.

I encourage her to take the reins and start trotting slowly with Galaxy around the pen, something the mare seems to be on board with as well since she starts walking before Tatum even gives the full signal. Tatum seems to be in love with Galaxy already, and I've never seen the horse I've trained for months be this content with anyone sitting on the saddle resting on her back.

She walks with grace and pride while Tatum continues to grin, her cheeks probably burning from it.

"When did you know you had a talent for this?" Tate asks after a while.

"Right after I came to Silver Creek Ranch. We had a senior horse coming in at the time who was very scared and traumatized by her old owners. She had injuries to her legs that made walking and standing very painful for her, so she was resting on the floor for a long time." The thought of Hestia makes a sad feeling settle in my chest. "I stayed with her for days, simply sat with her and fed her. We built a connection soon after. She trusted me and no one else," I go on, watching Tate's features soften.

"And that's when you knew?" she asks.

"Yes, that's when I knew. So, I got my licenses and training, and here I am," I finish, watching an unsure look cross her features.

"But why did you stay here? Why not go somewhere else with your training?"

"Because I made a difference here. I could help abused animals feel loved again, help them settle. Your father always takes in horses like Galaxy and Firefly, and they need someone," I explain while Tatum keeps walking in circles around the pen with Galaxy.

"You're a remarkable man, Aaron. I hope you know that," she says.

"You make me feel remarkable," I admit before urging her into a slow canter.

Minutes pass while Tatum enjoys herself, looking more at peace than I've ever seen her, except when she's sleeping in my arms.

"Aaron?" she says after she finally slows Galaxy into a trot again.

"Yes, sweetheart?" She urges Galaxy to a stop beside me, looking down at me with all of the emotion I felt earlier reflected in her eyes.

"I know I haven't said it before. I know I'm terrible at expressing my feelings in words, but I want you to know how happy you make me. Because you do. You make me so, so happy."

Her words almost cause me to stagger backward because, suddenly, everything she is feeling is directly shoved inside my chest. A lump forms in my throat, but I stop myself from clearing it.

"I feel the same way. You make me happier than I've been in a long time."

A long time being *ever*, but I don't tell her that. I don't want to make things weird by admitting that no one has ever made me feel as whole as she has.

"Fuck, fuck, fuck. Man, you gotta hide me," Beckett says as he storms up my backyard steps and to where I'm currently placing another chair beside the one I always sit in.

My body freezes as I try to come up with an excuse why I'm adding another chair *now*, something other than the fact that I want Tate to have somewhere to sit when she tires of sitting on my lap as we watch the sunrise together.

"What the hell are you doin'?" Beckett asks, and I force a nonchalant expression onto my face.

"Flynn was complaining he always has to sit on the floor, so I thought I'd do something nice for him for once," I lie, but Beck gives me an unsure look as he studies me for a few moments. Then, remembering his previous problem, he simply ignores what I'm doing and refocuses on his panic.

"Sage is visiting Tate, and I may or may not have completely embarrassed myself after we hooked up," Beckett says, falling into my chair where it stands beside the one I'm currently adjusting.

"What did you do?" I ask, crossing my arms in front of my chest as I stare him down. Beckett cringes, visually *cringes* like I've slapped him, before shaking his entire body from a big shiver that took over.

"If I tell you, you can't fuckin' laugh, Aaron. I swear, if you laugh, I'll knock a tooth out of your mouth," he warns, and I'm so intrigued now, there is no way I'm not hearing this story.

"Swear on my life, I'll do my absolute best not to laugh," I assure him, meaning every word.

Beckett sighs loudly before hiding his face behind his hands and mumbling, "She wanted to go for round two, but my dick was so spent, it wouldn't—" He points upward several times before placing his hand back in front of his face. I roll my lips to keep from laughing, not because of what he's saying, but the fact that I have so many old man jokes ready.

"Well, you know, with age, a man's—" He cuts me off by throwing the seating pillow he was sitting on at my head.

"You shut your damn mouth. I'm nowhere near the age where *that* becomes an issue," he says, shaking his head.

"Don't worry, Beck, that's what the little, blue pills are for," I assure him.

Flynn and Ian use that moment to walk around my house, clearly not bothering with the front door either. Olivia and Hadley trail behind them, talking about something I can't make out as my best mate suddenly appears in front of me.

"What are we talkin' about?" he asks as he flops down on Tate's chair.

"Beckett's performance issues when he slept with Sage," I say, watching the tall man shoot daggers my way. "Hey, you've shared way worse about my personal life," I remind him as I lean against the railing.

"You know that happens sometimes, right? It's normal, nothing to be embarrassed about," Ian assures Beck and places his hand on his shoulder.

"Well, it had never happened to me before, so it felt fuckin' embarrassing. Shit, I'm gonna have to hide from the woman until she's gone again," he points out, smacking his forehead with the palm of his hand.

"I think you're makin' a big deal outta nothin', Beck. So, you're getting old, what's the big deal?" Olivia adds, forcing a snicker out of me. I cough to cover it up, but Beckett catches me.

"Alright, how about we stop talkin' about my dick and instead focus on why Aaron and Tate are pretendin' they're not fuckin' like bunnies every time they're alone?"

All amusement leaves me as my eyes widen at his blatant, and accurate, assumption.

"What are you—" Ian chimes in before I have a chance to finish my question.

"Please, Aaron, we all see the way you're both looking at each other. It went from 'when are we finally gonna give in' to 'I can't wait to get you alone.' It's as obvious as Beckett's graying hair."

I almost smile at the way Beck slaps Ian's stomach in punishment for dragging his age back into this. Instead, my eyes move to Flynn, who is already staring at me. He knows. He's known for weeks. He knew as soon as we came back, but I was hoping to be able to keep this from everyone else for a bit longer.

"Don't worry, pretty boy, none of us are gonna tell Briggs. This stays between us until y'all are ready for everyone to know, but you're going to have to be more careful. If Briggs starts spendin' more time with the two of you, he's only gonna stay oblivious to the situation for so long," Hadley says, tying her brown locks into a loose bun and flashing me a sympathetic smile.

"So, you all knew?" They nod without hesitation. "And you thought you wouldn't tell me you knew and let us keep lying to you because of what? To give us time to adjust?" Again, they nod in complete synchronization.

"Listen, Aaron, we're your family. It's our job to know these things. Just like we all knew the second you saw her, that was it. You've never looked at anyone the way you look at her, and I doubt you ever will. I know you don't want us to see these things, but we do. We know you better than you know yourself." Olivia steps forward and places a hand on my arm, her fingers wrapping as far around my bicep as they can go before she squeezes.

"If Briggs finds out, it'll destroy everything I've built here. If he doesn't, I'll never be able to tell the world she's mine. What the hell am I supposed to do?" I ask, enjoying the fact that I can actually talk to all of them about this.

"How the fuck should we know?" Beckett asks, earning a smack to the arm from Flynn. He brings his eyes to mine, determination in them.

"What do you want your future to look like?"

I open my mouth to answer, but he shakes his head, stopping me.

"Really think about it. Think about how much the vision you've always had has now changed since Tatum. Think about what that means for yourself. Don't give me an answer you haven't thought through. Actually, don't give me an answer at all. You gotta figure it out for yourself, and that's gonna take time. Until you know, we're all keepin' our mouths shut. Briggs and the rest of Orchard Hill won't hear about it from us," he promises, but I look at Beckett with my brows furrowed and a doubtful expression placed on my face.

"Hey, I was the first one that figured it out. Well, until I found out Flynn and Olivia already knew, and I didn't tell anyone shit," he defends.

My head whips around to Olivia, who stares at the sky to avoid my irritated glance.

"To be fair, I didn't *know* until I walked in on the two of you naked, and Beck already had his suspicions before," she says, still pretending to admire the clouds as they pass above her.

"You what?" Beck asks before bursting into laughter. "Oh my God, y'all really don't know how to sneak around. Fuckin' amateurs," he mumbles as he wipes under his eyes.

"And you're so good at it that we never found out about you and..." I trail off, waiting for him to fill in the blanks, but his green eyes merely sparkle with mischief as he leans back in his chair and crosses his arms over his massive chest.

"Exactly," is all he says.

"You're a pain in the ass, Beckett," I grumble before Ian walks over to me and places an arm around my shoulders.

I really wish Tate was here right now so I could tell her we no longer have to hide in front of these jerks, that I can touch and kiss her now as long as Briggs isn't around.

"You look like you need a beer," Ian says, and I let out a snort in response.

"I think I need more than one."

Since I probably won't be kissing Tate tonight, I don't mind drinking until I'm tipsy enough to forget I'm going to have to tell her all of our efforts to hide our relationship have been for nothing

"Oh God, he's thinking again. Quick, get him some alcohol before he hurts himself," Flynn teases, and I let out a fake laugh before walking inside the house and grabbing the six-pack I put in the fridge a couple of weeks ago.

Then, I take a deep breath and try not to smile at the fact that I'm going to kiss Tatum in the barn tomorrow or when we're training with Galaxy again or whenever I'm sure her father isn't nearby.

It's a lot easier to fool one person than five members of my family.

CHAPTER 35
Tatum

SAGE IS SPRAWLED ACROSS my bed with Loki beside her, staring at her phone as she waits for me to get out of my shower. Her blue eyes fly to me as soon as I step into the room, a bright smile crossing her face. I don't trust it at all. She looks like she knows my deepest, darkest secret, and I take slow steps toward my closet, clutching my towel to my chest as I narrow my eyes at her.

"Why are you giving me that look?" she asks, propping herself up onto her elbows before petting Loki's stomach.

He's stretched out on his back, sleeping after our hard day at work. We spent all afternoon watering the flower fields and admiring the little sprouts. One of the sunflowers has even opened already, and I almost burst into very irrational tears at the sight of them.

"Because you know something, and I'm not sure I want you to know it," I say, slipping into my closet and rummaging around until I find a pair of underwear, some sweatpants, and another one of Aaron's very old shirts. It smells like him, making me nuzzle my face into the fabric.

"Your cowboy called you twice," she replies, her voice muffled as it fills my closet space.

"Which one?" I ask, flinching a little at the joke.

"Please, the one you can't stop mentioning every chance you get. Aaron did this, Aaron did that, Aaron and I..." She trails off while I make my way back into my bedroom, my cowboy's shirt now firmly hugging my upper body and filling my nose with his warm scent.

"It's because we're working on a project together, which, by the way, is going really well. We've placed an order for pumpkins recently, so we're going to have a pumpkin patch and events like pumpkin carvings in October after the flowers have wilted," I explain, trying to distract her. Sage, being who she is, doesn't let me.

"That sounds great. I'm very excited for you," she says.

We stare at each other for a few, long, uncomfortable seconds before she finally bursts out the one question I have no idea how the fuck to answer.

"Why the hell are you hiding the fact you're screwing *the hottest* man I've ever seen?" She gestures at me like I've committed the worst crime imaginable, and I cock a brow in response. "You might be a damn good liar, Tate, but I saw the hickeys on the top of your tits the second you stepped out of your bathroom."

And those aren't even the only marks Aaron has left on me.

"Remind me again why we're friends," I say as I drop onto the bed beside her and place my face in my hands to hide the blush creeping up my neck.

"Because distance makes the heart grow fonder," she teases, and I shove her a little.

Sage was here when I arrived at Silver Creek Ranch but disappeared the day after, mumbling something about Beckett and never wanting to see him again.

Plus, she's busy being a badass professional tennis player and has won four grand slams in her ten years of playing, so she doesn't have a lot of time for me.

"I'll be around more," she promises, sensing my change in mood.

"No, you won't be. And you shouldn't be either. You're very busy living out your dream, and I couldn't be prouder of you," I say with a genuine smile.

"Give me a few more years, and I'll be too tired to keep this up. The workout schedules are a fucking *pain*," she complains with a grunt. "And don't even get me started on the coach my mother assigned me. He's such a grumpy hardass, and I already have one of those," she says with a pointed look my way.

Before she knows what's happening, I grab my pillow and hit her in the face with it.

Sage falls asleep early, but I'm wide awake.

Tomorrow is the Sunday market, and I didn't check if Liv had a chance to fix the legs of two different tables that broke last week. I didn't ask Beckett if he washed the cloth we always tie to the bamboo poles for shade over the tables. I didn't do a hundred million different things that suddenly all seem extremely important.

So, I slide out of bed as silently as I can, my footsteps light as I move over to my bedroom door. Loki follows me without my asking him to, stretching once before slipping through the cracked door.

Dad's been trying to fix the small things that are falling apart in his house with some of the money we've been making with the market, but some things would cost too much.

My feet bring me into the kitchen where my father is sitting. His reading glasses rest on his nose as he scans his laptop screen with his eyebrows scrunched together in concern.

When he hears me, he lifts his head with a soft smile.

"Honeybee? Are you okay?" he asks, sitting up and gesturing to the seat beside him.

"Yeah, couldn't sleep," I admit, Loki trailing by my side and placing his head on my lap as soon as I'm sitting. "Why are you awake?" I ask, and Dad leans back in his chair, letting out a sigh so full of frustration, it hits me straight in the chest.

"The owners of Red Sky Ranch have made the bank an offer for Silver Creek Ranch," he blurts out, no warning, no preparation. He rips off the band-aid like I have no pain receptors.

Red Sky Ranch shares fences with Silver Creek Ranch in some places of the land. Since I came here, I've seen nothing but respect between the two farms. Landon has been very nice in every single conversation we've had. Bernard and Sofia, the owners of the farm, were helping with the Halloween decorations and partaking in the Sunday market every week.

Why would they do this? Why would they put more pressure on us?

"But they said we had time. We only need another month or two before we can make the farm visitable," I argue, thinking about the flowers that are slowly starting to bloom.

"If they have to choose between waitin' for money to come in and getting it from somewhere else now, which do you think they'll choose?" Dad asks, and I sink back in my chair, trying to figure out what the hell we're going to do.

An idea explodes to life in my head a few moments later.

"You signed a contract with the bank, right? I need to see it." I need to analyze every single word on those pages, find a way out of this.

"Don't bother, Tate. There is a clause that says if I fail to pay the mortgage for three months in a row, they will be able to put the ranch up on the market. It has been more than three months. They were being lenient out of respect for me, but they're not gonna keep this up when not enough money is comin' in," Dad replies, but I slip his laptop toward me, determined to find a loophole.

This is what I studied.

This is what I'm good at.

I gave it up because my seizures were triggered by extreme stress, but that doesn't mean I wasn't as good of a lawyer as my mother. I won every single case they gave me at the firm. I won cases no one thought could be won. This may not be a case yet, but I'll win it.

My dad is *not* losing Silver Creek Ranch.

And neither is everyone who has given blood, sweat, and tears for this place.

CHAPTER 36
Aaron

TATUM HAS BEEN MORE stressed in the past few weeks than I have ever seen her before. She's constantly looking over the contract Briggs signed with the bank to try and figure out how she can stop Red Sky Ranch from buying this place and ripping it away from right under our feet. Not to mention, her mother and sister are arriving tomorrow.

In other words, I'm worried about her.

She isn't sleeping, the dark circles underneath her hazel eyes are proof of that. She isn't drinking or eating enough, she admitted that to me herself. She is all over the place, evident by the way I have to say her name multiple times sometimes to get her attention. I try my best to remind her to drink when we're together, to give her food, and urge her to eat, but I can't be with her all the time.

Even though everyone except Briggs now knows we're dating, we still have to hide our relationship most of the time. Something else that Tate barely acknowledged, further proving that she's so lost in her head trying to come up with a solution.

My worry for my woman has me messing up at work, too. Ian gives me a strange look when I put the fresh pasture in the water feeder for the horses, taking the bucket from me and slapping me upside the head.

"Fuck, what was that for?" I ask, rubbing my head and shooting him a glare.

"To wake you up. This isn't the first time you were distracted today. Earlier, I watched you put on your saddle the wrong way around," he says, and I swallow hard. "Yeah, I witnessed it happenin', along with you trying to put your foot in the stirrup and realizing something wasn't right," he adds and shakes his head. "What's wrong, Aaron?"

"I'm fine." I'm not fine. I would very much like to go kill someone at Red Sky Ranch for stressing Tate and threatening to tear apart everything we've built here.

"I can help you bury the body," Ian offers. "You get a really murderous look when you think about anyone hurtin' Tate, do you know that?"

"It's not just Tate." Although she is currently my main priority. "It's everyone at Silver Creek Ranch. Do you think they will keep us here? No, they want to expand so that Bernard's fucking son can move in here and make it his place," I blurt out, anger making heat rise up my neck and cheeks.

"I know, but I believe in Tatum. She's got this."

"It shouldn't all be on her," I point out, earning an agreeing hum from Ian.

"No, it shouldn't be, and if there was something I could do, I would."

And he means it. I know he does because Ian has always been the kindest person out of all of us. Grumpy as hell, yes, but kind even more so. His heart is so big, he not only volunteers at the homeless shelter every Saturday, but he also hasn't told anyone about it. The only reason I know is because the nurses at the nursing home talk. He doesn't like to flaunt his good deeds like most people, to get recognition for them. Quite the opposite. He hates being put in the spotlight. He's a lot quieter than Flynn, Beckett and Olivia. He's more like Hads.

It's one of the million things they have in common.

"Do you mind helping me water the flowers and organize the patch of land we're going to use once the pumpkins arrive?" I ask because this is how we help Tate. We take some of the other tasks off her shoulders.

It's three o'clock on the dot as I wait for the nurse to lead me to wherever Nanna is today. It's wonderful outside, so she's probably in the garden, but I'm not allowed to simply go inside. There are certain procedures like them writing down my name, ensuring Nanna is able to see me today, and so on.

"She's in the garden," Freddy says, and I follow the nurse outside. "She's been asking for you today," he whispers to me a second before I see Nanna, a bandage still on her head from her fall weeks ago.

The doctor said she's healing well, albeit very slowly. Her eyes light up at the sight of me, and I almost cry from relief.

"Andrew," she says, sending a slicing sort of pain through my body. Andrew was my dad's name, her only child's name. I know I look a lot like him, but it was never enough for her to mistake me for my father.

"Hey, Mum."

"Come, my love. I've made tea," she says. I move without thinking, trying to get close to her while fighting back the pain and grief hitting me.

"What kind of tea is it?" I ask as I settle down in the chair beside hers.

She places her hands on my cheeks and kisses my left one, wiping it away a second later.

"Vanilla rooibos, your favorite," she says as she pours me a cup of my dad's favorite tea.

"So, tell me. What's new at work?" she asks, but I'm so unsure in which year her mind is stuck in, I simply smile.

"Nothing new," I assure her before sipping the tea, which I absolutely hate.

"No? Not even with that girl you're secretly dating?" *Secretly dating?*

"I'm not sure I know what—" She cuts me off before I can finish the sentence, her blue eyes rolling as she grins at me.

"You know who I'm talking about. Hannah, the short woman with black hair and blue eyes," she goes on, making my heart sink even further. *Mum...* "I know you're not allowed to be dating because of your workplace rules, but I think it's a shame you have to hide it."

How had she never told me this story before? My parents were hiding their relationship in order not to get fired from their jobs? I've never wanted to talk to them more, never felt closer to them.

"Well, it's dangerous. If they find out, I could lose my job," I say. "I have responsibilities. I have to take care of you, myself, my future," I blurt out, enjoying the way I get to lay all of my feelings out in front of me and knowing she won't give me the answer of a stranger. She'll give me the answer of a mother loving her son.

"Argh, who cares about one stupid job, Andrew? You can find another, which I suggest doing first before you decide you're ready to tell everyone you're dating." She gives me a small chuckle, but a cough follows it. I hand her her tea, and she takes a few sips.

"But my whole life is my job. How do I give that up?" I ask once I'm sure she's okay.

"Whatever you've built there can be built again. You've called Hannah the love of your life, and if that is truly how you feel, you shouldn't be hiding your love. No one wants to be kept a secret, especially not because of a job." Nanna leans back in her chair, her hands on her stomach as she looks at me.

For the first time today, I see what her illness is doing to her. She's lost so much weight. She looks tired like she hasn't slept in years. Her eyes are the ones I grew up staring into, but they're also not. Lorena Blaze is slipping further and further away from the world, and I realize she must be having a good day. A rare day. A day when she speaks and isn't lost in her head.

They tell me these stories, these realities I've been denying because I never see her like that. They don't let me come in when she isn't having a good day, and I know why. Nanna made them swear they wouldn't when she first got here.

Tears sting my eyes, but I blink them away.

"If she's your future, then she needs to be your present, too. You can't wait too long or else she'll slip right through your fingers," Nanna adds, breathing a little more heavily now than she was before.

"Do you want to lie down?" I ask, touching her arm gently. Nanna places her hand over mine as her eyes close. She sways in her seat a little before reopening them and staring at me. Uncertainty lingers in her gaze as she stares me straight in the eyes.

"Andrew? What are you doing here?"

Shit.

"I came to have tea with you," I say, but she shakes her head, something not making sense to her. "I think you made the tea a bit too strong," I add because it's one of the things Nanna used to tell me Dad said, and it made her want to smack the back of his head.

"I did not. I've been making tea longer than you've been alive, child," she says and lets out a huff while a breath of relief whooshes out of me.

I don't say anything as her eyes shift to the wildflowers they have in a dozen pots in the garden. I merely watch her, take her in as she admires the nature around her. Silence fills the space between us, but I enjoy it.

The limbo my head's in never eases. It's still a whirlwind of grief and relief that she's still here, denial and acceptance. Strange combinations that make me lightheaded when I try to address them, so I leave them be where they take up space inside of me.

"I used to have a husband." Her eyes are on me, but the familiarity has disappeared completely as she looks at me. "He died." Tears fill her eyes, forcing some back into mine.

"I'm sorry," I say, and she brings a smile to her face, so tired and exhausted.

"Don't be. I'm going to see him soon."

Her head tilts back to the flowers, but she doesn't hear me as I stand up, doesn't look over her shoulder to watch me leave, even as I offer her a sad, quiet goodbye.

"To Pluto and back," is the last thing I say before turning to walk away.

I want to hug her, but the woman sitting in front of me no longer recognizes me. And I doubt she ever will again.

CHAPTER 37
Tatum

AARON WAS VERY VAGUE about what he wants to do tonight. He said something about me dressing up the way I would if I was going out, but that was it. Olivia, Hads, and Beckett all give me their input on what I should wear even though I didn't ask any of them to help me with the outfit. However, since they found out Aaron and I are dating, they've been nothing but supportive about helping us sneak around to the best of their abilities.

"No, not the blue one. Wear the green," Beckett chimes in. "Aaron loves it when you wear green."

Bailey drags the green dress out of my closet before running over to her dad and handing it to him. He grins down at his daughter, the love and adoration he holds for her clear on his face.

"Not for me, peanut. For Tate," he says and points at me.

The little girl runs my way and places the dress in my arms so carefully, I realize she's scared of breaking it. Then, she runs back to Beckett, who pulls her against his chest.

Bailey looks absolutely tiny in her father's huge arms, especially when he places his chin on her head, crouching down in order to do so. It's like a brown bear hugging a squirrel.

"Why are you all here again?" I ask, crossing my arms in front of my chest.

"Because we told Old Man Briggs that we're takin' you out because you've been so stressed," Hads explains with a soft smile, her brown eyes sparkling with mischief.

"And in order not to suspect we're lyin', we are all sacrificing our evening to go to Boots & Beers," Liv chimes in, shooting Beckett a grin that he returns.

"Oh, thank you. I'm so grateful you lot are spending your Friday night doing something as unthinkable as going to the very same bar you spend every Friday night at," I say, and they all start laughing.

"Hurry up, would you? Aaron told us to have you ready by five, and I ain't getting yelled at because you're takin' forever," Beckett says, bouncing Bailey up and down on his thigh.

After I've slipped on the green summer dress that hugs all of my curves in a way I know will have Aaron on his knees, Hads shoves me down on a stool she got from downstairs and starts playing with my curls, straightening them out for the first time in... well, ever.

It frames my face differently than my curls, but it also makes me look fierce like I could take on the whole world. It's a nice contrast to how I'm feeling.

I'm lost. I've tried finding a loophole and went to speak to the bank to get them to give Dad more time, but they told me that if we can't manage to scrape the money together by the end of the month, they will be selling the property to Bernard and Sofia.

We're silent for a few moments while Hads finishes my makeup, grabbing a highlighter and a brush. She admires her work but frowns at something she sees in my eyes.

"You need to sleep more, Tatum. Your eyes are too red and you look like you're about to fall out of your chair," Hads says before handing me a glass of water and telling me to drink.

I have a feeling Aaron told all of them to remind me to drink and eat because they've been doting on me all day. But I'm too distracted by the fact that her concern is rooted not in the fear of me having a seizure while I'm with her, but merely a friend's concern. I know because apart from Aaron and Liv, I haven't told anyone about my epilepsy.

And, for the first time in my life, I feel like sharing it with everyone I see every day because of how safe and comfortable I feel with them.

"As soon as I find a solution, I'll sleep more," I promise her.

She applies the highlighter to my nose and cheekbones, then a little on my forehead, before spraying my face with the setting spray.

"Perfect," she mumbles as she steps out of the way and lets me admire her work.

It's a simple makeup look, but she's right. It's absolutely perfect. She's somehow managed to highlight all of my best features. My eyes shine brightly because of the brown and green she painted my eyelids with, and my lips are a dark nude shade.

"You're a magician," I say, and Hads lets out an excited giggle.

"Stop it. You're gonna make me blush," she says and waves away my comment.

Aaron looks mouthwatering.

He's wearing dark blue jeans that hug his ass so perfectly, I stare at it for a few moments too long. He's wearing a green button-up with the top three buttons undone, leaving a patch of his perfect, tan skin on display. A dark brown cowboy hat rests on his head, but his black locks come out underneath, framing his face. His blue eyes are even more so in the light of the afternoon sun. The whole outfit comes together with boots the same color as his hat and a buckle on his belt that I can't help but visualize pulling to bring his groin flat against my stomach.

I wish there were words for the way his eyes light up, soften, and turn molten with desire when he sees me. Like he couldn't be happier I was here. Like he can't believe I'm his and he's mine. Like he wants to rip this green, velvet summer dress right off my body.

His eyes trail from the top of my head, where the cowboy hat he got me rests, all the way to my feet, where I'm wearing the boots he bought me on our road trip, in a slow, thorough movement that has my toes curling and my knees a little weak. He stops for several seconds at my breasts, stomach, and thighs, his desire only burning brighter as he drinks in parts of me I used to be self-conscious about. Not anymore. Not for a long time.

"You are the most exquisite woman I've ever laid eyes on," Aaron says as Loki and I approach him. A blush creeps onto my cheeks, but I find myself smiling.

"Thank you," I reply and stop in front of him, careful not to get too close.

We're standing in front of his truck beside his little house, which means we're still running the risk of Dad being able to see us. Aaron doesn't seem to care as he slides his arm around me and drags me against his chest, his other hand lifting to my throat and gently pulling my mouth to his. His kiss moves from sweet and tender to hungry and demanding. His tongue slips into my mouth, long enough to make my body ache to receive the same attention.

"Why did you just do that? We could be seen out here," I remind him when he pulls back, but he merely kisses me once, twice, three more times.

"Because not kissing you before our date would have been a crime," he says before opening the truck door for me.

Aaron holds out one of his big hands to help me up, and I take it with a smile. Loki follows me inside, wearing his service dog harness as Olivia told me to put on him.

Whatever it is we're doing tonight, Loki is going to be working.

Once Aaron's settled in the driver's seat, I lean over the console to press one more kiss to his lips, already missing the taste of him.

"You look incredible," I say, running one of my hands down his chest and placing it on the belt buckle I was eyeing earlier. "Downright sinful," I add as I attempt to lower my hand even further. Aaron grips my wrist, and I enjoy the way his jeans get tighter in the front at the possibility of me touching him.

"We have places to be, sweetheart, and no time for me to bend you over and fuck you in the backseat," he says, his voice low. I raise a brow, readjusting his hold on me until I'm the one guiding his hand where I want it to go, which is between my legs.

"You can drive and make me come, can't you?" I challenge, watching a smirk take over his face as he runs his thumb along the inside of my thigh. He goes higher and higher until his fingers reach my bare pussy.

"No panties, Tate?" he asks while I gasp from pleasure as his thumb rubs over my clit.

"Nope. Wanted to drive you wild," I manage to croak out before he slips two fingers deep inside of me.

"This is heaven, Tate," he says, shifting his car into reverse and turning the wheel one-handed. Meanwhile, his fingers continue to plunge inside of me, curling at the perfect spot and then rubbing over my clit.

"Fuck," I moan, my hands reaching for the door to hold onto it.

"Such a filthy girl, walking around without panties. Do you know how hard that makes me, baby? How badly I want to drag you onto my lap and shove my cock deep inside of you?" I cry out his name as his fingers play with my G-spot. "So fucking badly, Tate, it's all I can think about."

"We have time. Just a few minutes," I say, practically begging.

"But you have to be fast. Can you be fast?" he asks, and I give him several eager nods before he pulls off to the side of the road and keeps going until we're stopped underneath a tree. This is so reckless. Anyone who drives by could see us, but I don't care.

Reckless is exactly what Aaron and I are.

"Come on then, gorgeous. Use my cock to make yourself come," he says, making me unbuckle my seatbelt as he brings his seat as far back as possible.

I crawl over to him, straddling his lap and fumbling with the belt buckle. As soon as it's out of the way, along with his pants and boxers, I take his hard dick into my hands and give it a rough jerk that has his head falling back in a moan.

"Fucking hell, Tate," he curses.

I guide his cock against my pussy, anticipation storming through me as I roll my hips. His cock glides over my arousal, coating him in it. I rub the head of him over my clit, biting on my bottom lip as pleasure consumes me. Aaron's hands lift to my breasts, tugging down my dress until they bounce free. The head of his cock slips into my pussy, and I tense around the feel of him, so thick and hard.

"So, so breathtaking," he mumbles as he leans forward and sucks my left nipple into his mouth. He hisses out a breath as I take him all the way inside of me without warning, his teeth nipping at my nipple and making me shudder. "You hug my cock so well, sweetheart." The praise has another wave of pleasure rippling through me without warning.

Aaron's mouth moves to my other nipple while I push myself up and then slam back down on his cock, forcing moans out of both of us. I go faster and faster as desperation takes hold of me, and he guides my face down, tilting it to the side and pushing my cowboy hat up enough so our lips can meet.

His tongue slips into my mouth in a steady rhythm with his cock slipping in and out of me. His hands are now firmly placed on my ass, squeezing and spreading me wider before he thrusts up, meeting my movements.

"Fuck, fuck, fuck," I cry out, my own hands dropping to his chest for leverage.

I go even faster, fucking him even harder as my orgasm builds inside of me. My hips roll, my clit rubbing against his pelvis until I'm moaning and begging for him to make me come.

Aaron doesn't waste a second, doesn't make me wait. He merely shifts his thumb to my clit, rubbing as he urges me to sit up a little, and then thrusts inside of me several times. So deep and hard, my orgasm explodes through me. My body shudders through the sensation while Aaron's cock throbs and pulses inside of me, his own orgasm hitting him hard.

My forehead drops to his shoulder while I try to slow my breathing, my mind still in a haze as he kisses my temple. A smile takes over my whole face, satisfaction consuming me as I pull back and bring my mouth back to his.

CHAPTER 38
Aaron

I ADORE THE POST-ORGASM glow Tate always gets after we have sex. She smiles a little brighter and her eyes sparkle a little more. It feels like every single time I call her beautiful, it doesn't do her any justice because when I look at her, watch the various colors in her eyes fight for dominance in the afternoon sunlight, the meaning of the word gets rewritten entirely.

I smudged her lipstick with my rough kisses, so she leans forward now, studying herself in the small mirror of the sun visor as she reapplies it. She purses her lips, and I do my best to refocus on the road ahead of us.

Tate turns to me abruptly, lipstick still raised as she eyes my neck.

"Are we going somewhere people will know us?" she asks right as I pull the truck onto the highway.

"We're going into the city, so unless you think there will be anyone that recognizes you with your cowboy hat and boots on, we should be fine," I say with a small smirk.

Before I know what has hit me, she places her right hand on my throat, tilting my head to the side enough to place a kiss on my neck. Then, she pulls away and goes back to fixing her makeup. I raise my head to see my reflection in the rear-view mirror. A chuckle vibrates off my chest a moment later.

"Did you mark me?" Tate grins as she runs the lipstick over her bottom lip.

"Yep. You got a problem with that?" she challenges with a raised brow.

"Not even a little bit, sweetheart. You can mark me as much as you want. I belong to you." This answer seems to satisfy her even more because a blush creeps back onto her cheeks, painting her light skin a wonderful shade of pink.

"I can do whatever I want with you?" Tate asks as she leans back in her seat and drops the lipstick in her purse.

"Whatever you want."

"Careful, cowboy, you said we had places to be," she warns, leaning her head against the headrest to watch me.

"We do, sweetheart, but I also don't think I could deny you anything you asked for," I admit, forcing my eyes to stay on the road as I let my words process.

It's as close to a confession of love I've ever come. Despite being in my thirties, I've never fallen in love before. Not because I didn't want to, simply because I'd never met someone I envisioned myself falling for. I would think something was wrong with me since people always told me to fall in love as much as possible if it wasn't for the woman sitting right beside me. It feels like she shoved me off the damn love cliff without a single moment of hesitation, without it even being intentional. And while it wasn't on purpose, it's a million percent her fault for being exactly who she is.

Maybe I wasn't meant to fall in love more than once. Maybe I was meant to wait those thirty-one years for this woman that I can't get enough of. Because I'm falling and I'm falling so hard that I'm catching fire on the descent down.

I wonder if she's falling with me.

I fucking hope she is.

My hand slips onto her leg while I think about my feelings, my fingers digging into her thigh. She doesn't waste a second, slipping her hand over mine and lacing her fingers through mine. The wave of comfort a single touch of hers gives me is astonishing.

Even knowing she might leave me, run away because she's scared, I've never felt safer with another person.

Call me romantic or cheesy, I don't care. I cover Tate's eyes as we walk up to the sign in front of the concert venue where her favorite band's name is printed across it. *From Angels to Devils* is playing tonight, and I've been working on getting her tickets and arranging everything for tonight since she told me she couldn't go.

I lift my hands off her eyes, watching her blink several times to adjust to the light. Her gaze finds me first as she furrows her brows in confusion, but then it shifts to the sign, her jaw dropping as she takes in where we are.

"Aaron," she says, and I watch sadness take over her face before I've even had a chance to explain.

"I contacted the venue who contacted the band's management. They asked if there would be any flashing lights and assured me this show would not have any. I know you're also worried about feeling claustrophobic, so I asked them if we could stand in front of the gates separating the crowd from the stage, and they assured me we could. They were very forthcoming about the whole process."

Which is, of course, the bare fucking minimum because our society is made for able-bodied people and those who do not suffer from chronic illnesses.

"You've thought of everything, haven't you?" she asks, staring at the sign. "Even telling me to take Loki."

She pets her dog once, grabbing his leash tighter as she tries to take hold of her emotions and blinks away tears. My lips find the top of her head as I pull her to me.

"Please tell me I didn't do something wrong," I beg.

"You did something very, very thoughtful, Aaron. The most thoughtful gesture anyone has ever done, and I really don't know how to deal with that," she says with a small laugh that turns into a sob. "Fuck, no one's ever done anything even remotely close to this."

"It's about time you get used to me doing these sorts of things, Tate. Your happiness is my top priority," I say and kiss her. She melts against me, but we're ripped apart by screaming fans making their way past us.

"I guess that means we should get going," she tells me and squeezes my arm once. Then, her attention drifts to Loki, who is sitting by her side and looking up at her like the good boy he is.

We are let in through a separate door after I show them the pass the venue gave me. Tate takes everything in with a smile as we're allowed to go to the merch line first while none of the other guests are there yet. They haven't opened the gates, which means that besides the workers who are running around to get everything ready, it's only us.

We stroll over to the merchandise, Tate nuzzling herself against my side while I fling an arm around her waist and drag her closer. She studies the pieces of clothing, caps, and tote bags for a few minutes while I simply enjoy the way I get to touch her in public. I enjoy it so much, I'm grinning the entire time like I've been told I could take in all the stray dogs in the world and give them a better home. My hand flies to the necklace of the horse I got her, a small sign of my devotion that is always around her neck.

"Anything you want, I'll buy for you," I say. Before she can protest, I add, "I invited you on this date, so I get to buy you something."

She narrows her eyes at my logic but doesn't argue with me. She merely smiles, presses a kiss to my cheek, and thanks me several times. Tate chooses the band's t-shirt with their symbol—devil's horns with a halo on top of them—drawn on the left chest area and their name scribbled across the back. I also get her the tote bag and cap, making her bury her face in my side again to hide her happy smile.

"You're spoiling me, cowboy," she says as we make our way to the stage, showing our badges to the security people, who lead us to where we will be standing for the duration of the show.

"Not done yet, sweetheart, but the rest of the spoiling I'll do later when we're alone."

She gives me a wicked grin, pressing her ass against me and tilting her head back against my shoulder. Her neck is perfectly exposed to me, and I wish I could lean down and suck on her sensitive skin until a hickey blooms there. Mark her like she's marked me tonight.

I slip my arms around her instead. They rest right under her breasts because she's quite a bit shorter than me, but it also allows me to place my chin on the crown of her head while we wait for the rest of the people to fill the general admission and seating areas.

A few moments before the opening act comes on stage, I slip the noise-canceling dog headphones I brought Loki over his head, earning another look of complete adoration from Tate.

I'll never tire of the way this woman looks at me.

The opening act is phenomenal, but *From Angels to Devils* is even better. The group of four guys don't play the music I usually listen to, but I find myself mouthing along to the words of the songs I listened to while preparing for tonight. Tatum is jumping and dancing the entire time and when a slower, more emotional song starts streaming through the speakers, I catch a tear rolling down her cheek. I wipe it away, hugging her close to my chest once more as we sway to the music together.

"*'None of my demons and none of my faults,*" one of the guys, I believe his name is Harvey, sings. "'*Hold me back from making mine hers,*

Let me share my wildest dreams,

So they become something she feels,

Nothing I see is better than her. '"

The song comes to an end and Tate spins around to kiss me. It's the kind of kiss two people share that says more than any words ever could. It's almost like I can taste her feelings. She's grateful I brought her here. She's happy that she's been given the chance to see her favorite band live for the first time in her life.

And she loves me.

She hasn't said it, hasn't even used words that hinted at it, but this kiss? It holds a promise. I know she never thought she could give anyone a future with her, but she's giving me hers. She's giving me the one thing she's been too scared to ever let herself believe she could have, and I kiss her back as fiercely, promising her that my future is hers. Tate can have all of it. Every piece of me, past, present, and future.

Despite breaking the kiss, she doesn't move away from me again. She merely sings along to the words and sways her hips in my arms as they play their usual pop-rock songs again. Loki continues to sit beside Tate, looking a little more than adorable with the headband-looking headphones to cover his ears.

The rest of the concert passes in a blur, and we get to leave through a back exit that a security person shows us to avoid Tate feeling claustrophobic in the giant wave of people making their way outside.

By the time we reach the car, she's yawning and smiling and telling me every little thing she adored, like Harvey and Will, the lead singer, harmonizing at the end of her favorite song or Harvey and Oliver having a battle between drums and bass.

The way her face lights up is worth every second I put into making this evening a reality.

We drive in silence for a while, listening to my country music playlist. Restless Road fills the car while she sings along to her favorite song of theirs, 'Go Get Her.' Her voice is still as angelic to me now as it was when I first heard it, and I'm convinced I could listen to this woman sing for the rest of my life and die a happy man.

"Okay, next time we have to do something you've always wanted to do. I told you about wanting to go to the concert, so it's only fair you tell me what you'd like to do and I'll arrange it," she says, clapping her hands together in determination.

My eyes drift from the road and to her briefly enough to see the same determination in her eyes.

"I've always wanted to go skydiving," I lie, watching the color drain from her face.

"Okay," she says a little breathlessly, and I burst into laughter.

"I'm kidding," I add, and she attempts to fight back her grin as she shoves my shoulder.

"Be serious, Aaron. I want to take you somewhere you've always wanted to go," she says, her voice so serious, my eyes slip to hers to see the pout on her lips.

"Fine, let me think," I offer as I place my hand back on her thigh.

She takes it in both of hers, lifting it to her mouth to place several kisses on the back of it before hugging it to her chest. My heart stutters and warms. It's that little display of affection that makes me realize exactly what I've always wanted but haven't let myself think about doing, especially not with someone else.

"I want us to go to Australia, to Brisbane where I grew up," I admit out loud.

"Let's go when winter hits here, then it'll be nice and warm in Australia," she replies without hesitation.

We stop at a red light, and I look over to see if she really means it, that she's planning so far ahead already, but Tate was waiting for me to search her face, already having tilted it my way so I could inspect it. There is no deceit there. She means it.

And I'm about to mean every single word I say.

"Tate, I—"

I'm cut off by the sound of sirens approaching behind us. I react fast, pulling to the side of the road so they can roar past us. Panic grabs a hold of me as I watch three more firetrucks rush past us, turning the corner toward Silver Creek Ranch.

"Fuck," I curse before stepping on the gas and following them.

"Aaron," Tate says, her hand flying to her mouth. "My dad. Bailey! They're at the house."

"I know. Hold on," I say, increasing the speed even more as we chase behind the firetrucks and toward the ranch.

It's dark outside because it's one in the morning, allowing us to see the flames long before we're even close to the farm. Smoke fills the sky, making my stomach turn.

Not again.

Please, not again.

We don't get a second to be glad the main house isn't burning when we catch sight of what *is* on fire. It's not the barn or any of our houses, thank God, but it's not great either. Goddammit, it's not good on any level.

The field of flowers Tate and I were working on is up in flames, fire consuming every single sprout and flower there. The sunflowers, the ones that were starting to show already, looking for the sun to help them grow, are gone. The lavender patch is on fire, too. There is nothing left, nothing at all of the one thing that might have saved this ranch from being torn away from us.

I park the truck far enough away, but Tate jumps out a second later, running toward where the firefighters are. Too lost in my thoughts, I realize it way too fucking late, but I still run after her, catching her before she gets too close. My arms wrap around her, catching her mid-run and pulling her straight back against my chest.

"Nooo!" she cries, sobbing so hard that tears jump into my eyes, too.

Tate sinks to her knees, and I follow, holding her through her sobs before we both sink backward even further. My legs are on either side of her while she cries and cries and cries. And, fuck, I'm crying, too. I'm crying as I watch our last hope go up in flames, watch her dream burn to nothing but ash right in front of us without being able to do anything about it.

CHAPTER 39
Tatum

I CAN'T MOVE, NOT even when I see Dad approaching us. It should worry me that he'll see me in Aaron's arms or my lipstick stain still stuck to Aaron's neck, but none of it matters. I can't even manage to stop crying. How the fuck would I get out of Aaron's arms right now? He's the only thing tethering me to reality, my rock as my project to keep this ranch from being sold is ripped away from underneath my feet.

Aaron's arms are bands of steel around me, holding me against him steadily. It's more of a comfort than anything else would be in this situation, but it doesn't slow my tears either. I've never experienced this much heartbreak all at once.

It's unbearable.

Dad squats down in front of me, his hands grabbing my knees to get my attention. My sobs have slowed enough so that I can hear him, but I'm still crying violently at the sight in front of us.

"Honeybee, please, take a deep breath. Everything will be okay," he promises, but I don't see how anything could ever be okay for us at Silver Creek Ranch. And I can't shake the feeling that this is my fault. That my ambition had whoever burned his crops setting fire to our field of flowers.

"I'm so sorry," I cry, feeling Aaron's arms tighten around me.

"This isn't your fault, sweetheart," my cowboy promises as he presses his face to the side of my head, clearly not caring about Dad being here either.

"He's right. This isn't on you. Now, breathe. I need you to calm down, honeybee. Get your blood pressure down, alright?" Dad says, and I do as I'm told when I hear the panic in his voice.

He's not worried about the flames destroying another patch of his land. He's worried about me having a seizure because of all of this. The thought is like getting an ice bucket poured over my head. My tears slow more and more with each second I stare into Dad's concerned eyes, with every stroke of Aaron's hands over my arms.

"Sir, could we have a word?" the chief firefighter asks, and Dad gives my cheek one comforting touch before standing up and walking toward the muscular man covered in tattoos.

"FUCK!" someone booms.

I turn my head in time to see Beckett kick the tire of his truck while Olivia and Hadley cover their mouths in utter horror. Ian's hand slips onto Hads shoulder in comfort and she bursts into tears, burying her face in his chest. Even Liv and Flynn exchange a look full of pain instead of disgust for once.

Beckett walks over to where Aaron and I are, but his eyes are glued to the fire as he drops to his knees, removing his cowboy hat and holding it to his chest. His hand lifts to Aaron's shoulder, but his gaze doesn't move to us until a minute later.

"Fuck," he repeats and shakes his head. "I'm so sorry."

"This is not the work of some teenagers. This is something much bigger than a disgusting prank," Ian says, cradling the back of Hadley's head as she sobs into his chest.

None of us is handling this situation well, watching a part of the place we love so much burn.

"I'm gonna kill whoever did this. Then, I'm gonna bury them right under those ashes," Olivia says from behind us, and I can't help but let out a sad laugh at that.

"I'll fuckin' help," Flynn says, and I notice he's inched a bit closer to her.

"If we knew who did this, we could tell Owen instead of killin' the person," Beckett reminds the two menaces behind him, but they merely shrug.

"Where's the fun in that?" Liv asks, crossing her arms in front of her chest and glaring at the flames.

"Where's Bailey?" I ask Beckett.

"Briggs called Linda. She's with her right now, but Bailey hasn't woken up from what I know so she's not witnessin' any of this," he replies, and I nod along to his words.

"That's good. She shouldn't see this," Aaron agrees.

Beckett stares at my cowboy for a moment, a small smile tugging at his lips.

"Are you aware you have Tate's lipstick stain on your neck or did you draw it on yourself?" he asks, and I point at the flames.

"Everything's going to shit, and *that*'s what you focus on?" I ask, but he simply laughs.

"Humor is my defense mechanism," he adds but I can tell he's in as much pain and anger and disappointment as the rest of us.

"Okay, I'm gonna ask the question no one here wants to ask. What the hell are we going to do now?"

Aaron and I exchange a look before I turn to Liv and say, "We have no idea."

Because of what happened, Mom decided to cancel her trip to Silver Creek Ranch, but Remi dropped everything to get here. She landed this morning, hugging me close to her chest and telling me how sorry she is about what happened. It doesn't help, but it's still nice to have her comfort.

"Do you think this is a good way to spend our time?" Remi says as we walk through the ashes of the flower field.

It's only been fifteen hours since everything happened, but the earth has already cooled as if nothing happened at all.

Aaron, Beckett, Flynn, Hads, Liv, and I already shoveled away some of the ashes to prevent them from flying into the creek and contaminating the water with it, but there is too much of it. We couldn't get it all.

"What are you looking for anyway?" Remi asks when I don't respond.

I watch Owen Grim's Dodge pull up next to my red Chevy truck, stepping out of it a moment later. "Holy hotness, who the hell is that?"

"Owen Grim, chief of police," I reply, ignoring the way she eyes my cowboy's old friend.

Owen is gorgeous. He has a warm brown skin tone, brown eyes and hair, sharp facial features, and a body to die for. The uniform hugs his slender waist and broad shoulders, but as much as I try to see what she sees, I haven't been able to truly admire anyone since my eyes found Aaron.

Loki nudges my leg as I walk further through the burned field, but I don't get far before the chief's voice fills my ears.

"Afternoon, ladies," he says, and my sister turns on her charm as she smirks at the police officer.

"Howdy, chief. To what do we owe this pleasure?" she asks, and I cock a brow at her in silent question as to what the hell she thinks she's doing. Owen gives Remi an unsure smile.

"You're standin' on it, darlin'. I'm here to figure out who the hell keeps settin' Silver Creek Ranch on fire," he explains as he walks toward me.

My sister is five foot ten with a curvy figure—close to mine, which is the only similarity we share—light skin, blonde hair, and blue eyes.

"How are you doin'?" Owen asks, looking down at my hand where I've been clutching a burned wildflower since I found it.

"That's a rather ridiculous question, don't you think, chief?" I ask, but I bring a small smile to my lips.

"Yeah, guess you're right. Pardon me," he says and places his hand on his chest before clearing his throat. "Have you found anythin' that shouldn't be here?" he asks, clearly sensing what it is I'm trying to do out here.

"Except for the stench of gasoline, no. Not yet."

But I haven't given up hope either. There must be something, anything that will give us a lead on who did this. We have to. Dad couldn't afford insurance after last time and even then they barely covered any of the damages, let alone the lasting ones. My head may hurt more than it ever has before because I barely slept last night, but nothing will stop me from figuring this out.

I have to.

"Alright, let's get to work then," Owen says, rolling up his sleeves and almost making Remi drool with his strong, veiny, muscular forearms. I roll my eyes at my sister as she starts flirting with the cop while I continue my search.

Sadness lingers in my chest as I stare down at the remnants of the sunflowers, wondering how anyone could be so cruel as to destroy a fucking field of flowers.

A light reflects off a shiny surface, temporarily blinding my left eye. It's gone as soon as it appears while I take a step forward. So, I take a step back again, searching for whatever it was. My eyes land on something silver.

It's a lighter.

And it looks damn familiar, too.

I pull out a tissue and pick up the lighter, eyeing it until I realize exactly where I've seen it before.

Until I remember who was holding it.

Before I have the chance to tell Owen and Remi what I've found, Loki starts poking my leg, two times in a row.

Fuck, not now!

But I don't have a choice in the matter.

I never do.

Loki leads me away from the ashes and I sink to the ground. My sense of touch becomes distorted and strange. My senses of smell and taste even more so. My left leg twitches as my focal-aware seizure takes hold of me.

Remi runs my way as fear consumes me, just like it always does. It doesn't matter if I've had seizures for as long as I can remember. They will never not set off a chain reaction of panic that turns into fear and then acceptance inside of me.

I haven't been eating or sleeping well. I should have known this was bound to catch up with me. Whenever I forget to take care of my body, when I get so stressed, it happens. It's the reason I quit my job and came to live here.

In these moments, right before my tonic-clonic seizure, I always scold myself for taking on so much without asking for help. I scold myself for being so careless with my health when I know it never ends well.

But this time, I also hear Dad's voice.

"If it gets too stressful, if you have a seizure because of this, you're off the project immediately. Deal?"

I promised him I'd be off the project. This seizure means he'll shut me out, he won't let me help anymore, even though I just found the key that could potentially solve everything. But there is nothing I can do now except lie on my side while Loki places himself right in front of me, always there when I need him most.

The last thing I think about before my body and mind shut down is how desperately I wish Aaron was here, and that scares me even more than my seizure does because I never want people to witness me like this.

CHAPTER 40

Aaron

BECKETT, OLIVIA, HADS, AND I spent the entire day in Orchard Hill, asking around if anyone saw anything last night, but they were as clueless as we were. Landon helped us too, walking into every single store on his list to see if he could find something suspicious, but we all came up with nothing. It was a frustrating process, especially because I know Tate is probably looking through the ashes right now, trying to find her own clues there.

I'm on my way to her when my phone suddenly rings, forcing my attention from the road ahead of me and down to check the caller ID. Briggs' name flashes on my screen, and I furrow my brows as I hit Answer.

"Yeah?" I say, leaning back in my seat and driving toward the main house.

The gravel groans underneath the weight of my truck, which is the only sound I hear for a long moment. Worry grabs my chest in a tight hold.

"Briggs, what's wrong?" Something deep inside of me knows what happened long before he finally manages to croak out the words.

"Tate had a seizure. She's alright now, restin' to ease the aftereffects, but I figured you'd wanna know," he says, the concern in his voice as clear as the fucking sky is right now.

He was damn right about me wanting to know.

"I'm on my way." I hang up before he can say another word, picking up speed.

Tate would be so pissed at me for being worried. She's had epilepsy most of her life. I can hear her voice so clearly, but it doesn't stop me from running up the front steps of the main house's porch and knocking aggressively on the front door. I need to see her, then I'll be fine. All I need is to see for myself that she's breathing and okay.

Briggs opens the door twenty torturous seconds later. I don't bother waiting for him to invite me in, I simply storm past him and toward the stairs.

He grabs my bicep and pulls me back. I'm startled by him getting physical instead of using words to stop me.

"What the hell, Briggs?" I ask, ripping my arm free and scowling at him. Yeah, for the first time in almost a decade, I'm scowling at the only parental figure who remembers me, but I don't give a fuck. He's keeping me from Tate, and right now, getting to her is all that matters.

"Are you and Tate secretly datin' or not? And don't even think about lyin' to me right now, son," he warns, placing his hand on my chest to stop me from reaching the stairs again.

"Get out of the way, Briggs. I might respect you, but if you don't let me go and see for myself that Tate's okay, I won't hesitate to move you out of the way."

There is so much anger built up inside of me because of this man. For the ultimatum. For trying to keep me from my sweetheart. For trying to keep us apart for good.

I have no more patience.

"I guess there's my answer." I move past him again, this time successfully.

"You can fire me later. Right now, I need a hug from my woman."

My feet bring me up the stairs faster than I thought possible as I take three at a time, desperation driving my movements. I throw her door open, trying to be gentle even as my heart races in my chest. When I find her bed empty, more irritation claws at me.

I make my way back downstairs, finding Briggs on his living room couch with a beer in his hand. I don't point out that it's barely lunchtime. He seems to need the drink.

"Where is she?" Briggs' gaze shoots to my face, and if I didn't know better, I'd think there was amusement sparkling in his eyes.

"Restin'," is his only reply before he takes a sip of his beer. I rub my temples with my index finger to get rid of the painful headache he's giving me.

"She's not in her bed." My hands slip onto my hips as I wait for him to give me something other than that strange expression.

"Sit, Aaron. Let's have a quick chat, and then I'll tell you where my daughter is. It'll be a much faster process than you storming out of here and runnin' around aimlessly," he points out.

"I already said I didn't care if you fired me. That means you and your goddamn ultimatum hold no power over me," I say, dropping into the armchair that's situated right in front of him.

"Humor me." I barely stop myself from rolling my eyes.

"Fine, ask your questions." If he wants information, I'll tell him whatever he wants to know if it means he'll tell me where Tate is.

"What is it that you want with her?" he asks, sipping his beer again and looking more stoic than ever before.

"Everything." Briggs' brows shoot up in response. "I want it all with her. I want a future with Tate, to grow old with her, to have a furry family with her, unless she wants to adopt a kid, then I'm on board with that, too. I want to move in with her, let her decorate our space however she wants to. I want to watch her fall asleep and then watch her eyes flutter as she wakes every morning. When we're both ready, I want her to be my wife and I want to be her husband. I want it all because I'm in love with her."

Briggs doesn't move a single inch.

"I love her so much, Briggs, that I don't care if you fire me. I'll figure out another way, I'll visit the animals I can't take with me. I'll find a new house and a new job. I just can't keep this a secret anymore, not when I want everyone to know." I stand up, too worked up to keep sitting.

This is the first time I've admitted out loud how in love I am, and I wish it wasn't to the man who's looking at me like he doesn't know me at all.

"I didn't want Tate or you to get hurt," is the first thing he finally says. "I thought this would spare your hearts, but, in reality, it did the opposite. I'm sorry. I shouldn't have threatened to fire you because I don't want to do that. You're family, Aaron," he adds, and I find myself getting hit by a wave of emotions so strong, it knocks the breath out of me for a moment. "I didn't want either of you heartbroken, but maybe neither of you will be. Maybe this will be exactly what both of you have always needed. A person to complete you."

"That's exactly who she is for me," I reply, staring Briggs dead in the eye to make sure he knows I'm serious.

"I can see that now, Aaron. Wish I would have seen it long before, too," he adds and rubs the back of his neck. "Not to mention, we're about to lose the farm, so I won't have to fire you. I won't be your employer anymore."

"We're going to find who did this," I assure him, but he waves me off.

He studies me for a moment, then shakes his head.

"Fuck am I glad it was you and not Beckett, Flynn, or Olivia," he says with a dry laugh, and I manage to crack a smile, too.

"As happy as I am that we're all good now, I'm going to need you to tell me where Tate is."

"She's at the barn." I nod once, staying one more moment to give him time to add what I can see in his features he wants to say. "Go get her."

Relief floods through my veins in an instant, leaving me lightheaded. A smile spreads across my face before I sprint out of the main house.

Ash is sniffing the flowers near the front porch, but when he sees me sprinting toward the barn, he chases after me. I notice Beckett, Hads, and Ian giving me funny looks but I don't care. I have to get to her. Wrap her up in my arms. Kiss her lips until she melts into me. Tell her I love her because it's about damn time she knows, too.

I push the barn doors open, ignoring the creaking we'll probably never get to fix now. And yet, none of it matters at this very moment.

None of it but Tate.

I find her sitting on the ground in Luna, Betty, and Angel's stable with her sister next to her, brushing as much of Luna's coat as she can reach with the mini cow's head on her lap. My entire focus is on Tate where she is on the ground, wiping at her tears.

When she finds me, something akin to panic crosses her face, making the same emotion shoot through me. Sensing we need a moment alone, Remi leaves the barn nodding only once in my direction.

"How are you feeling, sweetheart?" I ask, studying the blood vessels that have popped in her eyes and face. Her body looks so tired, and I notice she has little cuts from her nails in the palm of her hands.

"Every single joint in my body hurts, especially my ankles, and I have a massive headache," she replies, not quite meeting my gaze. "I bit my tongue a little too, so that's throbbing at the moment as well," she explains, staring at her hands.

"Is there anything I can get you?" I ask, but the expression she gives me is one full of uncertainty, regret, and guilt.

"Aaron—" she starts, but I cut her off, too scared of the words that will follow the soft, cautious way she said my name.

"Please, don't run away again. Please. Nothing has changed, not for me. I want this, I want us."

I'm so scared she'll leave me, I forget how to breathe. I know how Tate thinks. I know that because she had a seizure, it'll make reality come crashing back in and bring back her fear. I know her. I can see it in the way she watches me.

My next words spill out of me before she has the chance to speak.

"From the moment you drove that bright-red Chevy up the road leading to the main house, I knew. I knew you would be the first person I'd fall in love with. I could feel it deep inside of me. The only thing I didn't know until I was undoubtedly and consumingly in love with you was that you'd also be the last person I'd ever fall in love with. Because I don't want anyone else, Tate."

She lets out a sob, but I'm not done yet. There's one more thing I have to say.

"I'm in love with you. Not in spite of anything, not because of something, I just love you. So much so that breathing becomes impossible as soon as you're not near me. My heart beats more steadily when I'm next to you and, at the same time, the mere sight of you makes it stutter. *That* is how much you mean to me. *That* is why even if you run because you're scared, I'll run after you."

"Aaron, enough. Please," she says, making my heart drop.

Tate wipes her beautiful face, trying to slow the tears, and I sink to my knees in front of her. Luna raises her head but then plops it right back on Tate's lap while my sweetheart tries to collect herself.

"I'm sorry if I overwhelmed you," I manage to croak out, my voice barely audible.

"No, you didn't. That was the most wonderful love declaration, more wonderful than I could have ever hoped to receive. It's just—" She cuts off, staring up at the ceiling and blinking to get rid of the tears. "Fuck, why is this so hard?" she asks and lets out a teary laugh.

"Because you don't want to break up with me?"

"I don't want to break up with you, Aaron. I'm so in love with you, even now that I've never been more afraid, I don't have the strength to run away from you." A wave of relief hits me, taking my breath. "I'm not going anywhere. Whatever it is my future holds, whatever happens, I'm yours." I carefully lift Luna's head off Tate's lap to pull her into my arms and nuzzle my face in the crook of her neck. I inhale her scent, something floral and just Tatum.

"I love you, Tate," I say, placing my forehead to hers.

"To Pluto and back," she replies, almost making me stumble back.

"You remember?"

"Of course I do, Aaron. Every second of us, every piece of you, is important to me."

My lips are on hers as soon as she's finished speaking. Tate smiles against me, her arms wrapping around my neck as she melts against my chest. I place my hand on her hips, dragging her impossibly closer. I don't want a single inch between us. Not while I'm tasting her and every single one of her feelings. Not while I can finally hold her in my arms for everyone to see. Not while I'm so painfully in love with her.

The thought makes a happy sob bubble out of me, one I only manage to smother by breaking the kiss and burying my face in her neck again. Tatum's nails run down my nape as her head drops against my shoulder too.

We stay like that for what feels like forever, and despite probably not having a home, job, or future at Silver Creek Ranch soon, I can't bring myself to tear away from her yet. Instead, I press kisses to her neck as I rub a hand up and down her spine, feeling her shiver in my arms.

"Aaron?" she says, and I manage to raise my head when I hear the panic in her voice.

"What's wrong?" Worry fills me until her eyes find mine, determination now in them.

"I know who started the fire!" She fishes around in her cargo pants' pocket for a second before pulling out a silver lighter with a hawk drawn across the front. "Fuck, I didn't remember earlier because of my seizure, but this is it, Aaron. We have to give this to Owen." I furrow my brows, so she smiles at me. "I saw Landon light his cigarette with this lighter at the wood chopping competition at Boots & Beers. It's his, I'm one hundred percent sure," she says, hope blooming in her eyes, forcing some of it to course through me as well. I'd be more excited if Tate didn't look so damn tired.

"I know you never delegate until it's necessary, but please, let me do this. I need you to go home and rest." She's been too stressed these past few months, even more so in the past two weeks, and I need her to take a moment to breathe and reset.

"Okay," Tate says, meeting me halfway. "But take Olivia with you for backup," Tate adds with a grin, and I take her hand in mine as I lead her out of the barn, for the first time not scared of being discovered. No. I get to hold her hand for everyone to see now.

"I'll call her," I promise.

Once Tate has taken a shower and settled down in her bed, I give her one last kiss before making my way down the stairs to find Briggs asleep on the couch with his mouth wide open and snores leaving his throat. Remi is taking several photos of her dad in the unflattering position.

"Leverage," she explains, and I give her an amused smile.

"Send that to me. Now that he knows I'm dating Tate, I'll probably need it more than you." She snickers at that.

I pull my phone out of my pocket as I make my way outside, dialing Liv and then dialing Beckett. He may seem like a big teddy bear sometimes, but if Owen can't do anything with this lighter, then Beck's going to prove he's not as much teddy as he is violent, angry bear.

CHAPTER 41

Aaron

THE POLICE STATION IS almost entirely empty except for an officer at the front desk and a few walking past us to get to wherever they need to go. The *Orchard Hill Police Department* sign is written in bold, black letters behind the police officer welcoming us inside with a warm smile. Jeremy Wells is Helen and Ulma's son. He's also had the biggest crush on Olivia for as long as I can remember, which is probably why he starts blushing as soon as Liv flashes him one of her flirty smiles.

"Must you do that?" I whisper to her right as we approach the desk.

"Must? No. Want to? Absolutely. I love makin' men blush," she says and winks at me before focusing her attention on Jeremy.

I see his eyes skating over her face before lingering on her chest area where she left quite a few buttons undone. Beckett is grinning with his arms crossed in front of his chest as he watches Liv lean on the front desk.

"Hey, handsome. We need to speak to Officer Grim. Is he in?" she asks, smiling at him.

Jeremy is only three years younger than her, but the twenty-eight-year-old has always been on the shy side. Definitely easy prey for her.

"He's busy right now," Jeremy replies with an apologetic expression, trying his hardest not to stare at Liv's cleavage and failing desperately.

"Come on, Jer, this is important. You have to let us see him."

"I really can't. He asked not to be disturbed." Olivia pouts, but Beck runs a hand down the length of his face and shakes his head.

"This is ridiculous," is all he says before simply stepping around the front desk, knowing there is a reason why Jeremy isn't a field officer.

"Hey!" he calls after Beck and me, but Olivia distracts him by touching his arm and looking up at him with those bright green eyes of hers full of wicked promise.

Beckett throws the glass door to Owen's office open, ignoring the woman sitting across from the chief of police as he gets in his face.

"Considerin' you're the hand of justice or whatever the fuck they call you in this little town, you're damn hard to get to," the single dad says, looking every shade of angry.

"I'm in a meetin'," Owen says, pointing at the woman across from him.

"Pardon me, ma'am, but I have urgent police business to discuss with the chief," he says, giving her one of his charming smiles that she's very unimpressed with.

"Did your momma not teach you manners, boy?" the woman asks, her Southern accent subtle but still there, telling me she probably grew up around here but moved to a different city.

Beckett shrugs, his smile steady on his lips.

"My momma would probably lose it if she knew what I just did, but she ain't my biggest concern right now. Someone started a fire on our farm last night, and we know who it was," he explains as he gestures for me to give Owen the lighter.

The chief of police stands up as soon as he hears we have more information, his interest piqued. He wants to close this case as badly as we want to find who did this to Silver Creek Ranch. It's been almost a year since he opened it, since he started digging to try and find the person responsible.

"Momma, I apologize, but we're gonna have to finish lunch another day, if that's alright," Owen says, catching me by surprise. No one's ever seen Owen's mum.

"That's alright, Owen. I have to catch my flight anyway," she says and steps toward him to place an unsure hand on his arm. That's all the affection both of them show each other before she grabs her things, flashes one more scowl Beckett's way, and then disappears out the door.

"That's your mother?" he asks Owen, who flashes him a warning look.

"Yeah," he replies through gritted teeth.

"She's smokin'—" Owen grabs his gun and places it on the desk in front of him, effectively cutting off the rest of Beckett's sentence.

"We might only now be findin' common ground, but that's still my momma, so you better shut your mouth before I put you in handcuffs," he warns, and Beckett smirks immediately.

"Usually, I prefer being the one puttin' the handcuffs on, but I guess we can try your way, too." I smack my forehead with the palm of my hand.

"Can we get to arresting Landon fucking Cole, please?" I ask, pointing at the lighter.

"You sure it's his?" Owen asks as he crosses his desk, taking the silver device from me.

"Tate's sure, which means I am, too."

"Alright, I'll go question him and Bernard. I was suspicious of them since I found out they wanted to buy the ranch, but I didn't have anythin' to go on. Thanks to Tate, now we do." Owen reaches for his gun again, sliding it into the holster before grabbing his bulletproof vest.

"We wanna come," Beckett says, his arms crossed in front of his broad chest again.

"No. Y'all go home. I'll let you know what's happenin' as soon as I can."

Owen's tone lets us know there will be no discussion on the subject. It doesn't matter if we're friends or not. He has a job to do, and he can't do it with the both of us hanging around. We'd be a liability, and Beckett and I are not stubborn enough to not see that. We've done all we could, and now we wait. We wait for them to deny the accusation or admit what they did.

We have to be patient and trust Owen to do what he does best.

Fight for justice.

Tatum is curled against me on the couch at the main house, something I never thought would happen, while Briggs is finishing up dinner in the kitchen. She looks well-rested and is smiling happily at me while I tell her that the nursing home called me today and said that Nanna had a really good day. She ate, she laughed, and she went for a walk in the garden.

"I was thinking about visiting her again soon. Would you like to come with me?" I ask, running my thumb across Tate's cheek and stealing a kiss.

"I would love to, cowboy," she replies against my lips, deepening the kiss until someone clears their throat and forces her to pull away.

"Tate, Dad said he made green beans for you," Remi says as she drops onto the armchair across from us. A mischievous look plays on her face as she takes in the image of Tate and me. "So, Aaron, what are your intentions with my sister?" she says, mocking Briggs by using a voice similar to his. I lean down so my lips are right by Tatum's ears, cupping my hand over it and my mouth to make sure my woman is the only one who hears my response.

"Tonight, my intentions are to have a wonderful dinner and then have you coming on my mouth, screaming my name, for dessert." Tate's cheeks flash a bright red before she tilts her head to hide her face in my chest.

"Awww, gross," Remi replies as she looks around the room.

The front door swings open, Beckett storming through it with Bailey holding his hand. Remi jumps at the sound, whipping her head around to watch the mountain of a man covered in muscles and tattoos walk inside.

"Alright, what's for dinner?" Beckett asks while Bailey runs into the kitchen where she knows Briggs is. Her father's eyes land on Remi, surprise widening his eyes. "Who are you?" he asks, his casual charm long gone.

"Remi. Who the hell are you?" she asks with an unimpressed cock of her brow. Beckett takes a step toward her, an amused smile dancing onto his lips.

"If I play my cards right, sugar, I'm gonna be the best time of your life," he says and holds out his hand for her. "I'm Beckett."

"And I'm highly allergic to bad pickup lines. It's not happening, big guy." Remi stands up and walks back into the kitchen, leaving the armchair free for Beckett to plop into, a dreamy look in his eyes.

"Aaron, is there still space next to the grave Briggs is digging for you right now?" he asks, and I burst into laughter.

"Yeah, probably. Why?"

"Because I'm gonna marry his other daughter." Beckett leans back in the armchair and stares after Remi.

"Hate to break it to you, Beck, but my sister has a track record of only dating millionaires. Her last boyfriend was a billionaire, actually," Tate says, but he merely shrugs.

"Guess I gotta go make a million bucks. Shouldn't be too hard, right?" Tate chuckles at his ridiculous words, earning a soft smile from him.

I see it in his eyes then, in the way he looks at her. He loves Tatum. He loves her like he loves the rest of us. He loves her like he only loves very few people because he's too scared they'll leave him like his dad left. I knew Flynn, Hads, and Olivia loved Tate a while ago. It was obvious. Ian's so good at keeping his feelings under wraps that I'm never certain how he feels unless he tells me, but Beckett? When he cares about someone, it's obvious. He wears his heart on his sleeve around those he trusts.

"Why are you lookin' at me all weird?" Beck asks after a moment of me getting lost in my thoughts without even realizing Tate's eyes have closed again. I run my finger over her temple, but she doesn't move into the touch. Tate's definitely asleep again, the events of today catching up with her.

"Because you're looking at my girl like you've officially accepted her into our family," I point out, but he merely blows out a breath like I'm talking shit.

"You know I don't get attached to new people," he says right as Bailey drags Remi out of the kitchen and into the living room.

"Daddy! Daddy!" Bailey screams, and Tatum's eyes shoot open as she sits up to see where the sound is coming from. "Can Remi and I go draw outside?" she asks as Remi lifts a bucket of chalk to show Beckett what his daughter means.

"Yeah, peanut, you can." The two of them make their way outside right as Flynn and Olivia walk into the room.

"The next person to start a fire on this property will be me, Rafael, and it'll be so I can throw you in the flames," Liv says, and Flynn rolls his eyes dramatically.

"Do you even need to start a fire, *pesadilla*? Can't you just ask your master, *the devil*, to send some flames up?" my best friend asks, noticing Tate smiling at Liv and him. "You good, Tate?" he says as he walks over to her and places a hand on top of her head.

"Yeah, just tired. I had one of my seizures earlier and need some more rest," she explains, grinning up at him while Flynn clearly tries to keep his expression firmly set and not reveal his surprise. Beckett is a lot more successful than my best mate, whose mouth falls open a little at this new piece of information. "I have epilepsy," Tate explains, burying her face in my chest a second later to hide from the fact that she finally told them about her chronic illness.

I know how much it took to share this piece of herself, so I press a kiss to the top of her head. Flynn gives Beckett an unsure look while Liv smiles at Tate and me cuddling.

"Briggs is so going to murder you if he finds you like this," she sings as she drops down onto the armrest of the armchair Beck's sitting in.

"Nah, we had a heart-to-heart. I've got at least until Tate and I move in together before he ends me," I tease with a smile.

Ian and Hads walk through the door a few minutes later, not speaking or even looking in each other's direction. I'd ask what that's all about, but then Tatum stretches out her arms and sits up before Briggs walks into the living room to announce dinner is ready.

Beckett goes outside to get Bailey and Remi while Tate takes another moment to stand up. I rub her back, massaging it until she's melting against me. She tilts her head to kiss me once before Briggs calls out from the kitchen, telling us to get our asses in the chairs.

Dinner is long and filled with tension. All of us are waiting for Owen's phone call, for any update. No one speaks, not until Briggs breaks the silence with the one thing none of us wants to address.

"The bank accepted Bernard's offer to buy the ranch. Because I can't afford a new property, Bernard agreed to take in all of the animals." Briggs puts his fork down, looking each and every one of us dead in the eye before he adds, "He also agreed to employ all of you when he takes over. Your jobs are safe. Your incomes might change, but I hope they'll increase now that your employer has more means to support y'all."

My mouth opens as I attempt to speak, but it clicks shut a second later. All words have left me. I know what I want to say, but nothing's coming through my lips. Luckily, Ian has never been one to keep his mouth shut when something isn't right.

"No." Briggs turns his head toward Ian, quirking a confused brow.

"Why the heck not?" I almost laugh at the way Briggs censors himself because of the first-grader at the table.

"Because they burned your crops and the flower patch that would have been the savior of this farm. I'm not working for that asshole. Over my dead body." Ian shovels a forkful of pasta into his mouth while Beckett shoots him a glare for swearing in front of Bailey.

"Yeah, me neither, Briggs. I'm taking Pegasus and Bails, and we're leaving the second you are." Beckett runs a gentle hand over his daughter's hair.

"What about your house? Think about your daughter," Briggs urges, but Beck shrugs.

"My daughter will happily live with her grandmother until we find something else. And I'd rather not raise her anywhere near Bernard and Sofia."

"Yeah, I can't afford the living costs of our house by myself, so I'll probably move into Momma Moore's house, too," Flynn chimes in with a teasing smile.

"Liv and I aren't staying either." Since they live together, I'm not surprised Hads would blurt out this decision after only sharing a look with her best friend.

"You're all so dramatic," Remi says as she turns Briggs' way. "Listen, Dad, I know you're as stubborn as the horses you have on this ranch, but I have money, lots of it, and you're going to take enough to make sure you can get Silver Creek Ranch back." Surprise blooms in my chest. Briggs opens his mouth to argue, but Remi cuts him off. "Think about everyone else here, not just yourself. Are you willing to upend all of their lives because you don't want to take my money?" Remi asks, effectively shutting Briggs up. Well, at least while he processes her words.

"Why would you do this, ladybug? From a business point of view, this is a horrible idea," Briggs says.

Remi throws her napkin onto the table after wiping her mouth methodically, thinking about his answer before saying something that makes Tate gasp.

"Because I want to move here. I want to live here with my family. I've been away from all of you for too long," she says, and I watch Tate lean forward to study her sister.

"Really?" I can see tears fill Tate's eyes before she blinks them away rapidly.

"Yes. As much as I like being a business owner of a perfume empire, I think I'd enjoy investing in a smaller project, like yours," Remi says to Tate.

The sisters exchange soft smiles and my hand slips under the table and onto my woman's thigh. I squeeze it reassuringly, and she brings hers on top of mine, lacing her fingers through mine.

"Well, as much as I appreciate it, I don't think there's anything left that we can do. The contracts were signed this afternoon," Briggs adds and shakes his head. "Unless Owen pulls off a miracle, the ranch will officially be Bernard and Sofia's the day after tomorrow."

CHAPTER 42
Tatum

LOKI AND ASH ARE lying together, my dog's head on the other's back as they face the setting sun. I'm in Aaron's lap with his arms wrapped around me, his chin resting on my shoulder. Tears threaten to escape my eyes every once in a while, but I keep them at bay.

It's a strange sensation to lose a place you envisioned yourself growing old in. It's even stranger when it's the first place you ever really let yourself envision a future in. It's not like losing someone you love, but it's still grief. A different kind, but painful nonetheless.

"I'm not ready to leave," I admit as I watch the sunset, the creek reflecting the light in an explosion of glitter.

"Me neither," Aaron replies, kissing my bare shoulder as his arms tighten around me.

"I didn't just fall in love with you, Aaron. I fell in love with Silver Creek Ranch, too. Walking away from either one of you feels like I'm going against my survival instinct."

"Owen's going to pull through. He's going to get a confession out of Bernard and Landon and even Sofia," he says and kisses my shoulder again.

We fall back into silence as more sadness settles in my chest. There is so much I had dreamed of for this ranch, so much I wanted to do here. I wanted the ranch to flourish, to fix the barn doors with the money we'd make through the visitations from people in Orchard Hill and hopefully, eventually, from all around the country, too. I wanted to fix up the main house. I wanted so much, and yet, we had so little time for all of it.

"There is something I'd like to do before we leave," I say to Aaron, standing up and leaving the comfort of his arms.

His fingers wrap around my hands before I pull him straight against my chest. He hugs me close to him.

"Anything you want, Tatum, we'll do. Always."

Galaxy has become so comfortable with me, she seems to enjoy my company more and more every single day that I brush her. I have no idea how, but we're taking her wherever it is we're going. Her, Luna, Betty, Angel, Firefly, the llamas, and every other animal we can. Remi will help us. I know she will. After her declaration that she wants to move here and be with her family, I doubt there's anything she wouldn't do for us.

I saddle up Galaxy, ensuring everything is tight enough and that the saddle is perfectly secured before running my fingers over the material. No part of me has gotten over the fact that Aaron had this made especially for me and that it matches his saddle. He told me he loved me today, but he's been showing me how much I mean to him for a long time.

My eyes skip over Galaxy's back to where Aaron is saddling up Firefly, his horse nudging him every few seconds and distracting him until my sunshine cowboy is laughing. He runs one of his big hands down the length of Firefly's forehead and all the way to his nose.

"Ready?" I ask once we're both sitting in the saddles, Loki and Ash barking up at us.

"Ready," Aaron replies, so I lead Galaxy into a trot out of the barn.

Moments later, Aaron and I are both galloping side by side along Silver Creek, smiling at each other while we enjoy our sunset ride. If we don't get the chance to do this again, then I want to remember every second of it. The way the creek still sparkles. The way the summer air whips my hair back until I have to hold onto the cowboy hat Aaron bought me so it doesn't fly away. The way he takes his off entirely and tugs it under where his hand is on the horn of his saddle, reins firmly clutched in his grasp, too. The way I've never felt freer in my entire life.

His eyes keep drifting to me, watching the way my dress flies in the wind to reveal the shorts I'm wearing underneath and showing off my cowboy boots.

A few months ago, I was a woman wearing pantsuits. I was chained to work. I didn't know how to live a happy life.

Now?

Now I'm a woman who wears summer dresses, cowboy boots, and a cowboy hat while riding a horse along the most beautiful creek. I enjoy the work I'm doing here, even if mucking out the stables is *disgusting*. I finally figured out how to live a happy life.

They say people don't change, and maybe they're right. Maybe I haven't changed at all. Maybe I've simply embraced who I was all along.

Aaron and I slow Firefly and Galaxy a little, leading them to the creek where they dip their heads to drink. I pat Galaxy's neck a few times, praising her for being such a perfect horse. Aaron watches me with longing and adoration in his eyes.

"I love you," I say, watching his expression soften even more.

"To Pluto and back."

CHAPTER 43
Tatum

OWEN SHOWED UP AT the main house early this morning. He said he has news, but he's been sitting in front of Aaron, Dad, Remi, and me for the last two minutes saying nothing while sipping his coffee. To be fair, he looks like he needs it.

"For the love of everything that is good in this world, chief, spit it out," Remi says, and I slap her leg with the back of my hand. "What? The suspense is killing me. Did you get a confession or not?" my sister asks and slides the plate of cookies away as soon as Owen reaches for them.

"Considerin' I got a confession out of Bernard, who admitted Landon and him set fire to the crops *and* the flower field, I think I deserve a cookie," Owen says, looking all grumpy and moody.

"You what?" I blurt out, my heart skipping several beats as my hand flies to Dad's shoulder.

"Yup, they're behind bars as we speak, and they'll go to prison for arson. They'll be payin' for all of the damages and every cost associated with their crime, I'll make sure of it. Until then, the bank is going to nullify the contract Bernard and Sofia signed. You'll get to keep the ranch," Owen says, grabbing a cookie and shoving it into his mouth.

"You've been busy," Aaron says as relief courses through me.

"Yeah, well, this case was important to me. And scarin' the shit out of Bernard was a hell of a lotta fun," Owen explains, chuckling to himself as he relives what he did to get the confession.

"That's not very chief of police behavior, mate," Aaron reminds him, but Owen merely laughs.

"Well, whatever behavior it was, you're welcome." Owen smiles at Aaron before nodding at Dad, who reaches for my hand and presses it to his chest.

"We get to stay?" he asks Owen, clearly not processing what's happening.

"Yeah, Briggs. You get to stay. The damages will be paid, your mortgage will be paid, and any other consequences of their actions *will be paid*. It might make them bankrupt, but that ain't your problem. If anythin', it's what they deserve," Owen replies, taking another sip of his coffee before standing up and holding out his hand for Dad.

"Thank you," my father says, shaking the chief of police's hand.

"My pleasure. Now, if y'all excuse me, I need a shower, more food, and sleep," Owen adds. A yawn rips free, making him quickly cover his mouth out of politeness. "I fuckin' hate all the paperwork that goes with aresstin' someone." He shakes his head and walks toward the front door. "Oh, and you should probably get less nosy employees, Briggs."

Owen opens the door to reveal Liv and Beckett with their hands cupped around their ears, clearly having eavesdropped on the entire conversation. Hads, Flynn, and Ian are right behind them, too.

"We get to stay!" five voices scream at the same time before all of them fill the main house, Flynn wrapping Aaron in a hug, Liv and Hadley flinging their arms around me, Ian clapping Dad on the shoulder, and Beckett giving Remi a flirty smile. I almost laugh at the way my sister rolls her eyes but picks up a tired Bailey and places her on her hip.

"What do we do now?" Hads asks Briggs, and my dad brings a bright smile to his face before cupping her cheek.

"Now, we rebuild. We get back to work, and we're going to prepare the ranch for the Halloween-themed haunted maze, ridin' lessons, and taking pictures section. We go on with our ranch work as always because Silver Creek Ranch is ours, and no one's ever going to take it away," Dad says, earning a round of cheers from everyone present.

Liv and Hads let go of me a second before Aaron wraps me up in his arms and lifts my feet off the ground.

"We get to stay," I whisper to Aaron, and he grins down at me.

"Yeah, sweetheart, we get to stay."

His lips find mine while laughter booms through the room from the rest of our family as they discuss possibilities of what Owen did to get a confession out of Bernard. I have a feeling no matter what they attempt to come up with, Owen did something not entirely lawful to get the admission out of Bernard.

Whatever it is, it doesn't matter. All that matters is that we get to stay.

"Tate?" Aaron asks after breaking the kiss, my lips tingling.

"Yes, baby?" His eyes brighten before he presses another swift kiss to my cheek.

"How would you feel about coming to stay with me?" he asks, and I can't help the smile that breaks out across my face.

"For how long?" I ask, teasing him when I know what he means.

"For however long you want to stay." A smile, so soft and sweet it makes warmth spread through me, curls the corners of his mouth. "Preferably forever."

I press my mouth back against his before adding, "Forever sounds good to me."

Epilogue

Tatum

TWO MONTHS LATER

Lorena Blaze is one hell of a woman. This is the fourth time Aaron has taken me with him to visit her, but every time she sees me, she smiles. She has no idea who I am, can't remember who Aaron is either, but she welcomes us anyway. Every single time, she seems happy we're there.

Stories followed by stories are told, either by Aaron who wants to share something about our love story with his grandmother, or by her, who wants to tell us about the family she doesn't quite remember. Lorena talks about her late husband the most, something that makes Aaron smile the kind of smile one can only give someone who doesn't remember who they are.

But every time we see her, she speaks less. Talking seems to become more difficult for her as time passes. Her eyes are always bloodshot with dark circles underneath them. According to the nurses, she doesn't eat much anymore either, which is probably why she's even thinner today than the last time we visited her.

Aaron sees it, too.

Today, Lorena isn't speaking at all. She's watching the wildflowers slowly wither, petals falling onto the ground in a slow, swishing motion. Left to right, left to right, left to right, until there is nowhere left to go but the ground.

"Lorena," Aaron tries, but she doesn't react.

I don't know if she's ignoring him on purpose or if she's too lost in her thoughts to hear him. Aaron sucks in a sharp breath I can't hear but see before standing up and nodding several times.

"Let's go," my cowboy says, placing his cowboy hat back on his head before turning around to hide the tears in his eyes.

I stand up too, reaching out to grab my wallet and phone when her slender fingers wrap around my wrist. Her grip isn't strong, but I'm so surprised, she might as well have my hand in a steel grip.

"Take care of him," she says, and I look her straight in the eye as a wave of emotion floods straight through my chest. "Love him like no one else."

"To Pluto and back," I reply, which seems to satisfy her enough to offer me the smallest of smiles and turn her attention back to the wildflowers.

Aaron and I walk back to his truck holding hands. Loki is right by my side, focused as always. My cowboy is sad, but he still smiles at the people we stroll past, ever the sunshine.

He stops walking long enough to step in front of me, cupping my face in his hands and tilting my chin up so I'm staring into his blue eyes.

"I want you to know something," he says, his thumb caressing my left cheek.

"What's that, cowboy?"

"Meeting you is the best thing that's ever happened to me. You ease my pain and intensify all of my joy." His lips find mine, and I can't stop smiling against his mouth. "I still can't believe you agreed to move in with me, too. I'm not sure how I pulled that off," he says with a grin.

"I don't know either. I must have been sleep-deprived and not thinking clearly," I tease, but he merely pulls me into a fierce hug as he chuckles.

Moving in with Aaron was one of the best decisions I've ever made. We've been decorating our little house ever since, and he even got us Halloween decorations. Throw pillows with pumpkins and ghosts on it, porcelain figurines of skulls and ravens, and so many more things we've put up all over the place. I love Halloween. It's my second favorite holiday of the year, right after Christmas, but I've never taken the time to decorate the places I've lived in before. It's one of the many things I love about living with Aaron. Along with watching the sunrise and sunset every morning. Waking up to him. Watching Ash and Loki become best friends. Going to work together but working on separate jobs before coming home at night to spend the entire evening in each other's arms. Having as much sex as we want.

I love everything about living with my cowboy.

"We should get home. Tonight is going to be a long night," he says, kissing me one more time before continuing to lead me to his truck.

Tonight is Halloween. The ranch has been doing so well after we got the money from Bernard and Sofia, we finally started fixing up the main house and the barn. There are a lot of repairs to be done, but we've got time.

Remi has also decided to buy Red Sky Ranch after Bernard and Sofia went bankrupt. We're going to expand Silver Creek Ranch, so that we can grow new crops where Red Sky Ranch used to be. The other half of our ranch will remain the visitable portion.

Remi has no idea how running a ranch works, but Dad already promised to help and guide her as much as he can.

I tried talking to Remi a few days ago and see what the hell made her decide to buy a fucking ranch, but she just said she missed her family. No part of me believes her. There is something else she doesn't want to tell me, something that went awfully wrong. Unfortunately, my sister has an iron will. If she doesn't want to speak about something, she won't.

"Beckett's calling me," I say before answering and bringing the phone to my ear. "What's up, Beck?"

"You gotta get home *now!*" he barks before hanging up.

"Did you—"

"Hear Beckett being as dramatic as always? Yeah, sweetheart, I heard. I'm already hitting the gas," Aaron replies while my heart beats faster and faster.

The second the Silver Creek Ranch sign comes into view, the panic subsides. They set up signs leading from the main gate all the way to the house. Phrases like

"Enter At Your Own Risk" and "Beware: Monsters Ahead" stand out to me as we drive by. Aaron is chuckling at all of them, slowing down so we can admire the self-made posters.

"What have they been up to?" I hear myself asking, but Aaron shrugs.

"No clue, but I don't trust it. I don't trust them." The fondness in his voice tells a completely different story.

The sun is already setting, every day a little earlier as the months fly by. The lights we put up everywhere help people find their way to the maze. There are stands where Jamie set up camp to sell his baked goods, holiday-themed of course, and others where we charge a small admission fee for the visitors.

What catches most of my attention is my entire family standing in front of the main house, all of them dressed in costumes. Well, all but Dad.

Beckett looks amazing in his Hercules costume with Bailey dressed as Phil from the same movie. Flynn is dressed as his nickname's sake, Flynn Rider. Olivia is dressed as a robber, a balaclava over her face. Hads is dressed as a beautiful princess with flowers woven into her hair, and Ian is beside her, dressed like Prince Charming. Remi is dressed as Megara, which is something I'd very much like to ask her about, but seeing the scowl on her face, I'm guessing it wasn't by choice.

A smile blooms on my face at the sight of all of them.

"We got you some, too!" Hads announces as soon as Aaron and I are out of the car.

"I'm not wearing a costume you picked out," Aaron replies, but I turn to him with a pout. He catches my expression, his gaze softening before he turns back to our family and says, "It better be a good one."

Half an hour later, Silver Creek Ranch is filled with the people of Orchard Hill, who have also dressed up for the occasion. Aaron and I are now clad in matching costumes: Loki, the god of Mischief, and Heimdall. I'm wearing his favorite—well, the female version of Heimdall—while he's dressed as mine. I can't help eyeing my cowboy a little more because he looks absolutely delicious. It doesn't help that I used to have a crush on this fictional character.

"This is an absolute success. You outdid yourself," Ulma says as she and Helen approach. "I've never seen anythin' like this."

"Thank you, but this was a family effort. Everyone worked their asses off to make this happen," I say, pointing at where Aaron and Beckett are fixing a table leg and Olivia and Hads are collecting admission fees. Flynn and Ian are also running around, one of them taking pictures and the other supervising the pony riding lessons.

"But it's your vision, hun, and it came out fantastic. I already can't wait to see what you come up with for Christmas," Helen adds, and I smile at the short woman.

"Oh, Jamie made his famous pumpkin streusel. I need a piece," Ulma says before dragging her wife with her.

The rest of the night passes in a blissful blur. Before we know it, everyone has left and there are a million things that need to be taken care of. Dad tells all of us to leave everything the way it is because we can still clean up tomorrow morning.

"Where's Aaron?" I ask, and Beckett shoots me a mischievous grin.

"He's in the maze. You should go find him," he says. I give him a look, but he shrugs before walking away.

My feet bring me to the entrance of the maze, bales of hay on either side of me as I walk through it. It's quite easy to find your way through when you were the one to set it up. So, I keep going, finding my way to the center where Aaron is waiting for me.

"Come here," he says, holding out his hand for me. My mouth waters a little when I notice he's unbuttoned the vest of his costume enough to show off his tanned, muscular chest.

"What are we doing in here?" I ask as I step closer, slipping my hand into his. Aaron doesn't waste a second, bringing me right against his chest and kissing me.

"We're sneaking around," he replies between kisses, his hands slipping onto my hips before he guides me backward. The back of my knees hit a bale of hay, which he lifts me on top of. His hand slips onto my throat as he pulls me closer, kissing me hard. I grin against his lips in response.

"Aaron, did you get me to come in here just to fuck me?" I ask, running my nails down his abs until his grip on me tightens.

"Skirt up and panties down, sweetheart. Let me answer that question with my cock."

I do as I'm told while he kisses my neck, down my chest, and rips my corset apart to get to my nipples. He pulls the left one into his mouth before pinching the right one between his thumb and index finger. Pleasure sweeps through me while I slip my thong to the side.

"Been thinking about this all evening," he admits as he takes his cock out and carefully aligns himself with my entrance.

"I've been thinking about it since you put this costume on," I reply, and he grins down at me. He presses inside of me a little further, causing my eyes to fall shut.

"Eyes on me, Tate. Look at me while I slip inside this perfect pussy," he demands, and I force my eyes back open, watching him as he thrusts all the way inside of me. "Good girl," he praises, his mouth on mine as he fucks me in slow and steady strokes.

"Fuck," I moan. "I never want this to end, Aaron," I say, his thumb dropping to my clit where he rubs tight circles that have me trembling within seconds.

"We've got our whole lives, sweetheart, all the time in the world."

And, for the first time in my life, I believe that, too.

Bonus Epilogue

Aaron

MORE THAN A YEAR LATER

For the second year in a row, our Christmas events are a hit with everyone in Orchard Hill. This year, people from all around the country have come to visit too. We still have the same self-made decorations, the same lights hanging everywhere, snowflakes cut out and hung along the rope of lights too.

The past year has been a rollercoaster. We regrew our flower patch, and it was a huge success. The sunflower patch was the most popular, but they all enjoyed the wildflower picking and the lavender patch, too. Word spread so fast that the national news channel even did a segment about our event, which led to a couple of famous people attending as well. My jaw dropped so far to the floor when I saw Valentina Romana and Gabriel Biancheri as well as Adrian Romana and Nevaeh Fuchs strolling through the sunflower field. Tate almost fainted, but they were so nice, they let us take photos and even spoke to us for a while about our ranch.

Halloween went by smoothly. We had more decorations this year, more people that came from all around Tennessee to attend as well. It was a success. Crops have been growing well on the other half of Silver Creek Ranch, the part that used to be Red Sky Ranch. The repairs on the house are finished, but we're still working on renovating the barn.

Nanna passed away half a year ago. It's still uncomfortable to think about her, and I hardly ever manage to speak about the woman who raised me, but I'll get there. I'll get the strength to share stories about how wonderful she was again. I know she's resting now, that she's with her husband, but I miss her so much. Every single day. If it weren't for Tate, I think I would have fallen apart long ago.

"I'm so fucking nervous," I admit, watching Beckett raise his brow.

"Is this your first time?" He looks almost shocked, but I give him an unimpressed look.

"Yes, it's my first time. First and last," I state as I twist Nanna's ring between my fingers.

It's not extravagant in any way, but the small, green diamond only seems fitting for Tate. She's been wearing the necklace I gave her for one and a half years now, along with the earrings I got her half a year ago and the bracelet with a mini cow charm hanging from it. I can't wait to give her another piece of jewelry to add to her growing collection.

I love spoiling her.

"How much longer until she's here?" I ask, checking my watch once before turning to Flynn.

My best mate gives me an amused grin while Ian stands beside him, arms crossed in front of his chest and scowl firmly set on his face. Even Owen is here, too curious about witnessing all of this to be anywhere else. Not that any of them are allowed to stay here once Tatum arrives. They can hear about it later, but in the moment, I want it to only be her and me.

"Liv, Hads, and Remi are currently driving her past the signs you made."

Right, the signs leading from the Silver Creek Ranch one all the way to the main house. Signs I made that spelled out different reasons for why I love her. Her smile. Her warmth. Her kindness. Her intelligence. Her drive. Her determination. Her hair. Her lips. Her dreams. Her everything, pretty much.

Panic slips inside of my chest as I realize this is it. This is what we've been preparing for months now, wanting to make it nothing short of perfect. I place a hand on Luna's head before dropping Nanna's ring in the bag I tied to the loose band I placed around her neck. Her tail whips from left to right as she grazes on the grass she's standing on.

"She's gonna love this," Beck assures me as he points toward where Galaxy is standing, a sign taped to the saddle I put on her that reads "Marry" and Firefly has the matching "Me" glued to his saddle.

"Either she's gonna love it or she's gonna kick you to the curb," Briggs chimes in with a smile, and I scowl at him in response.

"Okay, all of you, leave," I instruct as I watch her red truck pull up. Olivia is driving it while Hads is covering Tate's eyes and Remi is holding her phone out of the window to record all of this.

The sun is setting, the chilly December air freezing my ears. I placed dried wildflower petals from the driveway all the way to where I'm standing in front of the booths we set up for the Christmas market. Luna is patient beside me, and Galaxy and Firefly are watching where Tatum is being led out of the truck and toward me. Remi is still filming, Hads has tears in her eyes, and Olivia is flashing me one of her mischievous smiles.

It's not that I'm worried Tate will say no. Not at all. I wouldn't be asking her to marry me if we hadn't discussed getting married and she said it's what she wanted too. I'm nervous this is not the way she wants to be proposed to.

And, okay, fuck, maybe I'm a little scared she'll change her mind if she hates what I arranged.

"What the hell is happening?" she asks as she raises her hands to make sure Hadley doesn't accidentally let her run into something.

"Patience, pretty lady," Hads says, guiding her further and further toward me until Tate is barely a few centimeters away from me. "Keep your eyes closed." Tate does as she's told, even after Hadley removes her palms from her eyes and steps away from us.

My hands reach out to touch her arms, slow and gentle as to not startle her, and she flashes me a bright smile as soon as my fingers curl around her arms.

"Hey, cowboy," she says, and I take a moment to adore the way she knows it's me without even looking.

"Hi, sweetheart. I'm going to ask you to open your eyes soon, okay?" She nods eagerly, and I bend down to kiss her smile before grabbing Luna's lead rope and guiding Tate to turn around, bringing her back to the signs Galaxy and Firefly are showcasing. "Okay, open," I say, and Tate's enchanting hazel eyes do as they are told. She focuses on me first before her attention drops to Luna.

"What's she doing here?" my future wife asks as she squats down to give Luna love.

"Maybe you should see what she has around her neck," I suggest, stepping behind her again so that once she has the ring, she'll see our horses.

Tate hesitates before raising her hands to the bag hanging around Luna's neck, and my heart rate skyrockets in response.

"Aaron, I know I'm going to find a ring in here, so if I start sobbing, I hope you are not recording it," she says with a laugh that I return while dropping onto my knee for her. Tate pulls the ring out of the little bag, whispering, "Oh my God," several times before she turns to me with tears in her eyes.

Her gaze drifts to Galaxy and Firefly, all of her emotions flooding through her and weakening her knees until she's kneeling too.

"Fuck, I never thought this would happen, let alone that I'd be crying," Tate says with a teary laugh, covering her face with her hands, the ring clasped between her thumb and index finger. "Fuck you, Aaron," she mumbles and wipes her tears, still laughing.

"You can do that later, sweetheart. For now, I need you to put that ring on your finger because I would very much like to marry you," I say, and she removes her hands from her face to show me the tears slipping down her cheeks.

"I haven't even said yes yet," she replies, giving me a naughty smile.

"I haven't properly asked yet," I say and take her face in my hands. "Will you marry me?" I press a kiss to her lips and lean back to watch a soft smile dance onto her face.

"Yes, cowboy. I'll marry you," she says, waiting for me to slip the ring onto her finger before she flings her arms around my neck and kisses me again.

A second later, our entire family swarms back outside, almost mowing us down to hug us and congratulate us.

Tate and I are at the center of their hug, smiling at each other as she whispers, "I love you."

"To Pluto and back."

The End

Sneak Peek of *Jump-Start* by Bridget L. Rose.
Jump-Start is the first novel in The Pitstop Series.

Chapter 1

Leonard

ANOTHER RACE. ANOTHER WIN. Another critic probably ready to jump on the mistake I made in the third corner during the opening lap.

I felt it in the car as soon as it happened. I didn't leave enough space for my rival, and teammate, so he went off track and lost first place. I can already see the headlines. 'Leonard Tick Only Wins Races By Cheating'. My entire life has been like this. Since I was a kid, people have attacked me and tried to tear me down. That's what happens when you're the first black race car driver in a predominantly white motorsport. I fucking love this sport, but there are so many things wrong with it. We still have a long way to go before we can truly be proud of it.

I jump out of my Formula One car, briefly appreciating the sleek black colour my team went with this year. My eyes fixate on the Grenzenlos symbol—two infinity symbols entangled—on top of the nose, a wave of nostalgia running through me. I won my first World Championship with this team and hope to win more in the future. We've come a long way over the years I've been a racer at Grenzenlos, and I couldn't be prouder of the team I have.

"Leonard!" the post-race interviewer—Jason Dirk, I believe—starts, and I stare at him with my lips pulled into a thin line.

Formula One has hardened me to the point of no return. One smile is all it takes for people to spin things out of proportion like I'm happy about the move I pulled in corner three, which inevitably led to my win. Sometimes shit like that happens, it's normal in an aggressive sport like racing, but reporters don't care about that when it comes to *me* making the mistake. I'm judged a lot more harshly than other drivers.

"You drove a great race today and managed your tyres well. What a way to start the season! How do you feel coming back as a World Champion?" he asks, and I suck in an inaudible, sharp breath.

"I feel great. My team and I have worked hard and restlessly over the break, which is why it's great to see it paying off already," I say, shaking my head at his next comment.

"That incident in turn three sure did help. How do you feel about that?" *I feel like I want to punch you in the face*, I think to myself, but except for me grabbing my towel a little harder, no one would suspect how much his question bothers me. That's why it's great to have a reputation for never smiling. It allows me to hide how I truly feel.

"I will have to review the incident before I can comment on what happened. From the car, it felt like a normal racing incident," I explain, wiping away the sweat dripping down the side of my forehead.

I'm exhausted.

Today was a hot and long race, and I can't wait to get back home and spend time with my family. After test-driving the car for the past few weeks and putting every available hour into training to get ready for the start of the season, I've barely seen them. My brothers, Mum, and Dad all miss me too—they make sure to remind me every day—and I have to get back to Benz, my three-year-old pitbull. I miss her. I miss everything about my home. Even that pain in the arse, Chi—

"Well, congratulations on your win. Let's move onto our second place," Jason says, and I step over to where my performance coach, Quinn, is standing.

"Great drive, kiddo," she says before my hand slips onto her shoulder. Quinn is my best friend in the entire world. She's hardly five years older than me, but insists on keeping that nickname.

"Yeah, you liked my move in corner three?" I ask, which causes her to laugh. We both know I'm joking in the only way I do—without showing it on my face—but she's enjoying my playful attitude very much.

"I did. Now go get your trophy, kiddo. I haven't got all day," she teases, and I pinch her side in response. She laughs loudly, the sound making a wonderful warmth spread through my chest.

Before I can make my way to the cool-down room, Adrian Romana, a Formula One rookie I've only met a few times, comes up to me, still wearing his helmet. He holds out his hand for me as he calls out a 'congrats' before pulling me into an excited hug and telling me how well I drove—from what he could see as I lapped him. I don't usually show affection to people, but this barely eighteen-year-old gives me no choice, and I don't mind it as much as I thought I would. Adrian's a good kid, maybe that's why.

"I'll see you later!" he says before letting himself get weighed, just like every driver has to after a race.

I wonder what the fuck has him so happy all the time, but it's nice. Having someone positive like him in my life might be good for me. The thought is pushed away by my pessimistic side before I can linger on it.

My tired and sore feet bring me to the cool-down room, where my teammate, Jonathan Kent, is taking small sips from the bottle of water they have ready for us. There are three podium-style tables at the front of the room, and I walk toward mine, seeing the cap with the number 1 on it. I place it on my head before taking my bottle and joining the other drivers.

Cameron Kion, Adrian's teammate, managed to come in third, and it has him smiling so brightly, I wish I knew if he's always this fucking happy too. Whoever paired them up wanted a sunshine driver line-up. They must be quite popular with the fans.

"Nice defence in the eighth corner on the second lap, Leonard," Cameron says, and I shift my attention to his blue eyes, giving him a slight nod.

"Nice work on your start," I reply, not used to anyone making small talk with me after the race.

The other drivers mostly keep their distance from me. It's always been like this, but I can't blame them either. My facial expression doesn't communicate 'hey, I'm approachable'. It communicates 'fuck off', I've made sure of it over the years.

"My throttle was fucking stuck in the first corner," Cameron goes on, and I raise both eyebrows in response. "Yeah, it was crazy. Thank God it unstuck itself after a terrifying five seconds," he says with a slight laugh that makes his chest move. I give him a thoughtful nod, so he moves over to his water bottle.

Dreadful silence fills the room, and I'm convinced I can hear Jonathan's stomach rumble from hunger. It makes me want to kick him. We don't have the closest of relationships. He can't stand me, and I've fantasised about strangling him on many occasions. He's a spoiled, arrogant brat, and I'm too serious for him. We don't match on any level, but fans go crazy for our rivalry. Last year, we were head-to-head in the Driver's Championship, but I beat him in the second-to-last race for good. The title fell on me, and he's hated me more since. I couldn't give less of a shit. As a matter of fact, I often have to suppress a grin when he tries to talk behind my back about how I cheated to get the title. He's such a bloody sore loser, it's hilarious.

"Let's go," someone says, and I stand up from the seats at the wall to follow them toward the podium area.

First, Cameron steps onto the podium, taking his place. Then follows Jonathan, who bumps his shoulder against mine on his way out knowing full well I won't be able to trip him in front of all of these people. I would love to though. I would also very much enjoy it if he fell right on top of that nose job he had five years ago. Arsehole.

I walk onto the podium, standing on the highest spot because I'm the winner of the fucking race. I should be happy. Starting the season off like this is what every driver dreams of, but, for some reason, a numbness has spread through my chest. It's incredibly unsettling and makes me suck in a sharp breath. *What the hell?*

A frightening question crosses my thoughts a second later.

Am I falling out of love with racing?

Acknowledgements

The first person I would like to thank is my Nonno. I wrote this book because I didn't know how to deal with my grief of seeing him lose his memories of his life and family. He was the kind of Nonno to always cheer me on in my dreams, telling everyone how proud he was of me, and I hope this book would make him very proud too. Because of his unwavering belief in me, like most of my family, was I able to chase dreams and write the books that thousands of people are reading. So, thank you, Nonno. I know I can never tell you how grateful I am, so I'm writing it in this book like the author I've become thanks to you.

Next, I would like to thank my furry son, JJ, for teaching me so much about epilepsy. He was diagnosed when he was three years old, and we've spent a lot of time navigating this new territory that no one in my life had ever been to, but I'm so grateful that even in the darkest times we had, we ended up learning so much about an illness that is not nearly talked about enough in our society. So, thank you, JJ, not only for being my son and loving me every day, but for teaching me things I would have never learned otherwise. This book is as much for you as it is for Nonno.

Next, I would like to thank Ams because without you, this book would not be published. I received so much negative feedback on the first draft that I truly didn't want to share this story anymore. But you were so patient with me and the feedback you helped me was everything I needed to build up the courage to rewrite the book and turn it into what it is today: something I'm immensely proud of.

I would like to to thank my beta readers who spent hours and hours reading and commenting in order to give me the feedback. A special thank you goes to Halie,

Sami, Gemma, Jess, Kayla, Solène, Makayla, Emma, and Tanisha. Thank you for everything.

As always, I'm so grateful for Vicky, Sophie, Martina, Alyssa, Sunel, Beth, Hali, Renee, Mais, Hannah, Brittani, Julia & Mareike, Victoria, Nesi, Jane, Ruth, Salma, Eliza, Mariah, Katherine, Isabella, Briana, and more amazing people who have supported me for so long. Being an author would be a million times harder without you.

Teigan and Esha, having you two as friends is one of the greatest gifts in the world. Teigan, thank you also for creating all of this beautiful art for this book, I am still obsessed with it.

Now, onto my favorite part of my acknowledgments, thanking my other half. To my sister, you are the greatest gift life could have ever given me. Without you, there would be no me. You are my soulmate in every way that counts, and I'm so eternally grateful that you've chosen to be my business partner in all of this. Thank you for spending your time reading my books and giggling over my fictional characters. I love you. Also, I hope this made you cry.

Lastly, I always want to thank my grandparents, mom, and Robyn and Miriam for being there every step of the way and being the kind of emotional support system everyone should have because it is the best thing in the world. I love you all, and I'm so very grateful you continue to read my books. All my love, Bridget

About the Author

BRIDGET L. ROSE IS a queer author currently located in Toronto, Canada. She was born in Germany and is half-Italian and half-German. During her teenage years, she was fortunate to live in Singapore and the USA as well.

Bridget fell in love with books from a young age, and soon discovered her passion for writing as well. Over the past two years, Bridget has written and self-published ten books. She writes contemporary romances, most of them set in the world of Formula One. Her first cowboy romance will be releasing in April 2025.

In her books she aims to be inclusive because of her own experiences of being queer and living with mental illnesses. Even nowadays, people still make assumptions and use stereotypes about queer people as well as people with mental illnesses, which she experiences daily as well. Bridget is passionate about changing the narratives on these subjects, especially in the romance market.

When Bridget is not busy writing, she loves to read and spend time with her family, including her two furry children JJ and Diego.

Books by Bridget L. Rose

The Pitstop Series

Jump-Start

**The Inside
of a Rainbow**

**Rush:
Part One & Two**

**Chase:
Part One & Two**

Reserved

Diffuse

**The Last
Championship
(Novella)**

**Straight to the
Chapel**

Silver Creek
Ranch Series

*From Angels
to Devils Series*

To Pluto & Back

From Devils to Angels